THE MAGICAL LANDS OF MIDENDHIL

THE MISSION OF THE LAST KEEPER

THE MAGICAL LANDS OF MIDENDHIL
THE MISSION OF THE LAST KEEPER

DAVIDE SIMON MAZZOLI

Translated by: Brunella Costagliola

IDUN

NASHVILLE, TENNESSEE

Idun is an imprint of W. Brand Publishing
j.brand@wbrandpub.com
www.wbrandpub.com

Cover Illustration: Paolo Barbieri
Art Direction: Davide Simon Mazzoli
Graphic design English Version: JuLee Brand

The Magical Lands of Midendhil / Davide Simon Mazzoli —first edition - English Version

Available in Hardcover, Paperback, Kindle, and eBook formats.
Hardcover ISBN: 978-1-956906-15-8
Paperback ISBN: 978-1-956906-16-5
eBook ISBN: 978-1-956906-17-2

Library of Congress Control Number: 2021952528

CONTENTS

To Leonardo, Alexander, and Alice

VAHALA

"*Shamballah!*"

The massive doors to the golden portal open wide, filling the temple with moonlight.

The man walks toward the center of the round room, his muscular body wrapped in a long, dark cape, and his face hidden under a large cowl. His bloody hands rest on his chest, and his eyes are glowing slits contrasting against his dark face. He slowly limps toward the center of the giant circle. The Mogonis Stone is right in front of him, pulsating with a bright light, releasing a deep, yet soft, sound.

"*Emmi bellovesus, imi bituriges . . .*"

Through gasps of pain, the man bows down to this immense power. A sudden cough shakes him, reopening a wound on his side. Blood drips down to the floor, as he curls up like a dying spider trying to ease the pain. Then, he carefully looks up at the stone. *Vril*, the Cosmic energy, begins to flow into his battered body, and in his defiant silence, he tastes the air with the tip of his tongue like a snake. He's finally defeated the enemy, now nothing can stop him. At last, the *Power of Creation* will be his.

He stands back up, brushing his hand over the pure bright sphere enveloped with electric webs of blue energy. He moves his cape to the side to reveal a long, thin sword, the blade of which is made of the most precious metal and honed to an unmatched sharpness. It is of such deadly beauty that it shines with its own bright aura. Ornate carvings, holes, and slots shape its form, giving it a graceful, yet powerful, appearance. Grasping the sword with both hands, he raises it above his head. A nighttime breeze blows through the metal incisions, making sounds and whistles that, for an instant, shake the whole temple.

"I, Sire Kenat, declare myself the new Great King!"

With a quick motion, he thrusts the sword deeply into the center of the Mogonis Stone, all the way to the hilt.

A beam of searing light explodes from the crooked globe and throws him back against the wall. An abrupt wind forms a vortex in the sanctuary; the beam of light radiates an unbearable heat. The ground begins to shake, and the air is filled with an agonizing high-pitched howl.

After an instant, silence returns as if the temple had been abandoned for millions of years. The Stone has been broken in half and eight streams of magma are flowing out of the deep cut in the globe red, green, light blue, purple, orange, yellow, blue, and white. The eight incandescent streams trickle down to the ground, magically taking the shape of eight small and bright spheres.

Kenat barely survives the aftermath of the explosion; the fire caused by the spell charred his flesh. Whatever bit of humanity left in him is now completely gone, dissolving with the spell. With his bony fingers, he touches his disfigured face. His nose is now nothing more than a flap of dried cartilage, and his eyes have become two fiery cavities in his naked skull. His strength, along with his powers, are leaving his body. But it doesn't matter. It's almost time. His destiny is about to be fulfilled.

The eight magical spheres are shining bright in front of him. Nearby, lay the two shattered halves of the Mogonis Stone. The skinless face of the sorcerer reveals a smile. The eight Sidhits, the power of the Universe, are now in his possession. He bends down to grab the result of his work when, once again, the ground shakes so violently that he is thrown down. The shattered stone comes to life. It vibrates, engulfing the sword that is still stuck into its heart and shines with a beam of fire so powerful it explodes through the ceiling. A new wave of energy shakes the temple.

Kenat is immobilized, shocked at the sight of the terrible violence he has unleashed The sky swirls into a whirlpool of clouds that surrounds the beam of fire, creating a vortex that attracts all the storms of the world. Pinned to the floor, the sorcerer fights against the invisible energy that pushes him down. He drags himself through the bursts of energy reverberating against the walls, trying to reach the Sidhits. Heavy rocks and debris fall on his body, but nothing can keep him from his destiny. Still dragging himself on the ground, ignoring his wounds, he stretches his bony fingers toward the spheres.

Suddenly, above all the chaos in the temple, Kenat hears the cry of a baby. He quickly turns toward the wailing sound. Fury burns on his monstrous face. He raises his hand.

"Nertos Och . . ."

He is unable to complete his curse; a powerful and unknown spell overtakes him with the strength of thunder . . .

chapter one

AWAKENING FROM A DREAM

. . .Bam!

I suddenly lift my head up as if a bomb had just gone off a few inches away from my ears. I am confused. What time is it? Where am I? My eyes feel heavy, but I can sense a shadow hovering over me. I try to focus on it as I touch my forehead.

My teacher, Miss Abona, is leaning down on my desk with her fist tight and her eyes gazing at my perplexed expression. Four words run through my mind: *I–am–in–trouble.*

"My compliments, Leonardo Ghebo! Is this how we behave in class?"

Embarrassed, I look at her without being able to utter a single word. In the background, the suppressed giggling of my classmates confuses me even more.

"So?"

"I'm not feeling very well . . ." I mumble through tight lips.

Her grimace immediately changes into a hideous smirk.

"You don't feel well?" she asks in a sarcastic tone.

Mastering my best *Living Dead* performance, I reposition my red hair in an attempt to look even more pale and make my act more believable.

"It's time for an oral exam!"

Dang, she didn't buy it. Sighing, I try to be brave as I walk up to the board with my head down. What rotten luck! This surely is going to turn into another F.

Miss Abona is standing right in front of me. Her drill sergeant attitude is making me feel even more inferior than I already do. I can't stand her. I truly believe that underneath her school teacher clothing hides a demon whose sole mission is to torture me. After all, she's been haunting me for

2 Davide Simon Mazzoli

years! First, as the principal of my elementary school, then as my private tutor from 6th to 8th grade. I know it seems crazy, but here she is again, as my 9th grade science teacher. Had I known she was going to be here, I would have surely gone to a different school.

I reach the gallows, grab a marker, and await my sentence. My face is so red it feels like it's on fire. I just hope that those freckles of mine are covering some of the blushing. For a few seconds, I stare at my tormentor, this poor excuse for a woman who shows me nothing but unkindness. Despite being a foot shorter than me, she fills me with turmoil like no other. Her scowl is outlined by a round and arrogant face. Her blue eyes are small and her mouth, perpetually pouting as if it were smelling something bad, is framed by a strip of mustache.

In a neurotic gesture, she pushes aside my notebook and pen, as she sits on my desk. She tilts her head to the side and looks at me with her usual condescending demeanor. It's clear that she views students as a pain, bothersome annoyances that come with the job, like pieces of dog poop for a gardener.

"Can you repeat to your classmates what I just explained?"

I wobble as I rest my shoulders against the wall.

Didn't you see me? I was sleeping!

"Yeah, sure . . ." I reply.

She grimaces, stretching her lips into a plastic smile. She looks like a big toad waiting for some stupid fly to come within range of its tongue.

"Today you explained that . . ."

I'm lost. As I quickly glance at the board, I see two giant concentric arcs scribbled that form some type of bridge. On the top corner, there is a circle, which could be the sun. Arrows go up and down, some bouncing off the curves, while others go right through them.

I've seen this before. But where?

I dust off my memory; I think it has something to do with planets. It reminds me of comic books I read, or even movies that I watched recently, you know, the kind that focus on a world close to destruction. Or maybe I've seen it on TV or the Internet? Perhaps I read it in the course book? Probably. It's in moments like this that I wish I had Google at my disposal. Heck, even Yahoo! answers would suffice right about now . . .

"So?" she insists.

"*Ehm . . . yes . . .*"

Come on, Leonardo, think. Think! So . . . there's the sun, which means these arrows could be its rays, maybe the heat . . . Some of those arrows bounce off that giant arc. Of course! They bounce off the atmosphere. Yes, the atmosphere! So, we must be talking about climate . . .

"Today you talked about the greenhouse effect . . .?"

I hold my breath. Miss Abona keeps staring at me with her arms crossed.

"Am I right? This is the representation of the greenhouse effect, isn't it?"

"Are you asking me, Mr. Ghebo?"

"No, no . . . this *is* the greenhouse effect. It's a statement."

"And then?" she asks.

Thank goodness for my memory! Alright now, moving on. My palms are so sweaty that I can feel the marker sliding out of my hands. I start saying everything I know and remember about the topic, trying to put all the words together in a sentence that will satisfy my tormentor.

"It's something to do with . . . climate."

"Yes . . ." she says nodding.

"It's a planet's ability to keep . . . some of the heat that . . . comes from the sun . . ."

"And what makes this process possible?"

"The atmosphere, which is kind of like a shell made of gas that . . ."

The teacher stops me by raising her hand. I know she's not happy that I'm actually able to explain these things.

"Can you tell me why we talk about problems caused by the greenhouse effect?" she asks.

"Because of the pollution . . . I think."

"And so?"

So *what*? Why does she have to make it so difficult on me? Why? I feel like there's a killer monster inside of me. A rage that lately has been pushing hard to come out, and it is becoming uncontrollable. Should I just try to calm down? Nope, too late. Here I go.

"I have no clue!" I suddenly yell, making all my classmates jump in shock.

Out of nowhere I throw the marker at my teacher, hitting her right in the eye. Then, before she can say or do anything, I jump on the desk, and I kick down everything that's on it. I step on her precious fountain pen and smash it hard with my foot as I hear it break under the pressure. I take her notebook where she writes about her students, and holding it up like a war trophy, I break it apart while letting out a powerful roar. I see her staring at me in shock as I take a few pages and start chewing on them, while others fall to the floor.

"What are you gonna say now, huh?" I ask her, while chewing on her notes.

"This is it, the greenhouse effect!"

This last sentence echoes in my head.

Then, I come back to reality. I am still standing here, immobile, by the board, with Miss Abona staring at me, annoyed that I have yet to answer her question. My classmates keep gazing at me in silence. All I see is a crowd of unfamiliar faces that pop out of the squalid green walls.

"So, what, Mr. Ghebo? Do you think you'll manage to answer by the end of the year?"

Once again, I hear their annoying giggles.

I am so irritated by them that I finally hear myself say: "Pollution causes global warming."

"And how come there are also instances of lowering temperatures?" she asks me immediately.

"*Mmh* . . . Equilibrium imbalance?" I attempt.

"Or maybe it's the beginning of the end?" the teacher replies with a bitter smile. "Alright, that's enough. Go back to your seat," she says in a harsh tone, as she smoothes the nun's skirt she wears every day.

Finally! The knot in my stomach is slowly going away. I'm safe, and after all, I didn't do so bad. The teacher gets up from my desk and walks back to her own. She doesn't say anything about how I did, but I am sure that, had I not been able to think on my feet, she would have simply destroyed me. Lucky for me, today she was robbed of an excuse for her sick pleasure of persecuting me. I don't care if she doesn't say anything. I'm just glad I got away with it.

I walk back to my seat, practically skipping through the backpacks left on the floor. I glance at the desk behind mine and see Maya, who returns my gaze with her usual blank stare. What is she thinking about?

Surely not me. We've known each other since we were kids, and even though I've been in love with her for many years now, I've never had the courage to actually tell her how I feel about her. What's the point anyway? I don't have a shot with her. We're best friends, nothing more. And for now, that's enough for me.

Maya is the most beautiful girl I've ever seen. She has her mother's Indian traits with gorgeous exotic facial features and golden skin tone. I could stare at her elegant profile for hours, losing myself in her jade green eyes. Oh, and her smell. It's the most amazing thing I have ever had the pleasure of inhaling, and she releases it every time she tosses her curly hair. She gives me butterflies. I know, I'm in trouble. Maya has no idea of my true feelings for her. I can't blame her. She is totally out of my league. I've been at this school for nine months now and people have come to know me as the "weird guy," the introvert who shies away from friendships.

Plus, everyone knows I'm an orphan. Bianca and Adam, my adoptive parents, are great people. They've been taking care of me since I was only a few days old. They've always treated me like I'm their son and have always given me everything I've ever wanted. I can't imagine my life without them, but since they told me the truth last summer, something inside of me has changed. Something has been pecking at my mind, breaking every certainty I have into a thousand pieces. And every day, I become angrier and more suspicious at the world. I don't think Mom and Dad know I feel this way. Maybe Maya has figured out there's something wrong with me because she's my best friend.

"Open your book to page 235." Miss Abona's words abruptly bring me back to reality.

"Chapter 8, paragraph 6. The greenhouse effect. You," she says, pointing her finger at a girl at the back of the room. "Read."

"The greenhouse effect is a natural phenomenon that . . ."

Booorrrring! This is really not helping my mood. I've also been feeling very sleepy lately and I'm not sure why. The sandwich I had for lunch earlier is like a fiery ball in my stomach, sitting in my gut like a boulder. Maybe having so much junk food wasn't my brightest decision. With my elbows on the desk, I rest my forehead in my hands, as I pretend to read the paragraph. I'm sure nobody will notice if I fall asleep this time. I just need a quick nap so I can recover from this weird haze I've been in. I slowly close my eyes and let the fog take over my brain.

Everything happens very quickly. A blinding light appears in my head as I feel pain between my eyes. In front of me, a cruel smile showcases a line of white, sharp teeth.

"*Where are yoooou?*" a voice whispers in my ear.

Its tone is so malicious that it terrifies me.

I jump up in fear. I look around to see who was talking to me, but no one is even looking my way. Everyone is focused on reading that paragraph. In an attempt to catch my breath, I look back at Maya who seems bored as she draws little tiny hearts in her notebook that make a frame around the name Simon. She catches me staring at her.

"What's up?" she whispers with a smile.

"Oh, nothing . . ."

I turn back, trying to figure out where the scary image I've just seen came from. Now, I'm definitely awake. I look down, pretending to follow the paragraph again. I'm totally lost, as I stare at the ink in the book. My ears are ringing, and my brain feels like it's doing flips in my head. What was that voice? I close my eyes and take a deep breath.

And there's that mouth, once again. Its lips are purple and its teeth are very shiny.

"My Master, Kenat, is looking for you . . ."

I can't take it any longer. I jump out of my chair as a chilling shiver goes down my spine.

"Is everything OK, Mr. Ghebo?" the teacher asks me.

"Yes, yes . . . thank you," I mutter.

"Maybe you should sleep a bit longer at night and a little less in class. Sound like a plan?"

And here goes the annoying giggling again.

"Please, keep reading," she tells the student. "And you, Mr. Ghebo, sit down."

The girl starts reading again.

"What in the world are you doing, Leo?!" Maya whispers behind me. "Get a grip!"

I sit back down as I feel hot flashes taking over. I caress my forehead and rub my eyes. Pitch black. All I see is deep blackness with blue and dark red patches.

Calm down. Relax. Breathe.

That girl's voice fills up the room, but I can't hear it anymore; it is now a faraway echo.

I instinctively grab a pencil and let it draw on the white pages of my notebook, completely enslaved by the need to focus on the images I see in my head. I am not sure *why* I am doing it, but I know it's important. It's been two weeks now that I've been drawing these . . . how do I put it . . . *nightmares?* I've basically filled pages and pages of these weird sketches, and they all look exactly the same, as if they were trying to represent the same things. My hand feels independent from my body as it moves over the paper. It's now drawing the majestic dome of the magic temple, the tall, white spires that reach the sky, and the dragon that bulges out over the gate. And then, it starts tracing the traits of that being. Kenat. His burned, thin body is covered in a cape made of gray feathers . . . no, wait, they aren't feathers. It's a cape made of dried wax. It reminds me of the waxy, dusty wings of moths.

I see Kenat walking inside the temple. For a moment, I feel as if I am standing right there in front of him, as if my drawing was staring at me. I suddenly hear that mawkish, sibilant voice again.

"*Yessss . . . accept who you are . . . Embrace Master Kenat . . .*"

I close my eyes so tight they hurt.

Suddenly, the bell rings, waking me up.

Class is dismissed.

"Alright, your homework tonight is to study the whole chapter!" Miss Abona says in her usual superior tone as students rush out of the room. I, however, have to move slowly. I feel as if the ground is shaking under my feet.

"It's just my imagination. It's just stress caused by finals," I tell myself as I grind my teeth.

"What's wrong with you today?" Maya asks me while getting her backpack ready to go.

"I'm just tired," I reply, trying to downplay the situation. "I'm just a little tired."

I feel weird, but I try to smile so I don't worry her.

"I know that Miss Abona's class is always a drag but come on . . . you can't lose it like that during her lectures," she laughs, shaking her head.

I get hit by her smell. *Ahh*, a breath of fresh air!

"I have to stop by the secretary's office," she says. "Catch you later in the yard?"

"Sure."

I watch her leave. Feeling stunned, I go to close my notebook when . . . *Bam*! My teacher's stubby fingers land once again on my desk. With a tug, she grabs the drawings, and without uttering a word, she pulls them right under her nose. I can feel my stomach knotting and dropping to the floor. I look around and realize that the classroom has completely emptied out. It's just us now. Miss Abona keeps staring at my drawings, squinting in disbelief.

"It's just something I drew back ho . . ."

She doesn't let me complete my lie. She puts my notebook in her pocket. I open my mouth to speak, but she suddenly turns around, gives me this deadly gaze, and walks out the room.

"Great," I say under my breath. "Now, I really am in trouble."

As I try to pack up the last few things on my desk, a wave of heat overcomes me once again. This time it's much stronger. I fall on the chair behind me and I get sucked into a black vortex.

A tall and graceful figure appears from the darkness of the cave and walks toward the chasm below. The hole is so vast I can't see where it starts and where it ends, the darkness so thick that I can't distinguish anything.

The figure stands tall, covered in a long black gown made of the same gloomy murkiness that surrounds it. It sighs, as if waiting for something. Bulging blue veins web its huge forehead, framed by shoulder-length black hair. Its skin is whiter than a skull, its eyes reflect the most violent, homicidal madness ever imagined. Its eyes, sunk deep into purple cavities, are red like blood, standing out starkly against the milky white sclera. Its stare is paralyzing. A stare that doesn't allow any chance of escape.

Its cape flutters in a soft, warm breeze, revealing its corpse-like feet. It smiles. Its skinny face is distorted by a cruel grin. Its purple lips barely hiding gleaming, predatory teeth. The once soft breeze coming from deep within the cave is now a powerful, scorching hot wind. The demon opens its arms, letting the wind blow smoke coils out of his clothes.

"Master Kenat, Antédios carries news," it says in a sharp whisper.

A puff and a red gleam. A fiery beam crosses the darkness of the cave. The ground begins to shake and lava starts gushing from the clefts in the rocks, flowing down the chasm, and forming an incandescent lake. The fiery blazes reveal the pale face of the demon, who stands tall and straight with its evil grin.

A deep voice that could almost be a roar fills the hot air, shaking the rocks.

"Did you find him?"

The demon nods, kneeling down to the blazing flames.

"Master, the boy has come forth."

A stream of lava gushes from the center of the lake, reaching the ceiling. A quiet and deep laughter echoes in the emptiness.

"Antédios . . ."

"Master . . ."

"Pay attention," says the voice. "I want the boy. And you know I won't accept failure."

"I won't let you down, Sire. Our spies are everywhere. The light is shining once again. We are just waiting to contact him."

"Find him and bring him to me!"

The surface of the fiery lake is agitated.

"Yes, Master. My senses tell me he's in the human world. I think he is . . ."

"Leonardo!"

I wake up suddenly. I'm lying on the floor, with my head resting on my backpack. I see Mike, the janitor, standing over me, with his puffy face covered in a soft beard.

"What happened?" I hazily ask.

"I'm not sure, you tell me. I came in here and found you lying down," he explains.

I sit up, realizing I'm a sweaty mess.

"Careful . . ." he says, helping me straighten my backpack. "Would you like a glass of water?"

"No, thank you." I'm totally disoriented.

"Are you OK?"

I stare into space, thinking back on the nightmare I just had. What the heck was that?

"Leonardo? What's wrong?"

"Nothing, I'm feeling better now . . ."

I can tell he's doubtful, but I am not telling a lie; I am feeling better. It's as if I sweat out whatever it was that was causing me harm. My eyes are teary, though. Mike notices it too.

"You know you can trust me . . ."

It's true. Mike is the only person I have been able to build a healthy relationship with during this first year of high school. I look into his pure, honest eyes and see a troubled expression.

"I'm fine, truly," I reassure him.

"You're not being honest," he says, helping me stand up. "Tell me, how was your day?"

"*Blah* . . ."

"What do you mean?"

"Miss Abona . . . she's always on my case. She hates me."

A serene smile comes though his bushy, white beard.

"Oh, come on, don't say that. She's just doing her job. She's not as bad as she seems . . . although, at times, even I want to strangle her!"

He then stands up straight, doing his best impression of my science teacher. "Mike, I see these good-for-nothing students wasting their time in the hall. Make them go away."

We both break out in laughter, which releases the tension. As always, Mike is able to make me feel better.

"Don't you think it'd be better to call your parents so they can pick you up?"

"*Nah,* it's OK. I'll see you tomorrow."

"Take care and be careful."

The hallway is almost empty. The afternoon light shines through the skylights on the ceiling, illuminating pillars of dust throughout the hall. I walk through that intangible colonnade, making it vibrate with every step.

I can't wait to get out of here.

chapter two

FOOD JAMBOREE

The sun blinds me as I walk out the door. School is about to end for the year and the holidays are approaching. A cool breeze blows over the hills, biting days away from summer. Miss Abona may be right, after all; climate is changing, and the world is along for the ride.

Completely lost in my thoughts, I walk down the stairs and blend in with all the other students who are mingling in the yard. I'm feeling better now, and that dizziness I experienced before is gone. I chew on a stick of mint-flavored gum as I hurry toward my scooter. Maya is waiting for me, sitting comfortably on her flamingo pink Vespa.

"Where have you been?" she asks, nervously drumming her fingers on her helmet.

"I was with Mike," I reply without giving away too many details.

"Again? Did he give you the third degree as always?"

"No, no. He just wanted to know how I was doing."

"That guy just can't mind his own business, can he?"

"Are you jealous of Mike?" I jeer, as I nudge her with my elbow.

She doesn't smile. Rather, she sighs and keeps quiet. Her mind is elsewhere, and her fingers are now fidgeting with the bracelet that her mother gave her as a good-luck charm. The breeze swirls her brown curls that shine with golden highlights. Something's up with her. Is it going to be more bad news for yours truly?

"I was supposed to go on a date with Simon yesterday afternoon," she says suddenly. "But he stood me up and hasn't called since . . ."

I have butterflies in my stomach, although they feel more like a colony of fierce giant bats. I try hard to hide a grin of pleasure, as a sneaky sensation of happiness is taking over me.

"I'm sorry," I lie. "But I told you, Simon is not the right guy for you."

"You really think so?"

"Yes, absolutely! He's too old, too stupid. And those prison-style tattoos . . ."

"I think they are sexy."

Low blow. But I'm not backing down. I counterpunch.

"Sexy or not, I don't find him entertaining."

"Too bad, he'd like to meet you . . ."

"Well, thanks, but that doesn't change anything. To me he'll always be an idiot. What do you even have in common with someone like him? You deserve better!"

A veil of sadness covers her face, but it's quickly wiped away by her smile that makes her shine with an unusual light. She places her hand behind my neck, pulling me closer to her. My stomach is in knots because I know that, in that very moment, it is finally about to happen. Maya is about to kiss me. Panicking, I swallow my gum, almost choking on it. I hold my breath and swallow. I pucker up . . . How are my lips supposed to feel like? Soft, tense? Panic! I move slowly and . . .

"Thank you, Leo," she says, leaning her forehead close to mine. "You're the brother I never had."

And there it is. The spell is broken, freeing the butterflies that had managed to get from my stomach all the way up to my throat. The same old story of the brother, the best friend, the guardian angel. When are you going to finally see me as more than what I am? More than what we are?

"What would I do without you?"

"I'm not sure," I try to regain my composure, in the hopes that she hasn't noticed anything. "Perhaps you'd have your heart broken by some self-absorbed, overrated Macho Man."

Maya laughs, tilting her head back like only she can. My eyes rest on her neck, and I stare at the little round mole under her jaw. I deeply breathe her in.

Yep, I've totally fallen for her, and I don't think I can resist much longer. I know it.

"What's so funny?"

A rusty voice catches us off guard and ruins the moment we were having: it's Diego Crippa, a troublemaking, obnoxious, spoiled brat who's still in high school even though he's twenty years old.

"Nothing that concerns you," she says in a firm voice, while putting on her helmet.

"How dare you . . ."

A nervous Crippa is pursing his lips. I'm about to burst out in laughter, but I restrain myself from doing so. I remain still, in silence.

"You're kinda sassy," he grumbles, as he looks at her in a semi-captivating way. "Wanna go out with me? I'll come pick you up with my new wheels if you tell me where you live." He then hits the button of the car remote he was playing with, and he turns on the headlights of his brand new, shiny, sporty convertible, which is parked right in front of us.

"So? What do you say?"

"I say, *no, thanks.* I have plans with him this afternoon," she replies, nodding toward me.

Oh man, this is not going well . . .

"Him?" he asks with a disgusted expression. "This *nobody's* son? And where is he taking you?"

"What we do is none of your business," she responds, annoyed. "Let's go, Leo," she says as she rides toward the gate.

I try to pretend nothing happened, but I heard him. A *nobody's* son . . .

I feel the weight of every single word I want to say to this jerk rushing up my throat and I'd love nothing more than to open the dam and let them fly, but I force myself to follow

Maya's advice. I go to start my scooter when I smell Crippa's nasty cigarette breath on my neck. I stand still with my head down and my hands gripping the handlebars.

"Watch out, Ghebo, 'cause you are pissing in my yard," he mumbles in my ear. "Boys like you, I eat 'em for breakfast and fart 'em out later. You got that?"

I remain still, without uttering a single word. I don't want to give him the satisfaction of acknowledgement.

"She comes to you only when she needs something. Just wait till she finds someone better and she'll forget you ever existed. You're just a *nobody's* son, and those like you don't deserve anything!"

A *nobody's* son. That word echoes painfully in my head. Maya has already left and I can't afford to let Crippa bother me any longer. Even though I want to kick his butt right now, I realize that he's big, definitely much bigger than me. It wouldn't go well for me if I stooped to his level. I know that because just over a month ago I happened to be at the receiving end of his right hook and it turned out to be an experience I'm not proud of and that I'd rather forget. Out of nowhere, Crippa provoked me, hit me, and then threw me across the school yard. That day I went back home with a shiner, a swollen lip, and a severely bruised ego. Staring at the handlebars, I strap on my helmet and choose to fight back with my own weapons.

"Crippa, let it go. Today's not a good day," I tell him nonchalantly.

"Wh . . .?"

I twist the throttle and get the heck out of there before he has a chance to finish.

"Ghebo! Hey, *nobody's son*, where do you think you're going? I'm not done with you!"

Despite the cold breeze, it's really nice outside today, maybe one of the nicest days we've had so far. The sun is shining high, peaking through the clouds that are scattered through the blue sky. Taking shortcuts through the narrow roads that intertwine across the old break houses, I reach Maya and we stop at the red light, side by side.

"Want to race to your house?" she teases, hitting the throttle.

"No, Maya, you know I don't like to do that."

"You're such a pansy. Has anyone ever told you to let loose from time to time?"

"Constantly," I smile, raising my eyebrows.

"Then let's go!"

The green light flashes and Maya floors it, burning rubber, crisscrossing through the cars that are ahead of us. I can't help but look at her as she rides smoothly through the narrow streets, almost killing a cat.

"Watch out!" I yell.

She brushes me off with a quick hand gesture and keeps going. It's clear that to her a race is a race, without taking into account that today is Wednesday, which means that my mom has been busy getting everything ready for our weekly Food Jamboree, a special event in which the entire Ghebo family gets together to taste one of her bizarre recipes. Only rule is, you've got to eat everything. It's actually more of a threat than a rule, given my mother's not so great culinary skills. I honestly can't remember the last time she cooked something decent.

Yet, Maya loves these gatherings. Maybe it's because she is reminded of what it's like to have a family, something that, unfortunately, she no longer has. Shanti, her mother, died almost a year ago. She took her own life by overdosing on a whole lot of sleeping pills. In the months before her death, she hadn't been acting like herself; she kept saying she was bothered by strange things she could see around her. She seemed distressed, maybe even depressed, but nobody took the situation seriously.

Nobody actually thought it could escalate to that point and Maya still hasn't been able to make peace with that. That was the day her family broke apart. Her father constantly travels for work, and to make things worse, he got remarried. I have yet to have the pleasure—or displeasure—to meet the new wife. But, from what I've been told, she sounds like a real witch. Maya is lonely and I think I'm the only person who can empathize with what she's going through. Although, we've been dealing with our pain in two very different ways: I have become much more introverted, while she's been trying hard to escape reality. But I think that being orphans has strengthened our friendship, and we've become closer than ever.

. . . *You're a nobody's son.*

Crippa's words are still painfully echoing in my head.

"Come on, you slow poke!" Maya yells all of a sudden.

I brush off these troubling thoughts and accelerate, trying to keep up with her. I pass a guy on a bike, one on foot, and even a mail truck. We ride past the mayor's house, making his hunting dogs bark, and in a matter of seconds, we reach the vineyards that adorn the green hills. The air is brisk and it smells of wet grass. Finally, we turn on to the street leading to my house, a rustic, brick Tuscan-style house that sits on top of a hill.

"I won!" Maya says proudly, jumping off the scooter.

"It's alright . . ."

"I'm sorry, Ghebo, but you are going to be punished for this defeat!"

"What punishment?" I ask her in a dull tone.

"I'm gonna have to think about that . . . what's wrong? Why do you look so down?"

"Nothing," I murmur.

"Is it because of what Crippa said?"

I take my helmet off but don't say anything. My copper hair falls in front of my eyes.

"Don't waste your energy on that idiot, OK?"

I stand still like a statue.

"*OK?*" she asks again, in a serious tone.

I turn around, looking in the distance toward the immense valley. The wind messes my hair, now all in disarray, and I don't try to stop it.

"Leo, you know no one understands you better than I do, right?" she asks, still standing behind me. "You can't allow that idiot to hurt you."

"I know . . ."

I feel her fingers brushing against mine, her hand holding mine; I squeeze it tight. We stay there, facing the sun, just like that, in silence. There's no need to say anything. We just let the moment go by on its own.

"You and me, Leo. You and me against the world," she whispers, still admiring the clouds that race toward the horizon.

"Yes. You and me," I echo her.

Silence once again. These are the moments between us that I cherish the most. Moments when we take off our masks, letting our true selves come out: two lonely people, lost in a vast ocean of faces who stare at us, but don't understand us. The human heart is an immense universe that can keep all our secrets and anguishes; an abyss in which, from time to time, you are lucky enough to find a friendly voice and a hand to hold on to when you need it the most.

"You know what? I've made up my mind," she says, sounding amused.

"About what?" I ask in fear.

"Your punishment. I won, so tonight we're gonna watch *Dirty Dancing!*"

chapter three

SOUP-A-LOUP

As soon as we step inside the house, Maggie, my adorable dachshund, greets us with zoomies.

"Easy, Maggie. Good girl!" I tell her, petting her head.

"Leo, Maya, is that you guys?" a voice calls from down the hall.

We follow the voice all the way to the brick kitchen, where we find Bianca, my adoptive mother, standing in front of the cast iron stove. She has a tall, slim figure, with light blue eyes and a pronounced, straight nose, which she claims is the bane of her existence.

"Hey," I say, tapping with my knuckles on the door frame.

She quickly appears from behind the pile of pots and pans, which are all ready to go for the dinner prep.

"Welcome back, guys!"

"How are you, Bianca?" Maya says, with a big smile on her face.

"I'm great, how about you two? How was school? Any news?"

"Nope," I answer quickly. "Nothing new."

I prefer not to tell her about what happened with Miss Abona and my fainting. I know she'd worry and I'm not going to give her any more reason to give me one of her usual lectures.

"So, what's for dinner?" Maya asks, coming to my rescue.

"Yeah, right, what's for dinner?"

"A real treat. Do you guys have any homework?"

"Well, actually we should . . ."

"Nothing for tomorrow," Maya interrupts me.

"Awesome! Then go wash your hands and come help me out. I just need some help with manual labor in the kitchen . . ."

"But, Mom . . ." I huff, falling into the chair.

"Don't mind him, Bianca," Maya says while dragging me by the arm all the way to the sink. "Just tell us what we have to do."

"Cut up the beets and peel the potatoes. I'm making Soup-A-Loup."

"Soup-A-Loup? What is *that*?" I inquire with skepticism.

"It's a recipe I invented myself by taking a little bit of this and that."

"That's great . . ."

I'm really not in the mood to cook, but my protesting gets me nowhere. When my mom and Maya fixate on something, there's nothing I can do but go along with it. So, I arm myself with all my good will, take the apron hanging on the wall, and I begin to peel potatoes. In the meanwhile, Maya is cutting the beets, splattering purple liquid everywhere, and my mother is chopping ribs and smoked sausages that she places in a pan to simmer, along with a mishmash of herbs, carrots, and Cipollini onions.

In moments, the kitchen turns into a disaster of greasy pans and dirty dishes, but it is also engulfed with an exquisite smell of stewed meat and spices. The smell is inviting, giving me hope that it will be just as tasty. Could it be that this Food Jamboree will finally have a happy ending?

Then, the phone rings.

I pick up the phone: "Hello?"

The only thing I hear on the other side of the line is someone breathing, immediately followed by a *click.*

"Who was it?" my mother asks.

"I don't know, they hung up."

As I am about to go back to my potatoes, the phone rings again.

"Hello?"

A sigh once again, only this time sounding much more nervous.

"Who is it?" I ask.

Click.

"Did they hang up again?" my mom asks.

"Yes . . . Who in the world is this idiot getting a kick out of playing this game?"

The phone rings for the third time.

"Alright, now I'll show 'em!" I jump up, bothered.

"No, wait!" My mother stops me, drying her hands on her apron. "I'll answer."

Before I have a chance to rebut, she takes the receiver out of my hands.

"Hello?" A moment of pause. "Oh. It's you."

I can see her becoming tense and turning away, giving me her back.

"No, I can't right now. I'm cooking . . . No . . . No, I really can't, bye."

"Who was it?" I ask out of curiosity.

"Nobody, just a telemarketer," she answers nonchalantly, placing the last of the beets in the pan to simmer. "So, where were we? Oh yes, now it's time to prep for the savoy cabbage . . . Leonardo, how is it going with the potatoes?"

The phone rings again. We look at each other without saying a word. My mom looks somber.

"What do I do? Should I answer and rip them a new one?" I ask her.

"Don't worry, it's probably the telemarketer again," she says in a cold tone.

We let the phone ring for what seems like forever. Whoever is on the other side of the line doesn't show any sign of backing down. I go to answer when all the bulbs in the chandelier, which was off, start exploding in a series of deafening pops, making us jump up in fear. In the confusion, my mother bumps into the pot full of sausage grease, which falls on the floor with a *thud*. Maggie immediately dashes toward it with blinding speed, her tongue hanging out.

"Whoops! Dang it! Leo, get the dog."

"Whoa, what the heck is going on?" Maya bolts.

"Maybe something has gone off . . . maybe the control unit downtown," I hypothesize.

"But all the lights were off," Maya points out quickly.

I notice that my mom is staring at me with an expression that promises nothing good.

"What? What did I say?"

The phone has yet to stop ringing and the big pot with the boiling soup is starting to bubble over, sizzling on the stove.

"Wait here," she tells us, bothered. "I'll go answer this damn call."

I observe my mother walking quickly to the living room. I hear her lift up the receiver and speaking softly. More curious than ever, I grab the receiver in the kitchen, covering the mouthpiece with my hand.

"What are you doing, Leo?!" Maya hisses, as she turns the heat down on the soup.

"*Shhh*," I gesture, placing my ear on the receiver.

"I've already told you this is not a good time," my mother says.

"But it's important!" I hear somebody lamenting in a bitter voice that sounds familiar to me, but I can't put a face to it.

"Not now. That's enough, bye!" my mom concludes, abruptly.

I slowly place the receiver back and I wait for her to come back in the kitchen as if nothing happened. Maya is looking at me, without comprehending what is going on.

"Who was it?" I ask with fake naiveté.

"Your Uncle Victor. He called to say that he wouldn't be joining us tonight," she replies, avoiding eye contact with me.

"My uncle?"

"Yes, he said he had a prior commitment."

Wait a minute! What is she talking about? I'm sure that it was a woman on the phone. So, who was it? What did she want? And more importantly, *why* is she lying to me? A million questions are crowding my brain, unable to find answers.

The afternoon goes by without any more surprises. Even though Mom almost lets the soup stick to the pot a couple of times, and the beets were slightly overcooked, we manage to finish cooking without too many hiccups. As I begin to clean the mess on my cutting board from the four hundred pounds of potatoes I peeled, Maya is helping my mom whip up some sort of white cream, which does not look very appetizing, and toast the croutons for the soup.

Although the days have begun to stretch out, the evening dusk quickly starts to creep into the house, and we light a myriad of candles to have some light. We scatter them around, and within a few minutes, the kitchen glows with magical atmosphere. The grandfather clock in the living room begins to ring. It bellows out eight melodious gong strikes, and almost simultaneously, I hear the front door open to a loud din of laughter and jokes.

"Hello Bianca!" I recognize the voices of Anthony and Christopher, two of my dad's cousins.

"What a smell! What have you cooked?" my father asks, trying to enter the kitchen.

"It's a surprise," Mom answers, pushing him away with her foot. "It is forbidden to come in here!"

I see a smile on my dad's face.

"Hi guys! How's it going?"

"Hey Dad!"

"What's up with all the candles?" he asks, astounded.

"We had a mishap," my mom's tone of voice suddenly lowers. I can't hear exactly what they are saying, but I can clearly grasp a few words: this afternoon, call, urgent. I notice that my dad's facial expression immediately changes, becoming serious. I tiptoe closer and stealthily sneak behind my mom's back at the exact moment that she turns to close the door.

"*Ah!*" she shouts startled, almost perforating my eardrums.

"Leonardo! You almost gave me a heart attack!" she pants, leaning against the wall.

"And you almost made my ears explode."

"What were you thinking, sneaking up behind me like a spy?"

"I'm sorry, I wasn't trying to scare you. I just wanted to say hi to Dad."

"Alright, start taking drinks to the other room, I'll be right there with the soup."

What's going on?

Maya and I load everything up, and watching where we step, we walk through the hall all the way to the living room. The dining room is on the west end of the estate, with large glass doors that open wide on to the hillslope, overlooking the valley.

At the center of the room, there is a big table set for six people, and like every Wednesday evening, my mother has meticulously laid her most elegant, hand-embroidered table set.

In the living room, on the other side of the stone arch, my father Adam is animatedly telling something to his cousins: Chris, the youngest, and his brother Anthony, who we affectionately nicknamed "Big Guy." They have been both working at *Animagorium*, my dad's pet store, since I can remember, and even though they are brothers and both of them belong to the Ghebo family, they look nothing alike. Chris is short and thin, with the classic face of a rascal: a brunette with shifty eyes. Anthony is the total opposite: a big guy, bulky and commanding. He has huge hands and a small head, not well-proportioned to the rest of his Viking-like body. His expression is always serious, bordering on sulking, but it's just superficial, because, truth be told, he's a real jokester.

"Good evening, guys," I announce to get their attention.

"Are you ready for the Food Jamboree?"

"I'd say so!" my father says, as he begins to fumble with his cellphone.

"Hey there, guys! How's it going?" Chris asks.

"Not bad!" Maya smiles. "It could be worse . . ." she adds, sitting at the table.

"Attagirl!" the Big Guy intrudes, approaching us. "I like your optimism!"

I sit across from Anthony and I notice that the number of silver bracelets and rings on each finger has increased. I'm not surprised, he's obsessed. Chris thinks that, if Anthony keeps going this way, soon we will be able to use him as a Christmas tree. Given the number of decorations he already has, all he's missing is a string of lights and the star on the top of his head.

"I see you've bought some more doodads," I say, pointing out his hands.

"What? Oh, these?" Anthony asks. "Yep, I bought myself a few presents."

"When he's done with his fingers, he'll start with his toes," Chris jokes, amused.

Anthony immediately counteracts, muttering, "It's better if you mind your own business."

"'Nuff said, look what I found during my excursion last Sunday," Chris announces enthusiastically, placing a glass vase in front of us. Maya and I get closer to observe two weird flowers with blue-ish petals, sparse and thin, and with very long pistils, red like blood.

"What's this?" Maya asks, curious.

"What, you don't know? What do they teach you in school? These are flowers belonging to a very rare species of *Centaurea*!" he replies. "These are the magical herbs that, according to the legend, were used by Chiron the centaur, Achilles's teacher, to heal the wound caused by the poisoned arrow that that silly ole Hercules shot him with. I haven't been able to find them in years."

"Ah, got it!" I exclaim. "It's that type of cornflower you used to use to make the *Healmey*, right?"

"Whoa, you're all professors here. What's this Healmey?" Maya asks.

"You've never tried it?" Chris replies, astonished. "When you were little, did you never happen to hit your noggin here at la casa de Ghebo?"

"No. Unfortunately it's something I missed out on."

"It's a mix of herbs that Christopher makes," Anthony intervenes. "An ointment that we Ghebos apply on bumps to heal every pain."

"*Ointment . . .*" Chris mutters. "It's more of a miraculous *ointment*, thank you very much."

"Here, look," Anthony says, throwing Maya one of his neck pendants.

"What's this?" she asks as she catches it.

"Look inside."

Maya lays her hands on a flat, round, golden pendant, as big as the size of a quarter. Carved on the front is a strange symbol that resembles a sun with seven rays and small circles on the ends which contained weird symbols.

"How do I open it?"

"Press the button on the side."

"This," I indicate, pushing it.

With a delicate click, the tiny flap opens wide. The pungent odor of the Healmey overflows us instantly.

"The smell is certainly not inviting," she says, tilting her head back in surprise. "It stinks like tar."

"What?" Chris leans toward us. "You still had some of my balm and you didn't tell me anything?"

"You've never asked."

"Do you have any clue how hard it is to find these flowers?" he complains. "At least eight years have passed since I last saw them. I found these in a crevasse of Vetricia plateau, and only I know how long it took me to get them."

"You squeezed yourself into a crevasse?" Maya asks in disbelief.

"Yes, why?"

"My brother is a real daredevil, with a passion for herbalism, mountain climbing, and everything else in between," Anthony explains. "He often disappears for days, sometimes even weeks . . . he says that, by getting back to nature, he's able to find himself again."

"Exactly!" Chris exclaims.

"As soon as we start our summer vacation, I want to come with you," I tell him.

"Sure," he nods. "So what's up with you two? Any news?"

"Nothing new, same old story, same old people, and same old torture at home with that witch my dad married," Maya sighs, throwing the pendant back at Anthony, who catches it.

"She's always breathing down your neck, huh?" Chris asks.

"Breathing? Let's just say that she's clinging onto me like a flea on a dog."

"I'm starving," says my dad all of a sudden, although I thought he was still fumbling with his phone.

He's a round little man, a bit taller than me, with a corky nose and big eyes like an owl, encircled by a pair of glasses with large black frames.

"So, what's for dinner?" he adds.

"Don't worry, Bianca is on her way," Maya reassures him.

"Great! You know lately my meals have consisted of a little bit of broth and a mere, bland salad . . ."

"It's better this way!" Mom clangs, as she makes her triumphant entrance with the Soup-A-Loup. "You've put on a bit of a belly, my dear!"

My dad looks at us, with a goofy grimace, as the delicate smell of stewed meat and spices invades the room.

"Dear, this is not my belly, it's my wisdom."

"Sure, of course! Come on, enough with the chitchat, it's time to eat," she says matter-of-factly. She starts passing around steaming bowls, while Maya tops each one with a spoonful of white foam.

I tease her, hesitantly.

"What's this stuff? Whipped cream?"

"Leo, you know the rules. You've got to eat everything!" mom replies.

I choose to blindly dive in, but as soon as I take in the first few bites, I realize that the soup is exquisite. Tasty and original.

"It's . . . it's good," I say hesitantly.

Then, almost as if my words had paved the way for a whole path of compliments, I hear everyone else chime in.

A victorious smile spreads over my mother's lips. Satisfied, she finishes eating in silence and then disappears into the kitchen.

"The surprises are not over yet," she says, coming back to the dining room with the Cococuddle.

It's my number one favorite dessert, kinda like a tiramisu with cocoa, sweet mascarpone cream, cookies, and coconut milk. A real treat.

Mom approaches the table with a series of glasses made of chocolate, filled with Cococuddle covered in cocoa powder and coconut pralines. In a matter of exactly five seconds, there is no more dessert.

"Great," I say while standing up, feeling fat and happy. "It's time to pay my dues."

"Well said, Leo," Maya smiles.

"Meaning?" Chris asks.

"Tonight, I have to watch the umpteenth mushy movie . . ."

With teasing laughter behind us, Maya grabs my hand and drags me up the stairs that lead up to the bedrooms. I'm really not in the mood to watch *Dirty Dancing,* but the idea of snuggling up in bed next to her makes me hope something more might happen, even if I know it never will. But I can dream, can't I?

chapter four

STRANGE OWLS

"I'm warning you, my room is a real mess," I caution Maya, as we climb up the stairs.

"More than usual?"

"Yep, more than usual. I haven't had much time to tidy up these days."

"Too busy drawing monsters?"

I stop suddenly, stumbling on the steps.

"And how would you know?"

"Come on, Leo! Do you really think you can keep secrets from me?" she says, proceeding up the stairs.

Actually, yes. I have one right here, burning in my chest.

"I see and hear everything!" she adds with a smirk.

"And where exactly would you have seen them?"

"Between the pages of your notebook . . . you always leave it around."

"What?" I almost have a heart attack.

I feel so embarrassed. She probably thinks I'm totally bonkers, kind of like those crazy people in movies who fill up pages upon pages with monsters and nightmares and who sleep with their underwear on their head.

"What did you see? Which page?" I bombard her with questions.

"How the heck do I know?" she says, stopping right in front of my bedroom door. "You always draw the same stuff, the same hooded little monster."

I shove the door open with my hand.

"Yes . . . I know . . . it's just something I've been dreaming about . . ."

The reflection of the moonlight filtering through the window stretches onto my unmade bed. I turn the light on, leaving Maya literally out of breath.

"Oh my Gosh!" she exclaims, entering. "This time you've outdone yourself!"

Actually, Maya is right. I take a second look at my room and see that there's stuff everywhere: piles of clothes on the chair, scattered papers on the bed, books, comics, PlayStation videogames on the floor. A real mess. Clumsily and quickly, I begin to collect the dirty clothes, haphazardly throwing them in the closet.

"Did you know that ancient Egyptians used to consider a mess the matrix of new forms of structure?" I say, trying to gain some time and throwing my pool bag under the bed.

"Thanks for that little pearl of wisdom," she replies in an ironic tone. "Your mom doesn't say anything?"

"Don't get me started. She tortures me every time she comes in here . . ."

"If I were her, I'd hang you outside the window by your big toes . . ."

"Well thank goodness you're not her then," I laugh. "Why don't you get the movie all ready to go, while I try to spruce up the place a little bit."

"So *Dirty Dancing* is OK?"

"Do I have a say in it?"

"Not at all."

"So why do you even ask?" I mutter, as I snatch a piece of dried out candy I found under my desk and throw it at her.

"Hey, quit it!" she says, dodging it.

Out of the corner of my eye, I see her reaching for the shelf where I keep my books, my DVD collection, and about another million nick-nacks.

"Look at the mess you've got up here . . ."

"Shut up and grab the damn movie!" I tell her, as I continue to grab all the stuff scattered around. I pick up papers, fliers, and leaflets that are all over the floor and I hastily stack them on the desk. Some of those papers are covered with my nightmare sketches and since I don't want Maya to see them, I quickly sneak them under my ancient laptop.

"You know, I can't find it," Maya says, still looking through the shelf.

"Look for it! It's gotta be there somewhere."

I gather a few pieces of clothing that are draped over my furniture, two plastic bottles, and a crumpled up tissue. I pick up a couple of T-shirts that I threw on my nightstand, socks stuck behind the headboard, and a pair of jeans that I hung on the handle of the window and . . . my heart jumps up my throat so hard that I almost spit it out. I hold my breath for a moment. Squatting outside on the windowsill, with its slimy hands pressed against the windowpane, a creature is staring at me in the dark. I only see it for a second, but its huge reptile-like eyes terrify me. I scream, step back, stumble, and roll under the bed.

"What is it?" Maya shouts sounding scared, with the Blu-ray in her hand.

"Out there!" I stutter, with a dust bunny stuck on my lips.

"Out there what? Where?"

"There!" I point to the windowpane, now empty. "There was a monster . . . a thing!" I explain, my lips still trembling.

"A monster? . . . What the heck are you talking about?" Maya asks, getting closer to the window.

"No! Come here!"

"There's nothing there," she says, looking out the window.

"Come here!" I repeat, almost struggling to breathe.

"Knock it off, Leo," she says, turning around. "If you don't wanna watch the movie . . ."

"I'm not kidding! There really was something out there. I saw it!"

Suddenly, Maya opens the window.

"What are you doing?" I yell.

The chilly evening air hits my face, blowing away all papers that I put on the desk.

"See, there's nothing there . . ."

"Close it!" I stop her, jumping on her.

"Whoa, calm down . . ."

"There's something out there!" I tell her, almost shouting, as I close the window.

"What in the world do you think is out there? It's probably just an owl or some other nocturnal big ole bird."

"I know what an owl looks like," I blurt.

"Come on, let's watch the movie, and enough with the monster stories! You're being a real pain in the tuchus!" Maya grumbles, throwing the Blu-ray in the PlayStation.

I stand still for a few seconds, focused on the hilly vineyards that stretch up to my window.

"So? Are you coming?" she asks, cannonballing on the bed.

I lie down next to her, but my head is elsewhere. I am confused and scared. How can I stay sane if I keep seeing monsters everywhere? Should I stop watching horror movies? Or maybe I should quit playing videogames with zombies? Perhaps I'm just tired? Could it be the anxiety of the school year that is coming to an end? I mean, anxiety has already played tricks on me. I remember when I was ten years old, while dealing with placement tests in 5th grade, I used to wet the bed almost every night . . . perhaps this is the evolution of stress? I am not sure, but to be honest I'm kind of hoping that's all it is.

I sneak a look at Maya who, with the light blue reflection in her eyes, is watching the movie, weaving her head back and forth to the rhythm of "Be My Baby." I wish I could enjoy the moment, lying down with her and truly feeling like her *baby*. However, I can't help but peek through the window every five seconds. Time slowly goes by, and thank goodness, no more signs of the monster. Maya falls asleep halfway through the movie and I stay there, content to be her pillow.

Even though my arm is seriously going numb, I think these moments are truly special. I know she does it without even thinking about it, and even though I'm gonna have to have my arm amputated by the end of the evening, when she snuggles up with me like this, I can't help but feel important to her. It's as though in these specific moments I'm not *me*, but somebody else: someone I don't know, it's like an out-of-body experience. A guy who's happy, serene, and just a little less paranoid. I look at Maya. A tear is shining in the corner of her eye. Where are you now? In what world are you seeking solace to avoid thinking about your troubles?

"Leo, it's past eleven . . ." my mother informs me, peeking through the door.

"OK," I reply, inviting her to close the door with a gesture.

Maya slowly wakes up, stretching out.

"This movie is always amazing, isn't it?"

"Oh c'mon, you slept through the whole thing," I tell her, pumping my fist to get the blood flowing once again.

"Absolutely not! True, my eyes wcrc closed but I was listening the whole time."

"Sure, you were!" I push her with my foot while tickling her on the side.

"Stop it!" she says, curling into a ball to avoid the tickles. "I'm super tired tonight . . ."

She yawns, putting her shoes on. She hesitates for a moment. I can tell that her mind is elsewhere.

"What is it?"

"I can't stand the idea of having to go back home. I really don't wanna see that witch. I just hope she's already asleep."

"Your dad is away for work?" I ask, glancing at the window.

"You mean that stranger who stops by from time to time just so I can wash his dirty clothes?" she asks, following my line of sight. "Are you still thinking about that monster?"

"What? . . . No, I was just . . . I mean . . ."

The chilly air creeps in the room once again, and I stiffen up almost imperceptibly.

"OK, never mind. Let me close the window, so at least you stop thinking about silly things."

The crescent moon shines brightly in the sky and a strong wind blows, rustling the tops of the chestnut trees in the yard. We walk down the hall, quietly. Anthony and Chris have already left, Mom and Dad are in their room, getting ready for bed.

"Could you please thank your folks for me?" she asks.

"Sure," I reply, while opening the door.

"Goodnight, Leo. And be careful of those monsters on the roof!" she says, teasing me.

"I know you're joking, but I swear I saw something outside the window."

"Oh yeah, sure!" she giggles. "Monsters do not exist, Leo."

I nod without saying a word, and she gives me a peck on the cheek.

"I'll see you tomorrow at school," she says, as she walks away.

I snuggle into my sweatshirt, watching her get on her scooter and disappear through the vineyards, down the hill that leads to the town. I stay there for a few moments, pricking my ears and squinting my eyes so I can see better in the dark. The hooting of an owl echoes in the countryside, startling me. That's my monstrous creature. I've got to put a stop to my wild imagination. Maya is right, monsters do not exist.

chapter five

FUTURE AND PAST

Amber. It's the color you see when you look toward the sun with your eyes closed. Some say it's the color of our soul, others insist it's the color of Heaven. To me, it's the color of clear skies that anticipate the arrival of summer vacation.

Also today, a cool breeze is blowing, caressing the meadow and gently folding the petals of the first few daises we've seen this year. Laying down in the middle of the hillside, arms crossed under my head, I breathe in the fresh air that comes from the woods. The sun is much warmer today, and the grass is as soft as a pillow. Even though my eyes are closed, I can sense Maggie trotting around me like a bodyguard, jumping up and down from time to time in an attempt to catch a grasshopper.

It's exactly two past five on this wonderful day, and yes, I am happy to say that I'm finally feeling pretty good. Afflictions, nightmares, and sorrows are all part of my yesterday and for now, I've decided not to focus on them anymore. Or, at least, I can *try* not to focus on them. This morning, at school, everything went smoothly: no lectures and no surprise oral exams. Could it be because I didn't have a lesson with my science teacher? Actually, come to think about it, my problems only occur when I'm dealing with that harpy, Miss Abona. It's as if that woman is my nemesis, kinda like kryptonite for Superman. Whenever she's around, I'm always the victim of rotten luck.

I resurface from my thoughts, rubbing my back on the ground and digging a little valley beneath me in the grass as the weaving stalks tickle me. The sun kisses my forehead, pulling me away from my responsibilities. How could I possibly stay inside to do my homework on such a beautiful day? Plus, I have plans with Maya. Today, at school, she looked kinda down. I tried to make her laugh, but it didn't really help. I tried to ask her what had happened, but she kept giving me monosyllabic answers. She told me she preferred to talk to me in private.

No worries, Leo, I keep telling myself. *Don't get your hopes up!* Obviously, I'm not holding my breath. I'm sure she just wants to tell me, for the umpteenth time, about that dude who stood her up. I mean, it's his fault if she's so down now. And I'm gonna have to listen quietly while every single word she says stabs me in the heart.

Maya texted me to meet her at a spot we call "Ourhill," the hilltop behind my house where we've been going since we were kids. It's not really a special place, but we like to think of it as if it were. I've been waiting for her for the past thirty minutes but, so far, no sign of Maya. We said we'd meet at half past four, I'm sure of it. I check my phone again, scrolling through the texts. Yep, 4:30, no doubt.

I pick a daisy and I start to slowly chew on the stem. The sour taste of chlorophyll hits my tongue. I'm starting to get worried. Maybe Maya is in trouble with that old witch who lives in her house. I start picturing different scenarios of fights and arguments: flying dishes, slamming doors, and giant padlocks that are suddenly fastened, forever imprisoning my friend. I picture her crouched in a corner of the basement, desperately sobbing with her head between her knees and . . .

My phone pings and brings me back to reality. A text. It's Maya.

Simon called!! He asked me to meet him in 5 @ the town square 😊 😊 😊 😊 😊 😊!! I'm so freaking excited!!! See you at school. XOXO

What?! I sit down and read the text at least ten more times, to the point of exhaustion. I can feel my phone cracking under the pressure of my grip, as I picture Simon's tattooed neck in between my hands. The usual demonic rage takes over me, stiffening my every muscle.

"Damn it!" I growl, as I lay down on my back once again. How could this be? Is it possible that I am just her third wheel? The doubt, pardon, the *certainty* that to Maya I'm nothing more than a convenient replacement starts to burn inside of me like a huge fire. The words of that lowlife Crippa are echoing in my head: *Just wait till she finds someone better and she'll forget you ever existed.*

I can't just pretend that it didn't happen, even if Maya says I shouldn't pay attention to him; that big ole ape is right! To her, I'm nothing more than a shoulder to cry on.

"I'm *nobody's son* and I don't deserve anything," I repeat to myself, whispering.

Maya is just like everybody else; I am nothing to her. After all, if even my real parents have abandoned me, what can I actually expect from her?

I stare into the distance, focusing only on my pain. I'm not doing well. I'm *really* not doing well. I feel like I'm suffocating, but I try my hardest to quell my disappointment and the feeling of defeat that I am experiencing. I take a deep breath. I can't let myself go, otherwise it'll be over for me. I squeeze my eyelids shut so hard that I start to see red dots in front of me, as I keep listening to the sounds that come from the valley. The wind becomes stronger. Suddenly, I hear a *hissing* sound in my left ear, immediately followed by a *woosh*. Something passes within an inch of my face, sticking into the ground on my right. My eyes are wide open now. The sun is blinding me, but in the black shadow that hangs over me, I immediately recognize the proud figure of my Uncle Victor; in his hands, the stick that almost smashed my head.

"Uncle Vic! You almost gave me a heart attack!" I shout, sitting up.

It's as though he appeared from nowhere. His eyes are shining, his beard is ungroomed, and his smile is painted wide on his face. He really doesn't look like he's seventy years old.

"Warrior, have you forgotten all my teachings?"

"Not today, Uncle Vic! It's one of those days."

"Why? What happened?" he asks, bending down, already at Maggie's mercy, who's happy to see him.

"The usual stuff . . ."

"You mean that ignorant friend of yours . . . that Creepy boy?"

"I wish it was just that . . . and by the way, his name is Crippa, and he is definitely not my friend!" I reply, in a bothered tone.

"Did he belittle you again?"

"He tried to . . ."

"Why does he bully you? Have you tried talking to him?"

"Are you crazy?!" I exclaim. "He's jealous of Maya . . . he thinks he's got a shot with her, and he hates the fact that I'm her friend."

"But she's only got eyes for you, am I right?" he asks, nudging me in the side with his elbow.

I feel my head pounding, and my ears popping. Rage is boiling inside of me.

"Let's not talk about it," I say, holding back.

"Why?"

"If you could see what I have inside of me at this very moment, you wouldn't recognize me."

"Well then . . . *En garde!*" he jumps up, breaking a stick in half.

"Oh, come on, Uncle Vic . . . please . . ."

Nope, *nada*. Clearly, he didn't hear a word I said. He throws the other half of the stick at my feet and begins to move around me, brandishing his half-stick like a sword.

"Uncle Vic . . ." I complain.

"Quit whining."

He snaps forward and whacks me on the knuckles so hard that I see stars.

"Hey! This is an unfair match!"

"Stand up and fight! There is no such thing as an unfair match in battle. We are not playing here; we are fighting for our lives."

I stand up quickly, my fingers still burning. My uncle looks at me with this weird grin on his face. We move in circles, studying each other like two wolves ready to shred the opponent. A former professor of ancient literature and a big fan of the *Medieval Times*, Uncle Victor is one of the most well-known antiquarians in town. He turned the old rustic house where he lives into a museum, and as a real die-hard aficionado of duels and Medieval weapons, he has taught me everything he knows on the subject. So, while my peers were playing soccer, I spent my childhood simulating fights to the death with him: at first with wooden swords, then, once I was a bit older, with metal and padded ones.

"Uncle Vic, you know you shouldn't fight me when I'm so angry."

"*Woo*, I'm so scared . . . I'm about to wet my pants," he teases, swirling the stick.

Within a second, he makes a direct lunge to my side. I parry it, but I can't guard the second one, which touches me right in my ribs, making me stagger backward.

"Ouch!" I look at my uncle, with my eyes wide open. I can feel my thirst for revenge becoming stronger.

"Come on, you wimp! You'll let an old fart like me push you around?"

I let it go, freeing myself of all the nastiness pent up inside me: maybe it's just what I need. I make a feint, step right, and lunge straight to the torso. He parries my lunge, awkwardly leaving his right side unprotected, so I quickly turn to attack him on his shoulder. But he's faster than me, and our sticks cross in mid-air with a *snap* so powerful it makes my hands vibrate.

"Control yourself, Leo! Your rage won't make you a better warrior, just a more violent and clumsy one."

I spin to attack again, but he parries one more time, and with a quick move of his wrist, he counterattacks, pushing my weapon up, and leaving me defenseless. My stick flies out of my hands and lands on the ground a few feet away from me, leaving my uncle the opportunity to attack. He lunges in a series of left and right blows which I manage to skillfully guard.

"Are you crazy? If you stab me that hard, you'll kill me."

His stick draws a semicircle in the air, aiming at my shins. I jump up with both feet, and taking advantage of his miss, I spin around and trip him then snatch his stick as he falls on his back.

"The secret is to bend your rage to your will, so that it turns into strength," I pant, pointing his stick against his chest.

"Bravo, Leo . . ." he looks at me with shining eyes. "Well done, but you have to work more on your grip."

"Yes, I know, I should be more careful," I say, as I continue to spin the stick in my hands.

"Now, please help me up! I'm old, and between hits and sticks, my bones are creaking a bit," he says, reaching his hand out to me.

I go to help him up when, out of nowhere, he pulls me forward, placing his foot on my chest, and with one quick move, he makes me flip over him in a mid-air somersault. I land on my back with a *thud* so hard that it takes my breath away.

"Never let your guard down, warrior! Remember?" he laughs, crawling by my side.

"You got me!" I reply, laughing with him.

For a few moments, we just lie there next to each other, without uttering a single word. We stare at the movement of the clouds that form white shapes in the sky.

"Can I ask you something?" my voice breaks the silence.

I can sense uncertainty from his part. My uncle waits for a moment before answering me. He clears his throat, gaining some more time to think.

"Does it have to do with whatever's been bothering you lately?"

Caught! As always, he already knows everything.

"Well, actually, it's been quite a while," I sigh.

"Does it have to do with your past?"

"Yes. In these last few days, I've been constantly thinking about my parents. My *real* parents."

"And?"

"And I ask myself *why*. Why do you think they abandoned me?"

"I've already told you a million times, Leo. It happens."

"But I need to know why . . ."

My uncle sighs, staring at the sky, looking for the right words to say.

"You know, Leonardo, life is not always what we hope for. At times, you may find yourself in situations that you did not prepare for and go beyond your ability to comprehend."

"What do you mean?"

"Maybe your parents found themselves facing a problem so big we can't even imagine, and they knew they couldn't take care of you . . ."

"But what kind of problem can push a parent to abandon their own child?"

"Maybe your Mom and Dad were very young, and as such, they knew they weren't ready to raise you. So, they preferred to give you to people who were."

"Perhaps, I hate them anyway. They shouldn't have abandoned me."

My Uncle Victor doesn't reply. He prefers to remain silent, and so do I.

"I'm *nobody's* son, and that's the truth," I suddenly mutter.

"What are you even saying, Leonardo?" my uncle exclaims, quickly turning his head.

I can feel his eyes staring at me, harshly, like two boulders weighing down on me. Yet, I keep talking: "I know, I'm lucky to have my adoptive family, but I still feel abandoned."

"I hope that Adam and Bianca never hear you say those things, Leonardo. It would kill them," he says in a harsh tone.

"I know, that's why I'm telling you."

Silence fills the room for a moment. When he speaks again his tone is a bit softer.

"You know, I still remember the day you arrived in this family. You were just a newborn, and your head was full of hair, red like fire. We have loved you since the very first moment we saw you, Leo. You've changed our lives; you've given meaning to our future. Do you know what I'm saying?"

"I think so . . . thank you, Uncle."

I close my eyes, take a deep breath, and let the amber from the sun, and the peace from the garden, envelop me.

"In your opinion, why do you think Mom and Dad have finally decided to tell me the truth?" I mutter. "I mean, they could have not told me anything, and I would have never known."

"Because you have the right to . . . know," he whispers.

"But the truth is so painful."

"Oh, let it go!" he scolds me, sitting up. "Your life is not this huge nightmare you pretend it is. Don't act so pathetic!"

"I'm not pathetic!"

"Leonardo, it's hard to find shadows in a dark room, especially when there aren't any."

I sneer at him.

"And what would you know about my shadows?"

"I was your age once, and I know exactly how these things work. Your only problem is that you can't figure out how to tell Maya how you really feel about her."

"Is it that obvious?" I ask, crushed.

"I'm afraid so . . ."

"Today she stood me up to go out with an idiot."

"Well, she might have stood you up today, but she spends almost every other day and night with you. Have you ever thought about that?"

"But it doesn't mean anything. To her I'm just a friend."

"Be more confident. Things will change, you'll see."

"You really think so?"

"Friendship between a boy and a girl is a strange and amazing thing that, more often than not, turns into love. And keep in mind that, at your age, these kinds of friendships are never disinterested."

"I know, but I'm afraid that, in our case, the interest comes only from my side, and it may just be an unrequited love!" I say smiling, and my uncle chuckles. Then we both start laughing out loud and our voices dissolve in the wind.

How I hope he is right.

"Anyway, I'm so mad at her."

"You'll get over it . . ."

"And to think that last night, after the Food Jamboree, we cuddled up in my bed for two hours while watching a movie," I whisper, feeling a little embarrassed.

"You see?"

"Oh, speaking of last night . . . how come you didn't join us?"

"I spent the day in Florence at an auction."

"And you got word at the last minute?"

"What do you mean?" he asks, frowning.

"Why did you wait till the afternoon to call and tell us you weren't coming?"

"Well . . . truth is . . . who told you that?"

"Mom."

"Your mother told you I called her yesterday?"

"Actually . . . I was there when you called," I reply in a firm, confident tone, even though the truth is that it wasn't my Uncle Victor on the other side of the line.

I watch him biting his lip. He does it whenever he's in an awkward situation.

"Yes, I actually called at the last minute because I wasn't sure if I was going to stay in Florence for dinner."

Surprise! My uncle has chosen to go along with my mom's lie. But why? I am about to ask him a more difficult question to see if he cracks, but I can tell he has disengaged from our conversation. I follow his line of sight, and for a second, I see something run and then disappear in the nearby woods. Shivers run down my spine, as if my subconscious already knows what it is.

"What was that?" I quickly ask.

My uncle opens his mouth, but he doesn't get the chance to answer because Maggie hits the ground running.

"Maggie! Come back here!" I jump up, trying to catch her.

"Leonardo, wait!" my uncle shouts.

But it's too late, she's already run down the hill.

"Maggie, stop!" I yell.

I reach the valley, almost out of breath. Maggie is in front of me, standing still a few feet from the woods. It seems like she's gone crazy. She's a bundle of nerves, growling at something hidden behind a hedge of mastic trees.

"What is it? Did you see something?" I ask her, worried.

"Keep the dog back. It could bite," my uncle screams behind my back, as he leaps down the hill.

I try to calm Maggie down, but she doesn't listen to me; she keeps barking and growling.

"Come here, Maggie." I tell her, looking into the woods.

"Let's g . . ."

My mouth opens wide; I try to scream, but no sound comes out. A few feet from the edge of the woods, a monstrous creature is looking at me from behind the trunk of an oak tree. It's the same thing I saw yesterday outside my window. This time I can see it clearly. It is incredibly skinny and it looks like an alien. Its body is human-shaped, but its skin is green and hairless, with long thin amphibian limbs. Its oval-shaped head is bald with a flat nose and a protruding mouth, like a reptile. But the most frightening things are its eyes. Disturbing. Ravenous. The eyelids are two blades that move very quickly and in the middle of its yellow eyeballs there are two black chasm-like pupils.

"Leonardo, get away from there!" My uncle makes me jump in fear, as he grabs me by the shoulder. "Maggie, let's go!"

At the sight of my uncle, the creature wrinkles its nose, revealing sharp fangs, and with a jump, it disappears, camouflaged in the green forest.

"Uncle Vic, did you see it too?" I ask, terrified.

"What?"

I point toward the trees. I'm shaking like a leaf and I'm having a hard time keeping my finger straight.

"The monster . . . that creature!" I mutter, my mouth completely dry.

"Monster? . . . What in the world are you talking about?"

"There's a monster in the woods. Last night, it was outside my window and now it's there . . ."

My Uncle Victor places his arm behind my back, pulling me close to his chest.

"Not bad, Leo, not bad. You almost got me."

"I'm not making it up! Listen to me!" I exclaim, forcing myself out of his tight embrace.

"Come on, no more jokes."

"Uncle, I really did see something."

"Well, not all that we see actually turns out to be what we think we saw," he tells me with a serious expression. "Maybe it was just a wild boar, or maybe a deer, and in the shadow, you confused it for a monster. You know, imagination sometimes plays tricks on us, and well, you surely have a lot of it," he concludes, ruffling my hair.

"I guess, but to me it seemed so real . . ."

"Go home!" he says.

Confused, I walk up the slope, shivering and pulling my sweatshirt tight. What's wrong with me? Why do I keep seeing that *thing*? I turn around. My uncle is still there where I left him, and he's watching me. I wave goodbye. He answers by raising his hand. What's he doing? Why is he there keeping an eye on me? I scratch my head, call Maggie, and with the wind ruffling my hair, I walk up the path that takes me home. Yep, it's official: I'm really starting to get worried.

chapter six

THE YUTH

The sun is going down and the golden light of sunset lays on the meadows, drawing long shadows on the grass. I put on my blue hoodie, and bundled up, I walk with the backdrop of the pink, late-spring sky. I can't manage to get the image of that creature I've just seen out of my mind. It's the second time in two days. It's not normal. Not one bit. But the more I think about it, the more I believe my uncle is right. Imagination plays tricks at times. I clench my teeth as I come to terms with the absurdity of what I thought was real. *Monsters don't exist,* Maya's voice echoes in my head. I walk along the path that descends on the eastern side of the hill. Maggie is behind me hopping through the grass and trying to catch fireflies awakening at dusk.

On the horizon, through the vineyards that stretch as far as the eye can see, I can already spot the roof of my house. I recognize the color of the terracotta shingles, make out the little round window in the attic, as well as the chimney puffing gray clouds as always. I'm tired and sore, and the only thing I want to do right now is take a warm shower. I think back once again on what my uncle said. Maybe it is true. Maybe if I was more confident, things with Maya would change. Maybe I should just come clean and tell her how I feel about her.

Suddenly, I come to a halt, and Maggie with me. What if she just bursts out laughing? What if she tells me I repulse her? *Leonardo, you are just a friend to me and . . . blah, blah, blah* (where actually the *blahs* stand for *loser, lousy,* or even *cockroach*). Yep, that's the problem: she might brush me off and make a fool of me! I'd rather be buried alive.

Two crows fly across the piece of sky right above me and *PLOPP!* a drop of bird poop barely misses my head.

"Whoa, that was close!" I exclaim, taking a step back.

I hear the crows cawing and watch as they fly back toward the woods, down the valley. *Jerks.* I smile, as I can't help but think that, despite the rotten luck that I was almost pelted in the middle of a giant meadow, I was actually lucky not to end up being hit. Yes, I know, it's stupid, but this gives me enough hope to try and see things under a better light. But what if this wasn't the case? With Maya, I mean. I start walking again, a bit faster this time. Maybe, if I confronted her, she might start seeing me for who I am and she would understand that she could have everything she ever wanted with me: an accomplice, a best friend, and a great boyfriend. I can already picture it: me and her, lying on Ourhill with the dim light of the sunset as the background to our whispers, and the summer breeze blowing through our hair. As usual, we laugh and then we remain silent. We stare at each other for a moment. A kiss–delicate, intense. A kiss that brightens the whole world, or at least mine.

Alright, that's it. I've got to tell Maya how I feel. I have to talk to her right now. She should be home by now, but I take the dirt road that leads to her house. I am no longer walking. I'm running. While going downhill, my speed increases to the point that, before I'm even conscious of it, I'm actually rolling downhill. I finally stop when I reach the small chestnut tree right behind Maya's house. The prickly and sharp needles of the chestnut fruits, scattered everywhere on the ground from last fall, poke me all over, driving me crazy and making me itch. Shows you how lucky I am, *ha.* Maggie is right behind me, her tongue hanging out.

I stand up and brush off my filthy shoulders. My head is full of specks, my hands are filled with thorns, and my elbows and knees are covered in dirt and grass, like a little kid. Now this is just great! It had been years since I rolled downhill like a snowball in an avalanche. I just hope no one saw me. I look around me with caution, until a paralyzing, high-pitched laugh explodes from behind the trees right in front of me.

I could recognize that laugh anywhere. Maya.

With a terrible crushing feeling in my soul, I pick Maggie up, and tiptoeing, I slowly walk through the woods, stepping on wet leaves, careful not to step on sticks or anything that could draw their attention. I lean against the large trunk of a tree, and looking over the nearby clearing, I find myself in front of a scene that comes at me like a brick to the face. Maya and that dude, Simon, are lying in the middle of the meadow, next to each other, getting cozy and looking all lovey-dovey. They giggle and laugh like two sweethearts.

The dim light of the sunset is the background to their whispers; the summer breeze blowing through their hair . . . No! This was my dream, damn it! Jealousy nabs my heart and the butterflies that I feel in my stomach whenever I think of Maya are now dead, digested, and forgotten. The feelings have been replaced by a shapeless tangle, a mess of venomous snakes.

I feel the need to destroy, smash, and vent somehow. It's the first time I've felt such an intense sensation. So *dark* and forceful. This is not just rage, no it's something more. It's something that is hurting me, growing inside of me like a balloon pushing hard against my heart. I hold Maggie in a tight embrace. She squirms, but I hold her still.

"You know, I didn't think you were so nice," the dude says. "I thought you were gonna be like one those girls who are so full of themselves." He gently moves a curly, light lock of her hair from her forehead.

"Never judge a woman by her appearance," Maya twitters with a smile on her face.

A brief pause, a languid expression. A kiss. Something inside of me breaks. That kiss is passionate, greedy, and it lasts much longer than I can bear. With a step, I'm on to him. I grab that jerk by the hair, I lift him off the ground, and I throw him away in the bushes. I get close to Maya, lean over and kiss her.

A long, gentle kiss. The same one that I have dreamed of a million times.

"Why did you wait so long, Leo?" she asks me with a whisper as sweet as honey.

Maggie moves against my chest, making me slip back into reality. They are still glued together by the mouth in what must be a record. I lean with my back against the trunk, looking away. I can't keep staring. I just can't. I close my eyes and tilt my head back against the tree. The prickly bark pinches my nape. Yet, I keep pushing harder and harder, trying to feel pain to quell the pain in my heart. At this very moment, I wish I could just sink, disappear, disintegrate. I can feel the chestnut tree slowly creaking, then the *pops* become much more vigorous. I don't have time to find out what's going on. Suddenly there is a *crash*. The wood breaks and the trunk moves away from my back, tilting toward the two of them, who are still lying on the ground. I pull back, scared. The tree doesn't look rotten, so what the heck is going on? I just leaned against it, nothing more. I want to scream, warn Maya, but my words die inside my throat before I have the chance to release them. Maggie yelps. Then, a scream. "*Move!*" shouts Simon. Maya rolls away, pushed by the boy, just a second prior to the tree crashing on the ground. A pile of leaves on the ground doesn't allow me to see what is going on.

"Maya . . ." I call out.

But yet again, my voice won't come out. I hear a moan, then, Maya screams again. In that huge chaos, I can see my friend, safe, leaning over Simon who's still flat on the ground. In the impact, something must have hit his leg because a trail of blood is soaking through his jeans. Damn! He almost kicked the bucket . . .

"Simon! Stay still, don't move," Maya says, trying to reach her cellphone.

"No worries, it doesn't hurt," he calmly reassures her, looking around.

I hide just in time. Maya hugs him. She's scared, I can tell.

"You saved my life, do you get that?"

"Just another day at the office," that stupid creep replies, with a forced smile.

Instinctively, I would run to their rescue, to see if I could help, but something inside of me keeps me from doing so, telling me not to, to let things play out. I walk away in a state of shock, wobbling like a zombie. They don't need me, and it'd be better if I disappear before Maya sees me. Maggie is still in my arms. She's shaking like a leaf. She's disoriented, and so am I. I feel my eyes tearing up. I can barely hold back my tears. I am broken, dead, cheated, and destroyed. I don't know if I'll ever be able to recover from this. Why am I suffering so much?

I walk back on the same path that I ran on, only this time it's uphill and I'm holding a dog. I'm sweating, running out of breath, and the wind is blowing down my spine, making me shiver. My heart is in a thousand pieces, and no matter how hard I try, I can't figure out why.

Why can't you see me, Maya?

I drag myself to the front door. I am about to step inside when an out-of-place splash of color catches my eye. Parked in the corner of the front yard is the old red VW Beetle that belongs to my teacher, Miss Abona. What little blood I have left in my veins is now rushing down my legs. My stomach contracts. I take my hand off the door handle and slide into the rocky garden. I put Maggie down, then crawl through the Rhododendron and finally reach the dining room window. The dog is right behind me and is biting the hem of my sweatshirt, pestering me.

"Easy, Maggie," I whisper, scared to get caught.

I get near the window, just close enough to hear the voices coming from my house. Sitting with my back against the wall, I pick up my dachshund again, extending my ears in the hopes of overhearing something. It takes me less than a second to recognize Miss Abona's shrill voice filled with attitude.

" . . . And I can tell you that this is not even the first time."

"What do you mean?" I hear my dad's voice. "How come he's already home?"

"Leonardo often falls into a strange state of . . . how to put this . . . catalepsy," the witch adds. "Recently, I have caught him sleeping on the desk at least twice. As we know, this is definitely not a good sign."

"No, surely not," Mom intervenes.

"And I also caught him drawing this stuff . . ."

Great, she's showing them the papers she took away from me yesterday that are covered in my doodles.

"When did he make these?" my dad quickly asks.

"Yesterday . . ."

"Why didn't you tell us immediately?" he inquires.

"I tried to, I spent the whole afternoon calling you, but you didn't pick up and *she* didn't want to talk!"

"Yes . . ." Mom mutters. "You're right, it's *my* fault."

So, it *was* her! She was the one who called! She hung up because I picked up the phone and she didn't have the guts to talk to me. Filthy coward. Damned jerk.

"Look," Miss Abona replies. "He filled a whole notebook."

Silence. A deafening silence that is shuttered only by my mother's sobs. She's crying. I hate Miss Abona, since forever, and now I have one more reason.

"We knew it," Miss Abona the witch adds. "We knew this was going to happen sooner or later. It was just a matter of time."

"Yes!" my mom exclaims sadly. "But we also thought we had a bit more time!"

"Bianca, calm down," my dad comforts her. "Everything will be OK, you'll see. Maybe it's just an inkling. Maybe it's not time yet . . ."

"I really don't think so," that arrogant Miss Abona interrupts, "Everythi . . ."

"Hey!" my father stops her, raising his voice, "Shall I remind you; you're talking about our son!"

What? Why would my dad talk like that, especially to one of my teachers!

"Adam, try to stay calm," Miss Abona says with her usual bitter tone.

"I can't stay calm, alright?" my father replies in anger. "You can't come here with your snooty attitude . . ."

"Oh no! I really don't deserve to be treated this way!" Now it's the jerk who's raising her voice. "I'd like to remind you all that Leonardo is not your son. And I too . . ."

"Alright, calm down, you are taking this too far. This is not the time to quarrel," I hear a fourth person add.

A warm, gentle voice that, with major shock, I recognize immediately that it's Mike, the janitor at my school! But what is he doing here, at my house, with Miss Abona?

"Right now, we've got to stick together," the janitor adds. "The symptoms that Leonardo is showing are alarming and his nightmares are not a good thing. We have to be realistic. The boy is growing up and maybe his *Yuth* is starting to reveal itself."

My *what*? What the heck are they talking about?

"But how could this be?" I hear my dad question.

"I don't know," Mike answers, at a loss.

"But we can try to cover it up again, right?" Mom asks.

"We've done it so far, but if it has revealed itself now, there's nothing we can do about it."

A brief pause is broken only by my mother's weeping.

"Yesterday, after class, I found him passed out on the floor," Mike quickly reveals.

Traitor! That's the last thing I needed to add to my plate.

"What? Passed out?" my dad says, rattled and anxious.

"Yes, but I think it's just a consequence of what's happening."

"No, it's not possible . . . it just can't be!" I hear my mom say.

"Bianca, stop crying," the janitor scolds her with an awkwardly confident tone, as if they've known each other for a very long time. "We knew since day one that this was going to happen at some point."

"But he's just a kid!" she protests.

"You're right, but we can't just forget everything that is inside of him, and even we can't stop the inevitable," Mike explains. "Please, don't panic . . . I'm sure Leonardo won't give up."

"Where is he anyway?" Miss Abona asks with vigilance.

"He went up the hill. He was supposed to meet with Maya and maybe Victor," Mom replies, blowing her nose.

"Speaking of Victor . . . I'd rather he wasn't aware of all of this for now," Mike cautiously mutters.

What? Why would he have anything to do with my uncle and my family business?

"But why? It's not fair," Mom quickly disagrees.

"I get it," he abruptly replies. "But we all know where he stands on this matter. I think it's too early to tell him about it."

Tell him *what*? What's the matter? What the heck are you all talking about?

"So be it," Dad says. "Now go, it's late. Leonardo will be back soon, and I don't want him to find you two here. He would ask way too many questions."

Well, duh!

"Right," I hear the janitor agree.

"Let's stay on top of it," the teacher mutters. "We know all the risks associated with this. We have to be ready for the worst."

Worst? Worse than what? I feel like my brain is melting out of my ears like molten lead. I'm going crazy.

"Is the *Am-Arcanus* still on?" Mike asks.

"Absolutely," Mom replies. "We'll check later tonight, but for now you really should leave . . . and take away those drawings. I never want to see them again."

All of a sudden, I hear noises. Chairs being dragged on the floor, steps getting closer, and the door opening. My dad is walking those two snitches to their car.

I choose to stay a little longer here, curled up under the window, my arms wrapped around Maggie and my soul lost in emptiness. I go through everything that I've just heard, my dreams, my hallucinations, and I come to the only possible solution: I'm a whack job, I'm crazy! They talked about *symptoms,* they said they knew this day would come. Mike even mentioned my nightmares. But how would he know? I never told anyone! They used the word Yuth: is that the name of my disease? My cell phone starts to ring, muffled by my pocket, but who cares. I put it on vibrate, without checking who's calling. The move, however, loosens my grip on Maggie who, distracted by the noises coming from the front yard, squirms hard enough to free herself.

"Maggie, no!" I whisper.

I crawl through the bushes, watching from my hiding place: Dad, Mike, and Miss Abona are over there talking, standing in the fiery twilight on the horizon. When Maggie runs toward them, my dad becomes pale and starts to look around, scared that I might be nearby. Without even saying goodbye, the janitor and the teacher get in the car and skid away, spinning down the dirt road. *Cowards!*

I hide behind an azalea bush in bloom, staring at my father who, in pain, watches the old piece of red crap drive away. I am still here when my dad walks back inside the house, and I am still here when my mom starts crying again. Hopelessness is sucking the life out of me. I decide to stay here for a while longer, pretending that I never existed. It's my cellphone again. It vibrates. And I let it vibrate forever. Maybe a couple of seconds go by, or maybe a few minutes. The thing is that once I stand back up, my legs feel heavy, and my hands and feet are literally frozen. It's been dark for a while now and the cold air bites without mercy.

I walk inside the house, trying not to make any noise. The evening news theme song bursts from the living room and rumbles into all the other rooms. I follow the voice of the news anchor presenting the first news of the night, and I walk all the way to the stone arch in the living room. The logs in the fireplace are still popping, even though they are definitely close to becoming a pile of gray ash. The heat makes my face throb and feel flushed. Dad has his back to me, sitting on the dark green cloth armchair, with Maggie curled up on his lap. He's not watching TV; rather, he's gazing into space at something that probably only exists in his mind. From the bowl of the pipe he's smoking, rises small and uninterrupted puffs of a sweet aroma that fills the room, contrasting the fireplace smell. I can sense his tension at a physical level.

"Dad . . ."

He turns toward me. The sadness in his eyes clash against the smile on his face.

"Oh, there you are . . . where have you been?"

"Around," I quickly lie.

"Maggie's been here for a while," he says, nodding to the little one who's now asleep on his lap. "Your mother and I were wondering where you've been."

"I was up on the hill, then Maggie started running toward the house. I thought she was hungry."

"What happened to your pants?" he asks me, nodding at my knees dirty with mud and grass.

"I fell while running, klutz that I am . . ."

Dad forces a smile once again, thinning out his lips in a smirk that, I know, hides other thoughts. The more I stare at him, the more I realize that, in these past few hours, he looks like he's gotten at least ten years older. He's got an empty stare and purple bags under his eyes. I can sense my heart shrinking, feeling at the same time, both responsible and helpless for what he's going through. I swallow my guilty feelings away.

"You're smoking in the house," I point out, faking a calm expression to try and lift his spirit.

"What? *Ehm*, yes . . . it's alright for tonight," he says sadly, inhaling deeply from the pipe.

"Where's Mom?"

"Over there."

I walk to the kitchen. My mother is leaning with both hands on the sink, her head down on the dish sponge. A few locks of hair in disarray flow from her bun. I clear my throat to get her attention. She turns quickly as if suddenly awakened with a slap on her face, and with an instinctive gesture she tries to fix her hair, taking the attention away from the gloom that engulfs her.

"Hi, Leo. How was your afternoon?" she asks all at once, attempting to appear believable.

"Good, yours?"

"Were you with Maya?" she asks quickly, as she turns to keep washing the dirty dishes.

"No, she had other plans."

"So, what did you end up doing? Did you meet with your uncle? How's he doing?"

"He's fine . . . how about you though, how are you?" I ask her in a serious tone.

She drops her act immediately. She stops, lets the sponge fall out of her hand, and stays motionless for a few seconds. The voice of the news anchor on TV in the other room is the only sound we hear. Once she finally gathers enough courage to look at me, I can tell she's about to burst out in tears. She takes a step toward me. Her eyes fill.

"Leonardo . . ."

She hugs me tight without uttering another word. She lays her head on my shoulder, getting my neck all wet with her tears. I wish I could say something, but a lump in my throat stops my voice from coming out, leaving me still and embarrassed.

"Don't ever forget who you are," she whispers out of nowhere.

I slowly nod, not really knowing what to say. Then, she walks away, dries her eyes and attempts to smile.

"Come on, it's late! I've gotta put something on the stove, or who's gonna deal with your dad?" she says, matter-of-factly.

"What's going on, Mom?" I ask her, determined to face what now seems to be unavoidable.

She stops and stares at me. She hesitates for a moment, long enough to make me think that she's about to reveal something, but then the moment flees. On her face appears regret for having momentarily given in to her emotions. She sniffs, shakes her head, and chooses to lie to me once again.

"Don't mind it, Leo. I'm just a little sad," she says, shrugging.

I wish I could ask her more questions, but I choose to not push the issue. I can tell she's struggling, and I don't want to make her feel even worse.

"Look at you! You're a mess! Go take a shower while I get dinner ready," she ends the conversation, turning her back at me.

Dinner doesn't last long: soon, our table is covered by a veil of awkward silence that ties our tongues. If nobody asks, nobody has to answer.

I decide to seek refuge in my bedroom; so, I come up with an excuse and my parents seem to be relieved, as if they really didn't want me around.

I climb the stone staircase, crawling back into my room. Maggie follows me as usual. I throw myself on the bed, sinking into the duvet that the cold evening air demands. I'm exhausted. I can't recall a worse day in my whole life. I look around, hopeless. Blu-rays crowd the shelves, comic books are scattered everywhere, posters decorate the walls; yet nothing distracts me from all the thoughts that are filling my head.

I get up, restless, and stagger to my desk and old laptop. I push the power button and wait for the ancient piece of crap to wake up and start doing its thing, barely chugging along on its last legs.

Yuth. That's the name of my disease, right? Great, let's see if I can find anything about it on the Internet. I access the browser, get on Google and type *yuth* in all the versions that come to my mind. I try *iut*, then *iuth*, and then *yuth*. Nothing. I just find indie rock bands, a college in Saudi Arabia, and stuff like that. Nothing more. I try to search for it on Wikipedia and other websites of medicine and psychiatry. I scroll down the lists of names of several mental illnesses and various other pathologies, but I can't find anything remotely close to what I'm looking for. There are no traces of my damned disease. Maybe it's fate that I have to stay in the dark about everything.

I decide not to think about it anymore and I look for something to distract me. Facebook. I click on the home page. I have a handful of contacts here, former friends I haven't talked to in ages, and a few nerds from high school whom I barely know, so reading through my page takes me about five seconds. So many precious moments I waste scrolling through the pages sharing videogames, not-so-funny jokes, and lame images full of sappy love declarations.

Then there's Maya, the thorn in my heart. I snoop around her page to see if she's written anything about what happened this afternoon. Maybe a tear-jerking message? A dedication to her hero, Simon? Nope, nothing. No new post. The last one is from yesterday and it is a sharing of "Every Teardrop is a Waterfall" video by Coldplay. I start watching the video, leaning back against the chair. The music is really good; it feels like a summer night and beautiful, carefree moments. I think about me; I think about her. I think about what we could have been and what we have never been. Dreaming doesn't cost a thing.

The song ends quickly. Too quickly. I come back to reality and to my page. On top, underneath my profile photo, there's a question.

What's on your mind?

Answer: D-Y-I-N-G. Yep, I'm gonna write exactly what's on my mind. In capital letters, to make it more intense. I write it, but I know nobody is going to read it. I close everything and spin around on the chair, stretching my legs far enough that they hit against everything.

The whirlwind of crap that has been thrown at me, in these past few hours, is unbelievable, something to be recorded in the annals of black days. In just one afternoon, I've seen the girl of my dreams kiss an idiot, and to make matters worse, I have found out that I am destined for insanity.

And to think that I was actually happy today . . . damn me and my curiosity! I never should have eavesdropped on those conversations, and now I wouldn't know anything about my disease, if you can even call it that.

I get up and look outside the window, without moving the delicate linen curtains. I spy the countryside that extends beyond the windowpane, illuminated by the icy glow of the full moon that dances on every shape. The sky is embroidered with a thousand stars and not even one cloud dares to darken their light.

My cellphone again. It vibrates. This time, I check the screen. It's Maya. A message.

Where the hell are you? I've been looking for you the whole afternoon. I gotta talk to you. Call me!

I read it a couple of times. You have to talk to me? Talk to me about what? Of your adventure with Simon? No, thank you. I've had enough for today.

I throw my phone on the bed, letting my chest fill up with sorrow. I sink deep down to the abyss and then, once I've reached it, I lie on it, closing my eyes and letting myself die.

Something flashes in my mind. White. An incandescent light that hurts me like a cut. I shake my head and for a second, I regain control of my body. I don't know where I am anymore. I don't know who I am anymore. Amber. Amber fills my mind's eye.

A giant dome made of stone, with sparkling doors, appears right in front of me. Spires surround the temple and reach up to the sky. A big, stone dragon sits above the entrance, watching over it. The doors open heavily. Inside, in the center of a vast room, there is an ornate, round altar made of marble inlaid with gold. A giant crystal ball, pulsating with a searing and dazzling light, slowly turns on top.

The blue vault of the dome is immense and dark, lit here and there by big diamonds inlaid in the ceiling, drawing circles of light in the darkness. Now, the color amber begins to taint. It's getting darker. It's about to turn black. A man, or what was once a man, appears in front of me. Kenat walks in the middle of the room, appearing in all of his horrific power. The gray cloak falls from his shoulders, dragging past his feet and spilling over the floor. His bloody hands rest on his chest , and from the darkness of the hood, two cruel eyes sparkle and . . .

A sound, as sharp as the squeal of scrap metal, explodes in my head. I force my eyelids open. My eyes are pulsing and my ears are hurting. I find myself kneeling down on the floor, in front of a wall. In my hand, I am holding a black marker, and before me, right where my Iron Man poster should have been, on the light-colored plaster, there is now a drawing of Kenat's hooded figure! Underneath, in a scratchy calligraphy that does not belong to me, there is a sentence . . .

EMMI DUbi aesuS KENAT

I jump back, about to scream, throwing the marker on the floor. My hand is covered in black ink. What have I done? I quickly reach for a shirt abandoned on the bed, and desperately try to clean the wall. Nothing, the drawing won't come off, the sentence is indelible. I look around. I have got to cover it up or I'll get in trouble. I straighten up the poster, which is now hanging from the wall, and I put it back where it was, holding it in place with scotch tape. Baffled, I close the blinds, stealthily glancing one last time at the moon, which now seems to be staring at me, as if conscious of a truth that I am not aware of.

I get undressed, go to the bathroom, brush my teeth, and get into bed. I turn the light off, and for a few minutes, I listen to Maggie's calm breathing, as she is already asleep in her bed. *Calm down, Leo, calm down or else it's gonna be a huge mess.* I start tossing and turning, wrapping myself in the duvet like a burrito. I'm cold, but I'm sweating.

Is this possible? Is this another symptom of Yuth? Whatever it is, I can't keep going this way. I just can't. I have got to do something about this or else, I surely *will* be D-Y-I-N-G.

chapter seven

NIGHTMARES AND AFFLICTIONS

Tick, Tock . . . It's three o'clock and I have yet to fall asleep. I'm a bundle of nerves, and despite the duvet, I am still cold. I'm completely frozen. My legs are two stiff sticks; all I'm missing is a tag on my big toe and I'd look like a corpse. I don't know if the cold is only outside or from the block of ice that was once my heart. Thing is, I'm shivering. I walk around the room, groping in the dark. I hit the chair with my pinky toe, and hopping around muttering every bad word I know, I put on a pair of wool socks and a hand-me-down sweater from my dad.

Dinner feels like a twenty-pound rock weighing heavy in my stomach, and given all the anxiety, the cold and everything else, I don't think I have been able to digest anything at all. Actually, if I think about it, I start to feel sick. Outside, the wind is still blowing hard, the chestnut tree branches hitting against the windowpane, in a ghostly hypnotic *tap . . . tap . . . tap.* And to think that spring seemed to have finally arrived. With a leap, I get under the covers for what must be the fourth time tonight.

The moonlight peaks through the slits in the blinds, bringing out black shapes from the gloom. I'm trying to relax, but my brain is now mush enslaved by the images from this afternoon. I keep seeing Maya's face in loop. That kiss. I can hear her laughter, smooth as silk. And then fast-forward to Mike's voice. The revelations about my disease.

I put my hands under the pillow, grinding my teeth until my ears start to ring. My gaze wanders around the room, dwelling from time to time on the shapes that, in their own way, take me back to the past, to some of the most carefree moments. On the wall in front of me, the writing on the poster from the movie *Avatar* shines in the dark, merging with the cold light that is creeping everywhere. Beneath it, piled on the shelves, are silhouettes of my old stuffed animals that have simply become a dark audience, witnesses of a time that is now lost. A sad smile stretches over my lips.

I switch my focus, inch by inch, away until I reach the darkest corner of my room. I stare into the darkness, looking at the shape of I-don't-know-what, as my mind keeps going back and forth between memories and heartbreaks. I start picturing my future, locked up in a psychiatric ward; alone, wearing blue PJs, sitting on a chair that is nailed to the floor, staring at a window that opens onto a melancholic garden. What would Maya think of me if she knew what I am going through?

All of a sudden, I sense something moving. My pupils dilate in a spasm that almost rolls my eyes back in my head. I hear heavy breathing. Something is crawling toward me in the dark. My heart pounds with fear.

"Who's there?!"

I sit up, groping for the pull cord on the nightstand lamp. In front of me, two arms from the dark silhouette reach toward me. I can't find the light switch. The shadow comes forth. Long, thin fingers stretch out in the dark. I keep looking in terror. The small bottle of water that I keep next to my bed falls, rolling on the floor. A withheld laugh begins to *hiss*, blending with the noises of the wind.

"*My Sire, Kenat, wants you.*"

The voice is the same cruel one I have heard before.

"*Let Antédios touch you and I will know where you hide . . .*"

I am one step away from having a heart attack. The two smoky arms are on top of me, its fingers are prodding the air, almost touching me. I open my mouth to scream, but I can't. Finally, I find the switch. I turn the light on. The gleam blinds me, leaving black residue in my eyes. I close them and open them again. Nothing. The room is empty. It's just Maggie and me, just us.

I flop down on the pillow. My forehead, as well as my back, are all wet, while my heart is pounding like a drum that won't slow down. I reach off the bed to grab the bottle of water and guzzle it down. Heat waves keep hitting me, soaking my head with more sweat. It's as if I just got out of the shower. I really can't keep going like this.

I turn off the lamp and I pull the blankets over my ears. The situation is getting worse by the hour. My disease, this damn Yuth, is taking over; what will happen to me in a week? I turn around, trying to calm down. I keep my eyes closed and I start thinking of movie titles in my head, listing them by the actor. It's basically my version of counting sheep, a way to focus on something else. My breathing starts to go back to normal, and without realizing it, I begin to slip down the soft and warm slide of sleep.

I am now in limbo, when a sound coming from the hall wakes me up. My eyes snap open and focus on the ceiling, as I realize the noise had nothing to do with the wind. With caution, I move the duvet away from my ears, and I crane my neck toward the closed door, listening. The metallic *clinking* of keys, the mechanical *click* of the door lock and a *ssst* hisses so sharp it almost perforates my eardrums. My guts clench. I move slowly, my hands and feet feel tingly.

Once again, I look for the light cord. This time, I find it right away. I turn the light on. I see Maggie, sitting by the door, tense, and listening intently. OK, this time I didn't dream it. I get up, filled with shivers that are no longer caused by the cold. I walk toward the door, being careful not to make a sound. The floor is old and the smallest squeak could reveal my presence. I pick up the dog, open the door slowly as I keep listening attentively. More whispers coming from downstairs. I feel petrified, as my mind focuses on the image of two bad guys who, with masks on their faces and flashlights in hand are rummaging the drawers in the living room and the kitchen. I tiptoe to my parents' bedroom. I lean into the darkness.

"Dad . . ."

Silence. Nobody answers.

"Dad . . ." I repeat.

I step into their room, wobbling, and groping around. I look for my father's head as my fingers slide over the cold pillow.

"Mom . . ."

Nothing, the bed is empty. I go back to the hallway, and crawling along the wall, I look out from the staircase. Voices once again, this time a bit weaker and farther away. I'm going all in.

"Mom? . . . Dad? . . . Is that you guys?"

Silence. I slowly walk down the stairs. I'm shivering with fear. In what feels like an eternity, I finally reach the hall, which is dark and deserted. Everything looks normal as always: no intruder and no signs of a break-in. I look around, terrified that somebody might jump out of the dark, ready to stick a knife in my back, but nothing. No one's here.

Suddenly, I hear a slight *clink*: the keys in the lock are waving as if somebody has just touched them. Slowly, I peak through the small window that overlooks the front yard. My father and my mother are standing side by side, with their robes blowing lightly in the wind. They are standing there, immobile, looking up at the starry sky, as if waiting for something. What the heck are they doing out there this late at night? I am about to knock on the glass, when their clothes are flooded with a light that starts releasing bright golden sparks into the air. I see my mom raise her arm up to the sky, holding a small, translucent sphere.

"*Hava*," she says in a commanding tone.

The globe explodes with a blinding white light that almost immediately darkens to a sickly green color. Mom closes her eyes, and two big fairy wings appear on her back, which flap vigorously, lifting her a foot off the ground.

I shake my head to the point that I almost lose my balance. My hallucinations are becoming more convincing and now I can't even distinguish them from reality. I drag myself back to the staircase, when a sharp pain in my ribs pierces me from side to side, making me fall on the floor. Maggie yelps in my arms. That voice again.

"*Reveal yourself to Antédios . . . show me where you are . . .*"

The last thing I remember is the icy cold feel of the floor on which I collapse.

chapter eight

THE REAL STRENGTH

My ability to always be late for school is incredible. This morning, for example, I woke up late and my shoulder muscles were all sore. I'm not sure what I did last night but, between nightmares and everything else, I found myself with the duvet all rolled up on the floor and with my legs dangling from the mattress. Maybe it was because I got all agitated when I dreamed about my mom floating in the front yard? I don't know. And then, as if that wasn't enough already, my scooter left me on foot; it was dead, croaked out of the blue. Fortunately, my mom offered to drive me to school, but I'm late anyway, and to top it all off, first period is with Miss Abona.

I slowly knock on the door, barely touching it with my knuckles.

"Come in!" my teacher's voice roars.

"Good morning, sorry for being late but . . ."

"Go sit down," she interrupts me. "Ghebo, today is your lucky day," she says as she picks up the class attendance register. "The bell rang ten minutes ago, but I have yet to do the roll call."

Surprised, I nod to thank her and drag myself in the classroom. I'm a dead-man walking, an easy target, but the villian is strangely forgiving. She could easily scold me, keep me out in the hall for the whole hour, give me detention, ask me for a note signed by my folks, but instead, nothing, she doesn't care. Could she regret coming to my house, or maybe she pities me for being sick? Nah, I doubt it, her clemency is certainly due to a breakfast of bad news on morning TV. I'm sure of it! That woman, witch that she is, is pleased only by something tragic and evil. I stumble to my desk, being careful not to cross my classmates' stares. Maya's desk is empty. How come she's not at school? I sit down throwing my backpack on the floor. I take my book out, and as usual, I start pretending to listen to the lesson.

My morning continues without a hitch. Today is Friday, summer vacation is upon us, but no teacher seems to be slowing down: exams and lessons inexorably follow each other until the very last hour of class. Never-ending boredom.

Fortunately, my desk is by the window, which allows me to take a break from time to time, glancing at the yard.

I've been staring at a plant stem for the past ten minutes when I feel my pocket vibrate. I take my cellphone out of my pocket, and hiding it under the desk, I spy the bright display. A new text from Maya on Messenger.

I'm in the boys' bathroom on the third floor. Come here now!

Yes, ma'am, I tell myself. What the heck is she doing there? She doesn't show up to school and then she cuts class in the bathroom? It doesn't sound like a great plan . . .

After the teacher grants me permission to leave, I walk out of the classroom quietly, firm on my decision not to go back until the bell rings. I walk down the hall, passing like a shadow in front of the other classrooms. The first floor is Crippa's turf, and after the altercation we had the other day, it's best if he doesn't see me around.

"Well?" Miss Abona's cold voice echoes suddenly, breaking through the open door of a classroom just ahead.

"I'd like to know why you're always on my case."

Speak of the devil and he shall appear. It's Crippa.

"Because of your ignorance. You're a dunce, Crippa."

I can't resist. Maya is waiting for me, but I can't miss the show. I stand by the doorway, and I listen quietly, enjoying every word.

"I think you hate me 'cause I'm rich. You, with your meager schoolteacher salary can barely make ends meet and you can't accept the fact that one of your students can afford what you only dream about."

Frost. I can feel literal frost coming out of the classroom.

"Very well, Crippa, think what you want. However, life will teach you very soon that you need so much more than just daddy's money."

"Well, I can assure you that it's still very useful."

"Let's see if it can be used to avoid giving you detention to spend in the principal's office."

"This is your only weapon," Crippa puffs arrogantly.

"You're wrong. I'll also ask to meet with your father," the teacher rebuts with her usual calm tone.

"My dad is always out on business; you'll never reach him."

"He gave me his cellphone number. I can reach him any time I want."

"My father doesn't care about me." Now, in the ogre's voice I sense a bit of fear. "It's a waste of time calling him."

"You know your father cares a lot about your education. I am sure he won't be happy to learn about your latest achievements, Crippa. You flunked out again, like a dunce . . ." the teacher almost whispers the last words.

A *thud* of something landing after being thrown echoes through the classroom, followed by the sound of a chair being flipped. Crippa is losing his mind!

Alright, I think I've heard enough, now I better get out of here before I get in trouble. I quickly walk past the open door of the classroom, and being careful not to get caught, I walk straight through the hallway, climbing the flight of service stairs in the back through the narrow and dingy path leading to the bathroom on the third floor. The stench of a damp mop mixed with the smell of floor cleaner makes my nose twitch in a most annoying way.

"Where are you going, Leo?" It's Mike, who appears from down the hall.

"I'm going to the bathroom . . ."

"Why here?"

"Because the one downstairs is full of punks who smoke." I make it up. "And the smoke bothers me."

"Oh! Good to know. I'll go check it out right away!" he says quickly. "Everything OK, yeah?"

"Yes . . ." I reply, doubtful.

"OK, see ya later," he concludes, disappearing down the main stairway.

There, it's best if you get out of here. First you act like a friend and then you stab me in the back along with Miss Abona.

The bathroom on the third floor is empty, as usual.

"Maya? . . ." I ask, uncertain.

"I'm here," she says getting out of one of the bathroom stalls.

As mad as I am at her, I can't help but smile at her. Even though she looks tense, she's as beautiful as ever.

"What are you doing here? Do you know you could face a suspension if they find you here?"

"I gotta talk to you. I couldn't wait any longer," she tells me, getting closer.

"Why didn't you come to class?"

"That's exactly what I have to talk to you about," she says somber. "This morning I was too tired to come to school. I spent the night at the hospital."

"At the hospital? What happened?" I ask, feeling guilty.

"Yesterday, I had an accident . . ."

"An accident!?"

"Stop repeating everything I say," she admonishes me. "Yes, a tree fell on me, and if it wasn't for Simon, I'd probably be dead by now."

"No way!"

"I swear! He saved me and got hurt. Multiple fractures: tibia and fibula. I was at the hospital with him the entire night. Nothing serious, but he had surgery and has yet to wake up."

"Not bad," I let slip out.

"What?"

"I said *too bad* that he got hurt, but I'm glad it's nothing serious."

"Yes, fortunately," Maya whispers, running a hand through her hair.

We remain quiet for a moment, as I walk toward the faucet. What the heck does she expect from me? That I worry about that jerk?

I wash my hands and face with cold water and then, as if hypnotized, I stare at the running water.

"You don't have anything else to tell me? Can I go back to class?" I ask without looking at her.

"What?" She sounds disoriented. "Yeah . . . you can go."

I'd love to vent, vomit my feelings on her, but I know this is not the time to make a scene. Now it's crystal clear that there will never be anything more between us, so I should just give up.

"What the heck is wrong with you?"

"What do you mean?" I ask her, turning around.

"Yesterday afternoon I called and texted you a million times, but nothing. Not even a shred of an answer. I could have died, and you wouldn't have even known," she points out, fussing.

"But Simon was there, right? Your hero!" I tell her, giving her a bitter smile.

"Why are you behaving like this?"

"*This*, how?"

"Like *this*!" she exclaims extending her arms.

"Maybe it's because I'm tired of being your third wheel!" I suddenly blurt out. "Yesterday you had plans with me, but all it took was for a call from *him* to delete me from your schedule."

"But I told you," she tries to defend herself, mortified.

"Oh sure! With a text. You know what I do with your texts?"

"I didn't think you'd get offended! You know how important you are to me."

"No, I don't, you have never showed me in any way."

"You're so unfair, I thought that between us . . ."

A sudden *bang* and a curse shouted outside in the hall make
my blood run cold. I just have time enough to pull Maya into
one of the bathroom stalls, when the bathroom door slams
open. We get up on the toilet seat, and holding onto each other, we spy through the slit in the metal door. On the threshold,
we see Crippa the Creepy, dragging a note under his foot. The
same one he should have brought to the principal. His hair
is stringy with sweat and his face is beet red. He thinks he's
alone in the bathroom, so he starts shouting and kicking the
sink.

"Pathetic repressed ole spinster! I'll make you pay for this!
Just wait and see! I'll . . ."

He stops suddenly. He hesitates, distracted by the water
running in the sink, which I forgot to shut off. His tiny eyes
whizz around toward us, more accurately toward the closed
bathroom stalls. Oh no, if he catches us here, he's going to kill
us for sure. I draw back, leaning against the toilet pipe along
the wall.

"Is anyone there?" I hear him ask right outside our hideout.
"Is anyone there in the crapper?"

Maya looks at me puffing her lips in a grimace she always
makes before laughing. The water in the sink stops running. A
thud and the deafening sound of footsteps on the floor. I hear
heavy breathing vibrating less than a foot from us. Crippa, on
all fours and with his face planted on the floor, is checking
under every stall.

"Anyone here?" he says again.

I hold my breath, until I hear him get back up, snorting.
Thank goodness, idiot that he is, he hasn't even thought that
there might be somebody standing on the toilet. I hear his

footsteps getting farther away and his heavy voice mutter another round of unspeakable insults, followed by a bunch of horrific farts. I'm petrified, while Maya looks at me entertained as if we were at a comedy show. She finds the situation funny as heck, and when she acts like this, I can't stand her!

"It's just that idiot Crippa . . ." she whispers. "Let's get out of here and tell him to go get lost!"

I stop her, squeezing her lips between my thumb and index finger.

"Shut up . . ." I mouth and go back to spying through the slit in the door that hides us.

Crippa is with his back against the wall and his head bowed, looking at the floor. His eyes are unusually watery, as if a step away from crying. We can hear him sniffing, and believe it or not, he starts sobbing. At first slowly, then much harder. I try to stifle my breathing to the very minimum, while Maya, now having a full-on case of the giggles, holds her mouth shut with her hands. I stand still for several minutes, in the hope that Maya won't do anything stupid. Then, finally, I recognize the squeaking of the door that opens and closes shut. A few footsteps, the squeaking sound of rubber soles and running water from the bathroom sink turn into silence. We're alone. Finally, Crippa's gone. With a jump, I get off the toilet and out of our hideout.

"Can you believe it?" Maya asks, following me. "That guy is just a mess."

"It's his own business," I reply impolitely. "He's gotten what he deserves. Anyway, back to us . . ."

I turn around and it's as if a train hit me.

Sitting poised on the sink is Crippa who, with a cigarette hanging out of his mouth, is staring at us with his lips tight and the puzzled expression of someone who got caught red-handed.

"What are you doing here?"

"*Ehm* . . . What?" I mumble walking back, as the monster does the math.

"How long have you two been here for?" he roars, getting closer.

"Crippa, calm down," Maya intervenes, coming between us.

"You zip it!"

I immediately find myself with my back against the tiles on the wall and with my mouth completely dry. Blood: I feel like I can already taste it.

"Huh? Answer me!" he orders and slaps me right in the face. "How long have you been here for?"

"Let him go, you idiot!" I hear Maya say.

The skin on my cheek is stinging like a third-degree burn and my eyes start tearing up.

"I asked you a question!" he yells in my face, hitting me again. "How long have you been here for?"

"For a while!" I find myself answering. "Since before you started crying like a baby . . ."

The words are muffled in my throat, and I regret saying them even before I finish my sentence. Without warning, a fist hits me right in the stomach and makes me fold in half like paper. For a moment, I can't breathe, and the immense pain almost makes me fall to my knees. Maya is scared.

"Stop it!" I hear her yelling, hitting the ogre's back.

"Knock it off or I'll hit you too!" he threatens her. "And you? You'll let a girl defend you?" he asks, getting back to me.

Before I have a chance to recover, Crippa grabs me by the neck and shoves me again against the wall.

"So now you started spying on me, huh?"

"No . . ." I answer, still trying to catch my breath from the previous punch. "It was just a coincidence . . . I was in the bathroom before . . ."

I can't even finish my sentence when he grabs me by the hair and pulls me to the sink.

"You seem confused, maybe you should clear your head."

Without losing his grip, he opens one of the faucets and shoves my head under the icy cold water, pushing my nose down on the ceramic sink. Here it is. The taste of blood fills up my mouth.

"Please, let him go!" Maya begs.

I fidget around trying to break free, but Crippa's grip is so tight that there is no escape.

"You and your little friend will never utter a single word of what happened here, got it?"

"Yes . . ." I mutter, shaking.

"What?"

"Yessss!" I scream again as the icy cold water starts dripping down my back, soaking me completely.

Crippa pulls me up, and with a push, he throws me back against the wall. I slip, falling on my butt to the floor. The pain takes over my head and it constricts my lungs. My hair is soaked, just like my shirt. The beast slowly comes close to me, and with his usual sadistic smile, he bends over me, a few inches away from my nose.

"Got it?" he asks me in an icy whisper.

With his open palm, he shoves my head into the wall. I'm disoriented, I can no longer move.

Maya runs to my rescue, but Crippa is faster. He grabs her by the neck and throws her on the floor.

"I gave you a chance and you wasted it," he says, looking at her with disgust. "You choose to be with this *nobody's* son? Very well . . . accept the consequences, you tramp."

Crippa's words resound in my ears. I sense something tearing apart right by my sternum and an unknown strength begins to spread through every inch of my body, feeding off my rage. Everything happens very quickly. Without even thinking, I throw a punch at that slimeball's nose, tilting his head back; then, in cold-blood, and before he can react, I shove my open hand in the middle of his chest throwing him toward the opposite wall. The hit is so violent that Crippa's huge body is taken off the ground and flies over ten feet away, against the open sink that starts splashing water up to the ceiling. I get up and slowly walk toward him. I feel weird, invincible. Maya is immobile behind me, as if petrified. I close my eyes. I open them again.

Yes, this time it's all real. This time it's not my imagination. I see Crippa's face as white as a ghost.

"What happened?" he asks scared, feeling his swollen nose. "Look what you've done!"

"*Will you finally start keeping your mouth shut?*" I roar, squeezing his cheeks in a grip so tight it makes him stick his tongue out.

"No . . . I don't know! . . . Please, don't hit me!" he stutters, scared to death.

"*You promise not to torture us again?*"

"What? What are you talking about?" he starts crying, lost.

"*You promise not to torture us again?*" I ask again.

"I don't understand . . . I don't understand what you're say- ing! Why are you speaking this strange language . . ." he moans, terrified.

What? Language? What language? What the heck is this idiot talking about?

His eyes are wide as headlights, I have him in my grip and I am fiercely proud of it. I stare at him for a moment longer and then, inebriated by the power, I grab him by the collar of his Ralph Lauren polo shirt, jerking him close. Crippa screams in terror, as huge tears like giant pearls start rolling out of his eyes. The smell of his fear excites me. I want more. I want to hurt him, break him in half, destroy him, make him suffer. His pain is my pleasure. His desperation is my food . . .

"Let me go, Ghebo. I'm begging you!"

I immediately lose my grip and come back to myself. *What happened to me?* I look around, confused. My head spins as if I have a high fever. Maya is looking at me from a corner of the bathroom with a tense expression, unsure of whether to be scared or proud. I'm completely disoriented.

"You're a monster, Ghebo," Crippa keeps whining. "Look what you've done to me! You're a damn monster . . ."

At that moment, coming out of nowhere, Miss Abona appears right in front of us.

"What's going on here?" she asks with authority.

I'm standing up, soaking wet, with a drop of blood dripping from my mouth. In front of me, in a corner, is Maya and by my feet is Crippa, curled up on the flooded floor.

"He broke my nose . . . I can't breathe," whines the jerk as soon as he sees our teacher.

Oh boy, I sense trouble coming. With a step, Miss Abona walks near the sink. She closes the main valve, and the water gush slows down immediately.

"Get up, Crippa, and stop whining!" she tells him, without looking at him.

"I can't, I'm in too much pain."

The teacher grabs the bully by his polo shirt, and with a strength I didn't think she could have, pulls him up straight, making him grunt like a hunted hog.

"It serves you right. Now you know what it feels like to be on the other side of the fence."

"I'll tell my father everything and then you'll see what happens."

"Shut up and let me check your nose."

Crippa leans toward the woman, showing his nose, which seems to be a shapeless tuber. Miss Abona gives it a careful look. She squints her eyes and frowns, grimacing with tension.

"It's nothing. Here, take this and dab your nose for a while," she tells him, giving him a handkerchief. "Then go see Mike, the janitor. Tell him I sent you. He has an ointment that is just right for this type of pain."

"What? Ghebo broke my nose. You have to expel him!" the ogre shouts with his face all red from a mix of rage and fear. "He broke it, can't you see?" he asks, as he stops dabbing.

To be fair, within a matter of a few minutes, his nose has gotten swollen to the point of no return, and the dark shades around his eyes are now black circles kinda like those of a panda.

"Get moving, Crippa! You'll see; that ointment will make everything go away."

"But Ghebo can't walk free!" he whines, going back to his usual annoying attitude.

"Get out of here, Crippa," the teacher snaps at him in an icy cold tone.

I see Crippa grind his teeth, lingering over Maya and me for a moment and then, dazed, walks quickly away. Maya and I stay there, in suspense, while the teacher, who turned her back to us, stares at Crippa walking away.

"Young lady, if my memory serves me right, you're supposed to be absent today, correct?" she tells her without looking at her.

"Yes . . ." she says with a whisper.

"Good, then get out of here."

Maya nods at me and then disappears out the door.

"And you, Ghebo, don't you think it'd be better to go back to class?"

"Are we in trouble?"

"I'll let it go this time. Now clean up the blood you have on your mouth and get out of here."

What?! I can't believe this! It can't be happening. How will she ever be able to explain the disaster that's happened here? Without uttering a single word, I look at my reflection in the mirror of the bathroom. I slowly open the main valve of the faucet, and sticking my hand under the few drops, I wash my face. Miss Abona suddenly appears behind me.

"You saw us, didn't you?"

I feel paralyzed.

"What? . . ." I pretend not to understand her.

"At your house, yesterday, you saw us, didn't you?"

I turn around. Miss Abona is in front of me poker-faced.

"Appearances can often trick us, Leonardo. Things are not always what they seem," she says smiling.

I'm at a loss for words. What's she talking about? What's she saying through that grin? Is she actually smiling? Is she smiling at *me*? The bell signaling the end of class surprises us like a scream. We stare at each other for a few seconds, as the chitchat of the students overcomes our silence.

"I have to go," I whisper.

"Yes, maybe it's for the best."

I back out of the bathroom without turning my back to her, turn and run back to the classroom, going up stream like a salmon against all my classmates who are going down. I quickly throw my stuff in my backpack, and grabbing my sweatshirt, I walk toward the exit.

My cellphone vibrates, letting me know I have a new text from Maya.

You were great, Leo! I'll see you later, we gotta finish our conversation ☺ Love you.

chapter nine

THE TRUTH

As usual, the yard is teeming with students gathered like sheep. Kids loitering while they wait for the school bus and little fashion divas who walk down the sidewalk like a runway to attract adoring stares. With the wind blowing in my soaked hair, I walk quickly toward the gate. I don't have my scooter and I truly hope that someone remembers to come pick me up; I really don't feel like walking home looking like this. I can tell that a group of girls is staring at me. I catch a few hints of idle gossiping and a few strangled exclamations. Then a bespectacled dude that I don't know comes close to me and whispers, "You're awesome, Ghebo!"

Could it be that news of my prowess has already spread through the whole school? Well, good, I tell myself, maybe starting today everyone will start showing me some respect! I zip up my sweatshirt, pull up my hood, and walk toward the gate. The mighty horn of the Animagorium van overshadows every other noise and catches my attention. I raise my hand to answer Anthony, who has parked on the other side of the street. I am about to cross it when . . .

"Hey, Rusty!"

A squeaky voice calls for my attention. Leaning against the newsstand behind me, a woman squeezed into a tight, bright fuchsia mini dress smiles at me with a wink. Her hair is tied up in a bizarre eclectic red braid and rolled into a gigantic bun that is clearly unbalanced on her head. She has a grumpy expression and is leather-skinned from spending too much time in a tanning bed. I have no doubt; this is the witch that Maya's father married.

"I'm Maya's mom; would you happen to know her?"

What?! Why would she ask me that?

"Yes, she's a friend of mine," I say vaguely. "But I thought Maya's mom had passed away."

"Her first mother . . . I am the new one, the cool one," she replies in a coarse laughter.

I step back in disgust, which she obviously notices because she immediately changes her expression and tone of voice.

"Last night she didn't come home, and I don't see her here at school. Do you know where she is? She has a few chores left undone."

That's why she's worried; Maya has yet to finish her house chores.

"She left a while ago on her scooter. I think she went home."

"Oh, so she came to school this morning?" she asks, tilting her head to the side like a hen who just saw a worm wallow in the mud.

"Absolutely," I answer, lying to her face.

The woman stays there for a moment, staring at me as if stunned, with lips red like a lobster, pursed in an unpleasant grimace. The silence that comes of it, albeit short and passing, has something unhealthy and hideous behind it.

"Well, I should go."

"I like the color of your hair . . ."

"What?"

"Your hair . . ." she says, pointing to a tuft that sticks out of my hoodie. "I like the color. I noticed it immediately because where I come from nobody has natural red hair." She reaches to touch it, but I jerk away, almost losing my balance.

"I won't bite, you know . . ." she laughs again.

"Yes . . ." I tell her with a plastic grin. "Goodbye . . ."

"Wait a moment, why are you running away? Are you scared to talk to a pretty lady?"

"I'm not running away, but there's someone waiting for me," I explain, as I point and nod to Anthony on the other side of the road.

She follows my nod and sees the Big Guy who, despite the distance, does look like the giant that he is. With a circumspect giggle, the witch raises her hand to salute him.

"Is he your father?" she asks in a silky voice.

"No, he's my cousin . . ."

"By the way, my name is Cynthia," she introduces herself. "And you are? . . ."

"Nice to meet you, but I really have got to go now!" I tell her, stepping off the sidewalk.

"Well? You won't even shake my hand?"

"It's been a pleasure!" I walk away and pretend I didn't hear her.

"Till next time!"

I dodge two cars that almost run me over, I get honked at twice, a guy on a scooter yells "wimp" at me, and finally I reach the van. Anthony greets me a bit impatiently, "Hallelujah, Leo! Who the heck were you talking to? Your teacher?"

"Nah! She's the chick Maya's father brought home," I explain, jumping aboard.

"She's the famous *witch*?" he asks, spying beyond the road.

"That's the one."

"Well, what a chick!" he exclaims, then starts the engine.

"Christopher is not here?"

"Nope, he left yesterday morning for another adventure of his."

"Gotcha."

With a two-point turn, the van goes in reverse and then aligns itself on the right side of road. I pull my hoodie down, and as I scratch my head I absentmindedly turn to look out the window. Cynthia is still there where I left her, balanced firmly on her five-inch stilettos, her eyes glued on me. I feel as though her eyes are devouring me. That woman gives me goosebumps. What does she want from me? I hint a saluting gesture, just because the situation makes me uncomfortable. She replies with a weird giggle that lifts her wizened cheekbones. Bloodcurdling. What did Maya's father see in this one?

Within a few minutes, we are outside the little town, fully immersed in the light green of the hills. The radio is playing "Dream On" by Aerosmith, and Anthony, with his window rolled down, is drumming the rhythm on the steering wheel with a constant *clicking* of rings.

"Can you feel it, Leo, the smell of summer approaching?"

I sniff the air and shiver.

"Actually no, I can only feel an arctic cold."

Anthony turns toward me, noticing my wet head for the first time.

"What did you do? Did you take a shower with your clothes on?" he asks, rolling the window up.

"Nothing important, I had a run in with a jerk who needed to be taken care of," I reply, gloating.

"Did you drown him somewhere?"

"No, almost did though!" I laugh.

"Your mother told me about your scooter, what happened?"

"Darned if I know! It was working fine yesterday and then, out of nowhere, *bam*! It doesn't start anymore."

"What a mess."

"I'd say so. Without my scooter, I'm stuck at home."

"Oh, well, at least I'm here," he says, honking the horn twice. "Taxi service and personal chauffer!"

"Thanks, Anthony, but I've got to find a solution. Speaking of which, could you give me a hand later and help me bring the scooter to the mechanic downtown?"

"No."

I quickly turn toward him. He now has a serious frown on his face.

What did he say? I must have heard wrong.

"I beg your pardon? What did you say?"

"I said no."

"What do you mean, *no*?"

"I mean that, seeing as there are so many threats around us these days, I think it'd be better if we all started taking you around from now on. Whenever you want and wherever you want, no worries . . . there's no problem."

"You're kidding, right?" I ask, forcing myself to laugh. "Threats? What threats are you talking about?"

"Well, for starters, the traffic and . . . that bully, for example. Yep, that bully who keeps aiming at you outside the school. If I were to always come pick you up, then probably you wouldn't . . ."

"How do you know about that?" I ask him, shocking him.

"What?" he asks, with difficulty. "Well, I know about it because you just told me. Isn't he the guy who you came to blows with today?" He's almost stuttering now.

"Nope, I never said anything about a bully."

"What? . . . Oh well, anywho . . . don't you think it'd be nice and comfy going to school in a car instead of a scooter? Think of all the money from your allowance you'll save on gas, huh?"

Gas? Alright, I get it; he too is aware of my disease, and he doesn't want me to go around on a scooter. After all, I could become a danger, right?

"Am I right, Leo?" he asks me, turning toward me.

"Focus on the road, please."

"Yes, sure. The road . . . but aren't I right? Wouldn't it be a great way to save some cash?"

I let it go. To hell with everything and everyone.

"Sure," I whisper.

The climate in the vehicle slips into awkwardness. The thought that it is all nothing but a plan set forth by my folks is starting to echo in my head like a baseball bat against the wall, and the doubt that it was them who tampered with my scooter is quickly turning into a certainty.

"Look, I know everything," I suddenly say.

The van swerves and slams right into a pothole, making my head hit the window.

"Ouch!"

"Sorry Leo, I didn't see that hole."

I can tell he's now as stiff as a pole, his knuckles are turning white holding tight onto the steering wheel.

"There's no need to make anything up and tell me a bunch of lies," I admonish him.

"What lies?" Anthony pretends, again.

I can tell by the trembling in his voice that he is secretly hoping that I don't give him an answer.

"Never mind . . ."

Yeah, never mind. It's better this way. I'm afraid that, if I were to start speaking out today, my mouth would deliver only a whole list of unstoppable insults. The van stops right in the middle of the graveled courtyard, raising a cloud of dust that is immediately swept away by the wind. I jump out and go inside the house, without uttering a single word to Anthony.

"You aren't upset, are you?" he asks me, quickly coming behind me.

"Upset about what? For all the lies you told me?" I ask sarcastically, throwing my backpack on the bench.

"Good afternoon, Leonardo."

I almost have a heart attack. My mom and dad appear from the darkness under the staircase that goes down to the cellar.

"What are you guys doing there?" I ask, startled. "You almost gave me a heart attack!"

No answer. Their gloomy stares seem to foretell trouble ahead.

"Christopher?" my dad asks Anthony with his usual nice manners.

"Nothing. His cell phone is out of reach, and I can't contact him in any other way other than . . . well . . . the you-know-what way."

Dad nods before Anthony finishes the sentence.

"What did you do? Why are you soaked?" my mom asks worriedly, feeling my head and shoulders.

"Nothing, an accident."

"What kind of accident?" my dad quickly asks.

"He came to blows with his classmate," Anthony says, not minding his own business.

I glare at him. I really can't tell what's going on here.

"Go dry yourself before you get sick. Wait, let me give you a towel and a dry shirt," Mom says, disappearing upstairs.

"No, Mom, I can do it . . ."

"No," dad stops me, with a severe look on his face. "We need to talk . . ."

"If you say it with that expression, you scare me though," I say, forcing a smile. "The last time you used it was to tell me I wasn't your real son . . ."

As I talk, I observe the mopey faces of the two men. Mom comes back, breathless.

"Here you go," she says, handing me a towel and a dry shirt.

"So? Have you finally decided to tell me the truth about my disease?" I ask, while drying my hair and putting on my clean shirt.

My folks look at me with their eyes wide open. You weren't expecting this from me, were you? I am much smarter than you think I am.

"Disease? What disease are you talking about?"

"Stop pretending, come on! I heard you yesterday, I heard you talking with my teacher and the janitor. You were talking about *alarming symptoms.*"

My mother turns toward my dad, distressed. I can tell her big eyes are already watering up.

"Mom and I have to explain a few things to you, things that have to do with your life, your future . . ." Dad tells me with his usual warm tone.

"But you have to understand that we don't want to give you any kind of added responsibility," Mom follows up, even more agitated.

"No, we have to!" the Big Guy intervenes suddenly, feeling rueful.

"Anthony, wait!" Dad interrupts him abruptly. "We want to take it one step at a time. We all agree that it's time we talk to him, but let's do it the right way."

"But don't you think it's best if we see what Victor thinks? He wanted to wait," Anthony underlines.

"Victor is wrong!" Dad rebuts, almost screaming. "Our Am-Arcanus has warned us. Something is moving and we have to act before it's too late!"

"Enough!" The words come out of my mouth with no control. "Are you all crazy? *Act before it's too late* . . . what the heck are you all talking about!?" I ask, feeling blood rush to my head.

"Calm down, Leonardo," Dad says.

"No! I won't calm down! I'm fed up, tell me what's going on!"

"Come with me."

"Where?"

"To your room."

"What? . . ."

I follow him upstairs. Mom and Anthony are behind us as if following a funeral procession. Who's the dead guy? Me, obviously. I feel angry. I'm shivering from head to toe yet I'm gasping with rage like a werewolf.

"This morning we found this thing you drew," he tells me, moving aside to let me in.

The *Iron Man* poster is off the wall and reveals the obscene scribble that leaps from the clear background of the wall.

"What? . . . You went through my stuff?" Aghast, I see that my desk is also messier than usual. "Who gave you permission to go through my room!?"

Dad doesn't even hear me. He pushes me forward to the wall.

"Do you see him in your nightmares?" he asks me, with a tone that I barely recognize.

"You went through my stuff!" I scream without caring about what my father asked.

But Dad puts his hands on my face, and he holds me still, in front of the drawing. His fingers are pushing on my cheeks so hard that he makes me gag.

"Answer my question!"

"What? . . ."

I'm totally lost.

"Do you see him in your nightmares?"

"I don't know . . . what do you mean?" I put a hand against the wall, in the hopes that it will disintegrate under my touch.

"Leonardo, answer me!" he yells at me. "Do you see him in your nightmares!?"

"Let go of me!"

Maggie barks and jumps around us. She's scared and so am I. What's happening to my father? Am I the crazy one, or is he?

"Did you write this?" he asks, shaking me by the shoulders. "Did he tell you to write it? Did you say his name?" His tone is more and more frenetic. "Did you evoke him?"

Evoke? Evoke *what*? My brain is foggy.

"What are you talking about?! Leave me alone!"

"Adam, stop! You're hurting him," Mom intervenes, trying to free me.

"Bianca, we have to know! The Am-Arcanus went dark! You know all too well what that means. Our time is about to come to an end!"

"But this is not the way, Adam! You said it yourself, you wanted to take one step at a time," she tells him, taking his fingers off my arms. "You're just scaring him like this and that's all."

I free myself with a jerk and take a few steps back, scared. My father's grasp burns my skin, but my pride is what's truly injured. I feel rage and shame, as warm tears begin to stream down my cheeks.

"What's up with you all? What's this Arcanus?" I ask, feeling beside myself. "What the heck are you talking about?"

My dad's expression becomes different; dismay now blossoms on his face, dissolving the fit of rage. I see him. He's mortified.

"Forgive me. Everyone please, forgive me. Especially you, Leo."

He takes his glasses off and holding the tip of his nose between his thumb and index finger, he falls on the chair next to the desk.

"You see, Leonardo," Mom intervenes, attempting to lighten up the situation. "Dad and I need to know how long you've been dreaming about that . . . *thing* . . . do you understand me?"

Her tone is almost imploring. I take my eyes off her and I see that Anthony is behind me, staring at me quietly.

"And him? Couldn't you avoid making a scene in front of him?" I complain, focusing again on my mother. "Can't you see how embarrassing this is for me?"

"Adam . . ." my mother's voice is almost a whine.

"I wouldn't know where to begin," he mutters.

I know. I dry my eyes with the sleeve of my shirt, recovering that tiny bit of pride left in me. I know where to begin.

"You don't have to explain anything. I get it all," I freeze them, calmly. "I get what's going on. The symptoms of the disease are starting to show. You guys have noticed and have no idea how to tell me."

"Enough with that story!" my mother snaps. "You don't have a disease."

"Don't lie to me, Mom. There's no need to tell me anything else," I retort, walking toward the hall.

"Where are you going?" my father jumps out of the chair.

"Outside!" I reply without turning around.

"No. No walks for today."

I turn around, ice cold, looking directly at him.

"Why? You wanna punish me for what I am?"

"Don't be stupid . . ."

"Then why?" I ask, my voice furious.

"Because . . . Because I say so . . ."

Tears fog my sight, but I try to hold them back.

"Please, Leonardo," he begs. "I'm doing this for your own good. I'm your father and nobody else in the world could ever . . ."

"You are *not* my father," I interrupt him with a *hiss*. "Now go away. All of you, go away, out of my room!"

chapter ten

DARK NATURE

I throw the window wide open, letting the sun shine on me. Why am I not like everybody else? A normal kid, I mean. A regular guy, with a regular life. A regular future. The breeze flutters the curtains and the edges of the poster that is still hanging from the wall. The wind is whispering wild dreams to me. Today, more than yesterday, I wish I could disappear, dissolve, and forget about everything and everyone.

I turn around, kicking the folder of drawings that I have in front of me, launching it to the other side of the room. I let myself fall on the chair and I look at the desk that still shows signs of my parents' search. *Thanks a lot,* I think. I push myself back with my legs and I begin to spin in my chair like a top until I get dizzy. I run my fingers through my hair, as I press my open palms against my forehead, focusing on the crooked beams that go through the ceiling. A whimper catches my attention; it's Maggie who, from her bed, observes me with a stare. A lackluster smile relaxes me for a moment as I concentrate on new afflictions. The suffocating sensation I've been feeling since yesterday has now become constant. I'm stuck in a life that doesn't belong to me.

I need to talk to my Uncle Vic. I have got to see him and vent my feelings. Only he can understand me. Without thinking, I pick up Maggie and I climb over the ledge. It's not the first time I've done it; as a kid, I used to evade my folks' punishments by sneaking out the window, although at the time it was done within a, well . . .. different context. I proceed to the narrow-tiled roof that stretches beneath my ledge, cautiously walking to the wall that is next to the building. I reach it with a jump, then I walk in tightrope-fashion on top of the stony wall until I get to the grassy embankment that goes down to the edge of a meadow. I move very quickly and within a few seconds, I'm on the ground. I put Maggie down, and together we run crouched among the rows of vineyards that are all around the house.

The wind whips my face and fills my nostrils with the humid smell of rain and grass. Maggie, as usual, is ahead of me, hopping here and there among tufts of grass. We quickly arrive at Ourhill, the woods that surround my uncle's house are right beneath us.

"Come on, Maggie, let's go!"

I can feel my stomach grumble, but I try to quiet it down immediately. This is not the time to think about skipping lunch, I have too many questions that have gone unanswered for too long. I need answers, why can't anyone just tell me the truth? As bad as it may be, Bianca and Adam have got to face it, sooner or later. I would like to live the revelation of my disease with dignity; after all those years of silence, they owe me that much.

Clouds as black as night are rising on the horizon and threaten to conquer the valley. I stop to observe the sky for a moment; then, I run down the hill, taking the path in the woods. I weave through the whisks of genisteae in bloom, I go up on a small slope, and over a rocky outcropping that juts out of the ground like an ancient monolith.

My fingers crawl on the surface of the stone covered with moss and the light writings that, as a kid, I carved just for fun.

I, Leonardo Ghebo, proclaim myself Lord of this Forest.

A smile crinkles my lips, maybe I really am king of the forest. I know it like the back of my hand, and I know that, if I walk in this direction, and then I turn right at the big oak tree, I will get to my Uncle Victor's house within a few minutes. Once there, I will finally be able to . . .

My mind goes blank, and vertigo pulls the ground beneath my feet. I remain still, but I can't believe what I see. Right in front of me, there is a dark and gloomy swamp. A swamp that I have never seen before. The canopy of the trees is so thick that not even the sun's rays can penetrate, and the water is greenish, muddy, covered with a layer of algae. On the opposite bank, a huge tree with a wrinkled, twisted trunk rises from a tall rock that protrudes out of the stagnant pond. Its branches are bare and dry, like a tangle of stiff arms and legs, with roots that plunge into the putrid water. In the center of the trunk there is a gap with rough, jagged edges, with tendrils encircling it, as if their intent is to strangle what is still left of the tree. I look around, searching for Maggie. She was just here a minute ago, where has she gone?

"Maggie!" I try to call her, but my voice disappears as soon as I open my mouth, as if it has been absorbed by a black hole. A dark foreboding begins to fill my chest, scorching hot working down to my navel. I proceed with caution to the swamp when a tremor crosses it from side to side. The flat surface suddenly begins to ripple, as if something big were moving beneath it. Viscous bubbles start boiling up here and there, following submerged dark sickly-green-colored spherical shaped bodies that begin to push through the mire like buoys encrusted in mud. One, two, three, seven, ten . . . I can't keep up with the count. The swamp crawls with a swirl of shadows, and it releases a terrible stench that makes me sick to my stomach.

I step back as I try to figure out what is agitating beneath the rotting mire, when the answer bobs into view, paralyzing me with fear. Heads. The things that have emerged from the sewage are heads. About ten smooth skulls of a sickly greenish color with a greasy sheen. I see surfacing large foreheads, yellow eyes, and flat, reptile-like muzzles, curled up in frightening growls.

No, I can't believe this . . . it's those monsters again. I can feel my soul leaving my body. I try to run away, but my feet slide on the quagmire. I lose my balance and fall with a thump on my back, knocking the wind out of me. I look down, toward the puddle. The monsters are coming toward me. I crawl back, unable to breathe. I try to stand, but the soles of my shoes slide, making me slip closer to the shore. With my brain blazing with panic, I roll on my belly, and I look for something to hold on to. My fingers desperately dig into the mud.

"Help!" I am finally able to scream, with mire getting in my mouth. "Help!"

Something grabs me by my ankle. A clawed paw tears my pants and scrapes the skin of my shins, dragging me toward the marsh. Desperate, I keep tearing madly into the mud, until I find a solid root to grab on.

"It's just a hallucination . . . it's just a hallucination . . ." I repeat, as mud lumps slide through my teeth and over my tongue. The monster's claws dig deep into my flesh, and I scream in pain. I lose my grip on the root. Other creatures grab me, and they are dragging me down to the swamp. I am surrounded. I'm bleeding, the pain is excruciating, more intense than anything I can bear. One of the monsters climbs on the shore and hobbles toward me like a giant insect. Within a moment, it's on top of me. With its webbed paws it holds my wrists, while its bony knees press against my chest, pinning me down to the ground. Again, I can't breathe. The monster bends down almost close enough to brush against my nose, and it blows its warm breath that stinks of putrid nastiness into my face. Its eyes are two holes without a soul, and its shark-like jaws are lined with razor sharp teeth.

"It's all . . . ju . . . st a . . . dre . . . am," I mumble, squeezing my eyelids shut.

Suddenly, a chant begins to ring out in the forest. I open my eyes. The monster is still, turned toward the black tree, and as if called to order by a silent command it lets me go and it slides back into the murky waters of the swamp, along with the rest of the pack.

I scream. I scream again, until I no longer have a voice.

"Help me . . . somebody help me . . ." I scream as I look around.

But the chant, which now is a lament, keeps echoing in the forest, overwhelming every other noise. Not another soul, not another sound, no one can hear me now. I try to swallow, but I don't have any more saliva, my mouth feels like it is filled with sand. My calves are searing with the pain of torn skin and muscle, they hurt like crazy, but I have to react, I have to get out of here, and I have got to do it right now. I grab on to the nearby trunk, and despite the sharp pain that threatens to double me over, I stand back up. I walk back, limping, never taking my eyes off the creatures that now, tamed by the chant, sway in place like hypnotized beasts. I take a step back, then another and another one.

I'm almost out of their reach when behind me, I feel a bush. If only I could hop over it and start running, maybe I'd be safe. I feel the thick leaves of a mastic tree graze my fingers, its branches arching against my legs, stinging my wounds. One more step, and I am safe. I go to lift my foot when, all around me, the trunks begin to crack and the whole forest writhes as if trying to swallow me. Bundles of roots burst out of the ground, snapping against me like whips. I scream, or at least I try to scream again, but I am out of breath. I fall down. I roll. I try to dodge the tendrils. I turn on one side and then on the other, with the pain of my butchered calves blinding me. I rip away a few roots that are twisted around my waist, but it's not enough. The branches are wrapped around me like giant spider webs, and soon, they trap me into such a tight and powerful grip that I become immobile in the mud. I begin to squirm like a fish caught in the net but, the more I move around, the more they crush me. I give up, exhausted.

The chant, which never stopped, echoes behind me now. I feel it vibrating in my teeth, in my skull, and then down my spine. The voice has become warm, graceful, yet terrifying at the same time.

"Monsters don't exist . . ." I whisper, thinking back on Maya. "Monsters don't exist."

The chanting speeds up suddenly, and from the darkness of the slit in the tree trunk, comes out the singer. A woman. A woman with a regal air yet suffering at the same time. Thin, pointy ears stick out of her long, dark hair, that spreads over a worn-out robe, adorned with ornate floral embroidery which has become discolored by time. A long tear on the right reveals a glimpse of a pale, boney leg, insect-like in its thinness. With a slow and graceful pace that makes me think of a queen, she walks to the most protruding root of the tree. Her face is pale and emaciated; it hides features that allow me to imagine just how splendid it might have been in the past. Slowly, as if not aware of my presence, she sits with her feet floating in the air, and without missing a note, she starts to throw withered flowers in the marsh.

I try to move again, but the roots are crushing me, almost making me lose consciousness. My wounds are throbbing, and my head is about to explode. I look at the woman. Behind her, in the slit of the tree, a soft halo of white light throbs, becoming so intense that it is blinding. A roar thunders, bending the forest. My body vibrates as if crossed by an electrical discharge. I feel light, free, ripped away from that place and thrust into another universe.

A man, actually no, a creature is in front of me. Kenat is weak, exhausted. He drags his burned body, which is mutilated by the defeat, walking aimlessly. The face is monstrous and the clothes are a twisted heap of rags and ashes that glow like embers.

I see a fairy. A wonderful fairy sitting in front of a giant tree with a light trunk smooth like carved marble. The branches are laden with lilac blossoms, their smell is intense, a sublime sweetness full of joy. The fairy is singing with a voice as soothing as the cool stream. She sings a melancholic melody that speaks of defeated heroes and lost treasures, hypnotic music that suffuses me, body and soul.

A sudden pain pierces my temples. The bright sky is swallowed by darkness. Cold. It's cold and dark. Kenat is in front of me once again. Actually in front of us. I'm scared. Not of him, but of what is about to happen. I try to hold the fairy by the hand but she frees herself, becoming almost incorporeal. I see her running toward the wounded wizard, effortlessly picking him up from the ground and holding him tight. She kisses him.

"I will take care of you," *she whispers.* "Nobody will hurt you as long as you stay in the Oghandum."

Kenat smiles in his mask of pain and nods slowly.

"You and me, Hamadryad," *he whispers his response.* "You and me, forever."

I can hear Maya's voice in those words, an echo that seems centuries away. The white light again. The smell of blood. My mouth opens wide as if my jaw was dislocated.

My eyes snap open, I'm screaming. I am on the shore of the marsh once again, still trapped in the muddy tangle of the roots.

"This can't be real . . ."

The fairy, corrupted and now resembling a witch, is standing in silence, staring at me. The crooked line of her smile shows gray with rotten teeth. Her limbs begin to dissolve into a black, oily smoke, cascading down into the filthy swamp and churning the muck into a disturbing, writhing mass. The monsters are agitated, terrified. At the sight of the fairy's smoke, some of them jump out of the swamp, hiding in the bushes on the shore, while others submerge completely, disappearing in fetid eddies.

"None of this exists. None of this exists. It's just my imagination," I repeat as I try to free myself.

With a jerk, the tendrils begin to push me toward the swamp. Desperate, I toss and turn, pulling from every bit of strength that I have, but the roots continue to crush me; they begin to cut into the wounds on my legs.

"*Calm yourself, Leonardo . . .*" the demonic voice, with which I am now all too familiar, hisses from nowhere. "*Accept who you are. Accept who you were and who you will be. Resisting will only bring you ruin and desperation.*"

My lungs are burning. I wish I could scream, but each breath is harder to suck in. The roots that clamp my wrists creak. They are withdrawing, rustling and groaning, leaving my arms free. I jerk myself upright like a Jack in the Box, and I realize that my feet are already submerged in the muck. In a panic I snatch at the remaining roots wrapped around my legs, shaking and jerking like a mad man, yelling in terror. I scrabble faster, reflexively ripping at anything within reach while in the mire I see the black oily mass sliding toward me. I rip off the last few roots, I attempt to stand when two gray, ice cold hands shoot out of the swamp, pinning me to the bank by the shoulders. I try to scream, my mouth wide like a corpse, while in front of me emerges a head with long black hair, a sharp and scary face, distorted with a cruel smile that I immediately recognize. The demon tastes the moment, licking his black, thin lips with his tongue.

"*I finally found you,*" he tells me in a whisper.

A new pain explodes in my brain and burns through me like an infection. Only now I find the strength to scream.

The scream is lost in the wind. I sit up suddenly, my forehead is sweaty and my mind is numb with shock. Maggie is right next to me and she's licking my forehead. Confused, I look around. I am sitting on a bed of leaves in the middle of the path . . . The same path that I was walking on. My heart hammers in my chest. It feels like it will burst through my ribcage, and my breath rattles in my throat like a clogged drain.

A nightmare. It was all another horrible nightmare.

A light rain, cold as ice, is drizzling from the now dark sky, pattering on the leaves. I'm soaked. Again. Exhausted, in shock and confused, I let myself fall on my back. My sight blurs and the world fades in and out of focus. I'm still miffed at my parents and feeling cold, lonely, and uncertain. What made me think it was a good idea to go tell my uncle about what is happening? If I did it, he too would start looking at me as if I were going crazy, and that is the last thing I want. I take a deep breath and stand up, shivering at the thought of my obvious mental deterioration and the secrets I've kept bottled up. I don't want to go back home, but I can't stay here either, in the middle of nowhere. I don't know what to do.

Maggie chooses for me, running down the cold path that leads to Uncle Victor's house.

"Maggie, come here!" I yell, not able to stop her.

I have no other choice but to follow her.

chapter eleven

SECRETS AND LIES

The sharp snap of my Uncle Victor's fingers abruptly brings me back to reality.

"Hey, you there? Are you sure you're not hungry?" he asks looking concerned.

"I told you, I'm OK."

"Did something happen at home?"

"Nope, everything's great."

"You look pale and . . ."

"I was just thinking about something, it's nothing. Really."

Out of the corner of my eye, I notice my uncle, leaning against the edge of the sink, peering at me with the same penetrating look that my mother had the other day. I'm really not in the mood for confession, so I busy myself with sweeping up crumbs on the table.

"Would you at least like something to drink?"

"Water, please."

"Haven't you had enough of that on your way here?" he asks me, as he sets a bottle in front of me.

"I'd say so," I answer, shivering in the flannel shirt that he gave me.

"Are you cold? Would you like a sweater?"

"No, no . . . I'm fine, thank you."

"Are you sure you don't want anything else? Not even a warm *Panaka*?"

My mouth starts to water as soon as I think about it. My appetite is gone. I missed lunch and I'm in no mood for dinner, but I can never say no to Panaka.

"I'd love a Panaka, thank you," I mutter.

Once again, I sense my uncle's inquisitive gaze boring into me.

"There's something you're not telling me," he says, getting the milk, cocoa, and pots. "Come on, tell me."

"Nothing, Uncle Vic," I protest. "I'm just a little tired . . ."

"Lovesick perhaps? Is it Maya?"

"Maya? Nah, she has nothing to do with this."

For a few minutes, we lapse into silence as my uncle busies himself preparing Panaka. He clearly wants to know what I'm thinking, and I concentrate hard at keeping my face blank.

"Here it is!" he says with a flourish, handing me a cup full of thick hot chocolate topped with whipped cream and vanilla-flavored powdered sugar.

"This should help you get back on your feet and erase that mopey face you're wearing."

"I don't have a mopey face."

"Yes, you do! You're the spitting image of Mopey, the eighth dwarf!"

I lean over the pot, and I take in a deep breath of the aroma wafting up from it.

"*Mmm.* Smells delicious, Uncle Vic," I mumble. "Your hot chocolate always hits the spot."

"I know, kid! That's why Panaka was invented: to heal the broken hearts of young boys in love. Just like you!"

I begin to enjoy the beverage, attacking the whipped cream with my spoon until I reach the warm, dark chocolate. The sweet smell intoxicates me, and with each spoonful of cream I feel something inside me relax. Panaka is not just a hot chocolate, but something more. It is something extraordinary that, thanks to the secret ingredient that my Uncle Vic calls Biobio, truly helps heal every pain. Though I savor the sweet liquid with small sips, it seems that I empty the cup in seconds. I'm already feeling much better, confident, and much calmer.

"Would you like anything else?" my uncle asks me.

"No thank you, I'm good."

"Alright, then just wait for me in the living room. I want to show you something I bought the other day in Florence."

"OK," I reply, unenthusiastically.

I walk down the hallway, followed by the click-clack sound of Maggie's paws on the floor. As usual, she won't let me out of her sight for a minute.

"Put on some music!" my uncle yells from the kitchen.

Rumbles of thunder from the storm raging outside shake the walls as I proceed in the dark, walking past dark rooms. The storm is getting worse by the minute, and if it keeps its strength, I don't think I'll be able to get back home. Oh well, I can just sleep here.

As I step into the living room, I switch on the lights. The lights flicker for a long moment, giving the large living room a ghostly appearance. The room walls are covered with shelves full of antique books and shrines where armor, medieval helmets, metal gloves, pottery, chests and many other curious antique objects are proudly displayed. In the back of the room, mounted on the wall in front of me, there is an old mirror with a silver frame, surrounded by a bunch of ancient swords and broadswords, pikes, two shields, and a crossbow that is taller than I am. On each side of the door, arranged as if they were guardians, there are two sets of armor: one belonged to a samurai in the 1800s, while the other, the most important piece of the collection, was worn by a knight in the Holy Roman Empire in the 1500s and is made of black metal with silver trim. In the middle of the longest wall, placed between two leather couches, there is a large travertine fireplace that throws a pool of light into the room. Reddish firelight flickers over the ebony coffee table. On it, there is a small, taxidermied monitor lizard, an antique metal chessboard, and the usual clutter of knick-knacks.

I step further into the living room and throw a log onto the fire. It sizzles and pops then bursts into flame. I then start the old record player that sits on an old cabinet from

India. I carefully place the needle on the vinyl disk that is already sitting on the turntable, not caring which song I play. Exhausted, I let myself fall into the pillows that are stacked up on one of the two couches. Judy Garland's voice fills the air and the notes of "Somewhere Over the Rainbow" fill up the room, overtaking the rumbles from the storm and tap of the rain against the windowpanes.

Maggie hops onto the couch and curls up by my side. I gently pet her as I lose myself in the labyrinth of my thoughts. What am I going to do now? Should I confide in my uncle or keep it all inside? I don't know. The hallucination I experienced this afternoon has left me totally drained. I don't know what else to do. What else could I tell him?

Sighing, I turn toward the windows. Even if I were to find the courage to confide in my uncle, what would I tell him? How could I even bring up the topic? *Hey, Uncle Vic, have you heard the latest news? I'm going crazy!*

Someday I'll wish upon a star,

And wake up where the clouds are far behind me.

"Come on! Tell me what's wrong!" Suddenly, my Uncle Victor interrupts my thoughts.

"I've already told you that there is nothing wrong," I lie, rubbing my face. I am not ready to tell him the truth.

My uncle bites his lip, and he sits on the couch, in front of me.

"Have you already seen it?" he asks me out of nowhere.

"What?"

"My purchase!" he exclaims, nodding toward an object that is covered with a black cloth, sitting on the coffee table that separates us.

"No, actually I didn't even notice it."

With a fluid gesture, he uncovers the mysterious object.

"What is it?"

"Guess."

In front of me there is a murky, greenish crystal sphere, suspended on a strange dark metal pedestal adorned with three eagles placed in a circle, their wings wide open to form a ring and their claws stretched outwards. Based on the precious look of the sculpture, and the fact that the eyes of the birds look like embedded rubies, I guess that the object must be of great value. Useless, but pricey nonetheless.

"Well? No ideas?" he asks me.

"No, nothing," I mutter.

"It's a crystal sphere used for divination. They found it in a tomb that dates back to the Saxon period. It's a very rare piece, impossible to find."

"And how were you able to find it?"

"Your uncle is a man of many talents," he smiles, slyly. "Legend has it that ancient knights used these tools to gaze into the future and look for hidden perils. Extraordinary, isn't it?"

"Oh yes," I answer in monotone.

My uncle can quickly tell that my mind is elsewhere and not interested in his story. His smile fades.

"Is there something you would like to tell me?" he asks again, in a worried tone.

I hold my breath until I can no longer resist.

"In these last few days, strange things have been happening to me, horrible things that terrify me. I am not OK, not at all."

"What? What things?"

"I keep having these dreams . . . nightmares . . ."

I see him sitting up quickly, as if somebody had just thrown a bucket of icy cold water on him. I keep going, not concerned about his reaction.

"I am having a hard time sleeping. I can no longer distinguish between dreams and reality . . ."

"Maybe it's just a bit of stress," he guesses in a low tone.

"Yeah, maybe . . ." I reply without sounding convinced.

"Would you like to tell me what you dream about?"

"No," I tell him, lifting my head up. "I don't feel like talking about them."

My Uncle Vic grows pale, and his eyes are vacant, murky like the crystal ball that sits in front of us, Garland's singing stopped a while ago and the storm dominates the room with its roars.

"I know what you're thinking," I burst out suddenly. "But the truth is that . . ."

The words die on my lips. I look down again, embarrassed like never before. I was wrong, I made a mistake. I should have never confided in my uncle, he's the only person who still admires me.

"Do you think I'm going crazy?" I ask him in a hoarse whisper. "Uncle Vic, am I sick?"

"Sick? No, Leonardo, what are you talking about?" he asks me, frowning. "Have you told anyone else?"

"About what? My disease?"

"No, your dreams," he clarifies kindly.

"More or less . . ."

"More or less? What do you mean, more or less?"

"I have not been totally open with Dad and Mom, but they have figured it out anyway."

My uncle's stare turns as sharp as a knife. It almost scares me.

"What do you mean, *they have figured it out*? What have they told you?"

"Weird things . . . they've seen my drawings and . . ."

"Drawings? What drawings?" he interrupts me. His tone becomes increasingly agitated.

"Those scribbles I've done in the past few days. I drew what I saw in my nightmares."

"What do you see in your nightmares, Leonardo?" he asks me again.

"I told you I don't feel like talking about it."

"Did you dream of the monster you saw yesterday?"

"What?"

"The monster in the woods."

Without even noticing, I find myself covering my mouth with my hands. I nod, my eyes wide open. So, it's true; if my nightmares are obvious, this means that I am experiencing the symptoms of a well-known disease. Textbook psychosis! But why does nobody want to give it to me straight?

"Leo, allow me to help you. Confide in me."

I hesitate for a moment. I don't know what to say. I squirm as I sit on the couch. I suddenly break out in a sweat as if I were seated in a furnace and the couch becomes uncomfortable as if it has turned into a cactus.

I remain quiet, but my uncle persists.

"How long have you been dreaming about these things?"

"It's been two weeks."

"And what did Bianca and Adam say when they saw your drawings?"

"They asked me questions."

"What kind of questions?"

"I don't know! They talked about my life, my future. Dad got very agitated. I have never seen him like that."

I notice that, with every answer I give him, the muscles in my uncle's face contract in a tense grimace. It's clear that he wants to pull the truth out of me, like shrapnel from a wound. His expression makes it clear that there is nothing I can do but to let him.

"So why haven't they talked to me about this?" he roars.

"They said you wouldn't have approved . . ."

"What?!" He stands up, screaming, "They've kept it from me on purpose!"

A sudden heat wave coming from the fireplace forces me to turn away. The fire that, until a few minutes ago, was flickering happily, has now flared into raging flames that flood the whole living room with light.

"So, what have they told you?" Uncle Victor continues.

"Nothing. They've tried to explain to me, but I made them stop talking about it."

"Stay here. I'll go give your parents a call," he tells me as he disappears down the hallway that leads to the study.

I stay, collapsed on the couch, in silence. For a few seconds, I lay there, a nervous trembling running through me from head to toe. I finally regain control. I stand, listening for noise in the hallway, but the only sound I hear is a faint, heated mumbling, which informs me of the tone the conversation has taken. The fire in the fireplace shows no signs of dying down and the flames continue to flare up in an unnatural way. I observe distractedly, as I keep thinking about what's happened. I am nervous, and now more than ever, I understand that there is so much more to this than what I already know.

My pocket vibrates and my cellphone lights up. Of course, it's Maya on Messenger; she always writes me at the least appropriate times!

Where the heck are you?

I really don't feel like talking to her, not after the argument we had in the school bathroom. I wish I could just tell her it's my own business, but instead I choose to be diplomatic.

I'm at my uncle's.

A few seconds go by, then another message lights up my phone.

Today we didn't finish talking. Can we meet up tonight, after dinner? I can come to your place at, say 9:30?

Tonight? Haven't you seen the weather outside?

No, not tonight.

Beep.

Please. I need to talk to you 😣 . . .

Oh no, what should I tell her now?

As you wish.

I block the keyboard on my phone, and I put it back in my pocket, upset. I start pacing, unable to stay still. My head feels like a ripe watermelon that could burst at any minute. I let my gaze drift over the titles on a pile of books that sit on the table in front of me. Nothing. I stare at the names, but I can't read any. I just can't. *The truth.* It's the only thing I want to know and nobody, not even my uncle, seems to be ready to tell me. *The truth.*

All of a sudden, a sound similar to the jingling of Maya's charm bracelet catches my attention. I look around and I realize that the sound comes from the weird object that my Uncle Vic bought in Florence. I approach it stealthily and uncover it slowly. Incredible! In the heart of the stone is a shining sparkle that wasn't there before, a small light that pulses in sync with the clinking sound. How does it work? For a few seconds, I stand there, staring at it in awe, analyzing every little detail. The inside of the orb seems to be liquid: millions of small, golden specks orbit a miniature incandescent sun. What the heck is this thing?

I take a step back to gather my thoughts. I am still trying to pay attention to the hallway, and aside from the tapping of the rain that keeps hitting the windows, I can only hear my uncle's muffled voice still on the phone. I go back to the sphere, and dragged by curiosity, I forego caution and grab the stone, lifting it from its pedestal. The crystal doesn't feel like cold glass, instead it pulses with living heat. Holding it, I realize that the light is becoming brighter. For a moment, I relive the vision of my mother with her fairy wings, raising up to the sky a crystal orb identical to the one I have between my hands. Acting on an impulse I can't control, I imitate her, pronouncing the same weird word that I heard her say.

"*Hava* . . ."

In my head, a sharp metallic whistle explodes. It feels like my ears have been pierced with a needle. The ball becomes scorching hot and the light starts to quiver, erupting a vermillion red liquid that completely floods the whole sphere within seconds. I jerk back, jumping a foot off the ground and dropping the ball. The crystal falls to the floor and rolls a few inches still screeching like a wounded animal. After a moment it quiets.

I rub my eyes, incredulous. This time I am sure it wasn't a dream. Or maybe it was? *Calm down, Leo, calm down.* I carefully pick up the stone, barely touching it with my fingertips. I lift it up above my head, observing it against the light. On the inside, it is now opaque and murky like it was before, without a single sign. So, what did I see? A hallucination? Is this yet another psychotic episode? "It's just my imagination," I whisper, shivering, and I push it in the back of my mind. I place the globe back on its pedestal and walk out into the hall. In the darkness, a blade of light traces the contour of the door ajar to the room where my uncle is talking on the phone. I get closer, creeping like a shadow along the wall, and I listen intently.

I can clearly hear the words: "It seems to me that you're only thinking about the fact that he has to come back! You know all too well the risk that he runs."

"Let me be clear, I won't allow you to do anything of the sort."

"I know! But we can protect him. We can resist and keep him hidden; we still have time! His Yuth is still under our control."

His Yuth still under our control? What does that even mean?

"What!?"

The tone of Uncle Vic's voice suddenly becomes hesitant, almost shaky. I begin to scratch my neck, overtaken by a terrible itch. It happens every time I'm agitated: my skin crawls and I feel the sudden urge to rip my clothes off and start scratching myself raw.

"But, are you sure? Why didn't you tell me right away?"

Still scratching like crazy, I lean against the door frame and the old wood creaks. The sharp noise echoes in the hallway and my uncle stops abruptly.

"Wait a moment, stay on the line."

I hear footsteps. Uncle Victor is coming toward the door. I leap quickly like a cat, and with a couple of hops, I walk backward in the hallway, just in time to jump into the bathroom. The light of the study floods the hallway, my uncle's wary shadow looming on the floor. If he calls for me, I'm done. What should I do? Should I act like I just went to pee in the dark? Fortunately, the problem doesn't come up. He goes back to the study, this time closing the door firmly, muffling his voice as he picks up the phone.

I sneak out of the bathroom, more carefully than before. I tiptoe back to the living room, and grab the first book that I find and fall back on the couch, determined to give the impression that I have never left the room. Maggie, bothered, wanders to the kitchen.

A million questions crowd my mind.

Well, really just one in particular: *What is everyone hiding from me?*

chapter twelve

REVELATIONS

Uncle Vic comes back to the living room, walking with a fast, nervous pace, and he sits on the couch in front of me. I force a smile, not very convincingly, attempting to project a calm composure.

"So?" I ask softly.

"*Malleus Maleficarum* . . . I see that you delight yourself with important historical documents," he tells me, pointing to the cover of the book I have in my hands.

"What?"

"The book you are pretending to read is a famous manual of witch hunting that was written at the end of the 1500s."

"Why do you think I'm pretending to read?"

"This is a non-translated edition, and I don't suppose you can read Latin."

Busted. Congratulations, Leonardo, what a great impression you made! I lower the tome with an embarrassed smile. The light blazing from the fireplace dances on our faces. My uncle sighs deeply, leaning on the pillows; he looks up with his eyes closed, searching for the words to tell me. I break the silence before he can begin.

"Have you spoken to Dad?"

"Yes."

"And? . . ."

"He described your drawings." His words fall on me like a cleaver.

I lower my head, embarrassed.

"He told me that you wrote something next to the creature you drew. Is that what you see, Leonardo?"

"Yes," I answer.

"Has he spoken to you? Has he asked you to say his name?"

"What? Why do you all keep asking me the same thing?"

"It's important that you answer my question," he interrupts me abruptly. "Was he the one who asked you to write his name? Did you say it out loud?"

"No, I haven't said anything out loud and no, I don't even know how that scribble managed to get on the wall of my room," I reply, raising my chin defiantly.

"Well, so what happened?"

"And how would I know? I wasn't aware of what I was doing, until I opened my eyes and I saw that thing, that writing . . . *EmMi Du* . . . something . . . *Kenat.*"

My uncle's hand jerks to my mouth so quickly that I brace myself expecting a slap.

"*Prathayati!*" he screams instead, clenching his fingers in front of my lips.

At the sound of that command a beam of green light appears above my head and it quickly flickers, fleeing toward the window. Uncle Victor snatches it and throws it into the fireplace.

"*Lumpati!*" he commands, looking at that *thing* sizzling like bacon in a frying pan.

Within a few seconds, the beam of light dissolves in a green cloud that spews light and colorful smoke.

What? . . . No, this must be a hallucination. My mouth feels dry. And my brain, too.

"What the heck?!? . . ."

I don't even have the words to finish my sentence. I throw the book that I have in my hands up in the air, and with a jump, I scramble backward, retreating onto the couch then awkwardly flopping over the back. I duck behind the couch to hide from whatever miasma that . . . thing is putting into the air.

"Calm down, Leonardo . . . Calm down . . ." my uncle jumps up. "There's nothing to fear."

Nothing to fear? I resurface, still holding onto the back of the couch. My words come out all disconnected, in a jumble of verbs and nouns pouring out of me incoherently.

"What? You have . . . the light . . . you said . . . it burst . . . alive . . . smoke."

"Calm down and come here. Sit next to me," he invites me while reaching out his hand.

"No! Don't touch me!"

"Leonardo, it's just me, your Uncle Vic. You don't have to be scared of me."

"I'm not scared of you, but . . . you have to tell me . . . what was that . . . thing?"

"Magic."

I shake my head, trying to clear my mind. I must have misheard.

"Did you . . . did you say *magic*?"

"Yes, what you have just seen was a *revelatory spell*, followed by a *debilitating command*," he explains as if he was just listing the ingredients in a cake.

"A sp-s*pell*? . . . what?" I stutter.

"Please, come sit down here," he asks me again, venturing a step toward me.

"No!" I jolt in terror, pointing threateningly at him. "I told you not to come close to me!"

"OK, OK. Alright, I won't get close to you."

He goes back to sit on the other couch and sighs.

"You see, Leonardo, we do not say his name out loud because it is dangerous. You should never underestimate the power of a name, because it represents the essence of the Yuth from which is comes."

"Yuth," I parrot back dumbly, the revelations slowly penetrating through my panic clouded thoughts.

"Yes, the invocation of a name can open a direct connection between you and its owner. A signal that, in this case, I can assure you it'd be better to avoid."

"But what you just did was an actual . . ."

"Magic, spell, sorcery, call it what you want."

"And Yuth is? . . . What . . . what is the Yuth?"

"Within each of us there is a bright soul that throbs like a heart. It's an essence, the core of who we are. It's like a signature that distinguishes us and makes us unique."

"The Yuth?"

"Yes, the Yuth. Every living being or object," he explains, "has inside of them a, more or less, pure Yuth, which glows and pulses with life. Each Yuth has a different *pulsating luminescence* that changes according to the entity they embody: one Yuth might be dim in a stone or in a chessboard piece," he says, making a bishop twirl on the chessboard he has in front of him. "But splendid and brilliant if instead it were in a living being. Are you following me?"

I nod robotically; my overwhelmed mind is blanking again.

"Every Yuth is part of a much bigger energy web, which connects each and every one of us into being one with the universe," he continues, illustrating by lacing his fingers. "This is Vril, the power of life: a constant river-like flow that, like many trickling streams merging and cascading downhill feed and form the torrent, all life is connected by the merging threads to the Vril. Vril flows in all that surrounds us, it's the meeting between the energy of the sun and that of the earth. The merging creates a pulse, a rhythm that allows the very existence and even the creation of life."

I am sure my incredulity is written all over my face as I stare, mouth agape.

"Just now, speaking that name, you released in Vril a message, an invocation, something that, had it gotten to the wrong ears, it would have been our end. The revelatory spell that you witnessed made it possible for me to isolate where that portion of Vril in which your voice, a reflection of your Yuth, was, and with a simple debilitating command I destroyed it and I avoided that danger. That's why your parents and I feared that you had already voiced that . . . name."

"But . . . it was alive!"

"Of course, I told you. Everything that surrounds us is *life*," he says, clenching his fist rhythmically, mimicking the beating of the heart.

My throat feels like I have just choked down a mouthful of sand. I try to swallow, attempting to suck moisture from my parched tongue, but nothing, I have no more saliva.

"The message you wrote, the one you started to say, do you know what it means?"

I shake my head slowly.

"Think about it," my uncle whispers, without dropping eye contact. "Listen to your thoughts and let your intuition guide you. You know the language."

I frown, feeling lost, not knowing whether to try to calm down or to scream until my lungs explode. I start to protest, when I recall a clear image of the words that I scribbled on the wall.

I see the letters transforming, swirling, and lining up again, writing a sentence that, amazingly, I can read.

"I understand what I wrote," I breathe in awe.

The corners of my uncle's mouth are arching up in some type of smile.

"Of course you understand it."

"It means . . . *I am your dark god, the sacred . . .*"

He raises his hand interrupting me abruptly.

"Yes, Leonardo," he nods slowly. "The being you see in your nightmares is the one we call the Dark Lord, Master of Deception and Dark Hand of Death. The synthesis of everything that is evil."

I shiver, realizing I am now holding onto the back of the sofa with a white knuckled grip.

"You mean to tell me that . . . that thing actually exists?"

My uncle nods again, contracting his face in a sad grimace.

"No . . ." I bark a denial, shaking my head. "No! It can't be real! And that language? How come I can read it?"

"That is *your* language, Leonardo. Actually, it is *our* language."

"*Our* language?"

I understand less and less the more he explains, and I feel my guts wrench in horror.

"Come sit down, Leonardo, I will explain everything."

I hesitate for a moment, then I slowly go back to sit on the couch.

"So, you, from what . . . well . . . you say . . . you are a magician, right?" I ask timidly, without taking my eyes off of him.

"A wizard, to be precise. I am a wizard, just like the majority of the people who come from our world. We don't study to become who we are, as the magicians do; we are born this way. We have the gift to shape the Vril as we like and to affect the Yuth of all creation."

"*We* do?" I ask, croaking in a hoarse whisper, my mouth still too dry to speak.

Uncle Victor lets himself fall back on the couch, rubbing his temples.

"Fourteen years have gone by, or at least fourteen terrestrial years, since the day that I, Bianca, Adam, Anthony, Christopher, and well, nearly everybody else that you know, like your teacher, Miss Abona, and Mike, were put in charge of protecting you."

"Miss Abona? Christopher? Mom and Dad?" I leap to my feet in indignation. "You're *all* part of this?!"

"Please, calm down. Let me explain."

I feel my eyes fill with tears, more from desperation than fear.

"Sit down," he begs me. "Please."

I glare at him for a moment, then I sit back down.

"Who are you?" I ask him, my voice cracking as I try to yell.

"We are the Guardians, an order of magical creatures who are in charge of keeping the peace and the equilibrium among our people. There are seven of us, because seven are the realms we represent. Seven realms erected around the Kahatma, the Temple of Life: the place where the Yuth of the entire universe was once protected, the origin of the Vril."

"Temple of Life? Guardians?" I repeat. What is he talking about now?

"We are warriors, Leonardo. The protectors of our lands."

"And why are you here now? What do you want from me? And why have you been following me my entire life?"

"The enemy caught us off guard, relying on an alliance of unimaginable dark forces. The Viceroys who used to reign over the seven realms have been subjugated and the Great King . . . he's been killed. The Stone of Life has been destroyed, and the Powers of Existence have nearly been lost. The dragon Sindrag helped us save you, hiding you in this dimension."

"A dragon?"

"A dragon," Uncle Vic nods. "One of the Elohim, the worlds' creators. He ordered us to protect you, guard you, and get you ready."

"Get me ready for what?! " I exclaim after finally managing to swallow past the lump in my throat.

"Your destiny. You are a boy unlike all the others, Leonardo. You are the last hope of the Lands of Midendhil."

"Midendhil . . ." I echo the unfamiliar word.

The name of this faraway place slides in my mouth like honey and I feel a sensation of homesickness that takes my breath away.

"It's our world, the Hollow Earth, the heart of our universe. It is from there that reality itself originates. I know it's hard for you but, give me another moment to explain," he pleads.

I nod, barely breathing. My uncle's tense expression fades upon seeing my reaction, and I again see the serene face of the wacky middle-aged man I love.

"I swear, Leo, I never wanted this day to come. I hoped with all that I am that your life could be normal," he says, turning and staring deep into the flames burning low in the fireplace. "But, unfortunately, the reality is what it is. *He* has been looking for you ever since we escaped. With his evil powers he has infiltrated the flows of the Vril. This time he has done nothing but chase, track, and bait you. He used his memories to attract you. All those years, we have protected you, hiding the light and the pulse of your Yuth, and by doing so, kept you hidden, until now."

The dying flames dance in his eyes, making them sparkle in the deepening shadow of the room.

"Bianca and Adam discovered that your Yuth has broken through our spell, as evidenced by your drawings, awakening to the call of the Dark Lord . . . That's why you see him. I had guessed that you had started having extrasensory visions; that much was obvious. It was just your magic nature, sooner or later, it was going to wake up again after all . . ."

"Pardon? Just my *magic nature*?" I ask, baffled.

With a slight pause Uncle Vic continues, "But I thought that all this was just about your sightings of the *Kuspaf*, like the one you had yesterday in the forest."

"I knew it?" I cry. "You saw him too!"

"Yes," he says. "But I didn't give it that much thought, like I should have."

"And what was that . . . thing?" I feel the Panaka coming back up.

"Kuspafs are nightmares. Only a few of us can see them. You need to have the astral eye," he explains, pointing to his forehead.

"What about Maggie?"

"Animals can see everything, it's their gift."

"And you call this a gift?"

"Kuspafs are ethereal beings, parasites living off the Yuth of the living."

"I don't understand . . . what do they want from me?!"

"I suppose that the Dark Lord coerced them to look for you."

"He sent those monsters to kill me?" as I ask, my voice trembles.

"No, no . . . Kuspafs are frightening creatures, but harmless. As I've already told you, they are nightmares and nightmares cannot harm the living."

"So why would he send them to look for me?"

"The Enemy is using all the weapons at his disposal to find you. He has figured out that there is a spell on you that is meant to protect you, hide your Yuth, and more than likely, he used the Kuspafs to awaken your magical consciousness, so that you were the one to break the seal."

"I haven't broken anything."

"Unfortunately, you have, without even knowing it."

I find myself with my head between my knees, rubbing my nape with my fingers so hard that it hurts.

"So, now he can see me? I mean, he sees this soul of mine made of a pulsating light, correct?"

"Yes, your Yuth is now visible and sparkling, like a light-house in the night."

"Am I in danger?" I ask, worried. "Can they find me?"

"No, you are safe here. For the moment, the Kuspafs are not a threat, assuming that the Enemy only sent them."

"What do you mean?"

"Nothing. Let's cross that bridge when we get to it."

I lift my head up. I feel pale like the moon.

"Why me?"

"Because of your power."

"But I have no power!"

"The power of *Akasha*, the Last Keeper of Sidhits . . ."

I squint my eyes, incredulous, convinced that my brain is about to explode.

"Leonardo, you are the one who will bring the Sidhits to Midendhil. The universe is destined to die and with it, all the other worlds that belong to it. Its Yuth has been broken and only you can restore it."

"Sidhits?"

"They are the spheres of light that the Dark Lord tried to steal over a thousand years ago, in Midendhil years, that is. From what Adam told me about your drawings, I think that this is the memory he has chosen to share with you. The one he has chosen as recall. We call it *Vahala: the Shattering.*"

The roar of thunder and a lightning bolt striking the trees right outside the window makes me jump. The house is shaking to its foundation and a weird crunching sound pervades the room.

"Is that right, Leonardo? Is that what you saw in your dreams?"

Uncle Victor observes me with a tense expression. I get closer to him, while a weird consciousness swirls in my head, like a hurricane.

"These are only fantasies!" I explain in anger.

"No, Leonardo, it's not like that . . ."

"No! Uncle, stop it! This is just a joke, a series of stupid things that only seem real because of your magic trick, which you managed to pull off because of some hidden light in here," I scream, kicking the coffee table.

The chessboard and the monitor lizard fall down, the strange quartz sphere rolls away, and the other knick-knacks scatter around, falling off one on top of the other.

"Yes! It's just a very original story you came up with to make me believe I'm not crazy."

Uncle Victor closes his eyes.

"The truth is never simple and almost never right, Leonardo."

"Cut it out, uncle. You're not helping me! Do you really want me to believe I am the protagonist of a fairy tale?" I stop suddenly. "Because this is what we're talking about, isn't it? A magic world with elves, leprechauns, wizards, and dragons, right?"

"Actually, there is only one dragon in Midendhil, one of the Elohins. As I told you, its name is Sindrag, and he was the one who saved you fourteen years ago."

"Stop it!" I yell again.

"Leonardo, it's all true. He's been looking for you because he needs your power, he wants it more than anything else. Now the Enemy is weak, incomplete, and unable to rule Midendhil. The battle with Sindrag has worn him down, but it has not defeated him. He needs you to become whole again and he won't stop until he finds you."

"I told you to cut it out!" I scream out loud yet again. Then, I turn around breathless, and I start walking toward the door.

"Where are you going?"

"Away! I'm going far away from your stupid things."

"Stop for a moment."

"Maggie! Let's go!"

"Stop and listen to me!"

"Maggie!"

"I told you to stop!" my uncle roars, while the flames jet out of the fireplace and block my path.

"I know that all my efforts have been in vain," he continues with a disappointed tone. "You only believe in what you see and that is a big limitation, Leonardo. Do you really think that there is nothing more to what we have around us?"

"The world is not this wonderful place you always tried to portray, Uncle," I reply. "There is no room for fairy tales and magic. What you just told me has no logic to it."

"Logic is home to people who are unable to dream."

"And I wish I was one of them!" I turn around, mortified. "You know that? Lately my dreams have caused me a lot of trouble . . ."

We stare at each other in silence, empty and exhausted.

"Leonardo, I don't recognize you anymore. When have you stopped hoping?"

A little tiny tear draws a line down his face, immediately blending in with the silver hair of his beard. I release all of my anger and I stand there in silence, looking at him.

"Before you go, come with me for a moment, I want to show you something," he says in a hoarse voice. "Just this one thing and then, if you want, you can leave."

Without saying a word, I follow him to the mirror that is hung on the wall in the living room. My uncle stands right in front of it, without moving, his eyes glued to his reflection. For the first time in many years, I notice that, among the floral embroidery that decorate its frame, there are also strange words.

"*Arearcanto Leeuwerikare*," I read out loud, remaining completely absorbed for a moment. "It means, Prank of the Guardian."

I say it before I am even aware that I opened my mouth. It's unbelievable; how can I read and understand this language? Uncle Victor glances at me, a dry smile on his face, and then goes back to staring at the mirror: his hands on his hips, with a tight and firm grip.

"*AlosDagonis!* I need your help."

"Are you talking to me?" I ask quietly.

But it seems that my uncle doesn't even hear me, and he keeps staring at the mirror.

"Stop playing around, I need your help, it's urgent," he repeats, waving out of nowhere.

I have no idea what's going on, but I start to have this uncomfortable, awkward feeling as if suddenly I am aware of somebody watching us. I go to tell my uncle, when I see his reflected image with eyes wide open, his pupils turning toward me, as if pointing at me.

"You mean Leonardo?" he asks. "No worries, you can talk. He's one of us."

I don't have time to think when Uncle Victor's reflection becomes alive.

"*You could have told me right away, instead of acting like a crazy person!*" he whines.

"I just did it to make you understand that you could reveal yourself."

"*Great idea you had,*" he rebuts, whirling his arms like propellers. "*For all I know, you could have also gone completely cuckoo and disregarded our laws of secrecy.*"

My uncle looks at me and shakes his head.

"Thanks for your trust . . ."

All the logic that, till a second ago, I was trying to grab onto is now melting like snow in the sun. This surely cannot be a game of smoke and mirrors . . .

"*And who would he be?*" the reflection rebuts, pointing at me.

"This is Leonardo Ghebo," my uncle says with pride.

"*Leonardo? That Leonardo?*" the reflection repeats, visibly surprised. "*It's a huge honor meeting you. It's a great honor meeting both of you,*" he specifies, shaking hands with my double, who has appeared next to him.

Now, I'm really shocked.

"AlosDagonis, I need to get back that thing you have guarded for me," my uncle reminds him.

"*You mean the Runoben?*"

My uncle nods.

"*Alright, Dagonis. Wait a second!*"

I rub my temples, which are pulsating as if my heart has now moved up to my head.

"What is it?" I ask, whispering.

"I'd say it's the proof you were looking for."

"Who's Dagonis?"

"I am. It's my real name, while my reflection is AlosDagonis. Alos is, let's say, the title that precedes the name of every reflection."

While my uncle talks, I see AlosDagonis reappear in the refraction of the living room, holding a key with which he opens the door to a cupboard behind us, and taking a small metal box that is elegantly decorated.

"*Where would you like me to place it?*" he asks Uncle Victor.

"You can put it on the coffee table."

The reflection follows the request and goes back out the frame, next to my double who has never taken his eyes off me.

"Here you go! All done!" he says, satisfied.

My uncle turns around and me with him, hesitant and bewildered, noticing that indeed, on the ebony coffee table, there is now the same box I see in the mirror.

"Thank you."

"No problem, Dagonis, don't mention it," he answers in an ironic tone. *"Goodbye, Leonardo, I wish you good luck for your comeback,"* he adds, looking at me. *"And you, what would you say about a great Panaka?"* he asks my reflection, putting his arm around his shoulders.

"Sounds great!" he replies, giving me yet another crooked look.

My uncle and I stay there as we watch our two alter egos who, chitchatting, disappear from the silver frame.

"Reflections . . . they don't think about anything but eating and having fun!"

"Is this what you wanted to show me?" I ask my uncle, unable to take my eyes off the mirror.

"No. Come with me."

chapter thirteen

THE SIDHITS

I drag myself to the couch. Uncle Victor throws more wood on the fire that has now dissolved to embers and he sits down in front of me, between us, the box.

"*Tanois*," he says, pointing his index finger toward the fireplace.

Flames begin to flare up again. I look at him, disoriented, and I am now aware that there is nothing to understand but everything to accept.

"I want you to pay attention to my words," my uncle begins, very serious. "In here, in this box, the Sidhits are kept. Now I will give them to you, but you have to swear you will protect them at all costs. Agreed?"

My eyes wander in emptiness.

"Are you listening to me?"

"First, you have to explain to me what that was," I tell him, pointing to the mirror behind him.

"It's an *Arcàntodam*, also known as Secret Mirror. It's a very useful object if you have pricey things to hide."

"But what is it? Where is it from?"

"From the lands of Midendhil, of course. That one is an original Arcàntodam, bought many years ago from an old shop in the gnomes' village of *Arcàntoris*. But there are many others in this world, too. Once upon a time, our dimensions were connected and trade between wizards and human beings was very common."

"Our dimensions were connected?"

"Yes. Otherwise, how would you explain all the legends of dragons, magicians, mermaids, or the Loch Ness monster?"

I cover my face with both hands.

"I know, Leonardo. I know all too well that this is difficult, but in time it will all become normal, you'll see."

"In time it will all become normal?" I ask, keeping myself from bursting out in a hysterical laughter. "Yesterday I almost killed my best friend, making a tree fall on her," I say without shame. "At this point, it's obvious that it wasn't an accident, right?"

Uncle Victor remains silent, a silence that speaks louder than a thousand words.

"And then, what are we gonna do about that . . . *monstrous thingy* that is looking for me?" I ask, my voice filled with dismay.

"Don't you worry, for now we are safe," my uncle tries to reassure me. "The Enemy has seen your Yuth, maybe he even guessed that you are in this world, but he has yet to figure out where you are hiding. The astral universe and the real one move on two different levels and planes; finding you in reality is much more difficult than in your dreams."

I let myself fall back onto the couch. My uncle picks up the box in front of us. I notice the golden effigy of the dragon surrounded by floral embroidery that decorates the entire coffer. As if he had followed my eyes, my uncle lets his finger slide over the top and then takes out a curved needle that looks quite foreboding.

"Give me your hand . . ." he says, in a serious tone.

"Why? What do you want to do?"

"Trust me. It's just a spell for protection that we made to protect the box."

I am really not sure of what I am about to do, but I choose to trust him, and I give him my hand. He grabs it abruptly and with a quick move, he pricks my finger.

"*Oooouch!*" I yell, quickly bringing the wound to my mouth.

"No, don't!" he stops me. "Let a little blood come out . . . we need it for the spell."

Then he squeezes my fingertip till a ruby-red tear sparkles, dripping onto the forehead of the golden dragon.

"You see, Leonardo," he says, nodding toward the box. "This is the only way to open it. Your blood and your approval are the only key," he explains with a satisfactory look. "This too is an enchanted object of the gnomes of Arcàntoris. They call it *Runoben: the Box of Secrets.*"

While we talk, thin lines of blue light start to tread through the dense textures of the decorations. The dragon roars with a metallic sound, as the tendrils curl up, folding back on themselves like petals of a withered flower bud. Amazed, I crane my neck and look inside the box. On the red satin background, there is a heavily worn blue leather satchel embossed with a weird, triangular-shaped symbol that looks magical.

"And in here, there are the . . ."

"Sidhits." my uncle finishes for me.

In that very moment, a gnat cloud, filled with millions of these insects, swarm out of the box and overcomes me like a toxic cloud.

"On no! Stop!" I hear my Uncle Victor scream. "You crazy *homunculus*! Can't you see who you're attacking?"

I start swatting my hands around like a crazy person, trying to free myself from the swarm that is now starting to also sting me.

"Help me, Uncle Vic!" I scream in fear.

"Hold on, Leonardo," he orders me. "Stay still for a moment!"

As soon as I follow his order, his hand wriggles, closing a few inches from my nose and everything vanishes.

"There you are! Thought you could escape, did you?" I hear him grumble, retracting his arm.

To my surprise when I look up, I see that Uncle Victor has pinched the jacket collar of a skinny tiny little man with a very long nose who, is hanging in midair wildly throwing punches trying to free himself.

"What's that?"

"It's a *homunculus*. A little spirit created through magic."

"Lemme go, ya punk! Just wait till I free myself and you'll see what I'm capable of!" the tiny being yells as his hat falls over his eyes.

"I have no doubt, Sbacot. Your master would have never given you the Sidhits had he not been sure of your abilities."

The homunculus stops immediately. He lifts up his bicorn hat, and with a sharp twist, he turns himself toward my uncle. His small little round face brightens up.

"Dagonis! It's really you?"

"Yes, my little friend. And I am happy to see that time has not changed you one bit."

"Too bad I can't say the same for you . . ." he rebuts in a sarcastic tone.

"I see you are still as sweet and delightful as I remember you," my uncle snickers, letting him fall like a stone.

"Ouch!" the tiny being exclaims, landing on his behind.

"I thought tiny spirits could fly . . ."

"I actually can fly, thank you!" Sbacot clamors, taking off till he touches the tip of my uncle's nose with his little blue shoes. "See?"

"Knock it off, Sbacot," my uncle says, waving him away.

"Hey, watch your manners!" the homunculus barks, twirling midair like a top. "Speaking of which . . . can you tell me why you opened the Sacred Runoben?"

"Yes, of course. I would like to introduce you . . ."

"Stop!" he suddenly interrupts him. "Now that I think about it, you didn't open it . . . it was him!" he yells, throwing himself at me. "Tell me immediately why you did it! What do you want? What are you looking for? Are you a thief?"

"No, actually I . . ."

I step back without being able to put two words together. What is going on? Now I have to get a lecture from some kind of flying sprite?

"Sbacot, knock it off!" my uncle intervenes. "I opened the Runoben."

"*Sacred* Runoben!" the homunculus corrects him.

"Do you think this is the right way to behave?"

"Let me remind you that my job is to make sure that the Sacred Runoben doesn't fall into the wrong hands!"

"And you do so by attacking with your super annoying *càndemus*?"

"I sure do!"

"So, it was you?" I ask clumsily. "*Ehm . . .* I mean . . . that cloud of insects was you?"

Sbacot, looking all pompous, turns toward me: his legs are planted, and his hands are firmly placed on the sides of his burgundy jacket which is tied around his waist by a belt with a shiny buckle.

"Yessiree! And let me specify that those are not insects," he specifies irritated. "They are *càndemus*!"

"Càndemus? . . ."

My question immediately changes his proud grimace.

"Where did you find this fella?" he asks in a contemptuous tone, looking at Uncle Victor.

"Càndemus are small fragments of homunculus," my uncle explains without giving into the teasing of this jokester. "These creatures are able to multiply in swarms of small versions of themselves and are able to scare away even the fiercest of trolls."

"You betcha, Dagonis!" Sbacot exclaims. "Yes but, mind ya, not all homunculus can do it like I do. My càndemus are the best thing since sliced bread!"

"We know that very well, Sbacot."

"Okie dokie! After this lesson of *homunculogy*, could you please tell me who this fella is?" the tiny spirit repeats with an attitude.

"You haven't figured it out yet?"

Sbacot's wrinkly little eyes begin to carefully analyze me from head to toe.

"You mean that he . . ." he stops.

He hesitates for a moment, till an incredibly large smile suddenly spreads under his long, curved nose.

"I can't believe this . . . is that really him? Is he already so grown up?"

"Yes, time flies, my dear friend."

"So, you are . . . *him* . . . right?" he says, interrogating me as he moves closer.

I am not sure what to say, so I keep quiet.

"Yes," my uncle speaks for me. "He's the Last Keeper, the Akasha."

Out of nowhere, Sbacot's lungs explode with screams of joy and happiness. As if gone completely crazy, he starts to twirl midair, clapping his tiny hands and singing nursery rhymes that make no sense whatsoever.

"We gotta celebrate!" he yells suddenly. "*BidiBubble* is what we need! BidiBubble galore!" he yells, flickering around the room and knocking down everything in his path.

"Hey! Calm down, Sbacot . . . Calm down!" my uncle orders him.

But no force of nature can possibly stop him.

"BidiBubble! BidiBubble! BidiBubble!" he keeps repeating, undaunted.

"I don't have anymore! I don't even have a single bottle," my uncle says out loud, immediately cooling down Sbacot's enthusiasm.

"What do you mean, you don't have any? Whadda you drink?"

"Something else. There's more to life than just BidiBubble, you know."

"Yuck! I want to celebrate with BidiBubble," whines the homunculus kicking the chandelier. Then, turning toward me, he adds, "You like BidiBubble, right?"

"I don't know what Bidi . . ."

"What?! Where have you lived so far? Under a rock?"

"Sbacot! Leonardo has been living here. In this dimension, where there is no BidiBubble," my uncle explains, while he looks through the cupboard drawers.

"Is it possible that you actually ran out?"

"I'm checking, see?"

"What kind of wizard are you? Running out of BidiBubble . . ."

"Well, you know . . . fourteen years have gone by; I couldn't actually bring a life-long supply," Uncle Victor points out, searching in a dusty jar.

"I would have!"

"*I have a few bottles left,*" suddenly a voice coming from the mirror interrupts.

"Yippee!!!" immediately clamors Sbacot, clapping his tiny hands.

AlosDagonis, Uncle Victor's reflection, is by the frame holding strange little bottles filled with a sparkly liquid. Behind him is my alter ego, who is still observing me with that half smile you could just slap.

"Oh, thank you," Uncle Victor says, standing back up. "You saved us from all the craziness of this little brat."

"*Where shall I put them? On the coffee table is fine?*"

"Yes! Yes! Yes!" Sbacot shouts. "BidiBubble, BidiBubble, BidiBubble, BIDIBUBBLE!"

"Is it really that good?" I ask with a whisper.

The homunculus stops suddenly, as if he had just crashed into an invisible wall.

"Whaaaat!? Of course, it's good! It's the best thing that has ever existed, and after spending fourteen years locked up in a box, you see why my mouth is feeling kinda dry."

"You've spent the last fourteen years locked up in there?"

"Well, duh! Where else?" Sbacot asks me, as if I had just asked the dumbest question ever.

"*There you go!*"

In front of us, right next to the Runoben, I see three paunchy ampules filled with a light green, translucent liquid.

"Here it is!" Sbacot squeaks, jumping right in.

"Thank you, AlosDagonis, I owe ya," my uncle greets him.

I observe the scene without speaking: wizards, spells, magical mirrors and flying sprites! I feel as if suspended between two worlds. Uncle Victor uncorks the bottles, and he hands me one.

"Cheers!" Sbacot clamors, chugging it down so fast that he almost drowns.

I take a look at the beverage, losing myself in the many bubbles effervescing at the top.

"Take a sip," my uncle invites me.

The fresh and fizzy taste slides down my throat. This could very well be one of the most delicious drinks I have ever had!

"So, whaddya think?" Sbacot asks me. "Isn't that just fantabulous?"

"It's excellent."

"Well, after all, BidiBubble is the best *FizzyPeezy* of all Midendhil."

"Alright then," Uncle Victor intervenes, drying his lips. "Now that we have toasted and celebrated, I think it's time for the delivery."

"Righto, righto," Sbacot approves. "The delivery . . ."

Saying so, he glides over and leans against the box.

"Come on, come closer," he invites me, waving his tiny hands.

I stretch out toward him, and take a peek inside the box. The little blue leather sachet is still at the bottom.

"Take it," my uncle murmurs.

"Now?"

"Yes . . ."

My life flashes before my eyes in a sequence of photos that now don't really seem to be that bad. I find myself thinking back with nostalgia about my problems, my fears as a young man. I am suddenly overcome with agony, and I feel out of breath.

"I can't go on like this . . . no! I can't go on like this!"

"Hey, what's wrong?" Sbacot says confused.

"Don't worry, Leo, everything will be OK," my uncle intervenes, already conscious of what is about to happen.

"Everything will be OK?!?" I repeat. "OK what?! It has been days now that I have been tortured by nightmares, seeing things that only a madman could imagine!" I yell. "I started to believe I was crazy, that I was sick! I tried to come to terms with it and then . . ."

I interrupt myself and stare into space with my mouth open, ". . . And then I come here to vent with you and I find out about absurd things. Things that don't exist neither here nor there!" I scream, pointing at the box and the little sprite.

"Hey! Are you talkin' about me?" Sbacot asks, offended.

"Calm down, Leo," Uncle Victor tries to reassure me.

I stand up and turn my back on them.

"Where do you think you're going?" yells the homunculus.

I remain still without being able to say a word.

"What do you want me to say? That all this is nothing but a dream?" my uncle suddenly asks.

I feel my chest rise and lower furiously. I don't even know what I want anymore. I'm confused, confused like I have never been before.

"If only I could erase it all, I swear to you I would!" he adds.

I turn around. My face is flooded with the intermittent light of the flames from the fireplace. I ogle at the little spirit, who's got a face you just wanna slap, and slowly, without uttering a single word. I sit back down.

"Jeeze Louise! Crisis averted?" Sbacot makes fun of the situation, being so out of touch.

"Shut up!" my uncle growls, then he gives him a tiny little slap that almost makes him fall inside the box.

"Uncle Vic, tell me what I have to do," I whisper, pointing to the small leather sachet.

"Accept your destiny and let your heart be our guide. First of all, we have to go back to *Nayaka*, the star of Midendhil."

"Sss ... tar?"

"It's the light that brightens the Tower of the Guardians, heart of the academy of our order. There, we will meet other warriors ready to help us with our mission."

"And my family? My real parents are in Midendhil?"

"I can't talk about this," he quickly says. "I am forbidden."

"Forbidden?"

"Yes, for your own good ..."

My head explodes and throat shuts down with rage. I decide to remain calm, and with a strength that I didn't even know I had, I miraculously manage to do so.

"Why all those stories about them, then? Why all the lies?"

"What was I supposed to tell you?" my uncle asks, a sad expression covering his face.

"I don't know," I murmur.

Outside, the storm continues to rage on. The shutters slam violently, and the water pours relentlessly down the windowpanes.

"The delivery," Sbacot reminds us, bringing us back to reality. "We have to take care of the delivery. I can't stay on alert for another fourteen years!"

"Sbacot! This is not the time ..." says Uncle Victor.

But I surprise everybody, and with a heavy heart, I slowly grab the leather sachet and I take it out of the box. The homunculus begins to recite a dirge that has something sacred about it.

"*Yours is the strength, yours is the will.*
What once was will become what now is.
One creed and one I will unify them till the end."

The lights of the chandelier in the living room become dim, the fire disappears for a moment hiding in the embers, as a puff of warm air overcomes us, messing up our hair. I see Uncle Victor look around with religious reverence.

"And so it begins," he says in a solemn tone. "The power of Sidhits has awakened."

Suddenly, the sachet starts to sizzle in my palm and eight little shiny globes begin to pulsate and reveal themselves through the leather.

"What is going on?" I ask in fear, as I try to pull my hand back.

"Don't move," my uncle orders me, blocking my arm.

"Don't worry, they won't hurt you," adds Sbacot. "Go ahead, open it!"

I slowly pull at the drawstring that secures it, on which is engraved a perfect triangle, with a circle inscribed and three oblique lines that, starting out from the center, culminate with three disks. I stretch out the satchel, being careful to touch it as little as possible, while a strange, bright vapor begins to rise from the inside.

With the corner of my eye, I notice that Sbacot and my uncle are following my every move very carefully. I slowly move the leather edges and I finally see them: the eight bright spheres from the dream are here, right in front of me. Wonderful and shiny like colorful fiery balls surrounded by pulsating nebulae of bright energy.

"Can I touch them?" I ask astonished.

"Of course, you can. You have to!" Sbacot answers excitedly.

I open my hand and I let them roll on my palm. The Sidhits are warm and quivering, immediately releasing a weird sensation of wellbeing and satisfaction inside me. For a moment, everything makes sense to me, as if my life were a path that had already been established. My stare wanders in the glittering of the spheres and my thoughts fly far away to other times, other places. A new consciousness shines within me, showing me a whole world of sensations that I thought were lost.

I turn toward Uncle Victor who bows slightly.

Sbacot, excitedly flies around the coffee table.

"My mission has come to an end, Last Keeper. If you have no more duties for me to fulfill, I kindly ask you to grant me permission to go back to Midendhil."

And now what am I supposed to say? I look at my uncle, who nods his approval.

"Thank you, Sbacot. You may go home now," I mumble, still not very convinced.

The homunculus smiles. He turns his tiny hand toward his face, makes a fist and lets it slide down to his neck; then, with his eyes half closed, he pushes his open palm toward me.

"Goodbye, *Akasha*," he says, taking a bow. "May my Yuth enlighten your path."

With a soft puff, he disappears in a twirl, leaving behind him a pink cloud that smells like cotton candy.

"What was that gesture?" I ask bewildered.

"It's the greeting of Midendhil. A wish that will be with you throughout your journey."

"Meaning?"

"By turning his hand toward his face," he explains to me by mimicking it. "Sbacot has deprived himself of part of his Yuth, and by doing this," he says, pushing his palm toward me. "He gifted it to you, making yours even stronger."

"He gifted me his Yuth? His soul?"

"No," my uncle laughs. "He gave you part of himself, but the Yuth, unless it is completely drained, regenerates itself within a few hours."

"So, I didn't take anything from Sbacot?"

"No, don't worry."

I lie back with my head on the pillow, remaining silent and staring at the chandelier hanging on the ceiling rafters.

"I didn't think you would have accepted it," my uncle whispers unexpectedly while picking up the quartz sphere from the floor.

"Did I have other options?" I ask, placing the Sidhits back in the sachet.

"We always have options. But you chose to accept who you are, and this is very honorable of you."

I reply with an unconvincing grimace. The fireplace is ablaze with fire and light again, and if it wasn't for the Sidhits, the open box and the mess that Sbacot made, everything would appear as normal as always.

"I need explanations."

"I'll explain as much as I can," he answers calmly, while closing the Runoben with a spell.

"This afternoon I dreamed about those Kuspats."

"Kuspafs," my uncle corrects me, putting the box back in the cabinet.

"I was on the shore of the swamp and right in front of me there was a gigantic dead tree. The Oghandum, it said it was."

My uncle quickly lifts his head up, as a shadow flashes in his eyes. Then he sits back down next to me.

"The swamp was full of those monsters," I add. "They attacked me and when one of them tried to bite me, a singing woman, who came from the trunk, stopped him."

"Can you describe the woman?"

"Terrifying."

"And then? Did you see something else?"

"Yes . . ." I answer, tilting my head. "I saw the tree when it was still alive. The woman was different, too: she was beautiful, she looked like a fairy. Then he appeared, the Dark Lord that is . . . he was looking for help and she helped him."

"No . . ." Uncle Victor hisses, sighing. "It must be another memory of the Enemy, subsequent to our departure. It's another one of his traps."

"Who's that woman?"

"She's the queen of the hamadryads, fairies of the woods, the Keeper of the Door to the Tower of the Guardians. The

Enemy must have used her to hide after his defeat," he explains, punching the coffee table.

"You mean that place actually exists? That woman in that tree is actually real?"

"That woman *is* that tree."

"But in the dream, she was different from what I saw in my vision."

"From what you've told me, it seems that she's become a being without Yuth. Something terrible must have happened to her . . ."

"Now she's . . ."

"A specter, just like any creature without a soul," he explains, heartbroken.

I linger for a few minutes, lost in my thoughts.

"I just hope that our sanctuary is still protected, and that the Nayaka still shines," my uncle murmurs.

"But I don't think that what I saw was actually the Oghandum."

Uncle Victor seems petrified.

"What do you mean?"

"It was all just . . . fake, as if it had been staged."

"Fake? What do you mean?"

"The Oghandum all of a sudden turned into a scary man who seemed to know me. The same man that has been appearing in my dreams lately. He keeps trying to touch me."

My uncle's expression shrinks.

"Describe him . . ."

"Pale face, long and dark hair, evil smile, and merciless eyes."

My uncle suddenly holds his hand tight to his chest, as if having a heart attack.

"He didn't touch you, did he?" he asks me, jumping on me. "Did he touch you?"

"What? . . ."

I don't have the courage to answer.

"Did he touch you!?"

"Yes . . ."

He runs his hands through his hair, cursing. The fire flares up again out of the fireplace, like in hell.

"We don't have time to waste! Come on!" he says, running. "Keep the Sidhits hidden and don't ever show them to anybody."

"What's going on?" I ask terrified, putting the sachet in my pocket.

"They found us! It's just a matter of time now."

"What? They found us?" I scream. "How did they manage? You said this was a safe place! And they would have never found out that . . ."

"What you saw in your dreams was a dark demon!" For a moment, I see him out of breath. "His name is Antédios, the most terrible scourge of the Dark Lord. He controls the seven damned souls of the Viceroy of Midendhil, the Dumongorths. He is not a vision . . . he's real. He used the memories of the Enemy to get to you and by touching you, he made a direct contact with your Yuth. He won't stop until . . ."

Words die in his throat.

"Until . . . what?"

"We have to go back to Midendhil!" he shouts, grabbing the crystal from the eagles' pedestal.

Immediately, in its center, the candid light starts quivering again.

"What are you doing?"

"This is not a simple antique object, but an Am-Arcanus of Midendhil: a quartz crystal able to let us know when evil is near," he explains. "It lets us know when the Darkness is moving, but until it becomes red, we have nothing to worry about."

My heart skips a beat, and I become pale. My uncle notices it immediately.

"What's going on, Leonardo?"

"Earlier, when you were on the phone, I saw that thing turn red."

Uncle Victor quickly lifts the stone up toward the sky.

"*Hava!*"

The crystal rapidly fills up with a greenish liquid and within a second it turns into a fiery ball.

"We have to open the *Portal of the Annunaki!*" my uncle yells, leaving it on the ground.

"What do I have to do?!"

"Take my sword, I'll let everyone else know."

"Which sword?" I ask, running toward the wall where they are displayed.

"Not those ones! There, in the fireplace," he says in a hurry.

"What?"

My uncle looks at me with a stare lost in space, concentrating on reciting sentences under his breath. I look into the fireplace. In front of me, between the flames, appears a silver spinning top as big as a walnut, slowly twirling like a mercury-like blob. I stretch out my hand, but the fire burns me.

"How can I reach it?" I scream.

My uncle doesn't answer, busy doing what seems to be a very hard spell. I put my arm in again. This time I am more confident. I get close enough to handle the heat. The spinning top, out of nowhere, moves toward my hand and it turns out to be the knob of a handle. My fingers barely brush against it. It's scorching hot.

"Uncle Vic, what am I supposed to do?" I scream out loud, desperate.

When I turn, I see my uncle wrapped in an aura of light blue smoke.

"*Adara!*" I hear him scream, imperious.

At that command the bright fog leaves his body, at first turning into a sphere and then into his own likeness. I see his specter of light floating in front of him, as if waiting for an order.

"Fly! Tell the others. They are here."

The apparition begins to twirl on itself, and in a flash, it vanishes out the window, flying through the woods. Uncle Vic rubs his forehead, tired from the effort. I am shocked. With my stomach in knots, I turn to look back at the flames: the silver spinning top is still there. Out of desperation, I put my hands into the fire. I close my eyes, and holding my breath, I grab the sword handle with both hands. The fire crackles, but the warmth from the heat waves caresses me without burning me. I don't feel any pain, just a thrill that, for a moment, rushes through me, making me feel dizzy. I draw the sword with a heave and in front of my eyes appears a very long, incandescent blade, forged by fire. For a second, I have this weird sensation that I am holding something that is alive.

"Uncle Vic! The sword!"

At that very moment, a huge roar floods the room, shaking the walls and making all the cupboards fall. The books, the helmets, and all the other objects that Sbacot didn't manage to knock down are now scattered on the floor in a jumble of debris, metal and papers torn apart.

Maggie comes into the living room, barking.

"*What's happening, Dagonis?*" I hear the reflection in the mirror scream in fear.

Uncle Victor suddenly opens the window. The icy cold rain whips his face and soaks him completely. In that same instant, a meteor of fire hurtles through the sky and lands between the hills right beyond the woods. The crash of a second explosion overwhelms the fields again, shaking us as well.

"They are here, Leonardo! They are here, now!" my uncle shouts. "Run away into the woods! Run back home! Bianca and Adam will come to your rescue, and they will protect you. I will try to keep them at bay for as long as possible."

"But I . . ."

"There is no more time!" he stops me, pulling the sword from my hands.

"Maggie, come here!" I say, lost.

"Go!" he says, dragging me to the front door.

Completely unable to even think, I let him drag me like a stuffed animal.

"What about you?" I ask, choking.

"Don't you worry about me, I'll manage. Now go and protect the Sidhits! May my Yuth enlighten your path," he concludes, mimicking the awkward salute.

I imitate him the best I can. Our eyes meet one last time.

"Take care of yourself, Leo."

chapter fourteen

THE UNKNOWN WARRIOR

I run down the path. Maggie is running behind me, her tongue hanging out. My emotions are overwhelming me. I can't think straight, and I'm soaked to the bone from the rain.

"Come on!" I urge her, my lungs burning as I gasp for breath.

I turn to pick her up and I try to fit her under my shirt, glancing back at the closed door of my uncle's house. It's absurd, everything that is happening is absurd! I still can barely believe what just happened - is happening.

A crackling *hiss* floods the forest. In the patch of sky above me, I see through the tree branches another fireball hurtling through the darkness. It's getting close. It's getting much closer and . . . Crap! It's heading straight for my uncle's house. I feel dread building like I'm watching a train wreck in slow motion.

"Uncle Vic!" I yell, my my voice echoing in my ears.

I run back toward the house and stumble into a puddle, but I manage not to fall. I have to warn my uncle. The fiery meteorite is now above us. The fiery glow lights up the yard like a false daybreak. I'm just ten steps from the door.

"Uncle Viiiic!"

I'm blinded by a bright light. I hear a deafening *bang* and then feel a rumble that shakes everything. The cottage explodes in a shower of debris of stone, wood, and fire. The violence of the impact throws Maggie and me over the surrounding wall. A few trees are felled, and I almost get stuck under them. Ears ringing, and with flayed hands and knees and a stinging cut on my forehead, I pick myself up, bewildered. In front of me my uncle's house is gone; there is just a huge pile of debris.

"Noooo!" I scream.

I crawl through the leaves of the uprooted trees. Tears blur my sight. The sense of loss drains everything else from my mind. I feel hollow. Black plumes of smoke from the rubble are already clearing out under the lashing rain; I see the shadow of a man. Uncle Victor! He's alive! I try to stand up, when a chilling voice begins speaking, somehow drowning out every other sound, ominously hissing in that language that I now understand perfectly.

"*Where are you, bedeviled? Where are you?*"

The shadow is moving carefully, like a ghost floating over the ground. The hope I had has now turned to horror. That's not my uncle. I can see it clearly now. It's a thin, curved man, with a burgundy tunic under a darker cloak. Dragging himself, he moves about, looking for something among the charred debris of the cottage. For a moment, I can see his bulbous undefined features, and his droopy wrinkly eyes, inexplicably pulled toward his cheekbones.

I hear him cussing as he stands erect and starts kicking the smoky rocks that surround him. The neurotic movements and convulsive swaying of his long hair sticking out of the loose, dark, slouchy hat, make him look scary and ghoulish. I am terrified.

"Is he dead?" a shrill voice asks.

"I don't know. The body is not here."

I see a woman emerge from the darkness, strutting on high heels like a stork.

Fiery red hair and skimpy clothes: I can't believe this! It's Cynthia, Maya's stepmother. What is she doing here? The answer arrives before I can even finish formulating the question. Cynthia, reciting a sinister chant, begins to tear her appearance off her face, which comes loose as if it was made of tissue paper. She rips off her hair by the locks, taking off her nose, her teeth, and like a snake, she slips off her tanned facial skin. Within a few moments, I'm staring at a different woman, incredibly beautiful and scary. Straight and dark locks flow lightly onto her shoulders, and her big eyes, as black as the night, look around with renewed enthusiasm. It is as if, after her transformation, they were finally able to see things that weren't there before. I am still lying down under branches of a fallen tree, my chin in the mud to try and blend in and become invisible.

The woman, with a soft gesture of her index finger, tears off a piece of the darkness that surrounds us, and magically, she turns it into a large, soft cape that she wraps around herself, sighing with pleasure.

"Ahh . . . much better. I couldn't stand to live in the body of that human anymore."

She preens her hair, which comes out of the cowl, and she places one lock in front of her face.

"Too bad for the red color though. That, I really wish I could have kept. It looked so good on me."

"Cut it out, Silischia. Just help me look," the other figure croaks, sounding hysterical.

The woman quickly turns, twitching her nose in annoyance.

"You better hope that the boy is still alive or there won't be any mercy for you this time around, Feghin!"

"Shut up! He's not dead, he's just hiding."

"You better hope so," she hisses harshly.

"What about you? You had him right in front of you all this time and you weren't even able to actually see him."

"I assure you, Feghin, that it wasn't as easy as you might think. I just met the boy for the first time this morning."

So, it's true: these two have been looking for me. It's just a matter of time now. How long will it take them to find me? A couple of minutes at most. Yes. And when they find me, they will inflict some kind of atrocity on me. My throat is throbbing and I'm shivering, making my teeth chatter. I shove my fist into my mouth to stop the noise. I gage on the taste of dirt.

"You're wasting your time. He's not here!"

His voice is like a breath of fresh air. Uncle Victor! Standing not too far, on top of the mountain of debris, his proud figure appears, with his magic sword shining in his hands. I feel tears of relief forming in my eyes and bite down hard on my fist to stop from crying out in joy. Too hard. I don't even notice my hand start to bleed.

The two dark figures step back, surprised by the unexpected exclamation.

"You must be Dagonis," exclaims the woman, lowering her cowl; her pale face seems to glow in the darkness.

"Who are you?" Uncle Victor asks, keeping his defensive posture.

"You don't know us, but we know all about you," she replies.

"I said who are you!"

"I'm Silischia and he is Feghin. We come from Midendhil, and we ask you to help us in our mission."

I know I'm still in danger, but I feel paralyzed. I should crawl out of here, warn my folks, look for help . . . but I'm scared. So, I stay still.

"Our Lord Kenat knows how brave you are," Silischia continues, confidently walking toward Victor, "and he thinks it would be a great honor for us to have a supporter of your level."

"Zip it, witch!"

Suddenly, the gleaming blade shifts in the darkness and the sharp silver of my uncle's sword aims straight for the witch's throat. Feghin screams, preparing to utter a curse, but Silischia stops him with a neurotic shake of her head.

"I will never help you," my uncle says between his teeth. "Your Lord was and *will always be* shadow!"

"You foolish old wizard!" Silischia mocks him, scratching her skin with the tip of his sword. "Things are not as you think. Our world has changed, and our master is so much stronger than you could even imagine!"

I see my uncle push the blade deeper, increasing the pressure on the witch's throat.

"Lord Kenat has already many followers among your people, our people, of Lokegir."

With those words, my uncle's confidence seems to fade, and for a moment, he loosens the grip on his sword.

"I don't believe you! You can't possibly be wizards of Lokegir!"

"Yes, Dagonis. We are the heirs of your people, children of your children."

"*Prathayati!*" my uncle screams, raising a hand to the sky.

A beam of light shoots outside of his chest, and slithering in the air like a snake, it enters the bodies of Silischia and Feghin.

"What did I tell you? Can you feel it, Dagonis?" the witch hisses. "Our Yuths have recognized each other."

The expression on Uncle Victor's face is like he was dreaming. Without letting his guard down, he dissolves the beam of light, making it disappear into a void.

"As I've said, many things have changed. Our Lord Kenat has many allies. Now, a big portion of your people are faithful to him," Silischia insists.

"Fools!" he suddenly roars. "You have betrayed all our principles!"

"What principles? All the dogmas and democratic principles you believe in are nothing but a big ole pile of nonsense that has poisoned the minds of our people for millennia. Our master has opened our eyes; he has inspired us by allowing us to understand our real nature. We are superior, Dagonis; we are different from all the other creatures, we are the chosen ones."

A crazy gleam revives her stare.

"You're all fools . . ."

"No, Dagonis. We are the future."

"Fools! He has poisoned your mind. He's using you! You don't know what you're doing!" my uncle shouts, raising the blade even more, forcing Silischia to lift her chin up.

"You poor deluded . . ." she squeaks through her clenched teeth. "We overestimated your wisdom. You have no idea of the greatness of our Master. His purifying work has already begun. The prisons of the *Noux Caves* have been opened; trolls, *abulcus, mashuis*, beasts, and monsters have now been freed!

Chaos has already taken over, inciting hatred and revenge among all people. Soon, the war will begin, villages and towns will fight, destroying each other, making it very easy for us to take control."

Suddenly, my uncle lowers his weapon. Silischia falls on the ground, exhausted.

"Join us," she continues. "You won't regret it."

"You have to choose, Dagonis," Feghin growls, slowly getting closer to him. "You're either with us, or you're against us."

A pause. That silence, that wait, scares me to death. What is my uncle thinking about? He is not going to abandon me, is he?

"Fools!" he yells suddenly. "Your Master doesn't know gratitude."

"You're wrong, old-timer!" Feghin screams. "When the time comes, we, the chosen people of Lokegir, will reign by his side, and with him, we shall reshape the destiny of our world."

"There cannot be any second-in-charge next to the one you call Master."

"How dare you doubt him!" Silischia cries, shrill.

"Sometimes, truth kills."

"So, you won't help us?"

"I'll be dead before I allow the Last Keeper to end up with you!"

"So be it!" Feghin threatens. "*Leucos Du!*"

Two tongues of light blue fire are released from the palms of the wizard's hands weaving and looming through the darkness, racing toward my uncle.

"Try again!" he taunts in response as he counters the spell sending it to strike a nearby tree.

"*Dubi Lugù!*" Feghin screams again, this time assaulting Uncle Vic with a multitude of lightning bolts that wrap around the blade of his sword like a spider wraps its prey.

Uncle Vic twirls immediately onto himself, redirecting the lightning, and with a barely visible gesture, he points his index finger against the enemy.

"*Zamana!*"

A beam of white light shoots out of his pointed finger, hitting Feghin right in the chest. Sparks fly as he is sent crashing against the wall.

"*Gall Allium!*" Silischia chants, throwing her hands to the sky.

A stream of sparks bursts from her fingertips and ignites the wind. A fiery storm descends on Uncle Victor who doesn't have time to react. The sword flies from his hands as he is surrounded in a swirl of green flames. His strength falters and he falls to the ground.

"You're trapped!" screams Silischia, excited. "I did it! You pompous fool, you didn't think I was capable of such magic, did you!?"

Feghin stands up looking ragged: the spell that struck him has torn apart his tunic and has left his chest burned. He walks toward my uncle who, surrounded by the swirls of the curse, has curled up in the rubble, weak and powerless.

Get back up, Uncle Vic! Get back up!

"Everything alright, Feghin?" asks Silischia from behind her shoulders. "I smell burned wizard."

Feghin glares at her.

"Don't look at me like that. You're pathetic, Feghin . . ."

"Without me you wouldn't have been able to hit him!"

"If that makes you feel less useless then . . ."

The sorcerer crouches down beside my uncle.

"So, what now, Dagonis?" he asks, picking up the fallen sword. "You don't feel so confident and powerful now, do you?"

I look at my uncle as he looks up at his tormentor. His eyes are vacant, his face bloodless. I fear he can't resist much longer.

"Give us the boy and this stops here."

Terror takes my breath away. My uncle slowly shakes his head, his face fearless. Feghin wrinkles his lips in a grimace of pleasure. He makes a fist, increasing the intensity of the anathema cast by Silischia. I hear my uncle grumble under his breath, trying to fight the pain. Then he arches his back, and he curls up in a spasm. Tears fill my eyes.

"Can you feel it, Dagonis? Now you too can feel the fire burning your skin, can't you?" Feghin asks him.

"Slow down, Feghin," interrupts Silischia as she crawls toward her partner. "The curse is mine. I deserve to finish him."

"Shut up, witch. This is no time to play," he says with an icy tone, pushing her away with the blade that he's holding.

Her hate-filled stare stops on the weapon.

"Give me the sword. It doesn't belong to you! I am the one who defeated the Guardian."

"No," Feghin says harshly, as he happily observes the chiseled hilt. "Now this sword is mine."

"How dare you! If the Master knew . . ."

Feghin turns toward her.

"The Master is not here now, and he will never know about this, unless you feel like dying . . ."

Her shrill laughter momentarily covers the fury of the storm.

"Be careful, Feghin," she threatens. "You've always been a mediocre sorcerer. I can give you the same treatment I just gave him."

The two of them stare at each other in silence, like lions fighting over the carcass of the same prey.

From my hiding place, powerless, I keep on watching the scene. I want to intervene, but Uncle Victor has sacrificed himself to allow me to escape, and any attempts of rescuing him would render all his efforts useless. What could I possibly do against magic? I have never been this scared in my entire life.

All of sudden, something happens . . . I see my uncle move his arm, he stretches out and he fights against the curse. An adrenaline rush shakes me as I focus again on the two wizards who, unaware, keep on arguing.

Taking advantage of the moment of distraction, my uncle musters all the strength he can, lifting himself up on his elbows.

"Careful, Feghin. Don't challenge my patience," Silischia warns.

In that same moment, I see the witch's eyes jump over her pal, landing on the fiery vortex of her spell that is about to dissolve. She doesn't have time to react.

"*Ualos Wero*!" thunders Uncle Vic.

The swirl of fire that trapped him explodes in a rain of glittery sparkles, and like a giant hand, he snatches up his two opponents and violently throws them against the ruins of his home. I wish I could jump up and run to hug him, but I know it's not the time. I watch Uncle Victor pick up the magic sword that has fallen from Feghin's grip as he takes a fighting stance with fatigue.

"You still have a lot to learn," he says gravely. "Willpower is much stronger than any magic."

From behind the treetops where I'm hiding, I see the entire scene in slow motion; Uncle Victor is definitely gone, and in his place, there is an unknown, powerful warrior instead.

"Your master is truly evil, and I am not surprised that weak minds like yours have fallen for his treachery."

"Kill us, Dagonis!" Feghin challenges him. "We are powerless. We are defenseless. Come on, kill us the way you Guardians know how to!"

"Oh no," Uncle Vic replies. "In my life there has already been too much bloodshed. Things have changed and nobody is going to die tonight."

With a lightning move, he twirls his sword, and aims it at their shocked faces.

"This is *Disingur*, one of the Magic Swords that once belonged to the Viceroys of Midendhil, and that now belong to the order of the Seven Guardians."

The sword vibrates and it releases a powerful white light.

"The power of the Magic Swords is immense. They reflect the real shape of souls."

The light is so blinding that I can't keep my eyes open.

"Ask for forgiveness for all your wrongdoings and its power shall absolve you, thus saving your lives."

I lower my head, unable to keep watching. The gleam has become unbearable.

"Ask for forgiveness, and you shall receive mercy for all your crimes."

A deafening *hiss* and the chilling screams of Feghin and Silischia fill the valley and cover the rumble of thunder. Then, suddenly, silence. I lift my head up slowly. The light of the sword is becoming dim, revealing the heartbreaking vision of two broken-down old people slumped at Uncle Victor's feet.

Their facial features have become rumpled, deformed by a multitude of wrinkles and flabby folds of yellow skin, thin and withered. Silischia's hair is thin, gray and stringy, while Feghin's slouchy hat has fallen, revealing a nearly bald head, covered with a few strings of hair that fall down to his shoulders.

"What have you done to us, Dagonis!" Feghin growls, touching his face.

"I haven't done anything. You are now nothing more than the mirror of what your souls have been for a very long time."

The power of Disingur has inflicted on the two sorcerers all the pain they have caused and these two, unable to repent, represent the horror of their abominations.

Silischia sits up. She looks at her thin, wrinkly hands, exploding in a scream that fills the forest and gets lost in the night.

"Pick up what's left of your lives and get out of here."

Despite his triumph, I notice that my uncle is still on the defense, and he keeps scanning the horizon. I stand up and I almost get out of hiding, but something stops me.

Feghin and Silischia are standing up and keep staring at my uncle with an air of challenge. What's going on? Is it over yet?

For a moment, I feel as though the worst is yet to come.

chapter fifteen

PATHS IN THE DARK

"Where is he?" Uncle Victor asks suddenly. "I know all too well you didn't come here alone. You don't have the power to do so."

"It's true, Dagonis," Feghin laughs, bitterly. "You were able to beat us, but you know that you will never be able to beat him!"

I see my uncle close his eyes and around him the light blue halo from the spell I saw him cast begins to twirl.

"*Adara*," he recites, as his bright specter appears again.

"It's of no use to call for help. It's too late now," Silischia screams, angrily.

My uncle's spell turns into a pulse of light that quickly extends beyond the forest, toward my parents' house. In that same moment, a cold breeze comes and a mantle of frost freezes over everything that surrounds us.

"Now you'll see, Dagonis!" Feghin threatens him.

With a simple gesture of his fingers, Uncle Victor throws both sorcerers against the rubble of the house.

"In the doghouse," he orders, without even looking at them.

Gusts of wind now sweep the meadows. I place my hands over my ears, terrified of the ghostly sound coming from the woods. Uncle Victor holds onto the sword with renewed energy. The blaze is now shining again, enlightening his fearless face.

"Where are you, Antédios?" he shouts. "Come forth and fight!"

A solid, thick black fog creeps through the darkness, surrounding him. It's alive. It's lethal. Smoky spirals spring toward him attempting to crush him, but the light of the blade flashes in a sequence of blows that break them, making them disappear.

"Reveal yourself, you coward. Fight like a man," my uncle yells.

The dark fog surrounds him once again.

"But I am not a man . . ." the cruel voice that I know all too well and fear whispers hoarsely through the darkness.

"Come forth, demon!"

Darkness twists itself in a vortex, turning into the lean and athletic body of a pale and scary creature, wrapped in light vests made of dense black smoke.

My stomach is cramping and I'm about to throw up. I cringe and double over until my lips are touching the muddy ground. The monster of my nightmares is a step away from me.

"Tell me where the boy is," orders Antédios, making a fiery globe appear between his hands. "Tell me where you've hidden him and nobo . . ."

"Zamana!" Uncle Victor yells, as he releases from the tip of the sword a powerful beam of white light that Antédios dodges, disappearing in smoke.

"Bricta Noux!" yells the demon in return, throwing a globe of purple-ish fire at him.

The orb darts toward my uncle and barely misses him, crushing against a wall of the ruins that was my uncle's house. The impact causes a roar, which makes debris and rubble rain again.

Lightning bolts, flashes, and flares begin to fly with no order from one side of the battlefield to the other. Light beams of every color flash over my head, with spells so powerful they make my hair stand up straight. Every attack launched by my uncle forces Antédios to take a step back into the woods, but the demon doesn't seem to be worried about it: he parries and throws anathemas, as he grins in a face deforming grimace as if amused.

"Guardian!" he shouts, suddenly. "It's useless for you to keep fighting. You know that I don't have a Yuth for you to kill."

Uncle Victor, however, doesn't surrender.

"*Alcex!*" he orders instead, causing the rubble, and what is left of the furniture, to crash on his opponent.

"You fool! You're just wasting your energy," the demon warns him, laughing.

"I just need to keep at ba . . ."

"*Dubi Lugù!*" a shrill voice shouts out of nowhere, surprising Uncle Vic from behind.

My uncle turns right on time to parry Silischia's curse.

"*Nirasha!*" he shouts, throwing her in the forest.

Antédios bursts out laughing.

"By a hair, Dagonis!" he says, while unleashing a torrent of lightening on him.

Uncle Victor manages to counter it by twirling on himself, but the glow of the curse blinds him to the point that he doesn't notice that Feghin has crawled toward him. In a second that seems to last a lifetime, I see the sorcerer pop up from behind the rubble with both hands stretched out toward my uncle. With a thrust, I jump up.

"Uncle Vic, watch out!"

But it's too late.

"*Vaya!*"

I see a purple glow, the sword falling on the ground and Uncle Victor crashing to his knees in front of the demon.

"That is how all the heroes end up. On their knees, regretting all their choices," Antédios tells him, placing the blade of Disingur on my uncle's shoulder. "All this for the future of a world that you don't even know anymore."

"I didn't do it for Midendhil," my uncle hisses, "but for my nephew, Leonardo."

Laughter. Fluid movement of the sword. My uncle's head is cut off at the neck. His lifeless body slumps on its side, crumbling like a puppet.

Something inside of me is torn apart. Something that will never be whole again.

I realize that I am out of hiding. Antédios is looking at me. He smiles, intoxicated.

"Get him!" he orders his servants.

"He's mine!" yells Feghin, jumping on me.

I'm terrified. I fall to the ground. A few feet away from me, the sorcerer trudges through the rubble, with madman eyes and curled lips of a beast. I'm shocked, I can't move a muscle. I feel Feghin's skinny fingers grab me by the ankle and drag me out of the boughs that surround me.

"You can't escape me now!"

A *growl*. Something flies by the wizard. Maggie, with her teeth showing and her hair straight up on her back, leaps on his face. Feghin's hoarse cry explodes, forcing me to react. I get up unsteadily, as an unexpected gleam of blue light flashes a few inches from my head, hitting and charring the tree behind me. I turn around. The demon is staring at me, laughing.

"Don't bother trying to escape!"

"*Gall Allium,*" Silischia shouts.

I throw myself onto the ground, dodging the anathema that, hurtling above me, crashes on the same boughs that were hiding me. The green fire of magic lights up the forest, flames flare and devour the shrubs all around me.

"Careful not to kill him!" Antédios thunders. "Hurt him, but don't kill him!"

Walls of fire block my path. The demon comes closer. The Sidhits, as if aware of the danger, glow and shine through the cloth of my pants with their bright golden light.

"There they are!" Silischia howls excitedly. "He's got them with him. Let's seize them!"

I try to crawl away, when Feghin reappears with his face covered in blood.

"Come here! Come here!"

I twist with my nails in the mud, and I try hard to stand up before the sorcerer has the chance to grab me again. I throw myself over the curtain of fire, and then I run at breakneck speed down the paths that intertwine through the darkness of the forest.

I hear the demon laughing still, as the explosions of the anathemas are splashing all around me, forcing me to constantly deviate my escape.

"Over here. Block the path," Antédios orders.

"*Belovesux!*" yells Silischia.

A deafening shock overcomes my body and floods me with light. I barely manage to dodge the curse, but the repercussion of the explosions throws me on the ground. Stunned, I hold onto a branch, and I try to stand back up.

"Maybe I hit him!" the witch exults.

The dark fog of the demon envelopes me.

"Come on, Last Keeper," says Antédios, "surrender to my Lord Kenat."

A stream of smoke flies over me, but a gleam of light coming from the Sidhits erupts, defending me. Overwhelmed by a suffocating sensation of horror, I try to hold on to the last bit of courage that I still have in me.

"The Sidhits are protecting him!" Antédios shouts. "Hurry up, you fools! Go get him!"

The bottoms of my shoes sink in the mire of the undergrowth and the branches of brambles trap my legs, but I, unable to think, keep running without looking back.

"There. He's over there," Silischia chirps.

Thunderbolts and flames hail down again, hitting and charring trees and bushes. A blast of heat stops me. I start to turn when I see a ball of blue fire flash near me.

I close my eyes, and surrender.

"*Nayate!*"

Christopher appears, protecting me.

"Run, Leonardo!"

Flabbergasted, I start running again unable to utter a single word.

"Get out of the way, Guardian!" I hear Antédios scream behind my back.

I make a turn, taking a shortcut but, even with Christopher's help, a new barrage of thunderbolts follow me. My lungs feel as though they have been pierced by needles, and my side feels as if I've been bitten; it forces me to run hunched over. I finally see the rock with my inscription on it. If I manage to get there, I'll be safe: the rock will be my shield and will allow me to get ahead.

With a jump, I am behind the rock, but a curse slashes over my shoulder, throwing me on the ground. A terrible pain arches my back, and an invisible force shakes me like a mop. I feel my skin thicken and burn, my muscles atrophy, and my joints lock up. My fingers go numb and my tongue is knotted on itself. It's over. I close my eyes and hear the quick steps of those three who are coming after me. Where have Maggie and Christopher gone?

"You're ours now, boy," Feghin growls.

A cold and wet nose kisses my forehead. I open my eyes. It's Maggie; she's safe and sound.

"Get out of here," I tell her, my voice raspy.

From the darkness of the forest, my parents appear, holding two swords that look similar to my uncle's.

"Dad! . . . Mom! . . ." I murmur, unable to move.

"Don't worry, Leonardo," my father tells me, without losing sight of our enemies. "You're safe now."

"Careful, Guardians!" Antédios shouts. "It's not in your best interest to be against me."

My parents lift their swords and rip through the darkness of the woods.

"*Vidu Teutates!*"

These are the last words I hear before losing consciousness.

chapter sixteen

HIDING IN THE DARK

The rain hits my forehead. *No, it's not true, it's hitting the shades*, I tell myself and run the tops of my feet through the sheets. In the darkness, I smell the clean shirt I'm wearing and feel the soft warmth of the duvet that is covering me. I open my eyes, slowly.

I'm home. It was all just a bad dream, the umpteenth.

The yellow light of the backyard lamp peaks through the shades. It's nighttime. I look at the display of my alarm clock, but it's actually turned off.

What time is it? The rumble of thunder makes the windowpanes shake, taking me back outside, in the forest.

"It was just another horrible nightmare," I repeat, whispering.

I tap my forehead. The cut, scratches and injuries from the explosion and the escape have never been there. In the back of my mind, flames and spells dart once more. In the whirl of lights, I see my uncle succumbing again. His lifeless body falling to the ground. I scratch my nose harder than I should have. I've got to calm down . . .

I attempt to turn on my side when, suddenly, Maya pops up in my mind. Within a matter of seconds, I am lucid and awake. How could have I possibly forgotten about her? Didn't she have to come over at 9:30? And then, wait. Wait a minute, I tell myself, hold on! How in the world did I even end up in here? I have a memory lapse and I don't remember coming back home at all. Nightmares are getting tangled with reality, in a confusing blur that is driving me crazy. I can no longer distinguish where one begins and the other ends.

I grab my cellphone, on the nightstand. The bright screen almost blinds me. I squint. 8:47. What? It's only 9 p.m.? Why is it so dark? And what am I even doing already in bed? Maya will be knocking on the back door soon enough, and how embarrassing will it be to have my parents tell her I'm sleeping?

I sit up quickly, when a sharp pain takes my breath away and makes me let out a distressed wail. The burning sensation on my back returns to torture me with even more intensity than what I experienced in my nightmare. Without being able to think straight, I touch my side: my chest is completely wrapped with a soft gauze, soaked with a cool ointment that smells like tar. Healmey?

"But what . . .?"

A daunting uncertainty ungulfs me, taking my breath away. I feel as though an invisible hand is squeezing my neck and moving down my throat, all the way to my stomach. A retch bends me in half. I spit bile and saliva on the floor, as my sight turns foggy.

I stay immobile, on my knees, on the edge of my mattress.

Maybe it's all true, maybe my uncle . . . perished: No, it can't be. I look over at the dog bed. Maggie is not there. That's weird. Where is she? I get up, walking in the dark. A new pain stabs me in the back so hard that I have to catch the chair before I fall. I move cautiously. I grab a pair of jeans, a shirt, and my favorite blue sweatshirt that are on top of the desk. I put them on, grinding my teeth, trying to deflect the overwhelming pain.

I slowly open the door, but a *clink* makes me stop in my tracks. I glance over the entire room: in a corner, by the closet is a pile of soaked clothes. I recognize the flannel shirt that my uncle let me borrow. I get near the pile. There's that sound again; I hear it much closer now. I search through the clothes that are all wet and muddy, as a beam of warm light shines through the dark. Frantically, I look through the pockets, until my fingertips sink into a soft and warm bundle that I immediately recognize.

Shivering, I take it out and a golden light overcomes me. In my hands, I hold the light blue leather sachet with the eight Sidhits inside.

"It can't be true . . ."

There's a noise coming from downstairs. I stand up, ignoring my pain and carefully put the sachet in my sweatshirt pocket. I look out the door.

The hall is dark and eerily quiet. I take a few steps toward the brick staircase and look over at the empty foyer. Even though the house itself seems to be sleeping, I can still distinguish, among shadows, a sliver of light coming from the living room. Now I hear whispers. I lie on my stomach, still on the lookout while I try to figure out my next move when suddenly the front door slams wide open.

In that instant, I realize how much nicer it would have been to just stay in bed. Lit up by a flash of lightning and smelling of wet dog, a monstrous being of gigantic proportions enters the house. My heart is racing; I lie flat on the floor, like a cockroach. The beast, much larger than a bear, has huge paws and a long crest of dark hair that goes all the way down its back to its tail. Its head is like a tiger's if it wasn't for the two rows of horns on its nose that weave through its entire muzzle, tracing over its eyebrow arches ending right below a pair of feline-like ears.

I gasp but quickly stifle myself with both hands over my mouth. The monster turns toward me. Its yellow eyes shine in the darkness of the anteroom. I can barely restrain myself from shouting. I lower my head, cheek on the floor, seeking refuge in the darkness. The beast is sniffing the air and emitting deep, cavernous wheezing sounds. I'm dead, I know. I hear its claws scrape the floor; the beast is climbing the stairs. Only a few more seconds and my head will be sheared off my body with a single bite.

In a rush of courage, I find the strength to crawl back and sneak into the first room that opens onto the corridor.

"Don't you think it's better to close the door?"

A voice rings from the hall. The swish of the monster's hair and the stomping of his steps on the brick stairs come to a sudden stop. I carefully look around. The beast is standing still on the first steps and behind it, by the frame of the open door, the silhouette of my teacher, Miss Abona, can be seen between the flashes of lightning.

She is drenched and dripping water from her her black floppy bucket hat to her blue trench coat; the sheen makes her shine in the dark.

"Bianca told me of your spell of disorientation," she says quickly, closing the door. "An acceptable attempt, but I don't think the forest will be able to keep Antédios at bay much longer," she adds, drying her forehead with a handkerchief. "We have to get going. Where's Victor? How come he's not with you? He has to give the Sidhits to the Last Keeper . . ."

"The Sidhits have disappeared!" roars the monster.

"What!?"

"They're gone. I'm afraid they took them."

"What are you talking about? Where's Victor? How did they manage to get them?"

Without uttering another word, the beast lifts itself up on its back paws and raises its huge head, which nearly touches the ceiling. Magically, right in front of my eyes, it begins to change. Its mighty figure starts to thin out, paws convert into arms and legs, and the feline muzzle changes into the exhausted face of . . . my father!

I feel my blood pressure rise to the point that it burns: my eyes are bulging, as if ready they will jump out of my skull and my ears won't stop ringing. The truth about my adoptive parents feels like it slapped me across the face.

I see Dad wrap himself up in the brown fur coat that was magically created from the beast's cape, and shivering from the cold, rub his head, which is soaked from the rain.

"What did he tell you? What did Victor tell you?" asks Miss Abona, visibly agitated.

Dad looks up, an incredibly sad expression plastered on his face.

"Dagonis is no more."

My teacher tenses and remains silent.

"There was a battle, his house has been destroyed . . ." my father continues. "I found his body abandoned in the mud. Decapitated."

"What? We can't leave him there!"

"I tried to bring him here, but the place was already filling up with humans."

"Humans?"

"The explosion of the cottage caught the attention of those guys who live nearby. They had cellphones, maybe they even taped me while I was running away."

"The situation is hopeless," Miss Abona *hisses*. "The Sidhits are lost, Dagonis is gone . . . We have to get out of here!"

"*Sshhh* . . . quiet down, Leonardo is still sleeping."

"I'd say it's time we wake him up! We're in danger. He's in danger! We have to leave."

"Let him rest some more!" my dad contradicts her, his tone sharp. "He has a bad wound. The Healmey has mended all his small cuts, but the burn on his back must be the work of Antédios."

"We've got to talk to him, immediately."

"He's only a fourteen-year-old boy . . ."

"You know it's not like that. Stop behaving as if you were his father!"

"I *am* his father."

The tension in the air is almost tangible. The two stay quiet for a moment, staring at each other.

"We have to move with caution," my dad says, forcing himself to stay calm. "And try not to get scared."

"I am not *scared*," my teacher rebuts sharply.

They face off again.

"This is not the time to dwell on our disagreements," my father admonishes her. "Are the others here already?"

"They're over there. Mike is the only one who's not here yet," my teacher replies, as she glances outside the window.

"Caution, please."

Miss Abona gives him a condescending look. She puts her wet hat back on, and with a grimace, goes out into the storm again, slamming the door shut behind her.

I follow the sound of my dad's muffled steps walking through the corridor, beyond the kitchen. Carefully, I move out of my hideout, tiptoeing, I walk down the stairs toward the entrance. I have got to know. The time has come for me to learn the truth, and I want to hear it from my parents' mouths.

I peek through the windowpane that looks out onto the front yard. The silhouette of my science teacher is still like a statue, solid on her short and plump legs and with her gaze focused on the dark horizon. In one hand she holds a sword with a long and thick blade, while in the other, her fingers pulsate with light blue beams.

I proceed along the wall, until I walk by the kitchen door. The warm glow of the fireplace spreads over the floor of the corridor, piercing the darkness. My back still hurts, well actually, still hurts a *lot*, but this is not the time to let myself succumb to pain.

"Adam! Finally, you're back," I hear my mom's worried voice.

"But where's Victor?" Christopher is here too.

Silence, no answer. I walk on carefully, staying in the darkness, and spy the living room. The room is in shadow and only the flickering light from the fire illuminates it, making every shape flicker. My mother, pale as a ghost, is sitting, very stiffly, in the armchair; Maggie, who's more restless than I've ever seen her, is by her side. Standing up, leaning against the opposite wall, are my cousins: Christopher, with hollow eyes and a bad wound on his face, and Anthony, with his usual gloomy expression.

Dad, wrapped in his fur cape, walks toward the crackling flames.

"Did they catch him? Did they catch Victor?" Mom asks, her voice trembling.

Dad lets his emotions show and places his hands and forehead on the wooden mantel of the fireplace.

"Dagonis didn't make it . . ."

My mother winces, her hands tightening over her mouth and her eyes filling with tears.

"What do you mean, *he didn't make it*?" asks Christopher, shocked.

"He's gone. They killed him."

Silence falls on the entire room. A loud silence.

"What about the Sidhits?" Anthony interrupts, voicing the question that is on everybody's mind.

Dad shakes his head.

"What?!" Christopher jumps. "May the Great Dragon protect us all! It's over. It's truly over!"

"No!" Dad admonishes him. "This is not the time to give up. The Sidhits are lost, but Leonardo needs our help. Antédios hasn't left. He's still here and he's looking for him."

"But what can we do?" Anthony asks. "Without the Sidhits we can't open the Portal of Annunaki, and we know all too well that we don't stand a chance against the Dark Demon and the *Dumongorths*."

Dumongorths? The bedeviled souls of the seven Viceroys my uncle was talking about. I bite my nails and taste dirt.

"He's right," Christopher echoes, dabbing his wound. "We can weaken them, slow them down, but there is no spell that could possibly kill a lifeless creature. They'll get him in the end."

"No, Christopher!" Dad exclaims. "We won't allow it."

"We'll hide," says Mom, her voice still trembling. "We'll get him out of there . . . we'll change names, town, country . . .

We'll come up with something. We swore we'd protect him . . .
We SWORE. And we'll do it till the end . . . right?"

Her eyes, shocked, look for my dad's.

"Isn't that right, Adam?"

"Sure . . ."

My parents hold hands, each looking for strength in the
other.

"Yes, till the end," Christopher repeats slowly. "We are the
Guardians, and this is our duty. Till the end."

A *thud*. The front door flies wide open, pushing the smell
of rain all the way into the living room. Maggie starts to growl;
I turn with a jerk. Down the corridor, projected on the walls
of the anteroom, there are the shadows of two men who move
hesitantly as they chat.

With a jump I throw myself behind a cabinet, right before
Miss Abona and Mike walk right in front of me.

"Here I am," says the janitor, exhausted. "Sorry for being
late, I was attacked by a Dumongorth."

"Did they follow you?" Dad asks quickly.

"No, he was alone," explains the janitor, clearing his voice.

I crawl back to my hideout behind the brick arch. Miss
Abona takes her bucket hat off, and with a touch, she smooths
her wet hair and stands in one of her usual rigid poses. Mike,
short and curvy, is shocked, he carries the weighty gloom of
somebody who just fought for his life. His pants are dripping
water and blood on the carpet, and he excretes a weird smell
of soot.

"You're injured." Mom murmurs.

"It was a curse," Mike explains, letting himself fall into the
chair.

"We need to take care of it stat or it'll get worse."

"No, there's no time," he replies, taking his belt off, with
fatigue. "We have to get going, or it'll be the end for all of
us," he adds, tightening it around his wounded leg like a
tourniquet.

Briefly, the blood seems to stop flowing, but then the wound opens all the way down to the ankle, overwhelming him with pain.

"Stop it. We have to take care of you immediately," my mother scolds him, as she crouches to analyze the gash. "The curse grazed you, but the damage is enough to make you bleed to death."

"Bianca, we have no time."

"I know, but we have got to do something. *Teutax*!" she whispers, closing her eyes.

A warm light begins to draw a halo around the laceration, covering it with a thin, opalescent membrane wrapping around the wound like a bandage.

"It's not much, but at least we blocked the hemorrhage."

"Thank you, Bianca."

"The important thing is that he didn't follow you," Christopher reaffirms.

"No, don't worry. Nobody followed me," Mike mutters angrily, getting up and limping toward the window.

"Confound it! I never thought they could get here."

"Rest while you can," my mom suggests nervously.

The janitor doesn't seem to hear her. He moves the curtain to the side and spies beyond the fogged-up glass.

"Was the Dumongorth nearby?" Miss Abona asks coldly.

"No," he answers, as he keeps on scrutinizing the dark of the fields. "We clashed outside of town."

"It's weird that he was alone," Anthony thinks out loud, offering him a glass of what I believe to be bourbon. "They never move by themselves."

"That's true," Mike agrees, sipping the whiskey making his eyes squint. "But I think it might be due to the fact that they are looking for us."

"Where did he attack you?" Christopher asks, restless.

"On the road that borders Victor's forest and . . ." he stops all of a sudden, turning toward Dad.

"He's gone," Mom says sadly.

"I know . . ."

"We received his message, but it was too late," Dad explains, with fatigue. "He must have faced them alone."

"A desperate action . . ."

"And Dagonis knew he would have never been able to face them alone. But his sacrifice is what saved Leonardo. Without him, he would be in their hands by now."

Those words pierce right through me like scorching blades. Dad is right. If I had had the courage to help him, to intervene, to shift their focus on me, maybe those three monsters would have spared my uncle. I am the cause of his death. Tears come back and fog up my sight. My heart breaks, what I'm feeling is unbearable. I am stuck in a nightmare that I have no idea how to get out of.

With a crazy gleam in my eyes, I walk to the center of the room. The six Guardians all turn toward me, stunned, holding their breath.

"Leonardo, what are you doing up?" Mom quickly rushes toward me. "You're still too weak. You have got to rest!"

I take a couple steps forward. My head spins and the floor tilts under my feet like the deck of a ship.

Mike chugs down the bourbon that is left in the glass all at once, and shivering, limps slowly toward me. He stares at me; it's as if there was a fire between us.

"Victor told you the truth about us, didn't he?"

I nod.

"Are you aware of our mission?"

I nod again, but this time slowly. A tear slips down my cheek.

"Mike, it's all useless now," Dad intervenes. "Leave him alone, he's already gone through too much for one night. The Sidhits are lost, and our mission has failed. We have no more hope of going back to Midendhil."

"There's always hope," Mike rebuts, still staring at me.

"The Sidhits are gone! Don't you get that!? We have to get out of here. We must disappear."

Mike tries to reply, but his words fail him. Mom is behind me, tightly holding onto my shoulder.

"It can't end this way. It can't end like this . . ." Christopher murmurs in a corner, his hands in his hair.

"Stop it!" Miss Abona roars suddenly. "This is not the time to whine."

"Shut up! You've got to shut up!" Christopher quickly rebuts her with a broken tone. "I'm not like you! There's a heart beating in my chest, got it?"

"Buck up, you loser!"

"Hey, calm down," intervenes my dad, stepping in front of Christopher.

"Just be quiet, all of you!" my mother interrupts them, abruptly. "What's wrong with you? Arguing will only make us weaker."

The three calm down immediately. I am feeling extremely sick, like there's not even a drop of blood left in me. I can't do this, I just can't.

"Don't worry, Leo," Anthony says, after crouching down by my side. "We won't let anyone hurt you. Sidhits or no Sidhits, you will always be our Leonardo."

For a brief moment, my eyes rest on the puffy, hairy face of the Big Guy. *How many centuries have gone by since we just laughed happily together during our last Food Jamboree?* I have this awkward feeling of having an out-of-body experience, as if, in a way, I wasn't part of what is going on. I feel like I'm in a movie. A horrible movie, of which I don't want to know the ending.

"Leonardo, are you OK?" Dad asks me, worried.

A blue beam hurtles through the dark, beyond the windows.

"What was that?" Christopher asks, alarmed.

"I don't know, but beware," Dad replies, pulling his sword out of his cape.

The six Guardians place themselves in a circle around me, all of them with their weapons drawn, ready to fight. Once again, the light encircles the house, leaving a trail of fiery debris.

"Over there!" Miss Abona warns.

The room suddenly lights up with a blinding flash, a globe of light follows the ceiling and stops a few inches from my head.

"Watch out!" I hear someone screaming.

I bend down on the ground, as the Guardians get ready to attack.

"Stop!" Mike shouts. "Don't move, it's just a message, but . . . from whom?"

The sphere floats midair, right in front of me. It begins to pulsate, growing bigger, until it takes the form of my Uncle Victor. His specter looks around, and for a moment, it seems to have him back with us.

"*My dear friends, if you have received this message, it means that I didn't make it and that I'm dead.*"

I squeeze my fists tight, trying not to pass out.

"*But, what's truly important, is that the Last Keeper and the Sidhits are safe and ready to return.*"

The eyes of the spectrum focus on me, as if my uncle was actually able to see me.

"*Leonardo, I am sorry for how things have unfolded. You know how much I wanted to be by your side.*"

I start to choke up, tears streaming down my face.

"*Don't be sad, Leonardo. We are stars that shine brightly in the sky, each one with its own pace and path, but don't think that death is the end to everything. We are so much more than that.*"

The hand of the specter stretches out toward mine. I try to touch it, but all I manage to grab is air.

"*Be strong . . .*" Uncle Victor tells me before vanishing in a vortex of light blue glittery sparkles.

chapter seventeen

THE PORTAL OF ANNUNAKI

"The Sidhits?" Mike asks, shocked. "You . . . do you have the Sidhits?"

Like an automaton, I take my hand out of my sweatshirt pocket and I open it slowly in front of the flabbergasted stares of the Guardians. In my palm, the eight Sidhits shine brightly like fires.

"Oh, Great Dragon," Christopher yells happily. "I can't believe this!"

Mike's face lights up, letting out a nervous laugh from his bearded face.

"So, not all is lost," he exclaims.

Anthony comes forward, with a proud and powerful attitude that I don't recognize.

"Leonardo, we are your Guardians. We have the duty of taking you back to Midendhil," he says, slipping his necklace with the Healmey-filled pendant around my neck. "Keep it, it'll help you through your journey."

"Journey?"

"My name is Rox, *Knight Mellon* of the *Realm of Celicnon*," he adds, excited as a kid in a candy store.

"I am Epostero, a *Samaya* elf from the *Village of Tamon*," Christopher says, coming forth and running his fingers through his hair that, at his touch, turns golden.

"My name is Dubrona, a pirate of the *Tortuga of Aban*, at your service," Miss Abona says, giving me a cold smile.

"Lucilla, fairy of the *city of Iesin*," Mom adds.

"I am Kheli, a warrior of the *Berseker tribe of Druma*," Dad says.

"Bethod, a *lusogham* of the *village of Ialon*," Mike then introduces himself. "The one you knew as Uncle Victor was Dagonis, a wizard of the *city of Lokegir*."

I am petrified. All my words are lost in the torrent of the night's wind. I look at the faces of the people around me, they are all now staring at me as if waiting for my command. I move slowly. I close my hand and place the Sidhits back in my pocket.

"I didn't think Dagonis managed to give them to you," Dad says. "I was scared that they had stolen them."

"Uncle Vic...I mean...Dagonis gave them to me right before..."

I can't. I can't even say it.

"Leonardo, it's not your fault," Dad tries to console me. "Protecting you was his duty, *our* duty."

"But Uncle Victor is dead! He's dead because of me!" I cry out loud, as tears flood down my face. My sobbing takes my breath away. "They killed him, Dad, and I didn't do anything to prevent it."

He holds me tight against his chest. I feel him shaking. Mom joins in the hug as well and begins to sob, too. We are all crying. We are crying for Uncle Victor; we are crying for what is happening. We are crying because we are aware that, once this night is over, nothing will ever be the same.

"We've gotta hurry," Mike says suddenly, while placing a hand on my head. "We have to open the portal and help Leonardo escape. Antédios will be here in no time."

"You're right," Dad replies, drying his tears with the back of his hand. "Bianca, it's late, we gotta go."

Mom turns me to face her and holds my face between her hands. Her thumbs caress my cheeks, wiping away the tears that keep flowing.

"Sweetheart, whatever happens . . . *anything* . . . remember that we will always be by your side," she says emotionally. "I am your mom, and I will never abandon you, I will protect you with my own life . . . Got it?"

"Got it."

I hold her tight, in an embrace that only a mother and her son can fully comprehend. Tonight, my feelings of abandonment no longer exist, and I finally understand what it means to have a real family. The five men come closer around us.

"Bianca . . ." Mike intervenes.

Mom moves away slowly, and she forces herself to smile.

"You'll see, everything will be just fine," she repeats.

I try to keep holding her for a while longer, but Mike brings me back to reality.

"Guardians, get ready!" he orders. They flaunt a confidence that seems fake. The others nod along.

"Let's go outside and form a circle around Leonardo," Christopher suggests. "A circle that will protect him until the Portal of Annunaki is open."

My legs tremble with fear. Everything is happening way too fast for me to actually understand and accept it.

"No!" I scream.

"What's up with you, now?" Miss Abona asks me.

"I . . . I'm not ready. I don't wanna go anywhere."

"Leonardo," my father intervenes, calmly, "trust in us."

"But I don't know what to do. I don't even know what you guys are talking about. Maybe there's been a mistake; I am not the Last Keeper."

"Cut it out, Ghebo! This is not the time to whine!" Miss Abona fulminates me, knocking me down with a whack.

A sharp pain hits me in the back making me nauseated.

"Leonardo!" Mom exclaims.

"Don't get in the middle, Bianca," she pushes her away.

I see my mother step back, looking apologetic. Mike, Anthony, Christopher, and my father look seriously at me, perhaps even disappointedly. Fear is replaced by anger.

"You whine like a little girl," Miss Abona makes fun of me. "Where I grew up, we eat people like you for breakfast!"

Another jab folds me in half with pain, making me scream. I hear my mom sobbing.

"Leave me alone!" I yell at the harpy. "Who are you to treat me like this?"

"In all those years I have made your life very difficult, a real nightmare. As soon as I saw you defenseless, I would hit you, humiliate you, destroy you. Ghebo, I never liked weak people."

I shake with anger, and I know that soon enough I won't be able to control myself anymore. Miss Abona stoops in front of me, her face drenched with disgust. I look down in an effort to restrain my hatred.

"Look at me when I talk to you," she orders me, lifting my chin with two fingers.

Two huge tears streak down my face.

"Cry, Ghebo. You cry because you're scared."

"You're wrong. I'm not scared. I don't fear you or anybody else."

"Then show me! React like you always have. You have never lowered your head down, Ghebo, and you can't start now."

Miss Abona's cruel grin disappears, leaving room for an expression that I barely recognize.

"You are the Last Keeper, the Chosen One, and no mistake has been made," she tells me, helping me to stand back up. "Often, truth hides behind actions we can't comprehend, but this doesn't mean that we must doubt its authenticity."

I look around, swallowing hard. I can't run away anymore. Uncle Victor is gone, and as absurd as this is, I must find the strength and the courage to face my destiny, whatever it may be. I stay still, in an attempt to accept the big and unexplainable truth of my future.

"So, what will happen then?" I ask, whispering. "What will happen when I'm in Midendhil?"

"You'll find your path," Dad explains to me. "You are powerful, Leonardo; you are the only one who can save our world.

Soon you'll find that your wish is your command and that it's only up to you to believe that all this is possible."

"Trust in your strength, because the destiny of our world will depend on what you choose to be," Miss Abona concludes.

"But what can I do? I'm only fourteen."

"You have to believe in yourself, believe in Midendhil."

I look down, my heart full of emotions that I can't describe.

"Say it, Leonardo," Dad comes closer to me, slowly. "Say that you believe in Midendhil . . ."

My hand searches in my pocket and holds onto the Sidhits. This feeling of wholeness that I first felt at my uncle's house is now back to reassure me.

"I believe in Midendhil," I whisper, unsure.

"Louder, Leo."

"I believe in Midendhil!" I scream with all the breath I have in my body.

A sudden beam brightens my cheek, as a supernatural wind begins to blow in my face.

"What's going on?!" I ask, scared.

"Reminiscence, Leonardo," my dad reveals, enthusiastic. "Our world is calling you! The Portal of Annunaki is ready to be opened."

Suddenly, I hear the *thud* of the patio door that slams, a broken scream, and a faint jingle of charms. I turn quickly, seeing Maya in front of me, her soaked curls popping out of her pink hoodie. I totally forgot she was coming!

"There was an explosion . . . but what . . . what's . . .?"

The light that I'm emanating extinguishes, making me fall on the ground.

"Calm down, Maya, calm down," Mom tells her. "It's alright . . . you're safe with us."

Maya steps back, until she hits the wall. A couple of picture frames fall, crashing with a *thump*; there's glass everywhere.

"Leonardo, what's happening to you? Did they hurt you?" Maya asks, looking terrified.

"No, don't worry. It's all . . . OK," I reply, hesitant.

"What are you? What . . .?"

"It's just us, Maya," Dad tries to reassure her. "Your best friend's parents. You have nothing to fear."

"There was an explosion and he . . ."

"*Nidra!*" Mike exclaims, out of nowhere.

A light *snap* of his fingers and Maya falls to the floor, unconscious.

"What did you do to her?" I scream, throwing myself on her.

"Nothing bad, Leo . . . I just made her fall asleep."

"What will happen to her now?"

"Nothing," my father tells me, as he crouches down next to me. "Once she's up, she'll feel like it was all just a dream."

I look at her for a few seconds, moving the curls that fall around her face.

"Will I see her again?" I ask, whispering.

Dad doesn't answer; his sad smile doesn't give me any hope.

"We have to hurry," Anthony interrupts.

A *thud* shakes the house and stops our hearts. The storm raging outside suddenly becomes more violent: the rain begins to hit the windows all around the house and the wind howls, as if wanting to tear off the shutters. Maggie barks at the window that opens onto the dark meadows.

"Antédios is moving the storm against us," Christopher growls, looking outside. "I wouldn't be surprised if the roof blows away too and . . ."

He doesn't have time to finish the sentence when a sudden gust of wind shatters all the windowpanes. A dark energy overcomes the living room and hits the six Guardians, throwing them against the walls. A swirl of smoky fog, fast and whipping like a cobra, engulfs the room. I throw myself on Maya to protect her, but a tentacle of smoke grabs us both. It retreats to the ice-cold fields and takes us with it.

Immediately, the magic of the Sidhits opposes the obscure power of Antédios, but this time in a much weaker way. The soft light of their power flares up, shining in front of me. The spine-chilling scream of my mother, and the desperate barking from Maggie are the only sounds I can hear.

When I open my eyes, I am flat on the ground. My back is embedded in the muddy grass outside my house as a torrential rain pricks my face. Maya is next to me, still asleep from the spell. The magic of the Sidhits has once again managed to dissolve the evil and block the demon, but this time it was not enough. I wrench around toward my house: the glass is shattered, the windows are all dark, the roof has crashed down. Terrified, I look at the vortex of dark smoke that floats over my head in a terrifying swirl.

"Antédios . . ."

"Bravo," the fog replies, turning into the horrible sneer of the demon. "I see you are finally aware of my name."

In a rage, I squeeze my hands around the sachet that fills the pocket of my sweatshirt. A ray of light shines brightly, clearing the darkness over me for a moment.

"It's useless, boy. The magic of the Sidhits will not protect you forever. Your fear is blocking their power and soon, when your reality becomes theirs, it will be all over."

I tremble, not able to counteract. The lascivious face floats over me, suspended in the smoke that it's made of.

"Give me the Sidhits!"

"No! I'd rather die than see the Sidhits in your possession!"

The fog turns thicker, and Antédios's body appears through the smoky swirls. Silky black layers of clothing wrap around his pale, hairless body, and shiny flowing hair materializes from the darkness, sliding down his shoulders.

"You silly brat, don't pretend to be the hero with me."

"You'll have to get rid of me, like you did with my uncle!"

The demon stares grimly at me. A nervous tic wrinkles his nose and reveals all the hatred he has for me. I'm scared to death, but I must be strong, or it'll be over for all of us.

"I know a thousand ways to get rid of a creature without having to kill it," he *hisses*, pressing his bare foot on my chest. "Soon, you will be begging me to take your life."

"I'm not scared!" I lie, trying to free myself.

"You will be, little brat. You will be!"

With one eye, I see Maya is starting to move, touching her face with her hand.

"What . . . what happened?" she asks, whispering.

Mike's spell is wearing off quicker than I excepted. My gaze darts to Antédios's face.

"And what do we have here?" the demon asks, noticing her. "A human . . ."

"Don't get close to her!" I scream, trying to protect her with my body.

"Ohh, so we found the Last Keeper's weakness . . . *Torkam*," he smiles, moving his fingers over us.

At the sound of that word, waves of heat pass by me and hit Maya's arm. Her cry fills the night: a painful cry that makes my blood freeze. A burn appears on her wrist, forming a purplish blister that quickly spreads to her arm.

With a courage I didn't think I could muster, I throw myself against Antédios, ready to tackle him, but the demon darts to the side and I fall in the mud. His cruel laughter resounds in my head.

"Come with me boy, and I'll save your friend. I promise."

Maya writhes in convulsions, until she becomes unconscious again. I crawl next to her, totally panicking. The swelling has now reached her elbow, wrapping her arm in a dark, jelly bubble that grows under her skin. I don't know what to do, but I have got to find a way to save her.

"Why do you oppose me like this? Why are you forcing me to hurt you? I want to help you," Antédios *hisses*.

"You are Evil."

"But what is evil if not good that has been tortured by its own desire to exist? I am the key to your destiny, Akasha. Think about it."

"The Guardians will destroy you!"

Antédios's sharp guffaw floods me once again.

"Oh, you poor fool. Those fanatics have filled your head with silly ideas. If only you knew the truth . . ."

"No truth can come out of your mouth."

"Don't worry, Akasha, you'll uncover the truth sooner than you think," he says, directing both of his hands toward my head. "*Bricta Noux!*"

A purple flame *whizzes* past me.

"*Nayate!*" Miss Abona's voice rings out close to me.

At the sound of that second command a crystal ball appears around my body, protecting me. The demon's curse bounces off the magic shield with a screech so loud that it gives me goosebumps.

"Guardians . . ." Antédios murmurs nervously.

I turn around, surprised. The six Guardians have appeared behind me, and with an air of authority, are holding their magic swords.

"Deceived! It's too late now," Antédios screams, "*Leucos . . .*"

"*Zamana!*" Mike yells, blocking the demon.

A gush of white energy hits Antédios in the face, forcing him to howl like a wounded beast.

"Leonardo, run!" my mother screams, rushing toward me.

"You'll never have him. He's mine," Antédios yells, stepping in front of us.

"Guardians! Defend the Last Keeper!" Dad cries out loud.

"*Ualos Wero!*" the wizards scream all together, raising their weapons to the sky.

The blades of their swords beam a white light and create an energy wave that throws the demon back, into the darkness of the fields.

"Leo, are you OK?" Mom asks, "Are you hurt?"

I slowly open my eyes, still blinded by the glow released by the spell.

"Maya. He hit Maya. Can you help her?" I murmur.

"I can try . . ."

My mother looks at the wound. The blister has gone all the way up to her shoulder and now pulsates like a large jellyfish. She closes her eyes in concentration.

"*Teutax*," Mom whispers.

I see the jelly liquefy and Maya's skin turning smooth and intact. The burn is starting to subside, and the purplish blister shrinks to her wrist.

"I have managed to reduce the effect of the curse, but I wasn't able to eliminate it completely," she explains to me, tired from the effort.

"Is she going to be OK?"

"She needs to rest and to be seen as soon as possible . . ."

The other five Guardians come closer, forming a circle around us and facing outward.

"He's coming back!" Christopher yells.

A vortex of dark smoke surrounds us creating an impenetrable wall.

"Stay back!" Mike shouts.

I see my father turn his sword into something like a collar; he places it around his neck, and as soon as he does that, he transforms into that huge beast again. The creature's roar is louder than the thunder from the storm. A battle is about to begin.

"Mom . . . is that you, Mom?" Maya asks me, with her eyes rolling in the back of her head.

"Maya, it's me, Leo. Can you hear me? Maya!"

"Mom . . . I'm cold . . . where are you?"

"Take care of her, Leonardo," Mom tells me, before joining the other Guardians.

On her back, two long fairy wings appear again, the same ones I saw in what I thought was just a dream. The dark smoke swirls until it is only a few feet away from the circle the Guardians hold in defense. The demon's body reappears in the murky fog that extends into the meadows.

"Antédios! This is your last chance. Leave! You can't fight against the return of the Last Keeper," Mike threatens him.

Antédios bursts out in one of his convulsive cackles.

"Shut up, Guardians. The time for words is long gone," he retorts shrilly, raising his arms to the sky. "Get ready to face your destiny."

Screams and battle sounds resonate through the fields, along with the howling wind. Seven warriors, straight from the depths of hell, emerge from the darkness of the night. They are huge, protected by black armor, adorned with metal spikes and red capes that flow like flames from a fire.

"The Dumongorths . . ." Christopher *hisses.*

"Hold your positions," Anthony warns, with a voice that seems to come from the center of the Earth.

Suddenly, his chest puffs up to the point of tearing his shirt apart, his pants rip to shreds and he becomes over three feet taller. In front of my very eyes, Anthony transforms into a stone giant.

"Come on!" he challenges them. "Show us what you got."

The possessed warriors looking like decaying hunks of metal, lumber over to stand next to their summoner. Long, fiery capes are gashes of light in the dark, and their decrepit armor dully reflects light. Their heads are completely hidden behind terrifying helmets, topped with huge horns that intertwine forming macabre crowns. In unison, the Dumongorths move their capes, and with a deafening screech, unsheathe huge double-headed axes.

"Get ready to die!" the demon thunders, drawing Uncle Victor's sword from under his smoky cape. "Disingur belongs to us now! And soon, all your swords will follow its same destiny."

Antédios throws the sword to the Dumongorth closest to him who, as if invigorated, quickly ingnites into black flames. The blade turns darker, while a menacing growl echoes from beneath his horrible helmet.

I hold Maya and Maggie close to my chest.

"Don't worry, Maya. I'm here with you," I whisper in her ear.

But she doesn't hear me. She keeps whining, burning with a high fever.

Suddenly, the rain stops midair. The wind quiets down. Time seems to stop, and the sky turns even darker. Frost rises from the icy meadows, and an overwhelming feeling of doom infiltrates my heart. Maya starts shouting in the throes of a who-knows-what kind of nightmare.

With a simple gesture of his arm, Antédios releases the fury of the seven Dumongorths against the defense of the Guardians. The clash is extremely violent.

Spells and explosions flood the valley, slashing light streaks of red, blue, and white across the dark sky. In the confusion of running figures and constant bolt near misses, I manage to move through the trees and to drag Maya under a withered one.

I prop her up, and with my hands, I collect a bit of rain from the leaves around us. I try to get her to drink.

"Maya, resist . . ." I beg her.

I look around. In the tangling of wizards, warriors, demons, and magic, I see my mother floating midair, fighting with her spells and sword against a Dumongorth. A few feet away from her, Dad is still in beast form and defeats two more, crushing them under his majestic, clawed paws. Mike and Miss Abona fight against Antédios and another warrior, while a short distance from them, illuminated by flashes of sorcery bursts, Christopher and Anthony fight against three Dumongorths, no holds barred.

This is not possible! With horror, I realize that every time the Guardians manage to defeat a Dumongorth, it disappears only to reappear again a few feet away. This battle is crazy, a fatal mission, but the Guardians won't back down. They keep battling and fighting with incredible impetuosity.

"*Avarodha!*" Christopher shouts, blocking the axe of a Dumongorth. "Leonardo, we can't keep this up for much longer. Open the portal!"

"What do I have to do?"

Christopher doesn't have time to answer my question. A Dumongorth blocks the spell, and with a roar, plunges his ax toward Christopher's head.

"Watch out!" I exclaim, while Anthony runs to his aid and defeats the enemy.

Christopher stands up looking dizzy, half of his face covered in blood. He picks up his sword, and emitting an unnatural reserve, he's back in his position of defense.

"Let's get back together so we don't break the circle," Mike shouts, still busy with Antédios.

A curse hits the tree where I am hiding with Maya. We are now left uncovered, in the middle of a raging battle. I throw myself on my friend, I hold Maggie tight, and I look around in search of another hideout.

"Resist, Maya, hold on. All of this will be over soon."

A ray of red light from behind me hits my little dachshund and it stuns her.

"Maggie!" I cry out loud.

Before I can even turn, two ice-cold hands paralyze me and shut me up. I try to free myself, but my aggressor is too strong, and within seconds, I find myself being dragged toward the forest, along with Maya.

"You see, boy? In the end, we have captured you," Silischia's hoarse voice pierces sharply.

"Move, witch," Feghin admonishes her. "The Guardians could see us."

"So, what. They'll all be dead soon enough!"

I flail like a madman, trying to free myself, but Feghin's skinny fingers are digging into my shoulders with an inhuman strength.

"Dad," I try calling, but my voice won't come out.

I turn to Maya. Her eyes are wide open, though she is staring right through me, her fever is taking its toll on her mortality.

"Finally, this little brat is getting exactly what she deserves," Silischia murmurs, pulling her by the wrists. "Do you have any idea what it was like to live with this little rebel, Miss Know-it-All?"

"No, and I don't care," Feghin admonishes.

"I was super happy when I killed her mother," the witch adds flippantly.

I turn around, startled. I can't believe what I'm hearing.

"It was so much fun letting her believe that she had gone crazy. You should have seen how desperate she was every time she saw the monsters I would make appear in every corner of the house! Nonetheless, forcing her to swallow the whole bottle of painkillers wasn't as easy as I thought it was gonna be. That foolish woman kept thinking about not wanting to abandon this spoiled brat . . . Can you believe it?"

No! This can't be true. Silischia killed Maya's mom to take her place and get rid of me. She died because of *me*, only because of me.

A sense of desperation overtakes me and feels as if it is strangling my neck like a noose.

I start thrusting more violently now.

"I think her blood might turn out to be useful to us! Her Yuth could give us back the juvenescence that has been taken away from us," the witch hisses.

"Slaughter her, Silischia, but hurry up and help me keep the boy at bay!"

"Break his arms and you'll see how still he'll be," she suggests.

I feel Feghin's rough fingers slide down and grab my biceps. I hear him conjuring a spell when my bones begin to creak, and stabbing pains incapacitate my muscles. Electrified by the agony, I feel a rush of strength, rage, and unforgiving violence.

With a jerk, I grab onto the sorcerer's wrists.

"Hold him down, Silischia!" he shouts, "Hold him down!"

The witch leaves Maya and throws herself on me.

A dark flame burns my hands only to then be released onto the skinny yellow hands of the sorcerer who, as if pierced with a powerful shock, is thrown a few feet back, disappearing in the smoky curtain that surrounds us. Silischia moves to the side and letting go of the grip she has on me, falls onto Maya, who moans in pain.

I get back up slowly and turn toward the witch who, in terror, tries to crawl away from me. I feel weird: what once was is now only a distant memory of a dream that is fading away. I am invincible, just, and merciless. The black flame rises and burns my arms, shoulders, and head. The path of my revenge is now clear.

"Get ready to die, witch!" I roar, with a voice that I hardly recognize.

"*Coepturix!*" I hear shouting behind my back.

A bolt hits Silischia, and turning into a beam of silver light, it wraps around her body like a snake, immobilizing her. I turn toward the voice. My hands are already in position to kill. In front of me there's a fairy, a woman who is somehow entangled in my past. A past that now, however, no longer exists.

"Don't you dare block my path," I threaten her, while that dark flame keeps flaring in me, feeding my homicidal madness. "In the name of whatever you have been, don't force me to kill you."

"Leonardo . . ." she begs me.

That name. A chink opens in the armor of my mind. I hesitate. Judgment and fear begin to battle each other in my brain, fighting to gain control.

The fairy throws her arms around my neck, holding me tight, and regardless of the dark fire that persists on wrapping me up, rage begins to fade away, melting like snow in the sun. I come back to life, as if remerging from a nightmare-ridden sleep.

"What happened to me?" I scream in fear as soon as I see my hands on fire, but not burning.

My mom, however, doesn't want to let go. She keeps holding me, her eyes closed, reciting a lullaby that I can barely hear. We begin to shine bright with an intimate powerful glow that fights against my dark flames, finally bringing me back to reality.

"What happened?" I ask, whispering.

"Leonardo, come back into the circle and keep Maya next to you!" my mother, exhausted, tells me.

In that same instant, a thunderbolt strikes her, taking her breath away. Her eyes roll back, her wings fade away and her body crashes into the frost in the wet grass.

"Momma!"

I fall on my knees, next to her. Bloody tears are streaking down to her neck. I wipe them clean with my sleeve; I am unable to stop sobbing. Her fingers barely touch my face, her lips arching into a feeble smile.

"Being your mother has been the most beautiful thing in my whole life, Leonardo."

"Momma . . ."

"Don't be scared, sweetheart. Don't ever forget who you are."

Her grip becomes weaker and her empty gaze pierces through me. I lay my head on her chest and I weep desperately.

"Come on, get him!" croaks Antédios who, flanked by a couple of Dumongorths, is still busy fighting against two Guardians.

I turn toward them. Miss Abona and Mike take advantage of the demon's distraction and cast a spell on him that makes him fly backward.

The circle of dark smoke that surrounds us disappears immediately. The warrior that killed my mother is now running toward me. Mike and Miss Abona rush to protect me, but two more Dumongorths attack them from behind, forcing them to defend themselves. I remain emotionless, empty, cold as I stare at death.

The Dumongorth, now a few steps away from me, raises his ax over his head and drops the blade, screaming. The metal slices into my father's back, and still transformed as the beast, he defends me and intercepts the hit. His roar of pain floods the valley, while with a paw he manages to knock out the Dumongorth.

"Dad!" I exclaim, throwing myself on him.

"I'm here, Leonardo," he whispers, resuming his human form.

"Momma is . . ."

He holds me in his arms, as blood gushes from his side.

"Dad, you're hurt!"

"It's nothing, you just need to save yourself now."

Miss Abona runs toward us, then steps in front of us in a defense position.

"Leonardo, you have got to open the portal," she tells me without turning. "There is no time to waste."

I look at my teacher who is holding a shining sword, waiting for the Dumongorths who are quickly getting closer.

"Go," she orders us, agitated. "Adam, go with Leonardo and Maya and save them!"

"Come with us!" I tell him, shocked.

"Our duty is to protect you; you don't have to think about the rest."

For a moment, our eyes meet. She smiles at me.

"Good luck, Leo. May my Yuth enlighten your path."

As if in slow motion, I see her raising her arms to the sky and running toward the enemy, she turns into a giant wave of clear water that explodes, wiping out the Dumongorths. With a heavy heart, I understand that Miss Abona has sacrificed herself for us.

We lurch forward shaking, walking away from my mother's helpless body; not too far away is Maggie, still paralyzed. Dad is holding onto me and is having a hard time staying upright. We walk back to Maya, who is now almost lifeless. I turn, and amongst the bodies of dark warriors who are writhing on the ground after being swept up by Miss Abona's attack, I see Antédios staring at me with his demonic eyes.

"It's over," his voice is in my head.

With his usual evil smirk and threatening posture, he comes closer.

My gaze redirects to the battlefield. Mike, Christopher, and Anthony are still fighting against the Dumongorths. They are exhausted and their blows are getting weaker and weaker.

"Surrender, Keeper. All your Guardians will be dead soon and there is nothing you can do about it."

I search my pocket and pull out the Sidhits. The shiny spheres cut through the darkness.

"Yesssss," the demon *hisses*. "You finally understand your destiny."

On the palm of my hand the eight Sidhits are shining bright with a very powerful light that blocks Antédios from coming closer. I feel inspiration, a realization, a voice in my heart that tells me what to do.

"Yes! Finally, I now understand," I say with staccatoed speech.

With a confident gesture, I throw the spheres above my head. The Sidhits float midair, creating a vortex of light around us.

"Noooo! Dumongorths, stop the boy!"

The dark warriors, abandoning the battles against the Guardians, throw themselves against the maelstrom of light; but this, as powerful as the most dynamic spell, rejects them, throwing them on the ground. I pick Maya up in my arms, and with Dad barely hanging from my shoulders, I walk toward the light.

"Attack!" I hear Antédios shouting, furious. "We have to stop him before he opens the portal!"

The energy field created by the Sidhits begins to expand. Powerful thunderbolts strike the saturated dirt, creating violent tremors that shake the hill to the point of breaking it in half.

From the large and abyssal gaping breach, comes a column of smoke and flames.

"Noooooooo!!!!!!!" Antédios's howling echoes.

The ground begins to rise, making paths explode and knocking down part of the forest.

In front of my terrified stare, two giants made of stone, majestic and powerful, emerge from the depths of the earth. I fall to my knees and hold Maya even tighter in my arms.

The *Annunaki* bow down in front of us, supporting on their shoulders an arch made of dirt and rocks from which waterfalls flow. My mouth is wide open as I admire this wonderful yet terrifying display. Then, the furious screams of Antédios bring me back to reality, to the battle that still rages beyond the barrier created by the Sidhits.

The Dumongorths keep slamming the shiny wall, but now I no longer have a reason to fear them. Finally, everything is coming together, and in front of us, there is only light.

In front of us is Midendhil.

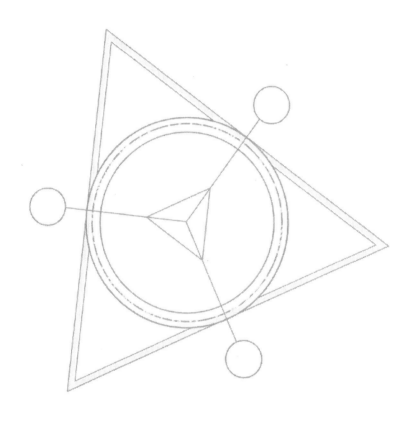

LORD OF MUSPELING

A gray fog floats through the trees of the forest and sprawls into the sinister night. The smell of smoke and sulfur coming from the cave is so strong it takes my breath away; the air feels like death, like being in a graveyard, as if this place hasn't seen a living being in centuries.

A faint ripping sound breaks the silence. A flame and two dark silhouettes appear out of thin air, motionless, as if trying to figure out where they are.

"We have been ordered to wait here," a female voice whispers. "We have to stay here and wait for the signal."

"What kind of signal?" asks the other silhouette.

"I don't know! He just told me to stay here and wait for the signal!"

The two hooded shadows crawl out of the opening in the clearing in front of the cave. Feghin, with his hand tight on his chest, swears at the pain his wound is causing him.

"Cut it out!" Silischia admonishes him.

"Witch, I fought all night long! I am injured and possibly cursed!" he replies, showing her his wrinkled hands. "I really don't feel like staying here."

"Stop whining! Antédios said that . . ."

"Antédios talks too much! He told us it was gonna be easy to get the boy and that we were surely gonna avoid fighting against the Guardians! And now look at us!"

"Shut up!" the witch interrupts him. "Your tongue causes more trouble than your magic. Even the stones have ears here!"

"So let them hear us! I can't . . ."

An inhuman cry rings out among the trees, freezing them in their place.

"I'm tired, witch. Do what you want, I'm going in."

Wounded, Feghin drags himself to the breach in the mountain, his wounded face turned to the scorching hot entrance.

"And what are you going to do?" she whispers behind him. "Going by yourself into the Muspeling? We don't know what's in there and . . ."

"I want to ask our Lord to give me my looks back."

"And you think he'll listen to us?"

"I don't know, but I wanna try," he replies, letting the portal swallow him.

The woman looks around and hesitates for a moment.

"Wait up! I'm coming with you."

"You changed your mind?"

"What do you think? That I enjoy staying in this shriveled shell?"

"What about Antédios? What do we do with his orders?"

"For all I care, he can choke on them. It's his fault we look like this now."

Without uttering another word, the two move forward, groping around in the tunnel and proceeding quietly, one next to the other, barely breathing.

Soon, their eyes begin to adjust to the absence of light, and they start distinguishing shapes. The path, worn smooth in the now solidified lava flow, delves deeper into the heart of the mountain through what once was the realm of Viceroy Bhakta, ruler of these lands during the time of the Great King. Statues and pillars lay in ruin as far as the eye can see, among magma rivulets that trace a ray system on the flagstone floor. A semi-sweet yet vulgar odor, like rotting meat, soon begins to permeate the sulfur smell. Silischia's eyes dilate like saucers at the sight of the massacred beast carcasses scattered throughout the path.

"Maybe we should have just waited outside."

"*Shhh* . . ." Feghin shuts her up, pointing to the cadaver of a huge quadruped not too far from them.

The immense chest of the beast is quartered, his bowels ripped apart. Silischia grabs her partner by his sleeve; inside the animal's stomach, two eyes shine bright. The sorcerers step back, one glued to the other, as a monstrous and semi-human being emerges from the dark, letting the dim light expose his diabolic form.

"A *mashuis* . . ." Silischia whispers.

A roar reveals the pointy fangs of the monster. It resembles a terrifying version of the old centaur with shiny hair hanging down in clumps from its big forehead and flowing onto its muscular chest that is covered in tattoos. Its lower half gleams in the darkness, resembling a giant scorpion.

Feghin and Silischia writhe, as the mashuis slowly comes closer, sounding like a jumble of armored paws. The sorcerers' arms are stretched out in front of them, ready to fight. The monster sneers, wiping its dirty, blood-crusted mouth.

"Well, well . . ." says a lumbered voice of one who is obviously not accustomed to speaking the language of men. "Fresh meat."

"*Albus Lugus!*" the two shout simultaneously, raising their fists now wrapped in flames.

"*Karkum,* sorcerers!" the creature roars in his language. "The fires of yours will stop me but not forever."

"Go away, creature of darkness!" Feghin barks.

The mashuis puffs his chest and releases a series of spine-chilling cries, to which he is answered with blood curdling screeches.

"He's calling other monsters," Silischia murmurs.

"*Hush!*"

"We should have stayed outside and waited for the signal!"

"I said *hush!*" Feghin reprimands her, as he walks away from the wall of the tunnel.

The witch quickly follows, as the flames of the spell become more intense, illuminating the most frightening situation they've ever been in.

From the multitude of dark caves along the walls that open onto the tunnel, dozens of hungry mashuis emerge. The two sorcerers, back-to-back, start spinning furiously.

"Retreat, monsters! Retreat now while you still can!" Feghin shouts.

A sudden and deep roar echoes in the dark. Silischia's burning fist extends into space and sheds light on a huge mashuis. He has a mature face, two big metallic rings pierce through his nostrils, and his eyes are as dark as two inky orbs.

"Do you really think you can run away from us?" says the mashuis, enunciating his every word.

"We are here for you! We are here to meet with your Lord!" says Feghin, trying to hide his fear.

"But here the only Lord of the mountain is me! RavaKhan, 'the Boneshredder,' leader of the mashuis of Muspeling."

"Don't lie!" the sorcerer replies. "You are just the *hybrids* that my Lord has placed as guards in front of his fortress!"

Howling sounds rise from the darkness. Mashuis' shadows quiver with rage, forming a circle around them.

"Fool!" RavaKhan growls. "How dare you come to my house and call me and my children hybrids?"

"Pardon the foolishness of this idiotic sorcerer, oh powerful mashuis," Silischia quickly says, pushing Feghin behind her. "We beg you to grant us permission to walk through. We are servants of your Lord, and we promise you will be rewarded."

The chilling cackles of the mashuis deafeningly echo through the tunnel and fill the ears of the sorcerers.

"Witch, we already have our reward," RavaKhan explains, licking his lips. "Skinny, but still acceptable!"

Horrifying cries, mixed with vaguely human screams, flood the cave. The black shadows of the monsters quickly dart. Feghin and Silischia, one after the other, follow the cries, moving with the cretons. One of the creatures jumps out of the darkness and shoots the poisoned harpoon at the end of his tail at Feghin.

"*Leucos Du!*" he clamors, throwing him against the rocks.

"Seize them! This meat is fresh!" RavaKhan guffaws, entertained.

Three more mashuis emerge from the shadow and flank them to attack them from the side. A sharp razor claw almost rakes Silischia's face.

"*Dagodurnux!*" she screams, raising her arms.

A thick, blue cloud lowers like a cloak from the ceiling of the cave and wraps the creature in an impalpable trap.

"Help me, Silischia!"

Feghin is busy with two more monsters that, unstoppable, keep getting closer to him and with their tails, block his every spell.

"*Palambi!*" she quickly clamors, transforming one of them into a blob of purple jelly.

But it's not enough: the other mashuis throws himself onto the sorcerer, his stinger aimed at the sorcerer's head.

"What's going on here?" suddenly asks a harsh voice.

The mashuis immediately retreats, as RavaKhan moves forward, his tail arching above him.

"We are following the orders of our Lord; we protect the path of Muspeling, demon."

"And you do so by tearing his servants to pieces?"

An arctic blast swirls through the tunnel of the volcano. Antédios appears out of nowhere, and even though he's shorter than the monster, his posture seems larger, exuding the confidence of somebody who has nothing to lose. As soon as they see the demon, all the mashuis retreat toward the walls, intimidated and crawling over the rocks that line the path.

All except for RavaKhan; the pack leader stands threateningly, lashing his tail like a whip.

"Stop it, mashuis. You know all too well that your poison is useless against those who have no Yuth."

"But I yearn to shred you to pieces."

With a sudden move, the demon's fingers lurch at the monster's throat, gripping it so tight his tongue protrudes from his mouth.

"Get out of the way, you dirty hybrids."

The harpoon from the mashuis's tail darts toward Antédios's head, forcing him to dissolve into smoke and reappear a short distance from where he was. RavaKhan shakes, his eyes filled with hatred.

"Go ahead, demon," he croaks, walking back into the darkness. "But after all the trouble you've caused in the other world, I wouldn't be so anxious to go see our Lord if I were you."

Antédios stays still, as if he were at a loss for words. For the first time, Feghin and Silischia see the faint shadow of fear flash across his face. Then, with authoritarian intensity, a guttural sound fills the tunnel. RavaKhan moves into the shadow, and behind him, his pack retreats toward the entrance of the cave.

"You, morons," Antédios rages toward the two sorcerers. "What did you think you were doing? Appearing before *him*, alone? Do you have a death wish?"

"We beg you to forgive us, Antédios," Feghin whines. "But we thought . . ."

"You *thought* . . ." the demon repeats coldly. "After what you've done tonight, I didn't know you two were actually able to *think*. You had the Last Keeper in your hands, and you let him go!"

"He transformed into a monster," Silischia intervenes.

"Shut up!" he roars, releasing a curse on them that makes them wail in pain. "And now get going, as it's almost dawn!"

The two sorcerers barely manage to stand up and keep up with the sinuous silhouette of the demon, who quickly advances into the depths of Muspeling. They proceed, passing ruins of more halls, when a sudden blaze blinds them.

"What's going on?" yells the witch, covering her eyes.

Antédios has stopped in front of a big door of light that, even though blinding, doesn't cast any light on anything surrounding it.

"Is this the dwelling of our Master?" Feghin asks, shrinking in fear next to the demon.

"Wait here," he answers laconically.

"But we wanted to ask . . ."

A single stare from the sorcerer is enough to silence them.

"Let it go, Feghin," Silischia murmurs. "Our turn will come."

Antédios, visibly agitated, raises his arms and emits an obscure monotone drone that immediately slams the door of the portal wide open.

A cloud of tarry smoke fills the air and coils around him, but the demon doesn't seem to be flustered by it, and advances with a firm step, letting the portal close behind him. He proceeds until he reaches the shore of a large lake of fire. From the walls, dozens of lava streams gush, in a display that is both majestic and terrifying at the same time.

He kneels slowly, in front of the hellish Majesty, while his face shows the shadow of fear.

"My Lord Kenat, Antédios brings news."

A flame erupts from the center of the magma lake touching the stone vault. The earth begins to tremble, the rock starts to crumble, and the magma becomes agitated. From the bubbling of the lake, on top of a stone rostrum, a massive golden throne slowly emerges, standing tall on the surface of lava. Sitting on it is a mummified cadaver, dressed in rags and wrapped with a big, gray cloak.

Antédios lowers his eyes to hide his thoughts.

A *hoot* echoes in the hall. A golden owl plunges from within the cavern, gliding toward the throne, finally taking its place on the backrest. In its beak is a shiny object; the owl, slowly and with calculated movements, slides it into the welcoming mouth of the cadaver.

A mystical breath expands in the cave, blowing back the clothes of the demon.

The raptor opens its wings, explodes, and dissolves into a sparkly rain. The Yuth blazes in the throat and slides down into the chest of the figure on the throne. Muscles, cartilage, and skin begin to shape around the remains of the cadaver and spread onto its dried-out bones filling the tunic and transforming the rags into regal clothes. The mummified face becomes radiant; the dry nose defines and the numb lips plump. Thin brown hair cascades down from the silver and amber crown that frames the forehead, softly flowing onto the large, bony shoulders. Then, as if electrified, the body writhes with violent convulsions: the lungs puff up with air, and two big blue eyes open wide, shining with the red reverberations from the fire. The being tilts and stretches his neck, making the nerves snap like withered twigs.

Two powerful hands come out of the clothes and hold onto the edges of the golden armrests of the throne. As wonderful as it appears, the vision remains terrifying: a creature, far away from his own past as a human man, is now more like a god.

Antédios sighs nervously; in front of him is the Dark Lord Kenat.

"My Lord, I beg your pardon for my failure . . . the boy has managed to return to Midendhil."

The fiery surface of the lake breaks apart and explodes into tall curtains of fire. The demon speaks quickly, trying to please his Master.

"But I have destroyed the Guardians and unleashed my spies everywhere."

"My dear, soulless friend," Kenat's voice sounds terribly warm and harmonious, like the calm before the storm. "My eyes are everywhere. I knew you failed even before you came back."

"My Lord . . ."

"I have already ordered my most faithful servants to carry out the duty that you, with everything I put at your disposal, were unable to fulfill."

Antédios lowers his head, humiliated.

"The mashuis, Antédios. I ordered RavaKhan to find the boy and bring him here. I think they are better suited than you, maybe even shrewder."

"But my Lord . . ."

"*Hush!*" The command echoes in the cave as if yelled from the mountain itself. Kenat's features flare with rage.

"I made a mistake in trusting you. I let you into my memories, I gave you the Dumongorths and you? Nothing! A complete failure!"

"The Dumongorths weren't able to . . ."

"Don't you dare make excuses for yourself!" Kenat stands up, reaching out into the air in front of him.

To that gesture, Antédios falls, as if hit by an invisible blade. A long, bloodless cut opens on his cheek.

"Your excuses make me sick."

"But the boy is powerful, my Lord. Way more powerful than we thought."

"Powerful, huh?" Kenat asks, leaving the question open.

With a hand gesture, he unrolls a fiery path that from the throne follows an arc all the way to the demon. He walks it with regal steps, and arrives in front of his servant, who is still groveling.

"He's just a boy with no guide and no knowledge of the magical arts."

"I am simply stating what I saw."

As soon as Kenat's bare feet touch the stone, interrupting the contact with fire, his features revert to the former decrepit body.

"Look at me, Antédios."

The demon looks up at his master: his facial features are already withered; his hair is falling out and his clothes have begun graying.

"How can I reign over his world, if I am not allowed to step away from the fire of Muspeling?"

"It's the Sidhits, my Lord. The boy is not only the Keeper, but also the owner."

"Don't try and interpret the ancient magic. The Sidhits don't have any owner!"

"But it's the power of the Sidhits that protects him. It's impossible to seize them without his consent."

The watery eyes of the mummy dilate with madness, his lips sneering in a smile revealing his black teeth.

"We shall see," Kenat *hisses*. "We shall see . . ."

chapter eighteen

THE MAGICAL LANDS OF MIDENDHIL

Amber. Amber light is in my eyes once again.

I rub my feet hoping to feel the softness of my sheets, but all I find is a rough surface, filled with spikey stones. My nose twitches. The smell of fresh laundry is replaced by the odor of wet dirt. I take a deep breath and find the strength to slightly open my eyelids.

My sight is blurry, lost in a confusion of light and colors. My hair is full of dirt and my soaked shirt sticks to my chest.

I slowly roll on my side, my back in agonizing pain and my legs twisted. Where am I? What happened?

"*Leonardo,*" a voice echoes inside my head. "*Leonardo, where are you?* "

I try to clear my mind, but I can't. I move blindly.

"*Leonardo, help me!*"

Help me? That plea flips a light inside my head; thoughts start to come together like pieces of a puzzle.

"Maya!"

I sit up abruptly, cowering with the pain jabbing from the burn on my back.

"Maya! . . . Dad!" I try calling, but nobody answers.

I touch my ripped jeans feeling my way up to the pocket of my sweatshirt. My fingers sink into the damp fabric, and quickly feel the dry soft leather. I carefully take out the small satchel, dumping the contents into the palm of my hand. The eight Sidhits palpitate brightly and release their pure light. For a moment, my back pain subsides, my tiredness goes away, and my sight is clear.

I look around again, cautious. No sign of Dad and Maya.

It's daytime, maybe afternoon. I am sitting in the middle of a forest that I don't know. The trees are tall, and the trunks go as far as the eyes can see, maze-like. Above my head, branches intertwine into canopies so dense that only a few rays of sun can peek through to the forest floor. Among the branches, I can see shadows of squirrels jumping from one tree to another, making melancholy squeaks.

An image comes back to my mind. It's an episode from my childhood, when my mother and I found a burrow in an old oak tree. It belonged to a couple of squirrels, whom we jokingly named Romeo and Juliet. The memory fades, breaking my heart. My mom is gone, and everything I have ever loved is now lost with her; my Uncle Victor is no more, and who knows what happened to the others. It actually happened. They sacrificed everything to save me, the Keeper of something I cannot even understand. Fear washes over me once again. I feel lost and lonely. What am I even doing here?

Still holding on to the Sidhits, I get up slowly, scared that I might literally break in half. I walk carefully, my bare feet aching. The squeaking of the squirrels is not the only sound that surrounds me, other sounds come from the forest: grunts, breathing, hurried movement among the leaves that are scattered on the ground. I try not to think about it. I convince myself that daylight, as weak as it is, keeps all dangerous animals at bay. My thought immediately goes to Maya, passed out who knows where, and to my dad, with an ax wound on his back. I start walking faster. Beasts or no beasts, I must find them before it's too late.

I start to walk on a dirt path. I turn behind the trunk of a curved tree, climbing over a tree root and hopping among the vast expanse of weird, colorful mushrooms. I am about to pull myself onto a rock when something sticks to my ankle. I teeter and grab a tree branch. With horror, I see that a couple of the mushrooms I just passed have grabbed onto my leg and are trying very hard to make me lose my balance.

I let go of the branch and resort to skipping in panic. I kick the air but nothing, the situation only gets worse. Three more mushrooms are now stuck to my calf, and within a few seconds, they knock me down like a chess pawn. I fall on my back, and a terrible pain grips me. Grinding my teeth, I try to get back up, but I can't. The mushrooms have surrounded me, and under their lumpy chapels, sprout a multitude of harpooned cords that, weaving around my chest, wrap me up like a piece of salami hanging in a deli.

"What the . . ." I murmur.

Alright, Leonardo. Calm down, nice and easy, I tell myself, as a couple of tiny guttural voices begin talking next to my head. I feel something crawling on my shirt, and with unsure steps it proceeds toward my face. Before I have a chance to formulate any hypothesis, a strange creature with a harsh demeanor appears an inch away from my nose: a puffy little sprite-like man, barely eight inches tall, with a broad-brimmed, lumpy mushroom hat of hazelnut color, which seems to be part of his head rather than an actual head covering. His face is wrinkled, armed with a handlebar mustache and a long, white beard divided into two pigtails. He's wearing clothes made of what seems to be leaves, tightened by a belt made with a knotted worm.

"*Gabu digu gabu bulu!?*" he tells me, pointing a wooden awl to my nose.

"What?" I ask, frowning.

"*Gabu digu gabu bulu!?*"

"I no . . . *comprehendo* . . . I go. You free me."

"*Bulu cucu!*" the creature yells.

Once again, I feel something crawling up toward my stomach then up toward my sternum. Behind the tiny man, two more mushroom people appear: the first one is tall and thin, with a big, curved nose and a light blue cap on his head, while the other is short and chubby, with a sly smile and an intense red mushroom cap. The two of them carry a big ampoule carved out of a pumpkin, which is releasing a sallow smoke with a stench I have never smelled before. Now I am starting to get scared.

"What do you think you're doing with that?"

"*Bulu guru gabu*," shouts the bearded sprite, giggling, while raising his awl to the sky.

To that command the other two lift the little flask and tilt it toward my mouth.

"Stop! No!" I scream, shaking my head to avoid whatever is in the ampoule.

The tiny cords break, and a myriad of little hands pull my hair, holding me still. No, this can't be! I have managed to survive a battle between demons and wizards, and now it can't possibly end this way, poisoned by a bunch of mushrooms, who would only be good for a nice risotto, if that.

"*Gabu digu?*" the creature asks.

I tighten my lips and squint my eyes as much as I can and keep squirming around like a snake. Then, in blind desperation, I arch my back abruptly. The three pests lose their balance and roll down onto the ground, creating a moment of hesitation within the rest of the group. I take full advantage of it, and with a couple of thrusts, I free myself and get up. The sprites, scared, run in a jumble of colorful caps. I pass them with a jump, I finally climb on the rock and run away as fast as I am able.

I'm shocked and scared. I know the place I am at right now is anything but ordinary, but I still didn't know I could get in trouble in such a short period of time. Suddenly, a thought overtakes me. I check the pocket of my sweatshirt with my hand. *Phew*, the Sidhits are still there.

I proceed into the forest, this time with more caution, not taking for granted what is around me: whether plants, mushrooms, or stones. I walk quietly and I stop from time to time to make sure nobody is following me. The grunts and noises have never ceased to surround me and it's becoming quite distressing.

I'm trying to figure out how to get through a cluster of bushes that blocks my path, when at the end of a clump of trees, in a small clearing, I spot a body lying in an awkward position: the hair is of a chocolate color and a trail of blood glistens on its back.

My heart begins to beat faster.

"Dad!"

I start to run, stumble, fall, and get back up. My feet no longer hurt and there is no grunt nor demonic mushroom that can possibly stop me.

I throw myself on the ground, next to him. I turn him around quickly, placing my ear on his chest. His heart is still beating. He's alive! Yes, he's beaten up, but he's alive.

"Dad . . ."

His eyes open slowly. With my sweatshirt sleeve I clean his forehead, then his face which is covered in dirt.

"How are you, Dad?"

"Leonardo, you are here . . ." He looks at me, surprised, as if afraid of not being able to see me anymore.

"How are you?"

"A bit beaten up, but OK . . . and you? Are you injured?"

His voice is weak. His hand almost touches my chin. I grab his hand and hold it tight between mine. I'm scared, but I try not to show him.

"No, Dad, I'm OK . . ."

"And the Sidhits?"

"They are safe."

"Help me sit up."

I gently hold him by his shoulders, supporting his back with caution. My hands sink into his cloak that is soaked with warm blood.

"Dad, you're still bleeding. We have to stop the hemorrhage immediately."

"We'll think about it later, Leonardo," he answers, coughing. "Where's Maya?"

"I don't know."

"You have to find her, and you have to do that right now." A trickle of blood slides down the corner of his mouth. "She could be in danger."

"But Dad, you . . ."

"No, don't worry about me," he interrupts me as if every breath he takes is torture. "We don't have much time. The Enemy may have already ordered his servants to look for us."

He coughs again. This time, it's more intense and painful.

"Dad, we have to find help, we have to . . ."

"You have to reach the Tower of the Guardians. Our order has not been broken. There, you will find warriors in training, maybe even new Guardians. Go to them and show them Anthony's pendant, the Azas, the symbol of our brotherhood."

"Why are you telling me all of this? You're coming with me, right?"

He forces a weak smile while he wipes the blood from his mouth with the back of his hand.

"Yes, Leonardo," he says slowly. "But what awaits us is a difficult mission. I have to tell you everything, in case something happens to me . . ."

"You'll get better, Dad."

"You must promise me that, no matter what happens, you will never forget who you are here, now, in front of me. Remember that the destiny of all the people you love depends on the man you will become."

I take his open palm and bring it to my face. He's cold and shivering.

"Dad, you're all I've got. Mom is gone and . . ."

"You have Maya, Leonardo."

I nod, swallowing hard.

"You have to go look for her," he whispers, turning on his side. "Take my sword."

"But you can't stay here by yourself."

"I know the deal. Take my sword," he tells me. He shows me a large and squat blade on which mysterious runes are engraved.

"No, you keep it. You're injured and you need protection."

"Leonardo, you have to . . ." His next cough takes his breath away.

"Resist, Dad. I'll be back with Maya and with all the help we need," I conclude without giving him a chance to rebut.

I kiss his head and I quickly go into the woods, without looking back.

I feel like crying again, but I hold it back. I do it for me, for my dad, or maybe just because it's the right thing to do. Will I be able to find help? For a moment, I am tempted to go back to him and hug him, have him tell me that everything will be OK, but I already know that, if I did it, I would never be able to find the strength to leave again.

Maya, I say under my breath. *Now I have to find Maya.*

chapter nineteen

THE FOREST OF NEMETON

I have been walking along paths and sliding down hills, overcoming crevasses for what seems to be an eternity. Doubt has turned to certainty; I am lost. I am surrounded by trees, trees, and more trees. I have no idea what time it is, but my stomach is growling, and my thirst is driving me crazy. I'd do just about anything for a cold soda or even a glass a water. I don't know how long I'll manage to hang on, but all I can think of is Maya. Just Maya. I have got to find her before it gets dark.

Fortunately, since leaving my dad, I haven't met any weird creatures, but creepy sounds have been following me the whole time. A few times, in the thick of the bushes, I thought I could see the glow of watchful, tiny little eyes and fleeting shadows, but I brushed it off as paranoia and I kept going.

My feet are now totally covered in blisters and the skin on my back still burns as if somebody had thrown acid on it. I need to sit down. Yes, I have to sit down for a moment, just long enough to catch my breath. I crouch down on the bump of a root sticking out from the underbrush and I gently massage the soles of my feet. I gaze at the expanse in front of me, searching, until a twinkle between the rocks and dried-out leaves gives me hope. I crawl on all fours toward it, holding my breath. I don't want to delude myself, but I think I already know what it is.

Moving the leaves, I slide my fingertips over the rocks and moss, and there it is. That's it! Maya's Rajasthan bracelet. The twirling of the red cotton is crusted in mud, but the three bells are intact. I shake it off to clean it, making the bells jingle.

From behind the wall of bushes, something echoes the same sound. It's like a scene straight out of a horror movie. I hesitate for an instant, then I shake the bracelet again. It replies immediately, and from two different spots in the woods. Undoubtably, I am surrounded.

Swallowing, I muster the courage, and with my stomach in knots, I walk into the bush. Images of huge spiders, ready to wrap me in their sticky cocoons, dominate my mind, but I resist. I resist for Maya. I make my way among the branches, holding them down with my feet, while the leaves smack me in the face. I tighten my lips, turn my head, and walk ahead when finally, lowering the last branch, I see her. Maya.

I rush to her side, tearing the branches that wrap around my ankles. She's unconscious, incredibly warm and she is breathing very fast, like a scared little bird. Her wrist is swollen, still marked by Antédios's curse. I have got to rescue her, and I must do it right now.

Even though I don't have much strength left in me, I try to pick her up. My muscles are burning up, pearling my forehead with sweat. I fall to the ground, exhausted.

"Help! Somebody, help us!"

I hear the jingle once again. In the heat of the moment, I had completely forgotten about that. I jerk my head, first right, then left, until I see a thin, tiny hand protruding from behind the tree trunk, and a little face with a lively grin.

"Who's there?"

It's as if I had given the green light to chaos. From every bush and shrub sprout fairies who are about fifteen inches tall, riding on long, red blades of grass. They begin to twirl in the air like tiny witches riding brooms, making the same harmonious jingle that guided me.

I am amazed and a little suspicious, but the show is wonderful. These creatures don't seem to be dangerous like those little mushroom-shaped nightmares. They appear to be slender maidens with very luminous pale complexions, the color of new spring leaves, and their delicate faces are illuminated by big almond-shaped eyes. Their ears are pointy, and from their flowing brown hair, goat-like horns stick out following the curve of the head down to their nape. From the end of the blades of grass they are riding on, a shiny dust is released, leaving a trail in the air with every move.

I stay there to admire them, enticed, while four of them fly over Maya, grabbing her by the wrists and ankles, lifting her up above my head.

"Hey, wait a minute . . ."

Their jingling gets stuck in my head, and it turns into a hypnotic melody, like one from a child's music box. One of the fairies comes close to me and rubs her nose against mine. Thirst, hunger, and exhaustion go away in an instant, and the pain in my back and feet disappears. I stand entranced, awakened miraculously as if only to follow Maya's body, which is now floating a few feet off the ground.

I keep moving forward, stunned, as I begin to approach a much darker area of the forest. I am not sure how long I have been walking, and without really noticing, I find myself in a vast clearing covered in shadow. The trees have black bark, and the trunks are strangled by red ivy that creeps over everything. Light has disappeared. I am sure that over there, somewhere beyond the dark foliage veil, the sun is shining bright in the sky.

The fairies delicately lay Maya on a rock and wait for me to reach them. I move the curls from her face. She's even warmer now.

"We need water."

The little creatures look at us with awkward, surprised expressions.

"Drink . . ." I gesture with my hand toward my mouth. "Can you understand me?"

I get closer to one of them. In her hands, she is holding what looks like the spiral shell of a snail.

"Don't worry, I don't want to scare you."

But, when I go to caress her, she distorts her face and opens a huge mouth, full of sharp teeth that snap an inch away from my finger. I jump back in fear, while she, once again looking like a gracious fairy, gently blows the shell. The piercing whistle pierces my eardrums and throws me to the ground. Even Maya shakes her head in a long, painful moan. The spell I was under is now broken. I quickly come back to myself and realize what a horrible, bleak place we now find ourselves in.

"What are you doing?"

Inhuman cries flood the forest. I keep my eyes on the trees and on Maya, while the tiny little monsters start moving in a circle like a school of piranhas.

Suddenly, I hear heavy breathing and a crunching sound above us. Pieces of bark rain down on me, in my hair and down my sweatshirt.

I look up, slowly, toward the tall branches. My heart skips a beat; monstrous creatures are crawling down the trunks, straight toward us. They are not huge spiders. Worse. They are terrifying women: witches, straight out of a child's worst nightmare. The tips of their green hair float in the air in front of their scary faces, hooked noses, and protruding chins. Their skin is made of bark, and instead of legs, they have some kind of long tentacle that, along with the claws of their hands, is used to crawl down the trees they hide in.

I run toward Maya, desperate. The witches stop a few feet from the ground, each one on their own trunk. They smell of decaying leaves on the forest floor; they smell of death.

"Well done, finfinellas," one of them says, with a bone chilling voice, looking at the swarm of fairies that is flying above us. "It looks like today's dinner is going to be much better than usual."

I feel into the pocket of my sweatshirt. The Sidhits! I grab them. I raise the little sachet above my head and a blinding light is immediately released, burning everybody's eyes, including mine.

Trying to be strong, I get up and pick up Maya. Slowly, I manage to focus on the nightmare that surrounds us. The fairies are withering on the ground, convulsing in terrible spasms, while the witches, fallen from the tree trunks, furiously scream, and painfully scratch their eyes.

I start to run, well actually, I try to run. With every step, the forest becomes darker, and the stinging vines of red ivy hang down from everywhere, blocking my path. Behind me, there are only screams of rage. I drag myself as much as I can, but the fairies manage to reach us quickly. They are no longer wondrous little creatures, but horrible monsters with voracious mouths that snap like shears all around us. Dodging them, I crouch down among the leaves, and I slide down a muddy path, making them lose my trail.

The blisters on my feet burn like fire and Maya slams in my arms like an inanimate puppet. I crawl on my knees among bushes with large shiny metallic leaves, until I reach the area that has the ruins of a huge statue in the center. The head is lying on the ground not too far from where I am, and the mouth seems to be a big enough hole where Maya and I can hide. I can barely stand but I start running desperately. I see the witches have also followed us; they jump from one tree to the other like monstrous spider monkeys. Only a few more seconds, and they'll see us. My body is shaking. My muscles feel like they are tearing apart, and my veins are on fire. I run through the clearing when something traps me. I look down at my feet and see that I am in a black quagmire, and it's crawling up my legs as if it were alive. I lean forward and flail like a madman, but nothing, the situation only gets worse. I take a good look at the hole where I was heading, and to my surprise, I see the silhouette of a man who is already hiding in there.

"Help!"

An old man, all nose and beard, with a hat crooked on the tip, comes of out the dark. He carefully observes me, Maya, and then the forest.

"Please, help us!"

I hear the witches screaming again, and the jingles of the fairies, who are now very close.

"Just take her . . . save her, I'm begging you," I tell him, extending Maya.

The man stretches his arms to get her, but suddenly the monstrous fairies pop out of the bushes and throw themselves at me, biting me and pulling my hair so hard I start tearing up.

Desperate, I look at the hole again: the man has disappeared and with him my last hope to save us. From the top of the trunks, the witches furiously jump down. They drag themselves on their hands, and within a matter of seconds, they surround us, some of them licking their lips, others groping Maya's legs with their long fingers.

"Stand back!" I scream, making them laugh.

One of them comes forward. She approaches us, hunchbacked, with a smile so cruel that it makes my blood run like ice through my veins. I hold Maya in my arms, while the witch stares at me, satisfied. Her needle-like pupils focus on my knees, sunken in the quagmire, and then on my face again. Delighted, the witch cackles as she tilts her head, dangling her hair-like filthy vines to the ground.

"Did you really think you could escape, my pretties?" her voice is sharp as a knife. "Oh no! Get ready for dinner . . . mommy is home!"

The swarm's excited laughter slays me. This time it's truly over.

chapter twenty

FALLING IN THE DARKNESS

My fear of ending up in a cocoon has come to fruition. I am trapped in a net made of woven vines, hanging from a branch at least thirty feet from the ground. Maya is in my same situation, and a bit further down, stuck like us, there is another strange creature with cloven feet and two horns on its head.

I am so scared that I can barely breathe. Fire glows below us illuminating the darkness of the clearing, projecting shadows of dancing witches celebrating their banquet onto the face of the statue. The songs and laughter are bone-chilling. Their silhouettes are contorted around the fire in a terrifying Black Sabbath, while those little monsters dressed as tiny fairies fly slowly in circles, waiting for dinner. I am alone, defenseless without the Sidhits; the witches left me in my underwear and threw all my stuff into a bush, including Aldo's pendant.

I shiver and turn toward Maya. Her face is pressed against the net and her eyes are wide open and vacant like a corpse.

"Maya . . ."

With an unprecedented effort, I manage to free my arm and stick it out of the net just enough to touch her. I shake her gently, but her stare is still glazed. I stretch so hard that my arm starts twitching, brushing against her nostrils; my freezing fingertips meet the warm, humid air of her breath. Yes, she's alive.

"Hey, you!"

Two eyes shine below me, in the darkness of the other prisoner's net.

"I can't move," the creature tells me with a limpid voice, almost feminine. "But you, with that free arm, could you grab the dagger I have behind my back to cut the cords?"

"Da . . . dagger?"

"Yes, dagger, you know what it is? It's hidden in my fur and the *mencans* didn't see it."

Mencans? Fur? I waver, swinging in my cocoon with my arm hanging down.

"Hurry up, Fireyhair! What do you wanna do? End up in the belly of one of those evil wooden witches?"

Hearing the wicked laughter of the hags for the umpteenth time makes the decision for me. I flip, pointing my head downward, stretching my arm as far as I can until I feel the cords of the net cutting into my armpit. My hand grabs onto the creature's net, my fingers frantically searching its fur.

"Up! Come on, we don't have all night."

My fingertips finally slide on a hard and smooth surface: the handle. I grab it, and without wasting any more time, I begin to saw away at the intricate tendrils that trap me, while the witches below us, unaware, keep their dances and rituals going.

"And then? What are we going to do once we are free? My friend can't hold herself up . . ."

"No worries, Fieryhair. I'll take care of her."

"Meaning?"

"Just cut, I'll take care of the rest!"

I have no other choice but to trust him, and encouraged by the confidence of my new acquaintance, within minutes I slash a hole big enough to stick my head through. Now both my hands are free, and I can move more easily.

"Come on, come on!" the creature urges me.

"I got it, I got it . . . One more second and . . ."

Something huge shakes our tree, making us swing like ripe fruit. Down among the red lianas that climb everywhere, I see a mass darker than nightfall, leaning against the trunk.

It's not a witch and more importantly, it totally ignores our presence. With a faint rustle, I see it tear apart a curtain of crimson ivy, crouch into the undergrowth and creep toward the fire. More silhouettes follow the creature, and coming out of the dark, they surround the camp in an instant.

The imprisoned creature looks at me with eyes wide open. I understand his message and go back to sawing, making other ropes break. Now the opening is big enough for my shoulders to pass through; I go through the hole when a roar stops my heart.

Beneath us the witches are screaming, screeching like the brakes of a train, while monstrous beings, half-human and half-scorpion, emerge from the forest, clutching them like an eagle with a fish. The fairies have already dispersed and the fire, as absurd as it sounds, has grown quieter.

"What are you celebrating, you dreg mencans?" one of the monsters growls.

"Oh nothing, powerful RavaKhan. My sisters and I were just celebrating the forest," the witch cowers, pretending to be as docile and innocent as a lamb.

"So why are the finfinellas flying above you? What prey have they given you?"

"Finfinellas? There are no finfinellas here."

With a flash, the monster grabs her by the hair and lifts her up above the ground, making her screech like a lobster thrust into boiling water.

"Powerful mashuis . . ." another witch comes forth, with her green locks falling in her face. "My sister, Belanunzia, is telling the truth."

The monster looks at her as if devouring her with his eyes. Then, his tail flickers, and in the blink of an eye, the barb of his tail pierces her throat injecting her full of poison. A silent scream petrifies on the face of the mencans as she falls to the ground.

"Who granted you permission to talk to me?" the evil monster hisses, while he watches her roll lifelessly in the flames of the fire.

The corpse burns quickly like dry wood and spreads a dense, toxic smoke that almost makes me cough. The shadows that surround the camp seem to laugh, while the mencans protest, pressing one against the other, with their long, clawed fingers in front of their faces, as if to protect themselves. The monster goes back to the witch hanging from his fist.

"Belanunzia, this is your name?"

The mencan nods.

"Are you the boss around here?"

The witch nods again.

"Mencan, I want to give you and your sisters a chance to live, so don't lie to me. What kind of prey did the finfinellas bring you?"

"A faun. A baby faun . . ." she says, her hands holding her hair. "We just finished eating it."

"Where are the remains?"

"There are none, there's nothing left . . . But, if you want, you can have his hands. They are over there, underneath that bush."

The monster grunts suspiciously and throws her to the ground. Belanunzia climbs back to the others using her wooden tentacle.

"We are looking for two man-cubs," the mashuis explains. "A boy and a girl. She has golden skin; he has hair the color of fire."

I tremble, and try to swallow, but I can't.

"Are you sure you didn't see them?"

"No, RavaKahn, honestly no. The prey of your hunt has not come by here . . ."

"They are not of my hunt, witch. The two humans belong to the Dark Lord and none of you better dare even twist a hair on them."

The ugly muzzle of the monster tilts down almost touching the long and shiny nose of the mencan.

"Is that clear?"

"Yes, RavaKhan."

He turns around, while behind him the witches are agitated, ogling each other. Belanunzia stops them with a neurotic gesture.

"What is it, dregs?" he roars, going back to them. "Is there something you'd like to tell me?"

"No, RavaKhan," Belanunzia rebuts quickly. "I have already told you everything."

The mashuis stares at her for a moment, thinking about her words. Then, slowly, he steps back, keeping his pitch-black eyes on them.

"Beware, mencans," he threatens them, walking back into the darkness of the forest. "If I find out that you lied to me, I'll come back to tear your hearts out of your chests, one by one."

Once again, I see the shadows crawling in the darkness and then, just like they appeared, the monsters disappear, swallowed by the nightfall.

The witches remain immobile, with their fearful eyes lost into space. With a crackle, the fire flares up again, licking away what is left of her sister's corpse. Belanunzia indulges in a dry and cruel laugh.

"You disgusting old shrew!" one of them suddenly says, her eyes as big as chasms and her fangs so long that they don't fit in her mouth. "Why didn't you give him the prey? Do you want him to kill us all?"

"Shut up, you fool! The mashuis could still be here," Belanunzia shushes.

"So let them hear me! You lied to them, so you will be the one to die."

"You really think so?"

Before she has the chance to rebut, Belanunzia jumps on her, scratching and biting like a rabid animal. All the others jump in the battle, and their camp is quickly turned into a brawl of merciless screams.

"I can't believe this . . . how could I possibly end up in this situation?"

"What are you waiting for? That they come and get us?"

I am brought back to reality by the one who must be the young faun they were talking about.

Without uttering a single word, I put the dagger between my teeth, hug the tree branch from which we are hanging, and counting only on the strength of my tired arms, I pull myself out of the net. Maya doesn't seem to notice, while the faun, who is now very agitated, keeps urging and begging me to get moving. I straddle the branch, and without asking more questions, I begin tearing his net apart.

"Come on, come on, come on!"

"You'll help me with my friend, right?"

"Yes, yes, but hurry up!"

Suddenly, a sound like the trumpeting of an elephant, erupts through the forest. The witches stop arguing and they turn toward the noise. From the darkness of the trees, comes the crashing of felled trunks and hellish screams. Deer, wild boar, squirrels, foxes, and other animals I have never seen before pour into the clearing as if running away from some unseen terror.

"*Drucaurus!!!*" one the mencan cries out loud, climbing on the tree in front of us.

Drucaurus? What's a *drucaurus*? I ask myself, exhausted.

"Oh no! This just keeps getting better," I hear the faun complain. "Come on Fieryhair, hurry up!!"

I stretch to look below just enough to see come out of the darkness the old man with the big nose, the one I saw earlier in the mouth of the statue. His beard is wrapped around his neck like a scarf, and he runs off laughing; with one hand holding the hat on his head and the other lifting the cloak off the ground.

"What's going on?"

"Keep cutting!"

The old man runs toward the group of mencans, who ignore him. Their eyes stare at the trees that are shaking. Leaves start to rain, and broken branches begin flying around. A few trunks crash down and from the dark shadow in the woods comes the huge face of a giant, whose skin is wrinkled like bark. His eyes reflect the fire, and his hair seems to be made of many small twigs full of leaves.

Shouts. *Growls.* The giant throws himself on the mencans, smashing, and squeezing them with his hand that seems tangled with roots. The witches quickly defend themselves, climbing on his broad back full of moss and trying to take down the enemy with bites and scratches. The battle is brutal.

The *pop* of the last rope brings me back to reality. Finally, I am able to open a large enough hole to let the faun's head through, horns and all.

"Help me get out," he tells me.

I stick the dagger back into my mouth and I pull him out of the net.

"Where do you think you're going?"

Attached to the trunk is Belanunzia, her tentacle wrapped like a snake around the branch we are hanging on, and her hungry eyes glued on me.

"Why does the Dark Lord want you? What powers are you hiding?"

Within a matter of seconds, she's on me. I dodge her and I roll onto my side. The faun slides out of my my hands and is now holding onto the branch with his fingers.

"Hang on!" I shout, pulling the dagger out of my mouth.

Under him, the drucaurus and the other mencans keep fighting in a jumble of monstrous bodies, which keeps going in and out of the cone of light from the fire.

"Come here, *warm blood*!" Belanunzia says. "Tell me why the Dark Lord wants you!"

Her claws scrape my stomach. I move with a jerk and grab the hilt of the dagger on the reverse side, keeping the blade on the outside just like Uncle Victor taught me. The mencan attacks me once again, but I twist, and my blow makes contact. Her painful screeching seems to cut through my head. The blade has slashed the bark on her shoulder, and a dense dark green sludge streams out of what seems to be a wound.

"You filthy cluster of flesh!"

With a parry, I stop her hand that is ready to tear off my face, but she charges with the other arm, aiming for my side. I dodge her again while the faun, still hanging in the void, manages to grab her by the face and pull her down. The witch wobbles, and slides but she is faster than us. Regardless of the surprise attack, she is able to grab onto the branch like a bat, swinging near the faun.

"You smelly hybrid, die!" she screams, grabbing him by the horns.

In that moment, a rock hits her right in the head and makes her crow out loud like a raven. Shocked, I look down and see the old man, all nose and beard, throwing rocks at her which once thrown, become bigger and bigger, like tennis balls.

"Hurry! I won't be able to keep her busy for much longer," he yells entertained, still hitting her.

I see the witch that keeps banging like a kettle drum, while the faun pulls himself up and reaches Maya's net.

"Fieryhair, let's free your friend."

I get to work quickly, and I start cutting the ropes with unbelievable speed. Within a few seconds, Maya is free. The faun picks her up on his shoulder, and with the agility of Spider Man, leaps quickly from the tree.

"Hurry up, Fieryhair."

"Hurry! We'll all be attacked soon!" the old man warns me, while a mencan hit by the giant flies over his head.

"How do I get down from here?"

"Jump!" the faun yells. "Grab the lianas and let yourself fall."

Jump? How can I possibly jump down from thirty feet high?!

In that moment, Belanunzia's hand grabs my ankle.

"You are mine . . . I want to know your secret!" she says.

I am emboldened by instant courage. I kick her in the face and jump, holding onto a couple of lianas, like Tarzan. For a second, it looks like everything is going just fine, but then my hands slide off and I fall like dead weight. I bounce off a branch, then another one, till I fall on a few ferns that fortunately cushion the blow. However, I hit so hard, it takes my breath away.

"Come on, come on you don't look so bad," I hear the old man say, as I feel two hands help me up.

A few feet away from me, the giant is still fighting the witches, scattering fire everywhere, while on the tree, Belanunzia screams like a banshee.

"Come on, let's go!" the old man yells in my ear. He now carries Maya on his shoulders. "We've had enough fun."

We've had *fun*? This guy is out of his mind!

"Here, this is your stuff," the faun says.

My head is spinning, and my sight is blurry. I get dressed in a hurry and check my pockets. The Sidhits bag is in place. Yes, all eight of them are here . . . I count them, touching each with my fingers.

"Now we must part ways, Fieryhair," the faun says, his face in the shadow. "Thank you and may my Yuth enlighten your path."

He does the weird greeting that people do around here, then with a jump he disappears among the bushes.

"And now? What do we do?" I ask the old man, while I put Aldo's pendant around my neck.

"Nothing . . . we run!"

Within a few seconds, I find myself running like a madman, pulled by a grandpa with the energy of a boy. The paths are dark, the forest is gloomy, and I no longer have the energy to think; I barely know who I am.

"Stop, please, I can't do this."

"No, Fieryhair, no! We can't stop. The mencans could reach us and I have no more stones to throw at them."

"I know, but I have no more energy to walk. I can hardly breathe."

"Oh, come on! Don't be a *skuok* now!"

"Skuok? . . . What's a skuok?"

"Oh, for all the smashed tops of *jimis*, let's not get caught up in idle chatter now! We have got to get going. My house is not too far from here and . . ."

"No, no, no! I have to go get my dad. He's waiting for me, he's injured!"

"Your father is here in the forest?"

"Yes, he's injured, and he needs help. We have to find him."

"Impossible."

"But he could die!"

"Well, so could your friend; she's burning up like a *zika* and if we don't get her temperature down . . ."

"What? . . ." I ask, my voice trembling.

"I don't think she'll make it through the night."

His statement hits me like a punch in the teeth. I look at Maya, her head leaning on the old man's shoulder. Her golden skin is so white that it almost glows.

"Let's go home, and after caring for your friend, I promise I'll go back to look for your father."

A noise resounds from somewhere in the forest.

"Mencans. They are after us already. We have no time to waste, let's go."

He grabs my wrist and forces me to start running again. We creep stealthily into a series of tunnels between brambles and bushes. We climb up cliffs, holding onto roots and branches, then slide down steep drop-offs, full of foliage and smelly ponds. I am tired, exhausted: my feet are like two pieces of shredded meat, my back burns and the scratches on my stomach have started to throb. Everything hurts.

"I don't feel well," I say, teetering. "I am about to pass out . . ."

"No, Fieryhair, not now . . . I wouldn't know how to carry you."

"I know, but I . . ."

I feel as if the blood is draining from my body. Cold sweat. I fall.

chapter twenty-one

CUDDLES AND CARESSES

The classroom is half empty; there are only a few students chitchatting while sitting on the desks in the back. I hear the noise of their snack wrappers, the smell of hot cocoa from the vending machine. It must be recess. I touch my face, my stomach, my back. Everything is fine, I'm OK. I have no wound, no cuts or burn . . . Is it possible this was all just a dream? I take a moment to think about it, until my smile quickly becomes neurotic laughter. My classmates are looking at me with their usual sense of superiority.

"What is it? Have you gone crazy all of a sudden?" Maya appears by my side.

Seeing her brings me immense happiness, and without thinking too much about it, I give her a big squeezy hug.

"You are fine! You are fine!"

"Yes, I was doing well till a second ago . . ." she pants, hitting me lightly on the back. "You are taking my breath away . . . I can't breathe!"

I let her go, but I keep holding her hands on my shoulders: my eyes get lost in hers. I can't wait any longer; I have already wasted too much time and only now can I see things clearly.

"What is it with you today?"

I don't care that we are at school, I don't care that in five minutes the bell rings and everybody is going to see us; I have spent my entire life thinking of others, now it's time to focus on me, well, on *us*.

I tilt my neck and pull Maya toward me like the *cool guys* in the movies. I close my eyes. Our lips meet. Finally, a kiss. The kiss I have been waiting for my whole life. Her lips are soft, and smell like coconut, with a tiny mustache that pricks me . . . *What? Mustache?* Maya doesn't have a mustache. I open my eyes, letting go slowly. I smile at her, as if nothing happened. She replies with the sweetest expression that fills my stomach with butterflies.

Her mouth is perfect, there's no mustache!

I try to go back to where we left off, when her hands stop my face forcefully.

"What are you doing?"

Without uttering a single word, she sticks out a huge, extremely long tongue and starts licking my cheek like a Saint Bernard. I move her to the side, looking for her eyes, but nothing, she is still on me, sniffing my ear.

"What are you doing, you silly *maju!*"

The image of Maya dissolves, and in front of me, appears the hairy muzzle of a bizarre animal, who is totally washing me off with its nasty, long, and warm tongue.

I sit up quickly, and I get off the table on which I am lying. I try not to scream. I breathe in and breathe out counting to five, but I can't hold it in.

"What in the world is going on here?!" I yell.

"Calm down, calm down, Fieryhair. It was a just a bit of cuddles from my Mela," exclaims the man, all nose and beard who, popping out of nowhere, tries to reassure me.

"And what's that?" I ask, pointing to the beast with a lion's mane that is looking at me while sitting beside its owner.

"I told you, it's Mela: a very affectionate *maju*. Forgive her, she's always a bit pushy with those she doesn't know," he explains, rubbing her big ole head just behind her high horns.

I look around, heartbroken. I am not in school, nor at home. I am in Midendhil, obviously, and the nightmare that I thought was just a nightmare is actually my real life, along with the Sidhits pulsating in my pocket.

I am in a room that is even messier than my own bedroom, full of dangling lanterns, books, alembics, and other weird objects hanging everywhere. The ceiling is low, supported by branches of some big trees that seem to be an integral part of the house, while the stone walls, coarsely plastered, are decorated here and there by a series of symbols and drawings that appear to be magical and mysterious.

The furnishings are spartan to say the least, with cupboards and shelves full of knickknacks and rolled-up parchments. The fire crackles in the fireplace, and a large cast iron cauldron with a series of jugs, pots, and kettles hangs above. My sweatshirt is there drying as well. I notice a myriad of doors and tiny gates on every wall, so I assume the shack is far larger than it seems.

"Where am I? What happened?"

"We are at my house," replies the old man who now, with no hat, exposes a round little head, almost completely bald. "You passed out, the mencans had almost reached us. It was Mela who carried you here."

"I passed out? . . . I don't remember."

"Of course, you don't, a mencan hit you!" he says, pointing to the bandages sticking out from my shirt. "Those evil witches are poisonous, and with a single scratch they are able to make even a *garfus* lose memory."

"Garfus?"

"Between the curse that hit your back and the wounds on your feet, it's a miracle you're alive."

In my head I hear a ringing bell, no, it's a deafening alarm.

"Maya!? Where's Maya? Is she OK? Is she feeling better?"

"Hold on, Fieryhair, calm down. Your friend is resting in the other room. She's still unconscious, but I managed to lower her temperature. She'll be fine."

"Can I see her?"

"Of course, but only after you've had something to drink and eat," he rebuts, disappearing into the pantry. "You don't want to faint again, do you?"

I follow him limping and I see him filling a couple of mugs with a bright green liquid, maybe it's Bidibubble.

"I'm incredibly thirsty," I tell him. "I haven't had anything to drink since . . . I don't even know. Too long."

"Here," he smiles, offering me one of the mugs.

I drink up without hesitation. Yep, it's Bidibubble: fresh, fizzy, and goes down so easily. I guzzle at least a pint, but I can't quench my thirst.

"May I please have some more?"

"Certainly," he tells me, pouring me another.

As I sip my drink, my eyes wander on the several types of cheeses, pies, sausages, and hams that are neatly kept in the pantry. My stomach growls.

"Hungry, huh?" he asks me. "One more minute and you'll feast like a king."

"Yes, but we have to go look for my dad."

"Your father is in good hands," he explains, cutting cheese.

"Whose hands?"

"After I took care of your friend, I went out looking for him. It was easy; I followed your tracks all the way to a clearing not too far from here."

"My tracks?"

"My dear boy, as you ran through the forest you left more tracks behind than a herd of mad *bodulas*."

"What are bodulas?"

"Your father is with the hamadryads. They are taking care of him."

"Hamadryads? They are . . . the fairies of the trees, right?"

"Of course, they are. Usually, they don't want to be bothered with things that don't affect them, and I don't understand why they are bending backward for your father. Either way, they surely are not the *sgallux*, so you can relax."

I sit down at the table without even bothering to ask about the sgallux, as I am sure that I still won't get an answer. Meanwhile, the old man starts setting the table as best as he can, with wooden plates and beat up cutlery, whistling an off-key tune. Mela, on the other hand is sitting next to me; I'm scratching the back of her ear like a dog, and she is looking at me, mesmerized.

"Come on Fieryhair! Start eating while I go grab two more mugs of BidiBubble."

"Actually, my name is Leonardo."

"Leonardo?" he says, coming back with the two huge mugs full of fresh BidiBubble. "What a weird name, I never heard it before. I'm Luis."

"Nice to meet you, Luis . . . and thank you."

"For what?"

"Well, for saving Maya and me . . ."

"Oh, that! No problem, I actually had a lot of fun. It had been a while since I last teased those nasty mencans."

I look down at the trays between us. At the sight of all these delicacies, my mouth starts to water. There's a bit of everything: bread rolls with olive oil and nuts, cheeses of every kind, chicken in gravy, pickles and pickled onions, sausages, bone-in ham, boiled eggs with mustard and parsley, baked potatoes, peas with bacon, and carrots with butter. I dig in ravenously, biting into the sausage and bread that tastes like it's fresh out of the oven.

"I see you have a good appetite," Luis smiles.

I eat to my heart's content, while Luis tells me about himself and what he does. I must say that he is quite chatty, and even though he looks like he's a hundred years old, he talks quickly and with the energy and enthusiasm of a kid my age. Fortunately, he doesn't seem to be interested in who I am and where I am from, and this makes me feel at ease. Maybe he's used to being alone and not having anybody to talk to; either way, he manages to tell me everything about himself within a few minutes.

He tells me he's a lusogham of the village of Ialon: a people of wizards who live in touch with nature, spending their existence meditating, writing, studying, and documenting everything that happens in Midendhil. As I listen to him, I am reminded of the night that this whole thing began, when Mike introduced himself as one of them: a lusogham, I mean.

Unlike his peers, Luis lives on his own, on the outskirts of the Forest of Nemeton, because he has been entrusted with protecting something very secret. Something he can't tell me about, something he can't help but mention every other word. Given the circumstances, I really don't care to know what Luis has, but he seems anxious to tell me about it at all costs. His behavior makes me chuckle. It reminds me of how I used to be as a kid, when on Christmas Eve night, unable to resist, I would blurt out to my mom what my dad and I had bought for her.

The memory of my mother resurfaces making my heart ache.

"Hey, what is it?" Luis asks me, witnessing my sudden change of expression.

Even though he's a good man, I decide it's way too early to fully trust him.

"Nothing, I'm just tired," I reply, wincing. "So, your job is to stay here and guard?"

"Yes, but in the meanwhile, I try to be helpful in other ways."

"Such as?"

"Rescuing creatures who run into trouble in the forest, for example."

"Like Maya and me?"

"Exactly, like you two. And I write. With all the free time I have on my hands, I was able to write my very own *Grimoire*."

"Grimoire?"

"Well, OK . . . not an *actual* Grimoire seeing as there are not that many spells. But I must say that the *bestiary* part, the one dedicated to all magical creatures, it's quite exhaustive."

He gets up and grabs a leather folder on the desk behind him.

"Have a look!" he tells me, satisfied.

On the smooth leather, above the golden words *Luis's Grimoire*, is engraved a drawing of a tree with clusters of red berries. I untie the ribbon and take out a bundle of parchments: pages and pages of drawings that show strange creatures, full of notes and details. There's just about everything: from the mencans to the drucaurus, from the finfinellas to a multitude of other weird animals. Among the various sketches, I also find recipes of what seem to be potions and formulas of spells. I must say that the order is far from impeccable, like the rest of the manual, most sentences appear messy or deleted, as if written by a third grader.

"*Ehm* . . . as you can see, I am not very good with spells," he anticipates, reading my mind.

In the last two pages, I see some sort of geographic map that has yet to be completed.

"This is Midendhil, right?"

"Yes . . . sort of, it's the Midendhil that I know. I've traveled it up and down in the past, and this is the result of my journey. This is second nature to lusogham, we have a tendency to document everything."

"Can I ask you something? What were you doing hiding in that statue's mouth?"

"I was picking some *sludgy*," he giggles making his mustache wiggle.

"Which is? . . ."

"It's that mud that trapped you."

"And what do you need that nasty stuff for?"

"I sell it. I put it in small vases, and I get it ready for the fair of the Yule Festival. Do you have any idea of how rare it is?"

"Don't tell me . . . and I ended up getting stuck in it," I murmur to myself. "And what do people use that nasty stuff for?"

"Well, it's very useful for house chores. If you train it, it can help you with a million things."

"Train a vase filled with mire?"

"Well, his Yuth is very bright . . . it's not like normal mud."

"Yuth, you said?"

With the same grace of an elephant, Mela interrupts our chat leaning her muzzle on the table. She looks at me again with those big, sweet hangdog eyes.

"What is wrong with her?" I ask.

"She's smitten! Well, and she knows we're done eating and she's asking permission to have the leftovers," Luis laughs, taking back his Grimoire. "Alright, go ahead. Eat what you want, enjoy."

In less than a second, her tongue darts on the table with the same speed of a frog's, grabbing every leftover, pickles included.

"Can we go see Maya now?"

"One moment," he replies, standing up. "I still have a few more treats to give you."

"No, thank you. I'm full."

"Don't say that quite yet," he adds, snooping around a cupboard. "Once you taste it, you'll be glad you have a mouth."

"Honestly, Luis. You are so kind, but I am really stuffed."

As if I had not even spoken, he pops up in front of me with two cast-iron pots no larger than a grapefruit, covered with a wax top.

"What's this stuff?" I ask.

"What? You don't know? These are the *Tamon's SugarPot*, creation of the Samaya elves."

"Samaya elves . . ." I repeat, thinking back on when Christopher turned his hair into gold, telling me he was one of them. "What are they?"

"Open the cauldron and you'll see," Luis invites me, taking the wax top off his.

I follow his lead and I am immediately hit with a candy smell that reminds me of when I was a kid. There are many flavors and shapes: gummy worms, minty spiders, strawberry mushrooms, licorice mice, sugar fish.

"Fun, isn't it?" Luis asks me, gulping an orange dragonfly. "In the cauldron you can find the sugary version of the ingredients that we use to make magic potions. See?" he says, unrolling a small parchment that was placed among the candies. "As a gift, you can find the recipes of the most famous potions . . . I collect them, see which ones you have!"

I eat a peach-flavored butterfly and I open my surprise with a sense of curiosity mixed with confusion. On the parchment, there is a sentence that makes absolutely no sense, but I understand quickly. *Midendhilian* has no more secrets for me.

"*Kamanira*, love potion . . ."

"Noooo! Me too . . . I already have three of those," Luis exclaims disappointedly, stuffing his mouth with candies.

I pick through my cauldron. I try a cherry-flavored bat wing, a sugar-covered lizard, till I find a round candy shaped like a yellow eye with a very small pupil.

"What's this?"

"That is a mencan's eye! It's delicious!"

"Mencan?" I exclaim, dropping it on the table.

"No, try it. Don't stop at the name . . . it tastes like lemon."

Just thinking about those witches makes me feel nauseous, but I try to be brave and taste the candy.

"So? Didn't I tell you?"

"Yes, it's actually pretty good."

It really is, I am not lying. It tastes like lemon, and it's sour like those fizzy candies that I used to buy at the Christmas Vendor Show.

"Speaking of mencans, what were you and your friend doing over there?"

And there it is; the question I've waited for him to ask. What do I tell him? Should I tell him everything? About Antédios, the portal, and so on?

"Your clothes are weird. You are not from here, are you?"

I shake my head, not knowing where to begin.

"Where are you from?"

I improvise and lie in my usual clumsy way.

"From a small village . . . overseas . . ." I mumble, thinking back to the map I saw earlier.

"What's the village called?"

"You don't know it, it's very small."

"Tell me anyway."

"New . . . York . . . it's called New York."

"New York? . . . No, never heard of it," he says. "It must be a far-away land because it's the first time that I've seen somebody with hair like yours."

"My hair?"

"The color. That fiery red is unbelievable . . . never seen anything like it before."

I smile, embarrassed, trying to avert my eyes to the small candy-filled cauldron.

"So, what brought you here, to the Forest of Nemeton?"

"Fate." I try to solve it by giving him a half-truth, "Truth is, we got lost. Dad and Maya were injured during our trip, and I was attacked by a group of evil beings shaped like mushrooms that . . ."

"You mean the jimis," he interrupts me, pulling a long pipe out of his sleeve.

"Jimis?"

"Yes, but they are not dangerous. They are actually kind sprites that help save wounded creatures we find in the forest," he explains, lighting up the tobacco.

"Well, they didn't seem that peaceful to me . . . They wanted to poison me."

"No way!" he laughs, flooding me with smoke. "The smelly concoction they serve is just a calming drink: it relaxes the creatures they are trying to help."

"Well, it didn't seem like an effective move to me."

"You try and rescue a wounded *durnax*, and then we'll talk about it," Luis giggles. "So, what happened?"

"Then I found my dad. He was injured, but he asked me to go and look for Maya. So, I ventured into the woods till I found her in the company of a group of fairies."

"The finfinellas . . ." he says, puffing smoke from the corner of his mouth.

"Yes, the mencans called them that."

"Never trust creatures who fly riding on something that does not have a brain of its own. The finfinellas are evil spirits who hunt for the mencans."

"And we actually fell into their trap, along with the faun . . . it was a faun who was with us, correct?"

"Yes, a young female faun to be precise; they are very capable warriors, although a bit too suspicious for my tastes. So, what else happened?"

"Then . . ." I stop, uncertain whether I should tell him about the mashuis or not.

"And then I came along with the drucaurus, right?"

"Yes," I nod, thankful that he interrupted. "Then you arrived."

"Catching the attention of the *drucaurus* was so much fun. You should have seen how mad he got when I burned his big toe."

"Oh, so you were the one who angered that monster?"

"Of course, otherwise he wouldn't have followed me."

"What's a drucaurus?"

"An oak giant, sworn enemy of the mencans. They really hate each other, and I knew that if I brought one to their camp, chaos would ensue," he tells me, laughing out loud like a child.

His laughter is contagious, and within a second, I find myself giggling as well. I know I really don't have much to laugh about right now, but I like Luis; he is very entertaining, and I need that now.

"Well, I'd say it's time we go see how your friend is doing. She was hit by a terrible curse, and it'll take time for her to recover."

I nod, hoping he won't ask me where the curse that hit Maya came from.

"Are you sure you want to stick with the story of that place, that 'New York'?" he suddenly asks me, emptying out the pipe in the fireplace. "Don't you want to tell me where you are really from?"

I hesitate for a moment, feeling embarrassed. I wish I could come up with something more believable, but I can't think of anything else; my mind is a blank.

"I know you didn't tell me the truth, but I get it. Actually, I am a bit of a chatterer and I have a tendency to spill out everything about me to the first person I meet. Between the two of us, I am the one at fault, don't worry," he reassures me, placing his hand on my shoulder. "When and if you'll ever feel like telling me who you are and where you are from, I will listen and I will offer you my help, should you ever need it."

"Thank you, Luis."

"Now, let's go see Maya."

chapter twenty-two

THE ANIMAGORIUM

I follow Luis under a red brick arch, and we pop out in a circular room with a domed ceiling and periscope in the center. Above us, floating midair, is a big, round mirror that perfectly reflects the sky outside the dome.

"Amazing!"

"This is the lusogham observatory . . ."

"Incredible, but what is it for?"

"In theory, I should use it to study the stars, but I have never been able to understand squat about divination or astrology," he confesses. "And to think that being able to read the sky could really help me with many things . . ."

"Such as?"

"Well, the future of the living is written in the path of the stars and knowing about what awaits me would be tremendously helpful."

"I hear you . . ."

"Come on, over here," he says.

We walk along a narrow corridor full of portraits, until we enter a small library lined with shelves from floor to ceiling. Dozens of books with yellowed pages and leather covers fly around like butterflies among the ceiling beams.

"Are you still out?" Luis asks, looking up. "Remember to put yourselves away in order of genre. Especially you two, *What's Boiling in the Cauldron?* and *Gut-wrenching Spells*," he says, talking to two worn-out manuals that are carousing by the chandelier full of dried wax. "I'm tired of always finding you between the botanic books!"

On the floor, in front of an old stove, there is a red velvet armchair with some sort of griffon puppy nestled between the armrests fast asleep. On the bookshelves, I see a constant coming and going of those evil sprites, all busy dusting.

"There they are! These are the little monsters who wanted to kill me!"

"I already told you that the jimis are peaceful creatures. See how cute they are? They are trying to put some order in my library . . . even though it's clearly impossible with these enchanted flying books," he starts complaining again, pointing his fist to the ceiling. "Let's get out of here before I lose my patience."

We walk past another door, and enter into an alchemist's laboratory, with bunches of herbs hanging from the ceiling to dry and a wall full of jars filled with colorful dusts and liquids. Hesitant, I get closer to the shelf, and scan all the labels on the bottles. There is a bit of everything: potions with crazy names like *Talkmaster, Climby-Clam, Popface*, and others with more mysterious names such as *Lugonox, Hidevirum*, or *Zilpavat*.

"These are all your creations?"

"Only a few . . . I'm still learning. For now, I just experiment with the simple ones and buy the more complicated ones."

"You have a million of them."

"Yes. As luck would have it, I have two sorcerer friends from Lokegir, masters of making filters and potions. Most of these come from their laboratory."

"Lokegir?" I repeat, vague. It's the name of the village that my Uncle Victor and the other two sorcerers mentioned.

"Yes, have you been there?" he asks me.

"No, I have just heard of it."

"Weird people live there, near Muspeling; some of them are not very trustworthy sorcerers, attracted by dark magic and stuff like that."

"Dark magic? So, are your friends sorcerers of this kind?"

"Who, Daron and Gwen? No, not at all! They are good people and very funny, too."

On a stone table I see a row of tin cans neatly aligned, on the elegant, hand-painted labels I read: *SLUDGY, your little muddy helper.* Here it is, that nasty container of animated mud.

Further down, there are small glass vases with strange ingredients inside, such as crystal flowers and those tiny rocks that Luis used to hit the mencans. High up on the shelves I see more vessels with flying insects and others filled with bulbs of pulsating light.

"Over here, Leonardo," he calls me, tapping with his knuckles on a closed small door with a million iron latches. "Please, don't speak loudly and move slowly. No sudden moves, OK?"

"OK . . ."

"My Animagorium is in here."

"Animagorium?" I ask, shocked.

That's the name of my dad's store!

"My dear, you have no clue about anything. You must truly come from a faraway land."

I shrug without saying a word.

"The Animagorium is the place where we take care of wounded creatures. Remember? We were talking about it earlier; I save injured animals that I find in the forest."

"Yes, I remember, but I don't understand what . . ."

Suddenly, my thoughts paralyze me.

"Is Maya here?"

"Of course."

"With other wounded beasts?"

"Yep," he nods, touches the latches which magically pop open.

"Is she here alone?"

"What do you mean alone? How can she be alone if she's with other injured creatures?"

I don't let him finish the sentence. With my heart beating out of my chest, I shove the door open and throw myself into the room. A sea of heads, big and small, quickly turn toward me, staring at me with eyes of all colors and dimensions. Oh boy, where in the world am I?

"Easy, Leonardo, easy does it. Otherwise, it's going to be a huge mess in here," Luis whispers.

I enter the spacious room, faintly lit by a cluster of incandescent spheres suspended from the ceiling. A maze of bookcases neatly showcasing nests, boxes with strawbale doghouses, baskets, dens, terrariums, and even bowls filled with clear water and muddy messes. A magical creature lives in each one of them, and all of them are looking at me.

"Welcome to my Animagorium," Luis says proudly. "As you can see, I take care of a bit of pretty much everything. From the *alicanto* to the garfus." He points to some type of peacock with purple feathers and something similar to a colorful ostrich with the face of a giraffe.

Then he moves on to show me an aquarium that seems empty.

"Can you see what's in here?" he asks me.

"No, I can't see anything."

"Of course," he laughs, throwing a handful of peeled shrimp into the water. "Because the *agane* can become invisible whenever they want."

The shellfish don't have time to reach the bottom of the tank before they are devoured with unimaginable voracity within a matter of seconds.

"What are they?"

"The agane are kind of mermaids' little sisters. They are smaller, but equally lethal."

"You mean that mermaids really exist and that they are . . . dangerous?"

"Of course, they are. They were here long before Midendhil existed. They live in the abyss of Lake Nerthuris, and I hope you never meet them."

"What about that instead?" I ask, pointing at a shy little fire that crackles in some kind of big lantern.

"In there is an *elemental* that . . ."

He almost finishes his sentence when a salamander alight with fire jumps out of the flames toward me.

"Watch out!"

I fall back letting out a scream, but this thing lands on my shoulder sticking to me as if it had been glued on. I drop on the floor and roll when I realize that the fire actually doesn't burn, and even more puzzling, it isn't even warm. I stay still, disoriented, looking for help from Luis.

"Can you do something?"

"Incredible . . ." he comes closer, looking at the salamander, while it rubs its muzzle on my cheek. "You should have caught on fire immediately. This is a *zika*, and even though it's wounded, it still is lethal to the touch."

"And you leave it there, in a box?"

"They never leave their fire; they die instantly. That's why she's here, the flames in which I found her were fading away."

"Would you mind helping get this thing off me?" I whisper through my teeth.

"Are you crazy? Nobody can touch a zika like that, with bare hands. We need a protective spell."

"So why is she not hurting me?"

"I have no idea, I should be asking you," he replies, looking at me suspiciously.

Could it be that the Sidhits are protecting me?

I notice that Luis has a wary look on his face. He's gloomy, frowning, as if he was trying to figure out what secrets I'm keeping. And this is not good, not good at all. I have got to avoid attracting any type of suspicion, for both of our sakes.

Without uttering a single word, I let the zika off my shoulder, pushing it back into the flames of her nest.

"So weird, Leonardo. *Sooooo* weird."

"Can we go see Maya now?" I ask, clearing my throat.

"Of course . . . right this way."

I follow him through the bookcases. I see that, hanging out to dry from a wire between two columns, are Maya's socks and her soaked sweatshirt. We walk past a huge terrarium with blue worms as big as arms, until we get to a more open space; in the center, there is a cot with her on it, unconscious.

"Maya!"

Her face is less pale. Her forehead is not as hot as it was before, and her lips hold a serene smile that brings me joy instantly.

"I dripped a little bit of Panaka on her lips," Luis explains. "It's a beverage that . . ."

"I know what Panaka is," I interrupt him without taking my eyes off Maya.

I move her hair from her forehead, and I caress her scratched-up face all the way down to her wrist, which is now wrapped in a clean bandage.

"How is she?"

"Better than before, that's for sure. She needs a lot of rest because her fever has yet to go away completely. The curse that hit her is nothing to take lightly. I see she's already been cured with an alter spell, but it'll take time to get rid of the curse fully."

"How long?"

"I am not sure; it depends on her."

I look through my pockets and take out her Rajasthan bracelet; it's in a poor state, dirty, and one of the bells is gone. I try to clean it up somehow. I slowly lift her arm and put it on her wrist, the one with the bandage.

"Can we do something about those wounds on her face?"

"I put an ointment of *bodula sprouts* to disinfect and alleviate the pain, but I couldn't put too much, it's a powerful extract and in large quantities can be fatal."

"You don't know of any spell that could heal the wounds?"

Luis turns quickly, almost hitting me in the eye with his big nose.

"Casting spells is no joke!" he says bothered. "Just because I am a wizard doesn't mean I can just do magic, you know?!"

"No, of course, but I thought that . . ."

"Well, you thought wrong!"

"Sorry Luis, I didn't mean to offend you."

"You didn't offend me, it's just that I don't like to talk about my spells. I am not good at them, OK? Are you all out to make me feel guilty about it?"

"I wasn't trying to make you feel guilty, I was simply asking because . . ."

"Yes, that's why I don't live in Ialon, that's why they shipped me here, to protect a silly little tree. For *them,* I am not worthy of being a member of their community."

"Who's *them?*"

"The other lusoghams, who else?" he shouts, moving in a circle.

The tone of his voice is starting to agitate all the creatures.

"Calm down, Luis. There is no need to get upset."

"Druir, our chief, wanted me with him," he continues, undaunted, not calming down. "But the village counsel decided that, if there ever was anybody who had to live like a hermit, that someone had to be me. The most inadequate lusogham of all time."

I grab him by his shoulders, and forcefully turn him toward me.

"I apologize, Luis. To me, your magic doesn't matter. You saved us and that's all that counts. I spent my life being judged by others and I would never dream of doing that to you now."

He immediately becomes quiet. A moan from Maya catches our attention. She's still sleeping, maybe dreaming, but her sleep is restless. My hand goes back to caressing her forehead.

"I have what we need," I suddenly exclaim, surprising even myself.

"What? Do you happen to know a curing spell?"

"No, but I have this!" I say, showing him the pendant that Anthony gave me.

Luis grabs it and looks at it in shock.

"It looks like Azas, the symbol of the Guardians of Midendhil. Where did you find it?"

"It's not important right now. Instead, look at what it's inside."

The ointment's smell of tar makes our nostrils twitch.

"I can't believe this," he says, giggling. "The Healmey, the legendary healing balm of the Guardians."

"Well, we should be able to heal all of Maya's wounds with this one, right?"

"Maybe not the curse, but surely everything else," he exclaims, spreading cream all over her face. "Only a few minutes, and your friend will have her gorgeous apsaras-like face back."

"What's *apsaras*?"

"The fairies who live in the city of Iesin. Absolutely gorgeous creatures . . ."

Yes, just like my mother was.

I sigh, relieved, and I notice that I am exhausted. I let myself fall onto the stool and I lay my head on the cot, right next to Maya.

"Tired, huh?" Luis asks me.

"Exhausted."

"I guess you don't want to come with me to see the maretak, do you?"

"What?"

"The maretak. That thing I keep."

"Wasn't it a secret?"

"Well, now we are friends, so it makes no more sense trying to hide it from you," he tells me. "I have to go and water it and I assure you that it's a wonderful thing to see."

"Tomorrow, Luis . . ."

"Yes, it's pretty late anyway," he points out, looking outside the window.

"Tomorrow I'd like to go see my father."

"Certainly, and then you two could stay here with me for a while, until you all have recovered properly."

"I appreciate it, Luis, but I think it'd be better if we left as soon as possible . . ."

"As you wish, Leonardo. Now come, I'll show you where you can stay."

"No, I'd rather stay here with her."

"Here, sitting on that stool?"

"Yes, it's perfect," I reply, closing my eyes as I caress Maya's cheeks. "It's absolutely perfect."

A numbness takes over me immediately. I feel Luis covering up my shoulders with a blanket. Then, just the sweet nothingness of sleep.

chapter twenty-three

NOCTURNAL FLYERS

I wake up suddenly as if somebody pulled me up by the hair. I have a headache, and the cries of the beasts jumping everywhere is not helping. The Animagorium has plunged into a chaos of *barks*, *chirps*, and bodies moving in the twilight. Every creature is out of its hole, and they are now running down the aisle, panicking.

"Hey! What's going on? Calm down, please," I say, determined to stop them out of fear more than anything else.

Some kind of little fox, with white and blue stripes, whizzes over my head, throwing itself on Maya for protection.

"You! What are you doing?" I yell, pulling its long tail. "Get out of there, immediately."

Suddenly, I hear some sort of deep roaring coming from outside: a muffled *thud* and the steps of something big that moves in the dark. The force of the creatures' *chirps* around me increases quickly and it becomes deafening; giant worms, now out of their terrarium, are writhing on the floor trying to dig a shelter, while the purple bird, the one that looks like a peacock, is flying all over the room, as if someone was after it trying to pull its neck. The terror I see in the animals' eyes starts to make me feel anxious. On my knees, I look out the window. It's pitch black outside, and I can't see anything, but I recognize a shadow crawling in the night: something big, actually huge. I attempt to lean over a little more when a hand touches my shoulder.

"What's going on?"

It's Luis who, crouching and wearing his pajamas, stares at me with puzzling eyes, looking for answers.

"I have no idea. The animals have become agitated . . . there's something out there, something huge."

I become fully aware of the situation when I hear my own words out loud. The fear that the mashuis or the mencans have found us starts to overcome me. Luis gets closer to the window with his nose pressed against the glass.

"I can't see anything, what's tha . . .?"

A roar shakes the glass, and our entire bodies. Two pairs of golden spheres appear in the dark. They are eyes: eyes with no soul that belong to two heads as big as a desk.

"*Wyverns*? . . . No, I can't believe this!"

"Wyverns?"

"These beasts haven't been seen around here for hundreds of years . . . how is it possible that they are here?"

Could it be that I am the reason why this happened? Is it possible that these monsters are here for me, unleashed by Kenat?

"They're moving," Luis whispers, still glued at the window-pane. "They are going to the back of the house!"

"So?"

"The *maretak*! They're here for the maretak," he shouts, jumping up. "We have got to stop them; we have got to stop them right now!"

"Maretak? Stop them? But how?"

He doesn't give me time to understand what it is that he wants to do as he rushes out. I place Maya in a safe spot, away from the window. I follow Luis through the laboratory, the library and down the hall, till we get in a small room with a bed that looks like a hammock, a fireplace and the walls full of cuckoo clocks. I see a small door that leads outside; Luis is already there, kneeling down next to the nearby window.

"*Shhh!* Come here and don't make any noise," he whispers. "Get down, get down here next to me."

I get closer. Mela comes by us quietly, her eyes filled with fear. The wyverns are making strange sounds, as if sniffing the air looking for something. We hear them roar and argue with each other, smacking their jaws in the air.

"So, are we ready? On my signal, we get out there and attack them," Luis says.

"What? Wait a minute, what do you want to do!? Attack those monsters?"

"Of course! We have to get them out of here before they get the maretak," he insists, brandishing a staff with a crystal sphere set on top of it.

"Have you seen how big they are? And consider that it's two of them!"

"And it's three of us!"

Mela steps back and hides her muzzle with her paws.

"You coward maju, wait till you ask me for something else!" he *hisses* at her. "Alright, it's two of us: you and me. Are you ready?" he asks, offering me a short sword with a large blade, consumed by rust.

"No! I'm not ready at all. Let's think about this for a second. Why do we have to risk our own lives for this stuff? What is it? Why is it so important?"

"The maretak is one of the last *plants of fire*."

"Meaning?"

"It's one of the *trees of good and evil* that only blooms once every thousand years. With its leaves of fire and from its wood, it's possible to make the elixir of eternal life, but also very dangerous poisons that are able to destroy the Yuth of everything and everyone."

"Seriously? But why do these beasts want it?"

"Maybe they are trying to steal it for somebody who gave them the order."

"Somebody *who*?"

"Somebody . . . it doesn't matter who."

"Let me see if I understand this, we are talking about something extremely dangerous here, something incredibly rare and enormously precious, and your friends have sent just you and Mela here to protect it?"

"Are you trying to say something?" he challenges me, coming closer.

"No, but in my opinion . . ."

The roars suddenly increase. We hear the crackling of broken wood and the fire that flares up.

"Oh, no! They are destroying the *Tricasses!*"

I get up slowly and spy through the windowpane; the image in front of my eyes takes my breath away. A few feet from us, there is a huge column made of the trunks of three big oaks, intertwined around a heart of green fire that, I guess, is the maretak. The top is a tangle of branches lapped by pale flames on which are climbing the silhouettes of two gigantic reptiles with long and thin necks, their tails dangling down to the ground. The spurs of their devil-like wings are stuck in the bark of the trees, and their big jaws are tearing the wood apart.

"I have to stop them!"

"Hold . . ."

Luis doesn't let me finish. He pushes the door wide open and throws himself against the monsters. I follow him, unwillingly, holding my sword tightly in my hands.

"Hey, you!" he screams, rotating the staff in front of him.

The wyverns turn toward us like poisonous snakes. Now I can see them clearly, with the light of the fire illuminating their horrible muzzles. Their skulls are parted in the middle by red ridges that go all the way down to the back, their jaws resemble gigantic traps, with sharp fangs that jut out of their mouths.

The biggest one jumps off the Tricasses and aims straight at us, with its tilted neck, its head grazing the ground and the wings spread wide open like a huge bat. I feel like I'm about to wet my pants, but Luis doesn't seem scared at all. With his beard tucked into the belt of his robe, he slams his staff on the ground three times, turning the crystal on top into a white ball of light. The big lizard barks, irritated by the glare.

"*Nirasha!*" he yells, aiming the staff at the wyvern.

But all that comes out from the shiny sphere is a weak stream of sparkles like blowing a raspberry. Luis doesn't give up.

"Come on, Leonardo! Get the attention of the other wyvern before they manage to catch the maretak," he screams while dodging whiplash from the beast's tail. "I'll take care of the rest."

"You'll take care of what? Are you crazy?"

"Leonardo! Don't be a maju! If you don't do it, we'll be food for these monsters!"

I nod as I rue the moment I decided to follow him out here. I start moving the sword, which now feels as heavy as an anvil, and I turn toward the other beast, ready to fight. Meanwhile, the wyvern has managed to create an opening in the wood and stick its muzzle into it, heedless of the maretak flames that are burning inside.

For a moment, I hear a giggle coming from behind me but, focused as I am, I don't dare take my eyes off the monster that I have right in front of me.

Intuitively, my hand touches my jeans to confirm where the Sidhits are; all it takes is this simple gesture to infuse me with confidence and a good amount of recklessness. I inhale a deep breath and I start running with the sword lifted above my head. A couple of hops, and with a faint scream, I hit the tail of the wyvern with the blade. Not even a scratch: the edge is blunt, its skin is leathery, and all I manage to do is to make it very, *very* mad.

The head of the big beast suddenly peeks out of the fire and lashes out against me. I step aside just in time, before its jaws tear my arms off. I run back terrified, as the wyvern comes toward me. Its eyes are revolving out of rage and its tongue darts between the fangs, dripping with slime.

"Luis, I think I have all its attention," I yell, my sword straight in front of me. "What do I do now?"

With an acrobatic jump, the wizard twirls midair, dodging the attack of the big lizard he's fighting against. Then, he lands on top of it, and with all the strength that he can muster, he whacks it over the big head with his stick. It rings out like a deafening hammer blow—steel on steel—making the monster collapse on the ground like dead weight.

"Here I am!" he tells me, running by my side.

The wyvern in front of us steps back, staring at us with pure hatred.

"*Shoo*! Go away, you ugly beast!" Luis threatens it, shaking the bright sphere of his staff in front of it. "Go back where you came from."

But the monster immediately launches an attack and confronts us with its wings spread-out and its mouth wide open, showing off its sharp fangs. I am shaking from head to toe, but Luis takes a single step, and by constantly forcing the light globe in front of the creature's eyes, he compels it to walk toward the forest.

Out of the corner of my eye, I catch a movement: it's the other wyvern who, recovered from the blow, is crawling onto the Tricasses again.

"Luis!"

His gaze darts toward the maretak and immediately assesses the situation. Quickly, he rotates his staff, grabs it like a bat, and twirling around, throws a huge blow to the muzzle of the beast that is in front of him, making it fall on the ground.

"Keep it at bay!" he orders me, while running toward the other one at the Tricasses, now totally broken.

"How?" I yell, staring at the wyvern that is collapsed on the ground.

But Luis has already engaged himself into full attack mode against the other beast who has half of its body wrapped in the flames of the maretak, and the head is stuck looking in the Tricasses.

"Get out of there!" he screams, hitting its back.

The big lizard throws him down with a paw, getting out of the flames with a fiery branch in its jaws.

"Nooo!" Luis cries, throwing himself against the creature.

With a flap of the wings, the wyvern lifts off the ground. Luis is holding onto its tail.

"Luis!!"

"I got it, Leonardo, I got it," he shouts, while climbing onto the ridges on its back. "I just have to grab the maretak!"

They fly high into the night sky, moving toward the mountains, their shadows against the yellow, crescent moon.

"Luis!!"

A cavernous breath shakes my soul. I look down only to meet the gaze of the other wyvern, now back on its paws.

"Good girl . . . calm down . . ."

The beast observes me for a moment. Then, squinting, it takes the time to sigh and attacks me with savage fury, uttering sounds so terrifying that all the blood in my veins seems to drain out. I start shouting like a madman, throw the sword on the ground and run back inside the house, with the wyvern following right behind me. I close the door just in time, but the creature knocks it down with its head and shoves me against the wall under a rain of wood and debris.

Its neck darts like an eel, but its wings are too wide for the doorframe, and this gives me time to get away. I run through the rooms like there's no tomorrow, as the monster begins to destroy the cabin and tries to get in through the roof. I run past the library with all the books flying around, agitated like flies, till I reach the alchemist's laboratory. Mela, who is now by my side, is shaking like a leaf, and despite her size, tries to hide in every nook she can find. The blows from the wyvern are getting stronger and stronger, making the whole house shake like there's an earthquake.

In the Animagorium, I am immediately welcomed by a huge mess of fallen shelves, destroyed nests, shattered glass, wood, and straw everywhere. The presence of those monsters must have driven the little animals totally crazy who, terrified, broke the window and fled into the forest. All that's left in the room is the creatures in the aquariums, the blue worms who are still shaking on the floor and Maya, obviously. She's still lying in the same position that I left her, and thank goodness, the animals didn't hurt her while rushing to flee the scene.

I have got to take her away from here, but where? I look around, trembling from the attack of the wyvern. Then, suddenly, silence. Not a noise, nor a roar. Nothing at all. Carefully, I peep through the broken window, but my gaze sinks into the darkness barely illuminated by the green fire that flares up behind the house. I listen for a few seconds. I lean closer toward the outside and *boom!*

Two golden eyes swoop down on me. The wyvern is right in front of me and throws me against the broken window. It sticks its open muzzle and snaps her jaws like a shark.

I move back, crawling toward Maya. The beast tears the frame apart, knocking down part of the wall, and pulling away a piece of the roof. I start throwing everything I can at it, but I am not able to stop it. It pushes itself through the opening, scratching its neck against the broken glass of the window. I see its fangs a few inches from my feet. I try to climb on the cot with Maya, but its thin and scorching hot tongue wraps around my leg, pulling me. I grab onto the cot, squirming.

"Help!"

My gaze darts across the floor, on the fallen shrine in which shines the fire of the salamander: she's frozen in the flames, with her yellow eyes focused on me.

"Come here, baby! Come here!"

My grip starts to slip. I try to hold on even tighter to the point that my fingers begin to cramp, but the wyvern is too strong. I am about to let go when I see the zika slide down toward me. I stretch my arm out, letting go of my grip. The wyvern pulls me outside, but I manage to grab the salamander and throw her right at its muzzle. At first nothing happens, but then flames flare up. The zika runs down its neck, then on its stomach, until it's holding onto the wyvern's wings. Soon, the monster is completely engulfed in flames. I hear it squealing as it tries to fly away. But it crashes on the house, then on the trees, till the fire becomes too strong.

It falls with a *thud* and me with it; I am just staring at the fire that consumes its horrific body. I can't believe that I was able to do that. I grab onto the cot again to pull myself up. Maya is doing well: not a scratch, nor a burn. Hopefully she hasn't even noticed what almost happened to us.

I am about to take a deep sigh of relief, when I sense a rattle behind me, followed by the stench of rotten meat. I turn around, nauseated, while from the broken ceiling a goblin with a thin and shallow face slides down. His eyes are white with no pupils, but his gaze seems rapacious. His hair is twisted in filthy dreadlocks, styled with feathers and small bones of who-knows-what creature, while its body is slim and athletic, wrapped in leather rags and beasts' fur. I walk back slowly and the goblin, crouched on the ground like a monkey, despite his blind eyes, follows my every move.

"I good. I no do nothing to you," I tell him, showing him the palms of my hands.

An icy-cold blade lands on my throat, forcing me to look up at the ceiling. The stench of filth of the second goblin behind me makes me gag.

"Well, well," sings the creature I have in front of me, walking toward me, almost dancing. "You don't wanna hurt us, huh? And yet, you've killed one of our wyverns. How about that? Do you know that now you owe us?"

"O-o-owe you?"

"You owe us," he repeats, dragging his voice and exploring me with his long fingers that seem to have been made only to strangle someone. "But don't worry, by selling you and your female we will earn enough to make up for what you made us lose. The *kapturs* could pay us very well for two young slaves like you."

His blind eyes dart over Maya's helpless body.

"Don't touch her!" I scream, scratching my skin against the blade.

"I see we have a young hero here," the goblin makes fun of me, sliding his filthy finger on my cheek all the way down to my lips. "Careful, boy, you are worth more alive than dead, but we are merchants who can easily settle for a little less."

His dead fisheyes stare into space, while his fingers still slide down my neck and past the blaze of the wyvern.

"What do we have here?" he asks, finding the Azas, Anthony's pendant.

As soon as he brushes his finger against it, the goblin changes expression and jumps up, gripping onto the ceiling like a cat. The pressure of the blade pushing against my neck becomes a little weaker after the surprise.

"Guardian! He's a Guardian! Slaughter him!"

I don't give the other one time to react. I elbow him in the stomach, move the blade away and duck, sliding far from him.

"Don't move!" threatens the first goblin, who is already by Maya, with the tip of his knife against her torso.

A shiver goes up my spine.

"No, please!"

"One more step and I cut her open, Guardian!"

"Please, let her go . . ."

Even totally blind, the creature stares at me, almost feeding off my fear.

"But you are not a Guardian. They would have never stopped if faced with this threat. They don't negotiate, they just kill."

"Let her go . . . take me instead but let her go."

I see the goblin nod to his pal who's behind me again. A hit to my back takes me off guard and makes me fall on my knees.

"This is for making us believe you were a Guardian."

I wobble, as two skinny yet muscular hands pull me back up and immobilize me again, this time with my arms behind my back.

"Who are you?" asks the goblin bending over Maya.

"I am nobody."

"Who did you steal that pendant from?"

I don't answer. Anything I could potentially say, would surely be the wrong thing anyway. The goblin hesitates for a moment.

"You know what I think?" he says.

My fingers begin to tingle; rage is coming back.

"That we could settle for you and for your stolen Azas. Your friend is wounded, maybe sick . . . she's useless. Might as well kill her and chop her up. She has beautiful hands, gorgeous hair, I'm sure we could use those things for something."

Like a storm, a dark strength overwhelms me and floods me with hatred. I sense my hands getting heated to the point that they start releasing purple flames. I spread my arms out and free myself with ease. I turn around, and with a simple move, I reduce to ashes the goblin who's holding me.

"Who are you?" I hear the other one stuttering with terror.

I move forward, towering over him. The dark fire engulfs me completely and gives the illusion that I am the most powerful being in the whole world. Nothing can oppose my will. Whatever made me human till a minute ago, is no longer in me; it's been burned by the flames, thus leaving death, horror, and destruction in its place.

The goblin falls off Maya's cot. His face covered with fear, he scoots back on his behind and crawls outside, beyond the broken wall.

"It's you! You are the Keeper of the Sidhits! The Akasha! You are the one the Dark Lord is looking for."

The sound of that name makes me shiver and awakens something in me that I thought was lost, something that for all those years has been kept a secret from me. A dark feeling rises inside of me, feeding into my thirst for revenge. I move further, burning everything that surrounds me. The goblin blows some kind of whistle and makes a squeaky sound that reminds me of an old vinyl record scratch. I throw myself on him to destroy him, but it's too late, from above, a wyvern grabs him by the shoulders and lifts him up mid-air.

"We'll see each other again, Keeper," he roars, crawling on his behind. "We'll see each other sooner than you think!"

With two flaps of its wings, the wyvern is a dark shadow in the starry sky. The roar of the beast echoes in the forest and disappears in the night, just as quietly as when it got here.

I sense the tension leaving my body, the rage is disappearing, but my muscles hurt from the repercussions of all we've been through. The feeling of anger that till a moment ago dominated my being has left me now, gone without leaving a trace. Whatever I did feels as if it belonged to someone else's story.

I look up at what lays before me: the house is destroyed, Luis has disappeared, but Maya is safe and that's all that really matters. I hobble toward her, and I stand still to look at her. I hold her hand squeezing it tight, going back to that afternoon outside my house.

"You and me, Maya. You and me against the world."

chapter twenty-four

PACKING UP

The wyvern kept burning all night long. I just stayed there, still like a statue, staring at the salamander who was spitting fireballs everywhere. I didn't even notice that the chirping of birds had begun to spread across the forest, driving out every shadow of fear. The black curtain has been torn apart, giving color to the emerald green of the trees, while the sliver of sky where Luis disappeared has first turned pink, then violet, and finally turquoise.

I haven't been able to sleep. I've been sitting here on this stool, watching over Maya with the hope of seeing Luis come back safe and sound.

What happened has truly taken a toll on me, leaving me without hope. Maya doesn't seem to be doing any better, my father is out there somewhere in the forest, and I am here, alone, and desperate. I am trying to be brave, but I can't.

Mela comes out from under a destroyed cabinet and sits down next to me wanting to be petted. I let myself go, nuzzling my head in her fur that smells like smoke.

"Don't worry, Mela," I tell her, scratching her ears. "One way or another, we'll be fine."

"You betcha!"

I jump up, with a smile from ear to ear.

"Luis!" I exclaim.

We don't give him time to respond; Mela and I run toward him and knock him down in a joyful tackle. While I hug him, Mela greets him by wagging her tail and drooling all over him.

"Slow down guys, easy! I am a little battered and bruised!" he laughs, happy to see that we too are safe and sound.

"Did you get the maretak back?" I ask him. I see that his beautiful robe is now nothing more than a piece of cloth and he has scratches all over his face.

"I've tried my best, but that ugly beast was able to knock me off while flying," he explains, rubbing his lower back. "It's a miracle I didn't break my neck."

His gaze gets lost in what is left of the house. The Animagorium is destroyed, the roof is smashed, and the walls are crumbled.

"You had it pretty rough, huh?"

"Yeah . . . we almost didn't make it."

"How about your friend?"

"She's safe."

"Do you think that any of my little animals might be . . ."

"I don't think so, they all managed to escape before it even started."

I see him breathing a sigh of relief.

"What's that?" he asks, nodding at the fire emitted by the little salamander. "Is that what I think it is?"

"I wouldn't be here had it not been for her. I threw her on the wyvern a second before I ended up in her jaws."

"Great move. There is no creature who can resist a zika's fire . . . except for you, that is," he reminds me with a half-smile that hides a whole lot of questions.

I feel like I should tell him about the attacks from the other creatures like those filthy goblins, but this would force me to reveal other things, maybe too many. Plus, I don't really remember what happened. It's as if somebody else had taken over my body for a moment, leaving me and my conscience sitting next to each other, watching helplessly.

I do remember one thing though. The goblin called me Keeper of Sidhits, Akasha; he recognized me, and this means that we are all in danger. We have got to leave as soon as possible.

"We don't have time to waste," Luis surprises me, as if he had just heard my thoughts. I follow him and quickly walk through the gap left by the wyvern, until we reach the cot where Maya is. He places his hand on her forehead and he checks her bandaged wrist.

"Unbelievable. Her fever is gone, and her wrist is no longer swollen," he says, unwrapping the bandage. "I didn't think it was possible to get better in such short time."

"What do you mean?"

"It takes a long time to fully recuperate from that kind of curse, but Maya's recovery has been very fast. Much faster than any other creature I know. How come?"

"I have no idea."

He looks at me, squinting.

"How's your back doing?"

"A little better, actually. It doesn't burn anymore."

"Can I see it?"

I lift up my shirt. Luis moves the bandages that wrap my abdomen.

"Your wound is gone."

"What?"

"Let me see your stomach."

I turn around shocked, forcing myself to smile.

"The scratch from the mencan has disappeared too," he observes, incredulous.

"You two are hiding many more secrets than I thought."

"Secrets? Nah, what secrets?"

Luis doesn't listen to me; instead, he focuses on what's left of his Animagorium.

"We have got to go," he whispers, biting his lip.

"OK, but where can we go?"

"To the Ialon village."

"What about my father?"

"The hamadryads' dwelling is on the way, but we have to hurry up. The wyverns could come back, and I need to speak to Druir; he has to know what happened here. The fauns have definitely lost control of the situation. They must understand that!"

"The fauns? What do they have to do with the wyverns?"

"They are the keepers of the Noux Caves, the prisons where, in ancient times, all the evil creatures that infested Midendhil were locked. But, a while ago, something terrible happened; their king was poisoned, and all the monsters freed themselves. That's why the forest is so dangerous."

"Who poisoned him?"

"Nobody knows."

Luis's serious tone leaves me speechless. Fauns, monsters, wyverns, sorcerers and all the plotting . . . *Where am I?*

"Let's go," he says, shaking me out of my thoughts. "Go over there and grab all the blankets you can find. We'll spend one night in the woods, and we have to be prepared. Meanwhile, I'll get all the supplies we need for the trip."

I follow his instructions, without wasting any time. The bedroom is not as destroyed as the Animagorium, but you can tell the wyvern has been in here too. The back door has been knocked down, revealing the maretak, faded and withered, completely devoid of its magical protection. All the weird cuckoo clocks that were on the walls are now shattered, and underneath the window where we hid only a few hours ago is nothing more than a hole in the wall.

I grab all the blankets I can find, as well as two pillows, which are on that strange hammock. With a huge pile of stuff in my arms, I walk backward down the hall, all the way to the Animagorium.

"Here you go, where should I put them?"

Luis has his back turned to me, crouching behind a fallen terrarium. He's grumbling and analyzing something I can't see.

"Luis?"

He gets up slowly, then turns around with the same mechanical movements of a robot. His brow showing his deep concentration.

"What's this?"

In his tightened hand he is holding the falcata sword with the curved and dark blade.

"What is the weapon of an abuclus doing in my house?"

"It's a long story," I swallow, trying to buy some time.

"I'm all ears."

I look at Maya, then at the disaster that surrounds us. I place the blankets and pillows on an overturned shelf, stacking them next to the Grimoire and the bags full of supplies gathered by Luis.

"After I set the wyvern on fire, two filthy creatures showed up. They looked like . . . goblins."

"Goblins? They are abuclus, Leonardo! Dang it, where do you come from?" he replies, exasperated.

"They were furious because I had killed one of their beasts."

"You mean the wyvern?"

"Yes, they said it belonged to them, that I owed them, and that the only way I was ever going to be able to repay their debt was if they sold me into slavery and chopped up Maya."

"How many were there?"

"Two."

"And how did you manage to save yourself? They are expert cutthroats, dangerous even for the best faun warrior."

And now what do I tell him? That I can't remember what happened and that the few images I do have in my head terrify me?

"Leonardo?"

"The pendant I have around my neck," I tell him quickly, touching it. "They fled when they saw it."

"The Azas," Luis whispers. "They thought you were a Guardian."

"Exactly."

"And the ashes in which I found the sword?" he asks me, pointing to the small dust pile by his feet.

"I'm not sure . . . it's just . . . ashes."

I didn't convince him. Not even one bit. He won't stop looking at me and I really don't like his expression.

"You see, Luis, I . . ."

A deafening scream catches me off guard and scares me to death. Maya is sitting up, still like a puppet, looking bewilderingly at us from her cot.

"*Maya!*"

"Leonardo! Where are we?"

"*How are you?*"

"Who's that?" she whispers.

"*He's Luis, a friend . . .*"

"I don't understand you," she says, on the verge of crying. "This is all a joke, right?"

"*Calm down, Maya, calm down,*" I try to reassure her. "*Everything's fine.*"

"Don't touch me! And stop talking to me like that. I want to go home."

"*Maya, let me explain . . .*"

"Stop it!" she cries out loud.

I turn around, looking for help in Luis.

"*Why can't she understand what I'm saying?*"

"*Actually, I don't understand her either. You are speaking my language, but your friend is just making a whole bunch of sounds that make no sense to me. Is she really talking?*"

"*You can't understand her?*"

"*Not at all. I know almost all the languages of Midendhil, but this is the first time I've heard this one.*"

"Leonardo, who's this old man dressed like a fool? And where are we?"

I wet my lips, trying to focus on properly modulating the words in what I thought was the only language I spoke.

"Don't worry, Maya. Everything is OK. Luis is our friend."

I see her smile melt into a grimace that is a mix of hopelessness and relief.

"Leonardo," she hugs me. "Tell me that everything I remember was just a bad dream."

I slowly move away from her.

"What do you remember?"

"I remember you, with a light in your chest." Her words are struggling to come out. "Your mother was trying to calm me down. Her voice . . . the darkness."

"Is that all?"

"No." I can see fear taking over in her eyes. "I remember a man. A monster made of smoke. Then, you and I in the grass, in the rain. He wanted something from you. Then he hit me. Pain. The pain was so strong, Leo. I thought I was going to die."

She bursts into tears and hugs me again. My guilt is causing the knot tightening my throat and the tears welling up in my eyes.

"*I have the solution!*" Luis interjects rudely.

I dry my tears, trying to keep it together.

"He's Luis, tonight he saved our lives."

"*What are you telling her?*" he asks me, curious.

I concentrate again, pushing myself to speak in his language this time.

"*I'm telling her that you are a friend and that you saved us. What about that solution you thought of?*"

"*Wait here, I'll be right back,*" he hurries, disappearing down the hall.

"So, it's all true? You don't belong to my world?"

I tilt my head and hint an uneasy smile.

"Where are we?"

"From what I can tell, we are in some kind of parallel dimension, in a place called Midendhil."

"Miden . . . dhil?"

I grab Luis's Grimoire and I search through the pages till I see the map; the word Midendhil appears in the center, under a curious dragon illustration. Maya looks down at the drawing and slides a finger on the yellowed parchment. A lone tear lines her face once again, setting off in me a sense of nostalgia and regret.

"Why am I here?" she asks me, keeping her eyes on the map.

"You were in the wrong place at the wrong time. Had I not brought you with me, you would have died."

"What happened to me?"

"You were hit by a curse. It was killing you."

"A curse? You mean, like 'magic'?"

I nod in silence. I hate having to tell her that all of this happened because of me.

"What do I have to do with all of this?"

"They did it to get to me."

Her mouth quivers. She doesn't look at me. She prefers to keep looking at the Grimoire. I feel my heart heavy in my chest like a boulder. I'm hurting, suffering so badly at the thought of what I am about to reveal to her. My words will destroy everything: our friendship, and everything we used to be. But I must tell her. She needs to know that the monsters who are after me didn't just limit themselves to hit her with a curse; they've done so much more. They killed her mother.

"Maya, there's more."

She looks up, staring at me. Her green eyes draw me in and her world becomes mine again.

"I don't know where to begin, but . . ."

"*Here is what we need!*" Luis comes back with a small bottle of dust as yellow as the sun.

"*What's that stuff?*"

"*Potion Talkmaster,*" he says. "*It only takes a pinch of this, and Maya will be able to speak like a daughter of Midendhil.*"

"*And what would she have to do?*"

"*Nothing much. It's made with flower fairy dust; she just needs to sprinkle a bit on herself.*"

"*It's not risky, is it?*"

"*Not even one bit, lusogham honor.*"

I take the small bottle, let the cap pop off and an excited murmur of indistinguishable languages spreads immediately in the air.

"What's that?" Maya asks, scared.

"It's magic dust that will allow you to speak and understand the language of this world."

"Mag . . . Dus . . . I don't need this!" she bounces back. "Get that stuff away from me. Don't even think about it."

"Maya, we can trust him. Luis is a friend."

"Not mine. I am not going to take that stuff! Please, Leonardo, I want to go home."

"*Blow it in her face,*" Luis suggests.

"*What?*"

"*In her face! Blow a little bit in her face. It'll be enough.*"

Maya is going to hate me for this, but she has nothing to fear, I am sure of it. I let a pinch of dust fall on my open palm, unleashing the voices even more.

"What do you think you're doing?"

"I'm sorry."

I blow the dust without hesitation, and I surround her with a cloud of the sparkly and chatty magic.

"*Are you crazy?! What have you done!?*"

"*Crazy,*" Luis repeats, clapping his hands in enjoyment. "Now I can understand you, Maya. Welcome to my home, I'm Luis."

Maya looks at me angrily, quickly going back to Luis who, in her eyes, must seem like some kind of lunatic old man.

"You can understand me?" she asks him with a trembling voice.

"Perfectly."

"Are you speaking my language?"

"Nope, you are speaking mine."

"I wanna go home."

"Yes, Leonardo told me you got lost. Don't worry, we'll ask Druir, the chief of my order, to help you out. He surely knows some sailor who can take you back to the village overseas."

"Over-what?"

"I'm sure of it too, Luis," I quickly intervene to end this conversation.

"Are you hungry, Maya? Do you need anything?" Luis says in a fatherly tone.

"I'm thirsty . . . I need something to drink, please."

"Coming right up!" he tells her, placing a jug in her hands. "While Leonardo helps me take care of everything for our trip, you get comfortable. There's food over there and drinks over here. The house is a bit of a mess, but you know, we had one of those nights . . ."

"Wait! Leonardo, don't leave me alone," she begs, grabbing my shirt.

"I'm here, I'm not going anywhere."

"Where are your folks?"

Luis leaves us alone, understanding the situation. I sit down on the cot next to her, speechless.

"Dad is injured. He's been taken care of by some fairies of the woods."

"Fai . . . ries?"

"Hamadryads, to be precise," I correct myself, feeling silly.

"And your mom?"

"Mom . . . didn't make it . . ."

Maya looks at me, placing her hand over her mouth. Her face is an open book, in which I read all the pain that is written.

"What happened?" she asks with a voice that comes from far away.

I don't speak. I can't. I remain focused on the toes on my bare, dirty feet. She grabs my hand and doesn't ask anything else. We remain just like that, in silence, next to each other, like we have always done.

Alone, in an unknown and hostile world.

chapter twenty-five

THE AKRANDA

"Guys, come on, the sun is already up," Luis calls us to order. "It's late and we have to get where we're going before dark."

I slowly turn toward Maya. Her gaze is still lost in space and her hands fidget with the charms of her bracelet.

"Is it OK if I go?" I whisper in her ear. "I have to help Luis get everything ready."

She doesn't even look at me as she nods slightly. It seems like she's afraid to move and break her train of thought as if she's trying to escape reality by creating an imaginary world where she can seek refuge.

I start getting things done by helping Luis fill up a sack with potions from the alchemical laboratory. I grab two vials of each, just like Luis instructed me to do, and I refrain from asking too many questions regarding the nature of the liquids that wriggle like they are alive or that freeze my hands like the *Hìdevirum*. I also grab a handful of the magical stones possessing the power of becoming bigger, and some of that diabolic mud, which hopefully won't free itself and cover us when we least expect it.

Hours fly by quickly and we continue preparations for the trip without too many hiccups. Though Mela takes advantage of a moment when nobody is close to Maya to jump on her lap, which terrifies Maya half to death.

Around mid-afternoon, we manage to freshen up a bit, get dressed and grab a bite to eat. Luis gives me a pair of soft leather boots, which are a real blessing for my battered feet. Finally, we are all ready to go, but Luis blocks the door.

"Wait a minute," he says, hurrying into the room where all the cuckoo clocks were. I see him touching the wall with his fingers, as if looking for something.

"What are you doing?" I ask him out of curiosity.

"What? Oh, nothing. I was just checking something."

I am perplexed, but I don't have time to dwell on it since Luis drags me back to the entrance and pushes me out of the house.

The sun is high in the sky, over the mountain tops, and everything is going according to plan. We quietly say goodbye to Luis's destroyed tiny house, and we embark on our journey. Next to us, the zika, now as big as a cat, burns in her fire and runs happily like a child in the park.

"My dear little friend," Luis tells her, adding small pieces of wood to her fire, "please take care of the house and try not to burn anything else."

The salamander starts doing flips as we walk into the forest with our sacks over our shoulders; no looking back. I am sure it must not be easy for Luis leaving his house like that, but he hides it well. With Mela by his side, he walks briskly, leading the way through the trees without hesitation.

"This way, Leonardo! If we keep walking this fast, we'll reach the hamadryads' dwelling before dusk," he tells me, euphoric. "I can't wait to meet your father."

"And I can't wait to introduce him to you," I smile, waiting for Maya to catch up. "Are you OK?" I ask Maya, helping her get over a tree trunk that blocks her path.

"Yes," she replies.

But I know it's not true. She still has a blank stare and keeps her hoodie pulled down all the way to almost cover her eyes.

We proceed in a single file: crossing over a few streams, through bushes, keeping our distance from the part of the forest that is full of red ivy. Luis talks incessantly the whole trip, describing everything we see in the teensiest detail, whether it's plants, animals, or mushrooms. At first, I kind of wanted to strangle him, but his enthusiasm is so contagious that I actually started to see the forest in a new light. Even Maya seems to have taken her mind off her troubles, relaxing and looking at her surroundings through different eyes. She's now asking questions about everything. It's as if, at last, we are able to appreciate the magic of everything that surrounds us, the unique places that only exist here in Midendhil.

For example, shortly after beginning our trip, we walked by a giant tree that looked like a weeping willow with huge bell-flowers descending from the branches all the way down to the ground. Teeny, tiny fairies, as small as butterflies, were flying through the fronds looking for pollen to pick and place in their miniature baskets. At first, I was concerned they were finfinellas, but Luis reassured me, telling me that they, unlike the others, are not dangerous; they are much smaller and don't fly riding on blades of grass. Actually, they have the most beautiful wings with such lively colors that even Maya was mesmerized.

Along the way, we even spotted a garfus, one of those animals that look like awkward ostriches with giraffe heads that, according to Luis, have an incredible memory. Then, we also located a jimis village, those annoying, mushroom-shaped little elves. It was an actual town, dug out of a stump of a withered tree, with a palace in the center and fief all around it. Luis insisted we stop by, so he could chitchat with the chief of those hotheads who, after a long incomprehensible pantomime, offered us three thimbles filled with a mysterious beverage made from honey. Obviously, after the experience I had with them, I really didn't feel like trying that stuff, but Luis basically forced me to. So, I gave in, and I must say that it wasn't half as bad as I thought it was going to be; the beverage was an energetic nectar, and tired as I was, it actually gave me strength.

We had barely left the village when we found ourselves in the middle of a pack of durnax, giant gorillas with pointy ears, horns, and long muzzles like gargoyles. They were feasting on ferns and leaves of several plants, and even though they seemed harmless, it was the only time I saw Luis tense up, which made me a bit anxious. Fortunately, the animals kept eating without even looking at us. Once we were far enough from them, Luis told us that the durnax are not dangerous but, if bothered, have been known to attack and smash their victims with no mercy.

Then, we came across a couple of unicorns who were drinking on the banks of a body of deep blue water. It truly was a mystical experience. Unicorns are not how I had always pictured them and have very few things in common with horses. They have slim and muscular bodies, long and robust necks, and a dragon-like muzzle. A straight goatee grows down from their chin, and the long mane flows like it was made of silk. They are bright white and their horn sparkles like quartz. I kept staring at them for a few minutes as if hypnotized, and Luis had to pull me away from the scene, bringing me back to reality.

Still enchanted by that celestial vision, I start walking as if on autopilot. I have no idea how long it's been since that last stop, but I know that the sun is about to set. The fronds of the trees are sparse now, allowing me to admire the gorgeous sky painted pink by the last few rays of light.

"We're here!" Luis exclaims, placing his sack on the ground.

The clearing around us is different from the ones we've crossed so far. Here, trees have lighter bark, resembling that of birch trees; the air smells of flowers and a strange golden glow shines in the leaves of the fronds all around us. The one thing that immediately catches my attention is that everything is still, like a photo in a magazine. The air seems to be a bit denser, and I truly feel like I am in some kind time warp.

"We've arrived?" Maya asks, sitting on the ground with Mela by her side.

"Yes, this is one of the Nemeton hamadryads' residencies."

"My dad is here?"

"He's inside one of those trees," he says, caressing one of the trunks.

"Inside?" Maya asks, flabbergasted.

"*Hmm hmm*," Luis nods with a slight arrogance.

"And what are we supposed to do now?"

"We wait. Soon, the hamadryads will come out to salute the sun," he says, looking at the sky.

In that exact moment, a soft melody spreads in the air. It really doesn't resemble anything human, and it reminds me of the wind, the sound it makes right before it starts raining. A feeling of sadness overtakes me, making my eyes tear up, but I don't know why.

I look at Maya, then Luis, and I realize that they too are having the same reaction.

"What's happening, Luis?"

"The *akranda*," he replies, barely moving his lips.

"What is it?"

"It's the dirge of the hamadryads."

A knot forms in my throat. From the trees, I see a procession of women, dressed in light, flowing dresses. Their hair is soft and shiny, decorated with flowers and green acanthus leaves. The dirge becomes even more penetrating. It's almost unbearable. I still can't make out the words they are saying, but I know they're singing about death and tragedies. One of them comes toward me. Her eyes are emerald green, and her face is diaphanous, torn by grief. In her hands, she holds my dad's sword.

"No . . . tell me it's not true."

I fall to my knees, and begin to sob out loud uncontrollably. What I feel is excruciatingly painful, and it's as if this place amplifies my every emotion.

Luis is next to me. His hand is on my shoulder. He's squeezing so hard that it hurts. In my head, I hear a woman's voice. It's the hamadryad in front of me; she's talking to me through magic. She's trying to comfort me and alleviate my pain. I can feel she's hurting, too; she's suffering for me, she's suffering like me.

I look at her, lost in her glistening eyes. She tells me about my parents, their mission, and the sacrifice they made to save me. In my head, there is no longer just her voice, I see images. An oath made a long time ago. Two hands welcoming a swaddled baby. Dad and Mom holding me tightly in a hug. I can physically feel their love as warmth extending throughout my body. A journey. The light at the end of a tunnel. There's a tower that gleams on the top. It's the Nayaka, the star of the Tower of the Guardians. This is where I will find answers to my questions. Amber; in my eyes there's amber light again. The voice tells me it's not over yet; one day, when everything is fulfilled, I will see the ones I love. I will see them all; the Keeper and the Guardians will be united once again.

The turmoil in my head is quieting down. With a hint of a smile, the hamadryad offers me the sword. Slowly, I take it with both hands, as if I were holding my father's remains. The blade slides out of its sheath with a twinkle that fades away quickly. For a moment, I thought I heard my dad's voice, and felt the warmth of his embrace. I slump down, leaning on my heels, my teary eyes focus on the sword.

"*You are special, Leonardo Ghebo,*" the warm voice adds. "*You are a star burning in the sky. A star whose fire can give life, but can also destroy.*" In my head, I have new visions; this time I witness war, pain, and death.

"*Shine, oh great Akasha. Shine bright, and don't let your darkness extinguish the light you have inside.*"

I lift my head up. The hamadryads are gone, leaving the smell of rain in the air. Luis is crying. Maya is shocked, pale. She is sobbing so hard she can't breathe.

Mela starts howling a painful cry toward the sky. We stay there, spirits crushed and prostrate on the ground waiting for the night to swallow us.

chapter twenty-six

SHADOWS IN THE NIGHT

I've been crying nonstop for at least two hours. I'm having a hard time breathing. I feel as though something is dragging me to the bottom of the ocean and I'm drowning. I knew my dad's wound was serious. A tiny voice in my head kept telling me from the moment I left him, but I didn't want to listen; I pretended like it didn't even exist, keeping it hushed because I hated the message. I didn't want to face reality. Now that my father is dead, regret is torturing me.

It was hard for Luis to ask me to get moving again. Had it been my choice, I would have just stayed there, in the hamadryads' clearing, forever. I have had enough of missions, Midendhil, the Sidhits, and everything else. I just want to go back home to my normal life. I couldn't care less about this place. Actually, I hate it! It's because of Midendhil that everyone's dead.

I force myself to walk, following my friends with my head down. Luis is ahead of us, moving along like a train in the night, illuminating our path with the glowing sphere of his staff. He tries to encourage us, but it is all quite useless. Maya is exhausted: after only a few minutes of walking, she sits down, bursting into tears again, unable to get back up. She's desperate, I can see it in her eyes. After her mother's passing, my family had basically become hers and I know that the pain she's feeling is very similar to mine.

Luis has tried to pick her up but, when he saw that I too was lagging, he surrendered. He's started a fire to warm us, laid a few blankets on the ground for the night, and prepared something to munch on. However, neither Maya nor I have been able to eat.

Without uttering a single word, I curl up on my bedroll; I pull the blanket all the way up to my head, holding tightly onto the sword, remaining still like a statue. Next to me, Maya tosses and turns until she falls into an agitated sleep. Luis is on guard duty, smoking his pipe, with his back leaning against a tree and his crossed legs resting on top of Mela.

And now, here we are on the brink, on one side is the desert, on the other, an endless dark abyss. Even the forest seems to be waiting for something: not a noise, not a verse, not even the chirping of crickets. Everything is silent, as if honoring my father's death.

In the quiet of the night, I remember his last words: *Don't forget who you are, find the Nayaka and the Tower of the Guardians.* He didn't want me to give up, yet I am ready to get out of here and forget about my promise. How can I possibly do that?

I escape in my thoughts, and I seek refuge in the memories of my past. I begin reminiscing of sunny days, family dinners, and carefree runs across the fields. Finally, I fall asleep.

Two hands wake me, shaking me, and pulling me up forcefully. I let out a cry that Luis quickly suffocates by covering my mouth.

"Wake Maya up, don't make any sounds," he whispers in my ear.

I look at him confused, but he's already bending over the sack full of potions, searching for something. Mela is very agitated and she's staring at the forest, showing her fangs with a low, continuous growl. I get close to Maya, and gently shake her. She barely opens her eyes, frowning.

"What is it?"

I immediately put my finger on her lips, and I place my other index over mine. Luis crouches down next to us and shows us the vial with a milk-like white liquid, on the glass is written: *Hidevirum.*

"Can you tell us what's going on?"

He doesn't answer me. With a pocketknife, he shaves the wax that seals the vial, making the cork pop up. A narrow plume of turquoise steam rises from the ampoule, flooding us with the scent of pine trees like wintertime in the woods.

"Drink up."

"What is it?"

"Drink up, there's no time to explain!"

Luis looks around worriedly, as if anticipating something will attack us from the bushes. His fearful expression is enough to convince me. I take a deep breath and drink the potion; it is freezing cold, and I can feel it slide down my throat all the way to my stomach. Maya does the same and then quickly gives the tiny bottle back to Luis. He drinks it too, then places a few drops on Mela's tongue.

"Leave everything here and get on that tree trunk," he tells us, pointing to the one behind us.

"But why?" Maya murmurs.

"We don't have time, come on!"

I pick up my dad's sword and I push Maya onto the limb. I follow her and then help Luis pull Mela up.

"Can you tell me what's happening now?" I murmur once I think we're safe. "What's that stuff you had us drink?"

As I look at him, I notice that Luis is fading. He's becoming invisible.

"You're disappearing!" I exclaim, terrified.

I turn toward Maya and see that the same thing is happening to her. I stare at her hands, dissolving before my eyes, when a bothersome freezing sensation permeates me. I feel light, too light. I look at my legs and arms, realizing that *my* body is becoming see-through too. The potion has turned us into shadows!

Shocked, I look around to figure out what's going on. A man is silently crawling out of the bushes sniffing the air like a beast, and holding a dagger shaped like a fang. He's wearing a linen skirt, a large metal collar, and gaiters made of purple feathers that remind me of those of the garfus. His dark skin, shining in the weak reflection of the fire, is decorated with white paint that make him look like a ghost in the night. A long braid falls over his shoulder, swaying with every movement. On all fours, he reaches the bedroll where I slept.

He *hisses*, reminding me of a nocturnal animal, while two more men, who look exactly like him, come out of the forest. They glance at each other in agreement, and taking a deep breath, they shriek loudly and assault our camp in a mad search with daggers raised, ready to slaughter. I hear Maya moan next to me. I try to hold her hand, but I keep grabbing air, passing right through her. I am terrified, and as usual, I begin to itch uncontrollably.

Suddenly, in the clearing, ten torches appear, and more men jump out of nowhere, pouring into our camp like an army of ants. Among them, I spot an older and more robust man, with a scar on his chest and his nostrils pierced with a curved bone. He must be their chief, because the paint on his body is different: it's red like blood, and it draws a skull on his face.

"They are not here, oh great *Dum*," one warrior croaks, while the others go through our belongings, stuffing their mouths with our food. "Our prey must have heard us coming."

The man doesn't even look at him. He walks toward the fire, bends down, and places his hands in the flames. As soon as they touch his skin, coals screech, but he doesn't seem to feel any pain.

"This fire was fueled not long ago," he says, observing his fingers. "They must be nearby. Look for them."

The group separates: their torches moving in the darkness of the forest petrifies me. I look toward Maya, then Luis. Their shadow forms are still. Maya is crouched against the trunk, while Luis is looking down, paying attention to their every move.

The chief, the one they call Dum, is the only one left in the clearing. He's standing there, like a statue: legs firmly planted on the ground, head tilted on one side, waiting for his men to find us.

"Where is our prey, my brother?" hissing like a snake a bitter voice says suddenly.

"The boy with the fiery hair is no longer here," Dum replies, still immobile.

I feel Luis' shadow quickly turn toward me; I can't see his face, but it's not hard to picture his expression. All my secrets and mysteries have been revealed in the worst possible way.

"Don't worry, brother. Something tells me he's very close."

From the depths of the forest, another figure emerges, he's thin, way too thin to be a man. His yellowed skin is taut and stretched over the bones of his skeleton, his face is emaciated and hairless, giving it the ghostly appearance of a skull. Unlike the warriors, his skirt is long, and it reaches his ankles, and he's wearing shoulder straps decorated with crow feathers. Around his waist is a belt, from which small human bones hang. He also has a metallic collar around his neck. He reminds me of a shaman.

"They left all their belongings in a hurry, as if they sensed we were coming," the chief adds, gazing at the fronds of the trees. "But they couldn't have gone too far."

"Move," the shaman says. "Let the spirits reveal the path to us."

The Dum follows orders, while his brother starts rummaging through the fire, scattering ashes all over the camp.

"*Tanot*," he whispers, barely opening his mouth.

At that command the coals disintegrate, turning into small sparkling reels that, spin in a spiral magically revealing the footprints we've left on the ground. Incandescent tracks begin appearing like a map all over the clearing, showing exactly where we came from, where we sat, and even where we slept. The Dum walks back to the center with an evil grimace that makes the painted red skull on his face glow. He bends down to study the tracks, touching them with his fingertips.

"They came from over there. It was three of them. The boy, his female, and an old man who is guiding them."

He moves a few feet away, still crouching.

"There's a maju with them. A young one. Female."

"Is anybody injured?"

"No, they are moving slowly, but not because they are injured," he mutters, dusting off footprints. "They are exhausted. They have eaten and slept. The boy was right here," he explains, pointing to my blankets. "The female over there, and the old man was on guard duty, leaning against that trunk."

I see the Dum move on his knees toward the spot where Luis had been sitting. He rummages through the leaves, bringing his index finger and thumb under his nose and sniffs.

"Long leaf tobacco for pipe," he murmurs to his brother, the magician.

"Lusogham . . ."

"The old man woke them up. They gathered here and then ..."

"What?" the shaman asks to his perplexed brother.

"They disappeared!"

The magician laughs out loud, showing off his skull-like smile.

"Maybe they heard us coming and chose to use a trick to become invisible," he explains, still laughing.

"Can you do something to find them?"

"The spells and potions that give invisibility are many and varied. It would take me too long to find the right counter-spell."

I turn around and see the sack with the Grimoire and the potions that Luis managed to hide in a hole in the trunk behind us, right before he got up here. If the savages find it, they would surely be able to figure out which vial we used.

"So?" the Dum asks, slowly standing up.

"We'll outsmart them! It's not difficult to understand where they're heading."

"Careful, brother, the forest is full of faun patrol and one fight could . . ."

"Antédios promised me new powers," the shaman interrupts him, getting close to him. "Why can't you understand that?"

As soon as I hear the name of the demon, I see Luis' shadow quiver.

"Don't you already have enough? Look at what you've become," the Dum murmurs, standing still. "Your vows have changed you; your magic is consuming you. You are not who you used to be!"

"It's true. I am now much better than I used to be. I am much more powerful than any other kaptur that ever lived, and you know that my dear brother, because I am even stronger than you."

"Your soul is yours, brother."

"Yes, you are correct, it's mine. Now call your men back, oh great Dum. Let's get back to the caravan and move toward the East. We have got to catch them before anyone else."

I see the two of them going into the forest, disappearing in the dark. We remain quiet to observe the torches that are moving away, as the tracks illuminated by the sorcery start to fade away. I feel a tingly sensation in my feet, then my hands and my head; my body is regaining opacity. I turn to look at Maya, who is terrified. She has her arms around her bent legs and her face hidden between her knees.

Then, I see Luis who is beginning to appear as well. His face appears like a ceramic mask hanging into space, but his eyes are already scanning me.

"You and I have got to talk, Leonardo. Don't you think it's time you told me the truth?"

chapter twenty-seven

INVISIBLE CAGES

"I am the Akasha, the Keeper of the Sidhits." This is how I revealed myself, placing the shiny spheres in front of Maya and Luis. Both of them, for obvious reasons, almost dropped dead.

We spent the night hiding in the tree, just to be safe, impatiently waiting for dawn. Hours went by quickly, even with my interrogation. It wasn't easy confessing everything because, on one hand Luis kept asking me questions, while on the other hand Maya, just sat there wide-eyed with fear with every revelation.

I had to disclose everything; no detail untold, no more excuses to hide the truth. I had to be completely honest to regain their trust. As soon as I began spilling the beans, Luis started panicking. He couldn't put two words together and kept repeating the same words without making any sense: Sidhits, Keeper, Guardians, prophecy.

Then, the "Bombarding of Questions" phase began. He wanted to know *everything* about *everybody*, so I started from the very beginning. I told him about my dreams and drawings, the scribble on the wall, my fight with Crippa, and all the revelations made by Uncle Victor. Then, I moved on to the battle, the two Lokegir sorcerers and those dark warriors, the Dumongorths. I informed him about Antédios and how my mother and all the others sacrificed their lives for me.

Every time I mentioned my parents, my uncle, or the Guardians in general, I noticed Luis glow with reverence, as if I were talking about living legends. Finally, I began describing all the misadventures that Maya and I have been through in Midendhil. However, when I came clean about that whole thing with the mashuis and the abuclus, the atmosphere became really tense.

Luis mumbled something and then he started to call me a sgallux who, by what I could tell, must not be the brightest bulb in the box. He started talking about the end of the world, the rising of the dark, and the Armageddon; then, out of nowhere, he climbed all the way up to one of the highest branches, leaving us scared and full of questions.

Once I finished narrating my story, an uncomfortable silence fell over us all, interrupted only by Mela's snoring in her sleep. Maya is terrified as if in shock, and keeps her eyes closed. Luis is already smoking his pipe, usually only his evening ritual. He is aloof, thinking while puffing smoke like a chimney.

With my legs dangling and the sword pressed to my side, I think back on everything that's happened wondering whether I did the right thing by revealing everything. What would Mom and Dad have thought of all of this? Would they have approved?

"May I?" Maya asks suddenly, sitting next to me.

"Of course."

We remain quiet. I perceive her desire to talk to me, but she's disoriented and doesn't really know how to act. It's like having a stranger by my side who is not good at making small talk.

"After realizing what we've been through last night, I'm glad I was unconscious for so long," she whispers.

I sigh and force a smile.

"Your health has always been my main concern, and I couldn't let anything bad happen to you because of my fate."

Silence again. Her feet dangle in space, just like mine.

"It's not your fault."

"You're here because of me."

"No, I'm here because the other night I wanted to come to your house," she raises her voice, looking at me. "I thought a lot about what you told me in the restroom at school."

"What? Don't even think about that. It was a lifetime ago."

"No, please, hear me out."

"This is not the right time to talk about it, we have other things to . . ."

"Yes, Leo, this is the right time," she interrupts me. "We are here risking our lives every second. We are in an unknown world where there are monsters coming after us. Maybe we'll die tomorrow. But I need to know; do you really think you don't matter to me?"

I look down, staring at her feet, now still as if waiting for my answer to move.

"That thought has crossed my mind a few times."

Maya lifts my chin, turning my head toward her. A light breeze tousles her curls.

"A thousand boys like Simon wouldn't make up for one Leonardo," she gives me a sad smile. "You're not just a friend. You are my family . . . you are all I have."

Slowly, her face comes closer to mine. I feel dizzy and my stomach is in knots. What's going on? The closer she gets, the more I back away. What am I doing?

"I want to go home," she says, looking straight ahead. "This place is not for us. We don't belong here."

"I know," I agree, clearing my throat. "I promise that I'll do my best to make sure you go home safe and sound."

"Wait . . . you mean me, alone?"

"I have to stay. I have to find out who I am and where I'm from."

"You have to stay? Why?"

"I owe it to my parents."

Silence yet again.

"And what if something were to happen to you? Leonardo, I'm not going anywhere without you."

"Nothing is going to happen to me, I promise."

"Don't make promises you can't keep. If Luis hadn't woken us in time last night, who knows what would have happened."

"I know."

"You can't handle responsibilities that aren't yours, Leo. Nothing has changed; you are always the same boy, the one I grew up with and the one I care about. How can you possibly face all of this on your own?"

"I have a mission . . ."

"*Mission*? What are you talking about?" Her gaze wanders into space as she nervously bites her lower lip. "Do you remember when we were kids and we decided to save all those hunting dogs from the mayor?" she says suddenly.

"Yes."

"That jerk had them in cages that were so small they weren't even able to turn around."

"We should have told my father and alerted the shelter."

"Instead, we ended up taking care of all of them by ourselves."

"I still have the scar from when I jumped over the fence; I almost killed myself."

"Oh c'mon! You're always exaggerating!" she giggles, placing her head on my shoulder. "Do you remember how we managed to open those cages?"

"With a stone. I threw a stone at the lock. It took one time and it magically opened."

She moves with a jerk, staring at me. "Magically?"

"I didn't mean it like that . . ."

"And then? Remember what happened?" she asks me, snuggling next to me again.

"How can I forget? When we opened the cages, those dogs just stayed there; they were free, but they didn't even know it. They didn't move, as if still locked in cages, invisible ones."

Maya moves away from me, slowly. "How can you be sure that this time will be different? What if, once you save this world, after you've put your life at risk for its inhabitants, *they* don't understand that they are free?"

I look at her, not knowing what to say.

"This time, it's not about jumping over the fence. This time, we risk our lives for real."

Her truth gets under my skin, and it fills me up with doubts and fears.

"Do you think your parents would be happy to see you dead because of one of those monsters?"

"No . . . they didn't want for any of this to happen."

"Let's go home, Leo," she whispers, holding my hand. "Midendhil will find another hero to sacrifice."

"But, what if there's no other hero?"

"Then just do it for me. I need you by my side. We have a whole life waiting for us, but not here."

Suddenly, a coughing sound brings us back to reality. Luis sits down next to me, holding his pipe and letting his legs hang down like ours.

"I'm shocked, Leonardo."

"I'm sorry."

"No, you don't understand. I'm shocked in a good way. There are legends that talk about you, prophecies that announce your arrival; *you, whose mission will restore equilibrium in Midendhil.* The Akasha, the chosen one. It's an honor for me to be by your side, and I am ready to follow you till the end!"

I glance at Maya, who looks at me in silence, trying to refrain herself from giving us her two cents.

"But I'm not sure that . . ."

"I now understand why you healed so quickly," he interrupts as usual. "Her wrist, your back, it's because of the Sidhits!"

"What do you mean?"

"Haven't you realized what kind of energy you are the Keeper of? The Sidhits are the pure essence of the *power of life* and their magic is capable of true miracles. For example, regeneration."

"Miracles? You mean I could have saved my father?"

He looks down, twirling the pipe in his hands.

"We'll never know."

I grab my father's sword that is behind me. I extract it from the sheath, placing the blade on my knees and letting my fingers slide across its length.

"I should have never left him alone, Luis."

"Who knows, Leonardo, maybe not even the Sidhits would have been able to save him," he replies, trying to comfort me. "And you did it to look for Maya. Without you, the mencans would have killed her."

Behind me, Maya cries silently. She places her head on my back and hugs me tight. I caress her gently, in hopes of easing any of her feelings of guilt.

"I'm sorry, Leo."

"It's not your fault, I told you."

I hold my breath. I think back on what happened and curse fate. In that very moment, my father's sword begins to shrink, the blade gets narrower and the hilt changes shape, becoming more elegant. The runes engraved in the metal light up as if being written with fire.

"Incredible," Luis whispers.

"What's happening?" I ask, scared.

"Don't worry, everything's fine. Your father's sword is talking to you."

"Talking?"

"This is Uerabog," he explains, reading the runes on the blade. "One of the seven Viceroy's legendary swords that later became loyal to the Guardians of Midendhil. It's a magic weapon, alive. Its Yuth shines like ours and it merges with the Guardian who owns it . . . with yours, Leonardo; it recognized you as its new owner and it changed its shape to adapt to you."

I grab it by the hilt and feel a tremor through my chest. I keep it straight ahead of me and I let the light reflection bounce off the blade.

"See? Now it's smaller and lighter, made just for your arm."

I strike a couple of blows into space and let the blade rotate just like Uncle Victor taught me. Yes, it's true, the sword seems to have been made just for me; it's no longer a weapon, but the continuation of my arm.

"Very well then!" Luis exclaims, rubbing his hands. "Now that you are all decked out, we can finally stop hiding in bushes and face our enemies head on!"

"Who were those savages last night?" Maya asks, popping up from behind my shoulder.

"Kapturs, a tribe of slave merchants. Bad people who are best to avoid, evil men who the fauns had managed to kick out of the forest a long time ago."

"Did you say men?" I ask puzzled, stopping the sword midair. "There are men here in Midendhil? I mean, people like us?"

"Well of course," Luis replies quite nonchalantly. "Humans were the chosen people of these lands. The Great King was a man, chosen by the four Elohims that created the world of Midendhil. The seven Viceroy were too, just like their entire ancestry."

"And now? They've all turned into kapturs?"

"No, not all of them. After the death of the Great King, their realm was destroyed, and its people dispersed."

"Dispersed?"

"Unfortunately, I don't know much about it. These are old legends, myths almost completely forgotten."

"It doesn't matter, just tell me what you know."

"Alright, let's see . . . do you remember that big statue where we first met?"

"Yes, the broken one."

"Yep, that's an example of what is left of the Great Realm. The equilibrium of the power of life was crushed during the Vahala era: the Shattering. When the Great King was killed and the Mogonis Stone broken, buildings and entire cities were destroyed, and they crumbled just like that," he tells me, snapping his fingers right in front of my eyes. "In one night."

"What about the other people, those ones who didn't become kapturs? Where are they?"

"Why do you want to know?"

"Because I need to know who I am and who my birth parents are."

Luis wets his lips, as if now conscious of being in a situation bigger than himself.

"Well, many of them died that same night, but legend has it that some of them saved themselves by crossing the seas, while others crossed mountains. However, most of them actually live in the ancient *Asardhil City,* capital of Midendhil. It's where the *Saudha,* the *Palace of a Thousand Statues,* residence of the Great King, was erected. To this day, there are songs that recount its splendor."

"But you just said that, after the Great King died, everything was destroyed."

"Yes, it's true. If the rumors are true, these people must live in a nightmare, hiding in ruins that rise on the banks of what once was a blue lake, but that now is just a big swamp. They call it *Nifleum,* the swamp of the dead. Dark magic dominates those places, and throughout Midendhil, this is the only place I recommend you never go."

"Why are these people there?"

"They're waiting. They're waiting for hope, a new Great King that could bring the reign of Midendhil back to its ancient splendor. Somebody who could find a remedy to the Vahala."

"Do you think that *somebody* could be me?"

"Well, maybe yes," he admits, shrugging.

"Do you know where to find the Nayaka?"

"The star of the Tower of the Guardians? No, I haven't got a clue. It's a secret place."

"So, Leo, you've made up your mind?" Maya intervenes, worried. "Everything I told you earlier means nothing to you? You want to stay here?"

Luis looks at me perplexed, trying to guess my thoughts.

"I need a bit more time, Maya."

She pauses for a moment, deep in thought; then, she nods slowly, perhaps comprehending that the choice I have to make is not necessarily the easiest one.

"Right, take your time," Luis says. "However, first we have to camouflage ourselves. Whatever your decision may be, Leonardo, we can't keep wandering through the forest like this; your hair attracts too much attention."

"And what am I supposed to do?"

"Let me look through the potions we brought. I should have something that we can use," he says, rummaging through the sack on the trunk. "Alright, let's see: *Dyate, Lugunox, Fairyskiny, Pititus, Greenhands.* Here we go. This is what we need," he concludes, throwing me a small ampoule.

"*Popface* . . . what's that?"

"It's a transfiguring potion that will change your appearance just enough for what we need."

"Mine too?" Maya tenses up.

"They're looking for a boy with red hair and a damsel with golden skin. We have got to cover our tracks."

"Is it safe?" she questions him.

"It's something I invented; you'll see what a marvel it is."

"What if we just used our hoodies?" I propose.

"Hurry! Drink up, we have to find another option for our clothes too," he says, pointing to the blankets left by the tree.

As always, I am the first one to test the beverage. I hold my breath and take a sip of that weird potion: it's a thick liquid that tastes so bitter it makes my face cringe.

"How is it?" Maya asks.

"No comment."

She drinks it too, then squints her eyes as if licking a lemon wedge.

"Alright guys let's get off the tree and start preparing to leave," Luis urges us, jumping off with Mela. As I descend the trunk, a series of shivers go through my head like electric shocks.

"Luis, are you sure that the thing you had us drink isn't dangerous?"

The wizard turns back with a smile so big it shows all his teeth.

"Relax! Look at that . . . it's already working."

I touch my head: my hair is soft, long, and combed behind my ears. I look up toward Maya who, with her skin as white as milk, is caressing her straight hair, which is a luminescent purple now.

"Do you see this?" she tries to refrain from smiling, showing off a tuft of hair. "My hair is purple . . . and straight!"

"Come on, Maya! We gotta go!" Luis calls her. "The kapturs may be gone, but I'd like to avoid ending up in the hands of some other ugly beast."

Maya, fearlessly, lets herself fall into my arms. I catch her with ease, and I realize I've become much stronger too.

"You're so handsome, Leo! You're all tan and with that white hair you look so dashing."

"White?" I exclaim with my hands in my hair. "What do you mean, white?"

"Well, you know, I don't have much say on the color of the hair," Luis warns us.

"But we'll get back to our normal looks, right?"

"Sure," he reassures me, patting me on the back. "Maybe . . . well, I hope."

"Whatever, Leo. You look so cool!" Maya says.

What? She said *cool*? Did I hear that right? I remain there, dazed, staring at her, while she runs her fingers through her hair.

"Alright guys, let's take care of the clothes."

In a jiffy, Luis, with his sharp athame, makes two perfect ponchos out of the woolen blanket that we quickly throw on, and cinch a piece of cord around our waists. After having a bit of trouble, I succeed in hanging the sheath of the sword on my new belt. We gather all the sacks emptied by the kapturs, we drink from the only bottle they left us, and finally, we start walking toward the Ialon village.

The more I think about it, the more confused I feel. I've got nothing; I can't decide. Should I stay or should I go? I'm sad, full of doubts and conscious that, no matter what happens, I won't be able to keep my promise. My heart is telling me to follow my destiny, my parents' desire, and to fulfill my mission. But my good sense is telling me to listen to Maya, be with her, don't abandon her and go back home with her.

Yes, *home* . . . a place that I no longer know how to define.

chapter twenty-eight

THE IALON VILLAGE

"How far is the village, Luis? I'm exhausted and this poncho is so itchy it's driving me insane," Maya complains while riding Mela.

"We're almost there, guys. We should be very close."

"Should be?" I repeat, tired. "Do you mean we're lost?"

"No, no . . . not at all," he mumbles, analyzing the bark of a few trees. "See? There isn't any moss here."

"So?"

"We made it!" he twirls his staff and points to a couple of trees not too far from us.

"Luis, I don't see anything."

"Well of course you don't . . . *Eburos Velo!*"

On that command the space between the two plants Luis pointed at loses depth and looks two dimensional like a photo glued to a wall, but it's actually a doorway. Right in front of our stunned eyes, the two doors into a magical passage open, revealing a path that gives entrance into a wonderful, lively village.

"So, what do you think?" Luis winks. "Not bad, huh?"

Maya gets off Mela and comes close to me, her fingers almost touching mine.

"Welcome to Ialon!" Luis exults, walking down the path.

We follow him with our mouths wide open, walking under a stone arc decorated with jasmines in bloom, and heading down a street that goes straight to the center of the village. Turrets, domes, wooden windmills, and brick houses one after the other, mingling with the trunks of the trees and climbing plants sprouting from everywhere. The road is narrow and crowded with old men wearing pointy hats, all engaged in preparations of what seems to be a big celebration. Green, red, and silver banners hang out windows and balconies, while wreaths of woven holly decorate the front door of each house. A few lusoghams, climbing on giant beanstalks, are putting on the finishing touches to golden garlands and strings of lanterns that adorn the roofs. Meanwhile, a group of sprites with horse-like mouths, is busy embellishing the tops of pine trees, which line the path, with yellow candles and golden bells.

Outside each house there are rows of wooden tables where some lusogham women are comfortably sitting as they intertwine colorful ribbons and embroidered flags and handkerchiefs. A few more are humming in the kitchens, busy preparing donuts, pies, and pastries that, once cooked, they place on the windowsills to cool down, releasing delicious aromas along the street.

"How come there's so much going on here?"

"They are getting ready for the Yule Festival," Luis replies. "It's one of the most important celebrations of the lusogham year. Remember? I told you about it."

"Yes, I remember. Is it tonight?"

"*Hmm-hmm*," he nods. "Come this way."

We walk down to what appears to be the central square of Ialon. Right in the middle, there is an extremely tall tree, which reminds me of the weeping willow we saw in the woods, and it is surrounded by a labyrinth of street vendors. Even though the celebrations have yet to begin, merchants are already busy attracting curious customers who have made their way through the pavilions. We hear them calling out their wares: "Orc warts for sale, free callus gum with every purchase," "Mandrake syrup to laugh and transform your friends into werewolves," and "Sweetfire bubbles to make you burp like a real dragon!"

I have to say there is just about everything imaginable in these stalls: from crystal balls to cauldrons full of ingredients for potions, from ampoules of magic extracts to self-cleaning bewitched clothing, watches telling everything but time, thief-biting shrines, and even a cart of arcàntodam—those enchanted mirrors. There are many surprises among the vendors, too. In fact, in addition to lusoghams, I see witches and wizards with very eccentric clothes, bearded gnomes, scarfaced sailors, ape-like men covered in bushy brown hair, a seven-foot-tall cyclops with a squishy nose and light blue skin. From what I can tell, this celebration is not just a tradition of Ialon, but also a good trading opportunity for other villages in Midendhil.

Not too far ahead of us, in a big colorful pavilion comes a commotion of *chirps* and *barks*, I see a big man with a very hairy body trying to tidy up among the sea of cages that surrounds him. It doesn't seem to be that easy though, especially because in each cage there's a magical animal that is moving and making noises like crazy. There truly is something for every taste: golden parrots that sing opera, purple and yellow iguanas that spit fire balls, little blue owls wrapped in rain clouds, and even green carrion crows whose backs are full of pink primulas.

"Those are *green phoenix* from Ceinok, the wooded barrier of the west," Luis tells me pointing at them. "It's thanks to their pollen, which is also used by fairies, that we are able to make invisibility potions, including Hìdevirum."

"What about those?" I ask, nodding at the little blue owls.

"They are *bretnos* from the Brumen Plains. Very fascinating birds capable of causing rain even in the desert. A while ago, I had the brilliant idea of keeping one of them at home with me, and well, I'll just say that I lived with water up to my knees!"

I smile as I glance at a big glass tub, illuminated by a few shiny crystals that pulsate at the bottom. Small octopi, who gleam in the light, are swimming and playing with tiny paper boats, making them sink as they sail through the waters.

"These are so cute."

312 Davide Simon Mazzoli

"Aquarium *Krakens*. I love this type of animal, but they require constant care because they eat at least thirty times a day," Luis explains, knocking on the glass tub.

A squeaking sound catches my attention. I look up and see small foxes hanging upside down by their tails, from a tall pole; they are similar to the white and blue ones I saw at Luis's Animagorium. There are about five specimens and each one with fur of a different color: yellow, orange, purple, pink, and blue.

"*Sgallux*," Luis whispers. "The stupidest animal there is."

"Why? They seem so adorable."

"Yes, they are adorable, but try to get one and you'll see what a mess they are. They crawl everywhere and chew on everything. The one I had pretty much destroyed everything I had, including a brick sink."

"Leonardo! Come see this!" says Maya, crouched by a cart emitting an abrasive melody from an old gramophone which is full of flowers and plants. "Look how wonderful!"

On the small table in front of her, placed among a series of stone cacti and big fluorescent green mushrooms, there are flowers that dance to the rhythm while releasing small puffs of perfume.

"Do you like them? Would you like a *dancing anemone*?" asks a female gnome, not much taller than a child, with goat-like ears and her hair wrapped in a bun. "Here at Old Megan's, you can find any type of magical plant. Would you like a carnivore sarracenia? They are amazing. They can bite a troll's finger right off."

"No, ma'am, thank you. We are just having a look around."

"Are you sure? What about a *love water lily*?" she asks, showing us a box full of rings made from intertwined twigs with starflowers on top instead of stones. "I picked them by the Arar, the Apsaras River; they don't fade, deteriorate, or lose their smell. What better way to celebrate the union of a lovely couple like you two?"

"Oh no," I smile, embarrassed. "We're not . . ."

"Would you please put the two white rings aside?" Maya interrupts me. "We'll stop by later to pick them up, when the celebration begins."

"Certainly," the gnome replies enthusiastically.

I turn toward Maya, with a smile that hides a thousand questions.

"What?" she asks, acting surprised. "We are incognito, Leo. We have to pretend to be someone we are not, until you decide what you want to do."

"Right . . ."

"Where's Luis?"

"Over there," I answer, pointing to a stall not far from us.

We walk up behind him, but he doesn't see us coming; he's too busy bargaining with a sailor who looks like a pirate. His cart reeks of fresh fish and on the table between them there is a long row of vases and glass cylinders filled with sludge and colorful liquids that move as if they were alive.

"Oh, there you are!" Luis welcomes us with a huge smile. "Here, this is for you," he tells me, placing a small sachet full of silver coins in my hand.

"Why?"

"I sold the sludgy I picked up and given the horrible experience you had with that thing; I want you to have the money."

"Thank you very much, but I can't possibly accept it."

"Nonsense, I insist. This way you can at least buy yourself some decent clothes. What do you think, Maya?"

"I think it's not a bad idea! We accept and we thank you, Luis," she giggles, grabbing the sachet from my hands.

"Alright then, it's a deal. Now come with me, I want to show you something."

We walk through the maze of street vendors, and arrive in the middle of the square, where there is that giant tree, the symbol of Ialon. It is even more majestic up close.

"This is *Jólnir,* father of all the other plants in the Nemeton Forest. This is the real hero of the Yule Festival. This is who we actually celebrate."

My eyes get lost on its height. The trunk is huge, and it is at least thirty feet tall, opening like an umbrella of yellowed fronds that, with each gush of wind, rain leaves all over the market. Millions of bluebells emerge from each branch, but they are withered and a faded blue color.

"Luis! What are you doing here?"

We find ourselves face to face with a chubby lusogham, who has a neatly groomed mustache and a curly goatee.

"Good morning, Egort," Luis snorts. "I was actually looking for you."

"Why did you leave your post? You know your orders and the Counsel wants you to . . ."

"I have to speak with Druir."

"Druir is too busy, and whatever it is that you have to tell him, you can simply talk to me about it. After all, I am his counselor and his successor, so feel free to speak to me."

Judging by Luis's contrite expression and Egort's arrogant attitude, I assume that the two of them don't really get along.

"The other night, my friends and I were attacked by a couple of abuclus and their wyverns. They destroyed my house and stole a maretak branch."

I notice that Egort turns pale like the moon. Luis goes on with his story satisfied by his acquaintance's concern.

"Last night we almost ended up in the hands of a kaptur tribe. There was a shaman among them. Plus, rumor has it there is a pack of mashuis in the forest."

"What about the other *thing*? . . ."

"Don't worry," Luis reassured him. "It's safe."

I immediately wonder about what it is they are referring to. Meanwhile, Egort nervously wets his lips attempting to regain his pompous posture.

"Well . . . I'll try to set up a meeting with Druir. Maybe after the festival, but I can't promise anything. Anyway, who are these two?" I see his squinty eyes study us from head to toe, until they stop and stare at the sword I keep on my side. "I don't think I've ever seen them around Ialon."

"Let me introduce you to Cadell and Mary, a couple of friends from a human village overseas."

"Interesting," Egort *hisses* with a snooty attitude. "May I ask precisely which village you're from?"

"Egort," Luis intervenes, "they've been travelling for a month, and as I just told you, these past few days haven't necessarily been easy on us. Please, let them be."

"Very well then."

"Instead, if you don't mind, I'd like for you to show them how welcoming lusoghams are and show my dear friends around the village."

"What about you?"

"I shall seek an audience with Druir."

"But I already told you that . . ."

"Let me take care of it, Egort. I was already with him when you were just a bud under a cabbage head."

"Fine," he replies with a fake smile. "What about that thing? Does it have to be with us?"

"No, don't worry. Mela will come with me."

"OK," he squeaks turning his back on us. "Lady and Gentleman, follow me."

Within a second, I find myself having to run after Egort as if somebody was coming after us. He is the worst guide in the whole wide world: arrogant and makes us feel guilty for every minute he has to spend with us. The situation is quite embarrassing, and I wonder why Luis has left us with this guy. Instead, Maya seems to be perfectly at ease. She stays in the back, stopping by every vendor in search of something to buy.

"Look, Le . . . Cadell! Look how wonderful!" she exclaims, pulling me to a green pavilion with clothes hanging outside.

A skinny witch, all decked out in a flamingo pink outfit, invites us in.

"Come on in, worthy friends. Here at Guya's you'll find exactly what you are looking for."

"What do you think, Cadell? I'm sure we'll find something nice to wear for tonight."

I look at Egort and I see him snorting as he adjusts his pointy hat, which is way too small for his big head.

"I'll wait for you right here," he whines, sitting on a nearby barrel. "Be quick, though."

Maya pushes me into the pavilion, following the owner who paves the way through veils and fabrics. The inside is huge, probably an illusion of a spell, and it's full of shelves that overflow with garments, shoes, tiaras, jewelry, scepters, and magic accessories of every kind. On each corner, there are ladders that roll between shelves as if hooked to invisible tracks, and large chandeliers hanging from the ceiling, giving the room a soft ambience.

In the blink of an eye, Maya overwhelms me with sweater vests, jackets, and woolen britches, and pushes me behind a curtain that is supposed to be a fitting room.

"Try them on!"

"Everything?" I ask uncertainly.

However, my question goes unanswered, as if I hadn't even spoken.

"I'd like to try this, this, and this one too," Maya chirps without letting go of the witch who is hopping up and down the stairs, with her stork-like skinny legs.

"This one as well, dear?" she asks, trying to remain steady on top of a wobbly shelf, as she shows her an amethyst-colored dress.

"Of course! It's so gorgeous . . ."

"Sorry, Ma . . . ry, but what am I supposed to do with all this stuff?" I ask her again.

"Try them on! C'mon, you wouldn't want to walk around with me in that horrible poncho, would you?" she replies coyly before disappearing into her dressing room.

I begin undressing and trying on random clothes. The britches are too constricted, and the jackets are a bit itchy. I put on a shirt and a green jerkin that goes all the way down to my knees. I tighten it up around my waist with a leather belt, on which I hang the sheath of Uerabog, my dad's sword. I feel the Sidhits vibrating in the sachet, and I place them in the jacket's pocket, well hidden.

I glance at my magical reflection in the magic silver mirror, noticing that I'm not too bad after all. "*I've seen better, but you are not that bad,*" it comments.

As soon as I step out of the fitting room, I am grabbed by the expert hands of the witch who, with a few gestures, straightens up the vest and a few wrinkles that puff up my side.

"Here you go! Now you are truly perfect," she exclaims.

"Mary, how's it going?" I ask her while putting my sweatshirt, jeans, and poncho in the sack that the kapturs emptied out.

"Almost done, I'm trying on the last one."

I look up and almost have a heart attack. She appears right in front of my eyes wearing the purple gown that gracefully falls to her ankles but tight around her waist with an entwined leather strap that hangs from the side. The color of the fabric matches her hair perfectly, making her look as beautiful as a fairy.

"So? What do you think?"

"Splendid," the witch replies, giggling at my dopey expression. "It fits you like a glove!"

"Yes, it's true," Maya agrees, looking at herself in the mirror. "And I also think that my . . . boyfriend looks ever so dreamy."

Boyfriend? That word gives me the heebie-jeebies. I know Maya is just pretending, but I feel that, for the first time, something is changing between us.

We finally get out of that pavilion after half an hour. Egort keeps huffing and puffing while he drags us along for the rest of the morning.

Luis is still nowhere to be found, and given how hungry we are, we decide to grab a bite to eat at the *Wet Troll* tavern, the best inn of the village. The atmosphere is welcoming and homey, and right in the middle of the room, among the wooden tables, there is a fountain with a giant troll statue. The monster has a cast iron bath on its head which creates a waterfall flowing all around.

The innkeeper greets us with three mugs filled with fresh BidiBubble, and good ole lusogham granny she is, starts feeding us the most exquisite treats of the day. On our table, she places all sorts of cured meat, pork chops in apple sauce, roast chicken with mashed potatoes, stuffed vegetables, and grilled cheese. As we dig into all the goodness, I spot two weird creatures staring at us with their big blue eyes and eavesdropping on our conversations. Perhaps they hope I don't notice them, but I, always on the lookout, see them immediately.

"You were really hungry, huh?" Egort asks.

"Yes, it had been a while since we had a decent meal," Maya replies, enjoying the last sip of BidiBubble.

"You had a long trip, didn't you? Where exactly are you from?"

"New York," I say quickly.

I see Maya trying to hide her big smile behind the mug, while Egort stares at the ceiling beams, as if trying to recall something.

"New York? Yes, maybe I've been there."

Once we are done with our lunch, we continue our tour along the streets of Ialon: we visit the big lusogham library, the observatory, the nursery of magical herbs, and a breeding of bodulas, the creatures Luis had often mentioned. The place is run by a lusogham named Fern who, without much ado, shows us the stables and the farm pastures. At first glance, the bodulas seem like quiet pachyderms with small horns and funny trunks, but then, taking a closer look, I notice that these creatures are actually more similar to plants than animals. Egort explains that their body is made of wood and that the lusogham use the sprouts that grow on their backs to make ointments and soothing potions, which they sell with great success.

We continue our journey all the way to the village borders, where there are what the lusoghams call the *birthing fields* and the *sleep gardens*: two truly incredible places that show me an interpretation of existence I didn't think possible.

The lusoghams' concept of life and death is not like that of other creatures'; to them, birth doesn't necessarily mean the beginning of life, and death doesn't mean the end. The thing is, lusoghams are born under cabbage heads, looking like multi-centenarians, whose features they keep for the rest of their existence. The birthing fields are well-kept places, which are constantly watered by a lusogham élite, thus keeping the soil soft and fresh all year round.

The sleep gardens, on the other hand, are what humans call cemeteries. However, you won't find tombstones or caskets, just lots and lots of trees, resembling the woods. Egort tells us that when lusoghams feel they have reached the end of their path, they retire in these gardens, sit on the ground and slowly turn into trees, choosing to live their lives in a different shape. To them, existence is a round cycle that keeps repeating itself, ascending their knowledge and the enlightenment of their Yuth.

Fascinating to say the least, even though being so close to creatures that are so far from my way of interpreting *life* makes me feel a bit light-headed.

"How elegant!" Luis reaches us, riding Mela. "Mary, you look stunning!"

"Thank you, Luis," Maya blushes, twirling around.

"About time!" Egort exclaims. "I thought you forgot about your friends. What did Druir say?"

"Ask him, he's waiting for you."

"Very well, then I have no time to waste," he rebuts before turning around and leaving without even saying goodbye.

"He's truly something," Maya murmurs staring at him as he walks away.

"Something tells me he doesn't find us amusing."

"Don't worry, Maya. Egort is always like that. Anyway, did you enjoy the village?"

"It's amazing, Luis," I interject and refocus the conversation. "What did Druir tell you regarding what's going on?"

"He listened to me and now he needs time to reflect . . ."

"What about us? Did you tell him about us?"

"One thing at a time, my boy. Druir is very old, I couldn't just shower him with questions. Did you already have lunch?"

"Yep, we're all set," I reply, not trying to hide my anxiety.

"Did you go visit Duadus?"

"Duadus? What's that?"

"He's the most famous Samaya elf in all Midendhil: creator of BidiBubble, SugarPot, and even Panaka."

I look at Maya; she's frowning and biting her thumb cuticles as she always does when she's nervous.

"Relax, guys. Everything will be fine, you'll see, we're safe here . . ."

chapter twenty-nine

DUADULAND

We follow Luis through small roads, until we get back to the central square. The Yule Festival has begun, and every pavilion is crowded with strange creatures, all busy with their shopping sprees. Distracted by everything going on around us, Maya and I end up knocking our heads against something incredibly hard: a giant man who is busy carrying a cage full of golden parrots.

"We beg your pardon," I say, massaging my forehead, but he doesn't seem to notice our presence.

He is really big, his skin is made of compact stone, and he is wearing so many jewels that he can hardly move. Suddenly, Anthony pops up in my mind and a melancholy smile crosses my lips.

"That was quite the knock, you guys! Are you OK?" Luis asks us.

"Yes, but where did that mountain of a man come from?" Maya inquires, following him with her eyes.

"He's a mellon, a stone giant from the Celicnon city."

"Why is he wearing so much jewelry?"

"Mellons believe that the vital essence of every creature resides on the exterior," he explains as we keep walking through the crowd. "They get all decked out with as many jewels as possible because they are convinced it will make them become better than what they are. However, truth is they are just a bunch of cuckoos."

"I knew one of them," I say, having a hard time keeping up with them. "He was a dear friend of mine, and he was anything but a cuckoo."

Luis stops quickly and stares at me.

"Guardians. You're talking about the Guardians, aren't you?" he murmurs. "I imagine there was a mellon among them."

"He was one of my best friends."

At that moment, we realize we are standing between two giant bellies of huge animals that almost crush us. I hear Maya scream and Mela becomes agitated.

"Hey, watch it!" Luis yells, hitting one of them on the back with his staff. "Couldn't you just keep your human form? I don't think it's a good idea going around the fair looking like this!"

The two beasts turn toward us, showing us their stocky and horned muzzles, similar to a rhinoceros.

"Sorry," they reply deeply in unison, and within a second, they turn into two chubby twins wrapped in gray leather cloaks and walk away blending in with the rest of the crowd.

"Unbelievable," Luis mumbles. "We're already walking all squished as it is, and these giant beasts just make it worse!"

"What were they?" Maya asks, her eyes wide open.

"Berseker warriors," I reply, leaving both of them speechless. "My father was one of them."

We finally arrive at the legendary Duadus, happy to see that it's not just one pavilion, but a whole section of the fair dedicated to yummy sweets. An arch made of giant sugary chopsticks supports the enchanted sign reading "*Duaduland*," with the puffy and happy animated face of an old elf inviting people to stop by and listing all the treats they sell.

"This way, you won't believe your eyes," Luis calls us, while Mela trots along.

The place is a rainbow of colors. Kiosks, so big they resemble actual buildings, are flooded with sweets and treats and scattered all around the arena.

I walk through the masses and all the way to the center stage, where Duadus himself, helped by a group of young and beautiful elves, is presenting the new and yummy *Wize-o Jello*. A banner placed above his head announces: *Jelly made* with *Jólnir tree's chlorophyll, will make you incredibly wise.* A small clause underneath warns that its effects will vanish once swallowed.

Moving on, I notice a cauldron-shaped pavilion where there are at least a hundred SugarPots, divided by types of ingredients. Another stand is showcasing a series of glass vases that are six feet tall, full of weird candies like *SweetFire Bubbles, Lemon Bombs, Violet-flavored Sugary Nails,* and *SmashingTeeth Dragées,* the latter which I guess are made of actual stone. Obviously, there is an entire area dedicated to the BidiBubble, Duadus's flagship, where elves offer a glass of the beverage to every bystander.

"Let's go to *Chocoduadus!*" Luis proposes, trying to hold back Mela who, starving as always, sniffs around eating everything off the floor.

"What is it?"

"It's the area devoted to chocolate. I'd like to get a bit of *Crunchy Granoly* and a Panaka bar."

"There are Panaka bars?"

"Of course! I told you, Duadus is the king of treats, and you can always find everything he makes."

"What's Panaka?" Maya asks out of curiosity.

"It's . . ."

"Don't tell her," Luis stops me. "I don't want to ruin the surprise."

We manage to cross the flood of wizards and creatures who keep cheering with BidiBubble, then we pass by the magical carousels area, near a group of boys who are having a burp-a-thon with SweetFire flames, and we finally arrive at Chocoduadus.

Here, the air is filled with sweet cocoa smell and there is one huge pavilion full of sequins with a big chocolate fountain at the entrance. On the inside, there is a stand where shelves are overflowing with bars and treats of every kind.

"Here you go," Luis says, offering Maya a chocolate bar. "This is Panaka."

Maya holds the bar, which sparkles as if embellished with golden specks. After the first bite, I see her face delighting under its magic spell.

"Would you like to try the new Animachocos?" a short elf asks us, handing us a tray full of chocolates shaped as magical Heraldry animals.

"What are they?" Luis asks, biting on a ram with curly horns.

"They are chocolates with an enchanted filling," the elf explains. "Each one of them has a different flavor and gift."

"Gift?" I ask, picking up a bee.

"Yes, the bee, for example, has a honey filling that releases energy and diligence, while the eagle has an orange and cinnamon filling, and it gifts you with better sight."

"What about the owl?" Maya asks, her eyes gleaming with curiosity.

"It tastes like violets and gives clairvoyance."

"Mine!" she exclaims, picking it up.

"Sorry, what about the ram?" Luis inquires, happily chewing on his chocolate.

"It's nut-flavored and it helps with growth."

"Growth of what?"

With a grimace, the elf looks at Luis's beard that is becoming longer by the second.

"Oh boy! Of all the flavors, I had to pick the silliest one," he complains, making us all laugh out loud.

I pop my honey-filled bee in my mouth, and as soon as I begin tasting it, I feel a strange energy within me, as well as an unstoppable desire to tidy up. I look around trying to suppress this urge, and I spot the two creatures we saw at the tavern, who are a few feet away, staring at us.

"Do you need anything?" I ask bothered, catching my friends' attention.

"Do you like those treats?" one of them comes toward me, walking on long skinny legs.

"What?"

"May we buy you some to ask for your forgiveness?" the other one asks.

"Of course, you can," Luis quickly replies, stepping between us. "Three boxes should do it."

"What do I have to forgive you for?"

They don't answer me, and without adding anything else, they bend over toward the elf with a few silver coins. I see they are not familiar with money, trying to touch it as little as possible, as if repulsed by it.

"They want us to forgive them for spying on us during lunch," Maya whispers.

"And how do you know about that? You didn't even notice them."

"I think it's the effect of the chocolate," she smiles, wrinkling her nose. "Clairvoyance, right?"

I look back at the two creatures: they are tall, very tall, with pale wrinkly skin and green stripes on their backs. They have short and matted mohawks, big blue eyes, and a monkey-like face with a pointy goatee. They don't have much on; they are basically just wearing a miniskirt that leaves their thighs uncovered, a belt, and big necklaces with rough stones. On their backs, they carry a wooden bow as big as I am and a quiver full of red-feathered arrows.

With a lively smile, they hand me the chocolate boxes, stretching out their arms and bowing their heads. I happily accept their gift, even though I feel slightly embarrassed. Who are these guys? What do they want?

"You might be asking yourselves who we are," one of them tells me, noticing my perplexed expression.

"Exactly," I reply.

"We are *vaneyaras*, from the Isara River tribe. My name is Kubra, and he's my brother Suma. We wanted to apologize for earlier, for bothering you during lunch."

I feel Maya touching me with her toes.

"We know you saw us, but we just couldn't help staring at you. Your Yuth is so bright, and we had never seen a human shine like that before. Where are you from?"

Luis places his hands on our shoulders, and in a very fatherly way, he pulls us closer to him, making us almost lose our balance.

"They are dear friends of mine. They come from New York, a small overseas village."

"New York? Never heard of it before. What brought you here to the Ialon village?"

"Leisure," Luis answers on our behalf. "They are here for the Yule Festival and to taste Duadus' treats."

"How come . . ."

"Now, if you don't mind, we should go get ready for the celebration," he interrupts them quickly.

"Of course," Kubra nods. "May our Yuth enlighten your path."

We mimic the Midendhil salute, and without ever looking back, we walk away quickly, blending in the crowd.

"Who were those two?" Maya asks, puzzled.

"We call them children of the forest. They are kind giants, protectors of the trees, but they can come across as being too nosy. They mean well, but they just don't know when to be quiet and mind their own business."

Walking around, I notice that the village is now full of those tall ancient creatures.

"What do we do now? Should we go see Druir?" Maya asks.

"Relax, Maya. The celebration is about to begin. Let's go drink something at the *Wet Troll* tavern and wait for dinner time."

chapter thirty

THE YULE FESTIVAL

At dusk, every street and square of the village takes on an even more magical ambience, illuminated only by lanterns and candles that decorate the tree canopies.

The fair is enveloped by a perfectly festive atmosphere, and the masses crowd the market roads. A few lusoghams begin placing long wooden tables around the Jólnir tree, positioning them in four large concentric circles. The flower fairies hang lamps and clove-decorated oranges on the tallest tree branches, while in the square, next to the *Wet Troll* tavern, a platoon of chefs is busy erecting a big kitchen, with wood-fired ovens and running water. Not far ahead, gnomes, led by Fern, the grumpy bodula farmer, have set up the dance floor with a stage for the orchestra. Lusogham ladies appear from every corner of the village, and without wasting any time, begin to set the tables with embroidered linens, placing earthenware pots, silverware, and a big mug for each person.

Since leaving Chocoduadus, Luis has remained sitting comfortably at the *Wet Troll* tavern, smoking his pipe and chitchatting with anyone who happens to walk by close enough. Maya and I, instead, have been strolling around the fair, taking it all in but, unfortunately, we haven't managed to find Megan's pavilion, the kind gnome who set aside those two rings for us. Exhausted, after more than an hour of walking, we give up. We pass by two witches who are arguing over a set of *self-stirring cups* and a *dancing sugar bowl*, when a loud bell resounds across the square, piercing my eardrums.

People around us quickly drop what they are doing and run toward the tables. Merchants put away all their belongings and close-up shop, blending in with the crowd going toward the Jòlnir.

"Come on, guys!" Luis shouts out of nowhere. "Let's go, I have reserved the best seats."

We follow him and slide along the flood of people until we get to our table. Two benches farther, I spot a wooden throne with an inlaid backrest. As people take their seats, sprites with horse-like muzzles bring fresh water jugs, iced BidiBubble, wheat beer, wine, and some other weird beverage.

"Who are they?" Maya asks Luis, pointing at the waiters.

"They are *dukkos*, sprites who live in symbiosis with lu-soghams. They're kind of like our assistants."

Chubby lusogham grannies, wearing flowery aprons and lace hairnets, start coming out of the kitchens, placing baskets of freshly baked bread, flat bread, crackers, and many more delicacies on the tables.

"Here you go, dear, start eating something," one of them tells me, pinching my cheek.

I fill up our mugs with BidiBubble and begin munching on a couple pieces of toast that have been fried in butter. We've been eating all day long, but I have to say it's hard to resist all these yummy goodies. I spot Maya throwing a couple of pieces of bread on the ground for Mela. For a moment, I'm lost in admiring her profile, wondering what in the world we are doing here. Only a few days ago, we were stuck behind our desks in school, and now?

"Cheers, my friends," Luis says.

"Luis! What are you doing here?"

Sitting across from us is a woman with yellow eyes and dark hair, dressed in a scarlet multi-layered flowy dress.

"Gwen! How are you?"

"I'm great! I wasn't expecting to see you here at the Yule Festival."

"Me neither, let's just say it was an unplanned trip. Let me introduce you to my friends. This is Cadell and . . . his wife . . . Mary."

"I'm Gwen." She shakes our hands, bending over the table.

"She's my friend from Lokegir I told you about, master of preparing illusions and potions," Luis explains.

"You're always too kind," she thanks him.

"Are you alone? Where's Daron?"

"He's around here somewhere with our son Gyln; he's helping him sell the *gulons* he caught a few days ago," she tells us, sipping on her drink. "Don't get me started on the trip we ended up having because of them. Those creatures are horrible."

"What are gulons?" I quietly ask Luis.

"They are some kind of soulless, nasty dogs that infest the Selga Woods. Truly unbelievable."

Maya and Gwen immediately click, chitchatting as if they were long-time friends. Gwen gives her a sachet of curious potions, including a magical nail polish that changes color according to the mood of the person who wears it. Soon, Daron and their son join us, and after brief introductions, they sit down and pour more BidiBubble for everyone. Daron is a wizard, tall and bulky, with a huge Viking-like mustache, while Gyln is a skinny boy, and younger than me. He doesn't talk much, and has his mother's honey-colored eyes, but his father's serious gaze.

It's incredible how, even here in Midendhil, I don't seem to fit in any conversation. I am the Last Keeper, the Akasha, yet I am still same old me: shy and awkward. Even Gyln, who seems more introverted than me, is able to put two words together with the berseker girl sitting next to him.

Bored, my eyes wander, looking at everyone around me. There are creatures of every kind: lusoghams, wizards, gnomes, samaya elves, mellons, bersekers, vaneyaras, pirates, hairy men, and cyclops. However, not even the shadow of a faun; weird, I thought they were keepers of the forest. Why aren't they here celebrating Yule like everyone else?

Suddenly, silence. Egort pops up between the tables, wearing a very elegant brown velvety suit, and walking toward the empty throne. Everybody claps and he is obviously enjoying his five minutes of fame with a huge smile plastered across his face. He clears his throat, fixes the fez on his head and with his usual pompous demeanor, speaks to the crowds.

"My brothers, children of Midendhil, please welcome Druir, father of all Nemeton lusoghams."

The squeaky sound of a small trumpet breaks the silence, and in that same moment, a palanquin carried on the shoulders of exhausted dukkos appears. On top of it, there is a slouched old man who sways like a puppet. No, that can't be Druir!

I spot his white beard and big red nose, common lusoghams' features. He's wearing a green outfit embroidered with gold, a pointy hat with a tilted tip from which hangs a lit lantern that bobbles nonstop. I notice his gaze: empty, hidden behind thick, curved eyeglasses that make his eyes appear larger than normal. I guess he's deaf, since he has a golden ear trumpet, which he uses every time somebody talks to him. The disappointment hits me like a slap in the face and makes me fall back on the bench. After everything Luis had told me, I thought I was going to meet a great wizard, able to help me, advise me on which path I should take. Instead, what I see is just a shabby old man, deaf as a doorknob and alert as a sgallux.

"So that would be Druir?" I ask Luis, without even moving my lips.

"Yes, our great Druir," he replies, ecstatic. "Father of us all."

I follow the dukkos who, paying attention to their every move, place the palanquin on the floor, and carefully, as if afraid to break him, help the wizard get out. Druir wobbles holding onto his staff, until he stops in front of his inlaid throne. He quietly stands still for a few seconds, observing each one of us with his big eyes. He looks at us but, given his condition, I highly doubt he can see anything past the end of his nose.

"Welcome, my dear brothers," he announces with a shaky voice. "Welcome to a brand-new Yule."

He pauses for such a long time that I assume he's fallen asleep; then, suddenly, he continues like a toy with low battery.

"Another year has gone by, and another cycle of life is coming to an end. However, I wish to remind you that, as always, for every old thing that ends, a brand new one begins."

He stops yet again, and for an instant, I feel as though behind those huge bottle-bottom glasses, his eyes are actually staring at me. I turn around and see that everybody at the table is in awe of him, as if entranced by his words. They are all so quiet you could hear a pin drop. I look back at Druir who now hesitates and appearing confused, as if just realizing where he is standing.

"What was I talking about," he murmurs to Egort.

"*Life cycles.* You were talking about life cycles."

"Oh yes, of course," he says with a smile. "Life cycles. For every death there is a life, so we shall not cry over those who leave us, but we shall rejoice over those who come to us."

My heart is still shattered over my parents' death, and I feel very uneasy listening to this speech.

"Enough words for now," the wizard concludes by raising his staff. "May the Yule celebrations begin."

A thunderous applause explodes, making all the lanterns over our heads swing. Maya and I glance at each other, feeling like fish out of water. Meanwhile, lusogham grannies and dukkos are flooding tables with lots of delicacies: wild boar pot roast, cheese with jam, onion and mushroom soups, sausages with sauce, baked pork chops with honey, eggs and fried chicken, polenta and cod fillets, corncobs with butter, French fries, and baked potatoes, and so much more.

In the blink of an eye, all the diners dive into the food, munching, chewing, and swallowing everything they can reach. It's a real binge-fest, and the more we eat, the more trays full of delicacies appear; the dukkos bring the trays while refilling jugs with BidiBubble and fresh beer. Like at every decent party, songs and choruses rise from one of the tables: it's the mellons who, with tuned voices, sing hymns, cheering and drinking straight from the jugs. Further down the table, near the orchestra stage, four happily buzzed gnomes put on a tumbler-like show that seems right out of the circus. Then, suddenly, an old toothless wizard stands on a table and begins twirling on one foot, shooting firecrackers out of his ears. After the first blast, the orchestra bagpipe begins a melody, followed by the rest of the band. The diners, who have gone totally wild, keep the rhythm with their feet and hands, while the old wizard twirls faster and faster, until he takes off like a helicopter and floats above our heads.

Luis is on cloud nine, and during the whole dinner, he drinks BidiBubble and chats up a storm with people sitting next to us, overwhelming everybody with his yackety-yak. Druir, on the other hand after taking a nap between courses, is joined by Duadus, the king of sweets. I can't even imagine what an elf like him could possibly have to say to such a cuckoo lusogham, but they have been babbling-on for quite a while now. Druir is listening looking very tired, pointing the ear trumpet to the elf's face while Duadus keeps yapping, moving his hands fervently along with his story.

"Would you like to dance?" Maya asks me.

"What?"

Before I have a chance to think about what she just asked me, I find myself in the middle of the dance floor, in front of the orchestra.

"Please, you know I can't dance. Let's sit back down, it's almost time for dessert."

Nope, my words fall on deaf ears. Maya giggles, making me spin around, and soon after, we are joined by other couples who start dancing as well. She's gorgeous, moving her hips in front of me, slightly tilting her head. She's looking at me, inviting me to mirror her moves, but I'm too embarrassed so I just stand there like a chicken, barely keeping time with my foot.

Suddenly, an elf with wheat blond hair and macho charisma steps between us. He turns his back to me and bowing so much that the tip of his nose touches the floor, invites Maya to dance with him. The moment she accepts by holding his hand I decide to put my foot down and move him out of the way. I mean, gosh, I am in another *world*, in another *life*, I've had a platoon of monsters coming after me, I think I can survive a few dancing steps.

"She's with me," I say, noticing Maya's face light up.

I hold her by the waist and let her twirl with the rhythm. I know my moves are a bit clumsy: sometimes I step on her feet, but she doesn't seem to mind. She watches me without saying a word. I have no idea what my feelings are trying to tell me, but I feel something inside of me; it's new, and maybe I've been looking for it my whole life. We dance around holding hands, stretching out our arms. She laughs, tilting her head back, while the light of the lanterns slides over her like a meteor shower. Her eyes sparkle, and for a moment, we both forget our troubles and tribulations.

The spell is broken by that old toothless man who is shooting firecrackers out of his ears; he grabs our hands, and he pulls us into a frenetic group dance. Maya is in front of me, and I keep my hands on her hips, feeling the warmth of her body through her dress. My thoughts move on to a brand-new future, different from what my destiny seems to be: she and I, our evenings spent at the movie theater, long walks, and endless conversations that last way into the night.

The weight of the truth I've been carrying around over her mother's death still sits heavily on my heart. I have to tell her; I can't keep this secret any longer. She has to know I am the reason for all her suffering. I make up my mind and pull her aside, away from all the dancing.

"Maya, we need to talk. There's something that . . ."

Her index finger on my lips shuts me up. I feel startled and a bit intimidated. I try to talk again, but she puts her arms around my neck. She kisses me.

I feel her soft and fresh lips that taste of BidiBubble. My hand is in her hair, while the other is on her waist and I pull her closer to me, holding her tight as I have always dreamed of doing. The music goes on with dances, shouts, and cheering, but the two of us are in another world—our own world. Then, she slowly backs away, our noses almost touching. She tilts her head, and with a smile, she moves a lock of white hair from my forehead.

"Are you willing to give up all of this?"

She kisses me again, before I have the chance to reply. I think that right now even if a bomb went off or Kenat were to appear, I wouldn't even notice. I could stay here and . . .

"Come up for air, boy! Your lady ain't a mermaid."

Luis. I don't know what prevented me from punching him. Could he possibly be more of a meddler? Maya looks at me; she holds back a smile and caresses her lips with her fingertips.

"What do you want?" I ask him.

"The big moment is upon us," Luis says, nodding at the circle of people surrounding Jólnir, the giant tree. "The ritual is about to start. Come with me."

He holds our hands and drags us through the crowd. I glance at Maya sadly, and she replies with a sweet grin, as if her eyes only see me. This must all be a dream, it's not possible that this is really happening.

Meanwhile, swarms of flower fairies fly over us, and in impeccable order, pick up all the oranges and lanterns hanging from the branches. A sudden uneasy feeling overwhelms me, bringing me back to reality. I look around, not really sure what I am searching for. Then, I see her. It's just for a second but it's enough to make my blood run cold. Pale and withered, Silischia appears among a thousand faces that animate the fair. It can't be true; we are safe here, Luis said so. Yet, I saw her: small and cruel, wrapped in her worn-out cape that makes her look like a big bat.

"Hey, what is it?" Maya asks me, aware of my worried expression.

I don't answer because I don't think I should worry her, but I keep looking around. I inspect each table, every person who chats or eats, but nothing. She has disappeared. I sigh, blaming all the stress I've been under.

"Well?" she says, caressing my hair.

"Nothing," I force a smile before I try to kiss her one more time. However, Luis interrupts us, yet again. Darn him and his timing!

"Here's Druir," he exclaims with joy.

Who cares! In this very second, I couldn't care less about that nutty ole man, but for some inexplicable reason, I can't help but follow his every move. I observe him as he dangerously wobbles toward the tree, supported only by his staff. The crowd is incredibly quiet; nobody makes a sound. Druir gets closer to the trunk, he caresses it whispering something, then he slightly taps it with the tip of his staff. The tap echoes in the silence, as a spiral of sparkles bursts out of the ground and wraps around the tree. I follow the vortex as it separates into a sunburst of sparks, flooding with light each and every twig of the tree. The leaves and the external tips of the fronds begin to sizzle and disappear into shiny puffs of dust, raining over our heads. The crowd, who has remained quiet so far, begins to stir, and within a moment, I am surrounded by a forest of raised arms with hands holding glasses, ampoules, and glass vases.

"Here, here!" Luis says, giving us two round vials.

"What are we supposed to do?" Maya asks.

"Do like everyone else and pick up a bit of the Yuth that Jólnir is gifting us."

We follow his instructions; the sparks raining from the tree reach us and enter straight into our ampoules. Stunned, I look up at the tree and see that also its trunk is slowly crumbling in shiny whiffs, and within seconds, the great Jólnir is reduced to no more than bright ashes.

"What happened?" I whisper, perplexed.

"Watch," Luis tells me, taking my vial of Yuth from my hands. Druir, still holding onto his staff, bends over the pile of bright ashes, sticks a finger in it and whispers something again. We all freeze, until we see a bud magically sprouting before our eyes: it's so bright that it's blinding. Druir steps back, as the bud quickly turns into a shrub and then a tree. The green stem grows thicker, covered in bark, without stopping its growth. It stands tall, opening its branches that are immediately full of leaves and bluebells. The canopy expands and it goes back to its previous width, this time green and luscious.

"The old has reborn to give light to the new," Druir exclaims, turning toward us.

His eyes sparkle with the reflection of the light that surrounds us. Screams and shouts of joy rise from the square, making my ears ring. Dancing and cheering start all over again, and the merchants open their shops one more time. Ialon is celebrating again, and I see only happy people all around me.

I observe Druir walking back to the throne. He's tired, exhausted, as if each move was taking a year away from his life.

"Do you want to talk to him?" Maya asks me.

"I'd like to try, even if I'm not sure it'll help."

I take a step toward him, but she grabs me by the vest.

"Now, you know what's right for us, don't you?"

I hesitate for a moment, then I choose to walk away without answering her. She understands and lets me go. The terror of making the wrong decision feels like a hand choking me. I know all too well that I wouldn't be able to reason right now, since there are two things on my mind: Maya and my fear of losing her. I feel so guilty toward my parents, but I try to erase my sense of regret by convincing myself that I am not the right person to take on the responsibility that has been thrown upon me. It's useless believing that I am. I'm just a fourteen-year-old boy who, till a few days ago, succumbed to the will of the school bully. I can't be the hero this world has been waiting for.

Druir is turned away from me, still busy in a conversation with Duadus. I get closer and clear my throat in an attempt to catch their attention. The lusogham observes me over his eyeglasses with a puzzled expression. He's much older and wrinklier than I thought, while the elf next to him doesn't resemble the happy-go-lucky face I saw this afternoon on the banner; on the contrary, he expression is tense and intimidating.

"I'm sorry to interrupt, but I'd like to . . ."

The sound of a horn prevents me from formulating my sentence, covering every song, laughter, and music. The celebration stops instantly, as the square is invaded by a group of giant faun warriors. They have big goat-like heads and strong bodies covered in leather and metal armor.

I sense a chill. I see the mellons tense up, backing each other, their hands already grabbing onto the hilt of their big swords. Among the fauns, their chief pushes through. He's a span taller than the rest, and his wide and muscular chest is crossed by two bulky leather straps, in the center is a large, golden medallion. His face is a combination of a man and animal, with big dark eyes that let his fierceness and bravery shine through.

His hair, thick like a mane, is braided and falls on the sides of his ram-like horns. I walk back, blending in the crowd, as the faun advances with a firm step toward Druir. In the silenced feast, his hooves snap on the square's. He stops in front of the lusogham: not a bow, nor a greeting. Druir examines him, without changing his empty expression; Duadus remains impassible, too. The faun taps his spear twice on the ground, as if demanding attention.

"Tharab," Druir greets him with a nod.

"I swore I would never again help the lusoghams, but for the sake of Nemeton and all the creatures who live there, you should know that a pack of mashuis is raiding the forest."

His words cause buzzing among the crowd.

"I know, I've already been informed," Druir tells him calmly.

"Disperse immediately! Go back to your houses. It's dangerous keeping up this façade."

Druir gives him a weak smile that makes me feel embarrassed for him. The faun bends his head forward, almost as if trying to challenge him, but then turns the other way. With a firm nod he orders his subordinates to proceed with their patrol.

"Don't underestimate me, lusogham," he tells him behind his back. "I'm not my father."

"No, unfortunately you're not," Druir whispers.

Without uttering another word, Tharab walks away followed by his aides and disappears into the night.

An almost palpable tension descends over the square. Behind me, people are mumbling, hissing, and calling the fauns derogatory names. Druir gives me a distracted gaze, which pierces through me as if I were a ghost. He gets up slowly and demands the attention of the crowd by clapping twice.

"Don't be sad, my children. Tonight belongs to Yule and no fear shall ruin our celebration."

Then, he addresses the orchestra with a twirl of a hand, they immediately start playing a cheerful tune. People are confused, but they seem to slowly forget what just happened and resume cheering, laughing, and dancing. Within a few minutes, the fauns' interruption seems erased from their minds.

I look for Maya and Luis; they are not far from me, next to two mellons who are busy arm wrestling. They nod at me, inciting me to try and talk to Druir again. I sigh, in the hopes of releasing the tension that is building inside me. I fix my sword that keeps knocking on my knee, and with firm steps, I move toward him. But the old lusogham has disappeared and sitting on the throne in his place is now Egort who is pretending to be in charge, chatting with an old witch.

I search for Druir through the square, and I spot him as he walks away on a small road. I go after him, pushing aside the masses. The old man with firecrackers in his ears is back at it, trying to make me dance once again, but I manage to get away and run after Druir.

I take the deserted street, away from all the celebrations. The house windows are all dark, the façades illuminated by the lanterns hanging from the roofs. I walk quickly, as an ominous feeling sinks deep in my heart. I'm sweating and my shirt is sticking to my back. I go past the library until I reach a small square by the edge of the village. In the center, I notice a large stump with a hollow shaft, a small swamp, and behind it all is a narrow path that leads to the forest. Druir is nowhere to be found. I feel goosebumps and I'm chilled to my bones.

"Leonardo, this is your human name, isn't it?"

I turn around, my heart freezes. Antédios, Feghin, and Silischia are in front of me. How's this possible? How did they manage to find me? I take a step back, unsheathing my dad's sword. A spark runs through the blade, making it vibrate.

"Good idea using a transfiguration spell, but it doesn't work with me," the demon tells me, tapping his temples. "I can see your Yuth, Last Keeper."

I lurch forward, pointing Uerabog straight at him. I'm desperate. My mind goes immediately to Maya.

"Calm down, Akasha. Nobody here wants to do you or your friends any harm," Antédios smiles.

Feghin and Silischia move to my sides. The demon stays in front of me as the spirals of smoke from his cape slither over me like snakes.

"What happened in the other world was unavoidable. My Lord has been trying to bring you back home since the Guardians kidnapped you. Those fools who raised you, filled your head with lies. You have the right to know who you really are."

"Shut up!" I scream, getting closer to him, my sword still aimed at him. "Don't you dare speak of them!"

"They are nothing to you," he calmly replies. "Look inside yourself, Leonardo. You know you are so much more than what you've been told. You know the great power that burns inside you."

I'm having a hard time breathing, but my grip on the blade is still firm. I swallow, but my mouth is too dry. I glance at Silischia, then Feghin, who are both staring at me, slowly nodding in silence.

"It's when that energy is released that you feel free, am I right? Strong and fearless, correct?"

"No, when that happens I . . . I'm not myself," my voice trembles, but I try my hardest to keep it steady.

"But you know, you can't resist what your heart wants because your mind justifies it."

I can't think straight, terror has taken over my thoughts and my heart is racing.

"Come with me. Give me the Sidhits and you'll discover who you really are," he tells me as if truly trying to help me and extends his hand. "Appearances often trick us, Leonardo. Things are not always what they seem."

I think back to Miss Abona and one of the last things she told me before sacrificing herself for me. I'm having a hard time breathing. This can't be it. It can't be real! The Guardians loved me; they would have never lied to me.

In the distance, behind the three of them, I see shadows of men. They are lusoghams. Among them, I recognize Fern, the bodula farmer. They run wielding their magic staffs that glow like lightning. Antédios notices their arrival as well. His expression changes, he's out of time. He walks toward me, as I keep stepping back.

"Trust me, Leonardo, and your life will become everything you've always dreamed."

I stumble and fall backward, ending up inside the hollow tree in the swamp. The lusoghams are here. I hear Fern screaming, then a white light shines through, breaking the darkness, while the demon and the two sorcerers disappear into a cloud of black smoke. I squirm trying to stay afloat, but a whirlpool swallows me and drags me down, into the abyss of the endless well.

chapter thirty-one

THE KALADAR

My mind is lost in a dark vortex, I hear my mother's voice calling me, a heartbreaking scream that I can't quiet. Uncle Victor is talking to me, too: *I never wanted this day to come.*

My temples throb, my lungs burn, I need oxygen, I'm drowning.

Suddenly a light, my head breaches the surface. I open my eyes and spit out water, desperately gasping for air. I'm alive, still inside that hollow trunk, but no longer in Ialon. How did I end up here?

Around me is an unknown forest, illuminated here and there by the gleam of flower fairies, who fly through the darkness of the bushes. I grab onto the edge of the stump, and using my arms as leverage, I push myself out of it. I fall onto the ground like a fish dumped out of a net, and that's when I see them: among trees, where the path leading up to the forest used to be, there are ruins of a majestic palace in white marble, completely covered with vegetation. Instead of the collapsed columns and arches, there are now enchanted fronds and roots, twirling in support of the remains of the building. The missing part of the dome, which covers the whole building, is a complex series of interwoven branches and leaves, and a large, triangular-shaped tympanum held by statues of two giants, surrounds the entrance.

Druir is standing at the door. He looks at me for a moment, then turns around and walks inside, disappearing into the darkness. I put Uerabog back in its sheath and follow him, trying to quell the urge I feel inside. I don't understand what's going on.

I cross the threshold, out of breath. I look right, then left, noticing that my clothes, maybe due to a spell, are drying quickly, becoming warm and soft. Without slowing down, I walk through the reception room, going up a stone stairway; I glance everywhere, but the lusogham seems to have disappeared into thin air. I find myself going around in circles, through dark and secret halls, like a labryinth.

I start running in panic, until I come across a light globe that floats in the middle of a passage: it's a bunch of flower fairies who, after dancing around my head, signal me to follow them. With my hand ready on my sword, I slide behind them until we reach a large smooth wall. A thin crack, as wide as a hair, traces the shape of an archway opening.

I see the fairies going right through it, and without further ado, I do the same. I close my eyes, and I walk with firm steps, trying hard not to think logically of what I am about to do. But reality hits me like a wrecking ball; the sturdy marble wall remains intact, while I hit my nose and head hard against it. I take a few steps back, perplexed, rubbing the bump that is rising on my forehead. The fissure that drew the entrance is no longer there and now the wall is a smooth surface of uncut rock.

"Don't try looking for a door that's not there."

A voice echoes in the empty hall. I spin around, unsheathing the sword.

"Who's there?" I yell, scared.

"Rather, think of where you'd like to be and forget about the obstacle in your path."

"Who are you? Reveal yourself!"

Out of the corner of my eye, I see a human shadow dart a few feet away from me. I turn around, ready to fight, but all I see is my own reflection in the big arcàntodam on the wall. He's staring back at me, with his usual attitude, mirroring my every move.

"What do you want?" I ask, getting closer.

The tips of our swords touch each other, separated only by the glass that divides our worlds.

"We often think that circumstances shape our decisions when it's actually the opposite. Will is the only thing that can change what's around us, and you should really understand that Leonardo."

I turn my back on him and walk back to the marble wall. *Will? Changing what's around us?* I put my sword back in its sheath, squint my eyes and focus on visualizing myself in front of an open door. After a few seconds, I hear the noise of flagstones moving, a gush of warm wind blows through my hair. I open my eyes with uncertainty, finding myself in front of a passage that leads to a round room.

"It didn't take much, did it?" I hear my reflection making fun of me.

I move forward, carefully. The atmosphere, here where I am, is different from the rest of the palace; I sense a somewhat regal and sacred ambience, which forces me to be very cautious. The room is illuminated by five big firepits, placed in a pentagon shape. Walls are covered with flaking frescos, and though vines climb everywhere, it seems clean and harmonious. In the center of the perfectly round fountain dug in the stone pavement, is the face of a huge statue emerging from the water's surface that reminds me of the portal of Annunaki. A long stairway leads to a white marble throne with a tall narrow backrest inlaid with precious rubies.

Suddenly, a tingling sensation envelopes my head. I touch my hair, and look at a lock that is fiery red again. I feel a weird sensation going through my chest muscles, as if I were more robust. Could it be that the Sidhits are actually transforming me?

"There's no need to hide your real identity, Leonardo," Druir comes forth from behind a column. He's now standing tall and proud, still holding onto his staff. "You are safe here, between these walls."

"How do you know who I am?"

"The stars showed me your arrival," he smiles, taking off his eyeglasses.

His eyes sparkle, now vigilant and attentive. I grimace, feeling as though someone is wringing my brain like a sponge. I'm shocked. The old, shabby lusogham is gone, replaced instead by this stately wizard, who beams with wisdom and power.

"Antédios is in the village," I tell him, almost whispering.

"He was in the village . . ."

"Were you the one who warned the other lusoghams?"

"The stars, again," he explains, pointing at the ceiling. "We already knew of his arrival."

"But you . . ."

"Did you picture me differently?"

I nod slowly.

"You know what? Sometimes, it's better to behave like a stupid wise man, than being mistaken for a wise stupid man. Stupid men are always so confident in their beliefs, while wise men live in doubt, and their uncertainties allow free will to those who seek advice."

I have no clue what he's trying to say, but it doesn't matter. I just need to sit down right now. I fall to the floor, with my open palms pressing hard against my eyes.

"Where are we?"

"We are at the antique mansion of Kratumat, Midendhil's greatest Viceroy, once Lord of these lands."

"But I fell in . . ."

". . . an old hollow trunk. Yes, I know, that's the passage that connects Midendhil to this *kaladar*."

"Kaladar?" I ask, returning his gaze.

"These are places of pure energy, suspended along the cracks of Vril: small worlds where the elders used to hide their secrets."

"So, this is not Midendhil? But I have got to . . . Maya . . ."

"Don't panic. We are still in Midendhil, just on a different plane."

"But we can go back to where we were, right?"

"Any time you'd like."

I rest my forehead on my knees and scratch my neck so hard it burns. I feel like I'm suffering from information overload: too much, too fast.

"What do the stars say about me?"

"Do you know why Luis brought you here to Ialon?" he replies with another question, leaning on his staff.

"Because he thinks you can help me find my way."

Druir crouches next to me. A smile on his lips, but his stare is somber and doesn't give me hope for the best.

"Which one do you think is your way?"

"My mission. Take the Sidhits to the Tower of the Guardians."

"This is what other people have told you to do. But I am asking you. I want to know what you feel, Leonardo. What do you think is your destiny?"

"I am very confused, and I fear finding out who I really am. I fear the Guardians didn't tell me the whole truth."

"You don't need anybody else to tell you the truth," he watches me with a sly grin. "You know what the stars have in store for you. After all, you've always known."

My eyes get lost in space. The shadow of my thoughts uncontrollably comes out of my mouth.

"I'm not the hero this world has been waiting for, am I?"

Druir looks down, as if in doubt.

"I'm sorry, boy," he tells me, sighing. "Being the chosen one is not a birthright, but a choice. I think that the real Akasha should sense that he is the one, and if you don't feel it in you, then I guess you are not him."

I feel strangely relieved, but also sad and disappointed.

"So, the Guardians were wrong?"

"Not necessarily. Things change with time and some of your choices have transformed certainties into riddles."

"What about all those mysteries surrounding me?"

"Why do you ask? Perhaps you are looking for different answers than those you've been given?" he rebuts, ogling me.

"No . . ."

I remain quiet, lost in my thoughts, while Druir pulls himself up with his staff.

"What about these? What am I supposed to do with them?" I ask, taking the sachet with the Sidhits out of my pocket.

"Nothing, they are no longer important."

"What?! Do you even know what they are?" I let them slide on my palm, but I realize that they have lost their light, now looking like useless marbles. "How is this possible?"

"Only the Akasha can guard their power and I'd say that now we have confirmation you are not the one," he tells me, closing my palm.

My disappointment is huge. My life has been turned upside down for nothing. What did my parents, my uncle, and everyone else die for? Was that just a big mistake? How could this be?

"You and your friend must meet with him immediately," Druir says out of nowhere.

"Meet who?"

"He's the only one who can take you back to your world safe and sound," he speaks as if he couldn't hear me, quickly heading toward the entrance.

"Meet who?" I ask again, going after him.

"Weldos, obviously. He's a great wizard, maybe the best one Midendhil has ever known. He's very old, and rumor has it, he now lives by the Isara River. That's where you have to go. Luis will take you there."

"But why do we have to leave right away?"

"The demon believes you are actually the Last Keeper, and he won't stop until he finds you. He knows you're here at Ialon and our spells cannot stop him for much longer. Antédios has magical powers we are not able to fight."

I look at the tiny rocks that were once the Sidhits. I hold them tight in my fist, and out of rage, I throw them in the fountain that's in the center of the room, making them bounce on the big stone head. Druir glances at me, nodding. He smiles trying to hide his sadness and disappointment.

"Tell me what I have to do."

chapter thirty-two

A SUDDEN DEPARTURE

As soon as I pop out the other side of the passage, two callused hands grab me and drag me out of the swamp.

"C'mon, boy!" a hasty voice pushes me.

It's Fern, the lusogham bodula farmer.

"What is it?"

"Druir," he abruptly interrupts me, "this morning he told me to come here and pick you up."

"This morning? How could he possibly?"

"The stars," he replies in a hurry, walking down the path.

Unlike other lusoghams, Fern has a bulkier body, almost muscular, and a tough-guy attitude that makes him seem like he's always about to slap somebody.

He walks ahead of me, with his clothes blowing in the wind. I'm having a hard time keeping up with him, especially because I'm soaked, my clothes stick to my body and my leather boots make an annoying suction-y noise with every step.

"I have to find Maya and Luis. Druir told me that . . ."

"I already know everything," he interrupts me as if annoyed, without slowing down.

The streets here in Ialon are deserted but, going forward, I spot a few lusoghams patrolling the village, brandishing their staffs like spears.

"We don't have much time. I fear the demon is still close by."

I nod nervously, rubbing my nose with my wet sleeve.

"Look for your friend. I'll take care of Luis."

In a moment, I find myself in the middle of the fair, squashed like a sardine between dancing and celebratory people who have no idea that there are monsters among us. Cheering is still going strong, and the tables are full of delicious treats.

I find Maya sitting between a beignet mountain and a three-tiered chocolate cake, still chatting up a storm with Gwen. Her skin complexion and her hair are still the same ones the potion gave her, and even though I've been gone for a while, she seems at ease.

"We gotta go," I appear in front of her, soaking wet.

The two women turn around surprised. Gwen's yellow eyes land on me full of curiosity, moving quickly over my red hair and pale face full of freckles. She studies me, as if trying to guess something.

"Leon . . . I mean . . . Cad . . . *ehm* . . ."

"There's no time," I grab her hand. "Come on."

I pull her away without offering any explanation and leave the witch sitting at the table by herself; she looks at us perplexed. We walk through the crowds, past the sugary arch of Duaduland and go straight to the road from which I came.

"Leonardo, what happened?"

I don't stop, nor do I answer her. I hold her wrist and pull her behind me.

"Can you at least tell me why you're all wet and you have red hair again?" she asks me in a firm voice, squirming out of my tight grip.

We are now face to face. Her expression is tense with suspicion.

"Antédios found us."

"What?!" she holds in a scream by covering her mouth with both hands.

A few patrol lusoghams appear at the corners of the street, coming out of the darkness when hearing our voices. They stare at us frowning for a few seconds, then go back into the shadows.

"We gotta go, we have to leave immediately," I say, grabbing her again. "Luis is waiting for us."

We run through empty streets; my boots provide rhythmic squeaks to accompany us. My clothes are hanging loose everywhere, while Maya is forced to lift her dress to avoid stumbling on it. We go past a tower from which hangs a quatrefoil-shaped sign, and we finally arrive at the hollow stump. Luis is there without Mela, animatedly arguing with Druir. Stiff as a pole, he is staring at Luis from behind his bottle-bottom glasses, listening intently. I spot the silhouettes of other lusoghams scattered around to protect us. Fern wisely coordinates their movements with firm gestures. Luis, on the other hand seems very agitated and speaks while waving his staff in the air, with so much animation that makes me fear for Druir's safety, more than once. I have a strong suspicion that things won't be as easy as I had hoped.

"Druir, I told you, I'm sure of it!" I hear Luis shout. "The boy is the Last Keeper. He showed me the Sidhits!"

Druir's eyes dart toward us. Luis becomes aware of our presence, and he stares at me with a dark expression I have never seen him display before; then he pushes me toward Druir as if I were a disputed object.

"Tell him, Leonardo. Tell him it's you, he doesn't believe me."

I hesitate embarrassed and look for support in Maya. She's frowning at me though, not sure of what to make of the situation.

"I'm sorry, Luis," I whisper, lowering my head.

"What?" he turns his back on me.

"So, this means we can go back home?" Maya exclaims, choking.

"Why do you do this?" Luis adds. "I saw them! I saw the Sidhits. I saw what you're capable of. You used that zika . . ."

He turns toward Druir again, pushing me aside in such a rough way that I fall.

". . . he used a zika to kill a wyvern," he tells him. "The boy is immune to her flames. Druir, you know very well that no creature is resistant to elemental fire!"

"Calm down, Luis," he says serenely. "The truth has been spoken to you from his own mouth. Leonardo is not who we have been waiting for."

"But how is that possible, I saw . . ."

"The demon Antédios was here at the village, and unfortunately, he too believes the boy is the Akasha," he tells him politely, his voice still sounding tranquil.

"Antédios?"

"You are in danger. You have to leave, and you have to do it now, before the Yule Festival ends. The vaneyaras have already been warned, and tonight, they will hide you in their *Nagha*."

I see Luis holding onto his staff so hard, his knuckles turn pale. He stares at me in shock, as if I had betrayed his trust, somehow. Maya is behind me, her face resting on my back, whispering an endless series of "thank yous." Although this is not the time, I can't stop thinking about her and her kiss. I'm so lost in my thoughts that I don't even realize Luis is still talking to me.

"Let him be, Luis. The decision has been made now," Druir intervenes.

The lusogham shrugs, overwhelmed by the events.

"I sent two of our brothers to look for Tharab and his fauns," Druir adds. "But I'm not sure they'll be able to convince them to come back to our aid."

"Why does that faun hate you so badly?" I ask.

"Tharab is his species's prince. He's King Cerneus's son," Luis explains without even glancing at us. "He's convinced a lusogham poisoned his father."

The revelation leaves me speechless. A lusogham murderer? Impossible! They are kind wizards, honest . . . I can't believe that one of them could have had the heart, and the strength, to defeat those warriors.

"You have to protect your friends and bring them to the only wizard who will be able to take them back to their world," Druir repeats. "He'll also help us understand what's going on in the forest."

Luis stares at him, gasping for air as if he couldn't breathe.

"Weldos? Please tell me you're not talking about the *Dark Wizard.*"

"He's the sole survivor of the ancient lineage and he's the only one who can provide us with the answers we have been looking for."

"This is crazy!" Luis yells, alarming other lusoghams around us. "Centuries have poisoned his mind. There are terrible rumors about him. They say he's become a human-looking dark god, and his black magic has become so powerful that he can evoke souls from the dead."

"You don't believe such silly stories, do you? No magic can do things like that."

"They say he has a monster guarding his dwelling."

"Trust me, Luis," Druir interrupts him, placing a hand on his shoulder. "Have I ever let you down?"

Luis shakes his head, his beard waving left and right.

"Behind the poisoning of the faun king and the wyvern attack there is something terrible that I can't figure out," he explains, becoming more serious. "The stars have been very quiet, they are not capable of shedding light on the shadows that crawl in the forest, but they showed me something . . . well, a face."

"The Dark Wizard."

"He's in everyone's destiny."

"But how can you possibly believe that he'll actually help us?"

"I don't believe so," Druir turns toward me with a weird smile. "But something makes me hope he will."

The closer we get to departure, the more tense we feel. I'm confused. Druir's words have forced me to think and become scared. We start walking in the dark, down paths in the forest that move around us as if they are alive. Here and there, in the reflection of the shining globe of Luis' staff, disturbing eyes gleam, disappearing in the shadow as we go past them. I try to ignore them, keeping my eyes on Luis' clothes that flow in front me. Behind us, in the distance, I can still hear sounds of the Yule Festival and often, I find myself thinking back with nostalgia on those moments spent at Ialon: the most precious moments of my life.

Since we left, Luis hasn't said a word to me. I'm not sure if it's because we have to be careful or because he's mad at me, perhaps more disappointed than mad. I guess the whole story of the Sidhits, the Guardians, and the Last Keeper had given him renewed hope, an illusion that has been taken away from him in a second. But if he's upset with me, what should Maya and I say to him? We found ourselves in a nightmare; we lost our parents and everything else we cared about and for what? What are we going to do when we go back? Where will we end up? More than likely, Maya's father is still under Silischia's curse, and we have nobody to help us. Will we end up in foster care? Or will be forced to run away our whole life? The future, which until a few hours ago seemed so bright and wonderful, is now turning dark and scorched.

All of a sudden, Luis stops, making us bump against his back.

"*Shhh . . .*" he whispers, pointing to an vague spot in front of him.

The darkness of the forest is pierced by the light of a flickering fire that burns nearby. Maya tries to talk, but Luis quickly shuts her mouth, turning off the faint glow from his staff with a single gesture. Shivers run up and down my spine, as we are swallowed by the darkness. The only reference point we have left is the fire Luis showed us. We walk toward the light. The white eyes that were staring at us appear once again, this time though, multiplied and in groups, perched on the branches above us. I try my hardest to ignore them, focusing on the glow that shines in front of me; slowly, I let it guide me to the clearing borders.

The flames' light dazzles me. At first, I have a hard time making out shapes but then I am terrified.

A few kapturs are crouched on the ground, sleeping like animals. My quick breaths make Luis turn toward me. I shake my head to let him know I'm fine. Maya squeezes my arm, her face pantomiming a voiceless scream. We move carefully and try to walk away from their camp, staring at them while doing so. I spot Dum, the chief of the warriors, close to the fire. He's asleep on his side holding onto his dagger, the red paint on his face glistening like blood. I hear him grunting while tossing and turning like a bothered beast in his sleep.

We go around the camp and past two big carts full of rusty cages. I recognize Belanunzia and three more mencans locked in one of them, whining. Next to the witches, in an aviary for birds, a few finfinellas without their flying blades of grass, climb up the bars, desperately looking for a way out. In another one, I spot some garfus as well as other creatures I have never seen before that remind me of black panthers. Then, in a much bigger cage, there's what appears to be a girl with long blue hair and pointy ears. She's sitting with her head down with long fairy wings on her back.

We attempt to climb over a trunk, which is blocking the way, when Luis stops us, showing us that it's actually a troll's leg. Thank goodness, I stop Maya from screaming out in terror by quickly putting my hand over her mouth. The monster is huge, and his skin seems to be made of rock. He's sleeping in such a weird position that he actually looks dead. He's drooling out of his mouth, and he stinks so bad that he reminds me of a trash dump during summertime.

Suddenly, a noise catches my attention. It's the shaman. He's awake, sitting by a second fire next to the other one. His lidless eyes are glued to the flames: his pupils black dots in the middle of his very white sclera, and the slit that is his mouth is moving quickly, reciting an atonement and continued dirge.

A tall flame flares up from the fire, as gas had been poured on it. Flames begin to move in slow motion and illuminate indistinguishable shapes. The shaman smiles with satisfaction, bending over the fire, as three silhouettes appear among the flames. Luis takes a step back, making us do the same behind his outstretched arm. What's going on? I glance at Maya, who is observing the scene with a quivering lip. I look again at the shaman. The silhouettes in the flames become clearer, more defined, and suddenly our faces appear in the fire.

"They are here!" the shaman yells out loud, kicking the other sleeping warriors. "Wake up, you pigs. The boy is here!"

Luis pushes us back and makes us hide in the darkness while the roar of the waking troll echoes throughout the forest. We move in the shadow, hoping to get out of there without being seen but one of the ugly beasts who was spying on us from the branches jumps on Maya. It's some kind of giant tick with a flabby body and a pair of powerful claws that snap like pincers.

"*Nirasha!*" Luis screams, but nothing comes out of his staff.

However, I have already unsheathed Uerabog, and with all my strength, I unleash a precise blow that kills the beast on the spot. I go near Maya, who's still shaking with fear, when a dagger darts between us and lands into the trunk next to us. The kapturs are awake and all over us!

"Hurry!" Luis says, crawling into a tunnel that opens from a hole in the ground.

We get down on our stomachs and slide in. I push Maya in front of me and I follow her, crawling on damp dirt. One of the kapturs grabs me by the ankle and tries to pull me out, but panic gives me strength to hit him with my sword, cutting his hand off by the wrist. His painful yelps break the night and explode the fury of his comrades who run after us. I hear them scatter behind me like cockroaches, getting closer and closer. The tunnel is narrow, but Luis' hand appears in front of us, first pulling Maya, then me, out of the tunnel. One of the kapturs pops up behind me, but my lusogham friend, with a firm tap of his staff, makes the arc of dirt above the opening crumble down, burying him under the landslide.

We start to run again like there's no tomorrow, while kapturs, holding onto their torches, come after us. Without slowing down, Luis searches his bag of potions, nonchalantly throwing a couple of them away, making them break on the ground. As soon as the liquids spill out, trees and bushes explode out of the ground, blocking the savages.

We stop to catch our breath, as Luis looks right, then left, in an attempt to figure out where we are. He nods at the rock outcropping that is not far from us, but in that very moment, huge hands grab us and swallow us up into the branches above our heads.

chapter thirty-three

A DIFFERENT DESTINY

I squirm around like a madman, trying to bite the giant fingers that cover my mouth. I can't see anything and the only thing I can think of is Maya. Where is she? What are they doing to her? Out of desperation, I move my sword, hitting the air, but even more hands now grab my wrist.

"Stop it, Leonardo," Luis unexpectedly whispers in my ear.

I calm down and wait, forcing myself to breathe. I feel around searching for Maya. I find her. She grips my hand in reply to my grip; she's OK. However, I'm still scared. I have no clue where we are, and most importantly, with whom! A minute ago, we were running away and then what happened?

In the darkness, I see faded lights. Under the tree where we are hiding, the flames from kapturs' torches move around, drawing beams in the dark. The savages have lost our tracks and desperately look for us, grunting like beasts.

The red glare of their fire bathes Luis and Maya, as well as on the three giant creatures who caught us. I spot their big blue eyes and their athletic bodies. They are vaneyaras! I recognize Kubra, his brother Suma, and a dark-haired female, whose features are much sweeter. Fear immediately vanishes. We are safe now, and even if it's quite dark, I can tell their position enables them to keep those huge ticks away.

Suddenly, Kubra moves his hand in an invitation to get on his back. What!? On his shoulders? Luis accepts without further ado and holds onto him like a backpack. Maya and I glance at each other, and then we imitate him. I get on Suma, while she grabs onto the female. With the same lightness of weightless creatures, the vaneyaras gracefully slide among branches, jumping from tree to tree without moving a single leaf. We fly over the savages' heads and they don't even notice us. Within a second, we are far away and the kapturs's fires appear to be distant dots.

We jump among canopies, ending up on branches of a giant tree that is on a cliff. Underneath us, the Nemeton Forest goes as far as the eyes can see, all the way to the mountains. After so much time spent in the darkness, I can finally see the sky, and a wonderful sensation of freedom fills my heart. The moon is high and bright, and the stars shine in the night sky.

A black river, piercing through the green valley, sparkles in the moonlight among the trees, resembling a big snake in the grass. Not far from its banks, I spot the light of seven fires that form a circle in the forest.

"That's Nagha," Kubra says. "What you see are the seven magical fires that protect our village. You'll be safe soon."

Actually, it takes us over two hours to get to the village. A terrible trip of bouncing, running, balancing over branches, and jumping into the air. When we finally set foot on the ground again, my legs wobble and my knees shake. I'm dizzy and the feeling of vertigo almost makes me throw up. I pat myself to make sure I'm still in one piece, realizing that our clothes are all dirty and torn, yet again. Maya, who now has her original looks back, is totally covered in mud and she seems exhausted.

"Welcome to our home," Kubra tells us. "This way, follow me."

Maya and I follow behind him, wavering, while Luis, jaunty as can be, walks away and chitchats with the vaneyaras. We walk on a dirt road that weaves through trees and tents. The seven firepits we saw from above are lighting our way. Their flames continually change colors, going from golden yellow to grass green and even ocean blue. The structure of their tents is quite simple, resembling those of Indigenous Americans, although much bigger. Every twenty steps, more or less, I spot trees with ladders and wooden platforms, where a few vaneyaras are stationed on guard duty. Nagha seems to be pretty much deserted and there's nobody in the streets, maybe because most of the tribe is still at Ialon, celebrating.

In the center of the village, on a plateau that comes out a few feet from the ground, there is a tent that's ten times bigger than the others, covered with blue leathers and decorated with stylized primitive stars and unicorns. Up from the point where the poles cross, a smoke column rises high, spreading ash in the wind.

Kubra, Suma, and Kirana—that's the name of the female vaneyara who accompanied us—pave the way to the entrance. Kubra moves the leather door, and with a smile, he invites us to enter.

The inside is warm and welcoming. The round room is wide, dimly lit by a majestic firepit that burns floating mid-air, painting dancing shadows on the oblique walls. Underneath, a pot of warm water, fed by steaming waterfalls, boils and froths. Lots and lots of soft pillows and inlaid wooden tables are placed over the carpets that surround the hot pot. Suma makes us aware of a very old vaneyara who is sitting among the pillows, meditating. She has a colorful cape on her shoulders, a green feather headdress from which sprout braids of white hair that go all the way down to her back.

Kubra signals us to wait; he gets close to the tribal chief and wakes her up gently, placing his hand on her shoulder. The vaneyara's eyes open wide and stare at us. Luis goes near her, making room among the cushions. He speaks to her for a moment, then invites us to join them.

"Welcome, my dear friends," she greets us. "May you find all the rest and protection that you seek here."

"Thank you, *holy* Janani," Luis replies, signaling us to bow down.

The attention of the vaneyara quickly moves from Luis to Maya, then rests on me; in her gaze, I detect surprise.

"You are the one the demon is after, aren't you?"

I nod with a bit of difficulty.

"Your Yuth shines powerfully."

"Well, actually I . . ."

She stops me by raising her hand.

"We vaneyaras do not tolerate secrets, especially if they belong to those who enter our Nagha. However, I feel you shouldn't tell me anything. I sense great conflict within you, and I do not wish for our hospitality to be a source of more tribulations. You are here to rest, and rest is what we shall provide you with. Not only for your body, but also for your soul."

She gets up slowly and lets her cape fall on the ground, revealing a tall, skinny, and wrinkly body. Her neck is wrapped in many stone necklaces that descend onto her shoulders and chest. Her legs are covered with an embroidered cloth skirt that goes down to her feet.

As soon as she claps her hands, three old females, like giant maidens, come by to help us get undressed. Within a matter of seconds, I find myself bare chested, wearing only my pants. I glance at my friends who have on just a white undergarment, which makes Luis look really silly, while Maya is a mesmerizing vision. The vaneyaras take away all our clothes, but I make sure to keep Uerabog with me. I wrap the belt around the sheath and place it on a pillow next to me.

The tribal chief throws a handful of salt in the tub, which she enters carefully, followed by Kubra, Suma and Kirana.

"Come," she invites us, opening her arms. "This is the Kanato's source. Every evening, we immerse ourselves here to cleanse our souls and bodies from tiredness and negative thoughts. You will see how much better you will feel after this bath."

We take her up on her offer and we enter all the way to our necks. The temperature is wonderful, and the water, frothy and fizzy, is just right. I close my eyes. The water is all the way up to my ears; it empties my mind of every image and sound.

We stay there for I don't know how long, in silence, everyone lost in their own thoughts. As we were told, all the trials and tribulations that were afflicting me now seem to have vanished in the pool.

After a while, we are handed towels to dry off, and heavy capes to cover up. Luis and Janani, followed by Kubra and Suma, go to a corner to smoke long pipes. Maya and I get comfortable amongst the pillows, ready to get some sleep, but we barely close our eyes when Kirana, the young vaneyara, offers to show us to our tent. A tent all to our own? I can't believe it! We wave goodbye to the rest of the group and follow the vaneyara outside through the village maze.

"Here, this is your *kora!*" she says, moving the leather that covers the entrance to a tent with yellow and green mosaic designs.

As soon as I step inside, I realize that this is a much smaller area than I thought: only the bare essentials, with three long vaneyara sleeping bags placed around a crackling fire. Near every bedroll, there is a wooden nightstand with a jug of fresh water, a glass, and an apple.

"If you need anything, you can find me in the blue kora nearby. Your clothes have been washed and mended. Tomorrow, the *mothers* will bring them back to you at dawn."

I thank and greet Kirana by mumbling something, while Maya looking pensive is already sitting down on her blankets, patting down her damp curls. I have no more energy to talk or even ask her anything. I lay down and I fall asleep as soon as I close my eyes.

"Are you sleeping?" Maya wakes me up suddenly.

"Almost . . . what's up?"

"I was thinking . . ."

I turn toward her. She's laying down on her back, staring into space.

"What are we going to do when we go back? Where will we live? And with whom?"

"I've been asking myself the same questions for a while now," I confess, trying to wipe the sleep from my eyes.

"And . . .?"

"I haven't been able to figure it out yet."

Silence engulfs us, but I feel that there is something left unsaid. Something is on her mind, preventing her to sleep and making her stiff like a statue.

"What about things between us?"

There it is. That's what she was thinking about.

"What?" I mumble, overwhelmed with dread.

"Everything is moving way too fast, don't you think?"

Fast? I don't think so given that I've been in love with you for years. I select my words carefully, trying not to reveal my true feelings.

"It was something natural and wonderful."

"I'm scared, Leo. I don't want to ruin what we have, our friendship."

"Maya, look at me," I tell her, heartbroken. "Do you really think that what happened could ruin things for us?"

Her eyes glisten and a tear streams down her face, ending up on the pillow. She can't even look me in the eyes and turns her back to me.

"Can we please forget about what happened at Ialon?" her voice delivers a fatal blow. I remain quiet for a moment, trying to absorb the hit.

"You only did it to convince me to go back, didn't you?" I ask bitterly.

"No!" she sits up suddenly, her eyes full of tears. "Don't you dare think that!"

"Why shouldn't I?"

She hesitates. Her gaze wanders around the tent, looking for excuses or maybe just logical explanations to justify her kiss.

"I don't know, Leonardo. Maybe I just really needed to feel like a normal girl again."

This time, I am the one to turn the other way.

"Try to understand. Look at where we are."

"It'll be over soon," I interrupt her abruptly. "I told you we are going back home, didn't I? So, let's end things here and do what you want. Let's forget about what happened."

I wait for her reply. I pray, hoping she'd say something. Anything. But nothing. The silence is heavy and empty. It's a silence that rings in my ears so loudly it hurts. I knew this couldn't be real. What a fool I was. For a moment, I forgot who I really am.

Once finding out about the chosen one and all those lies I believed for awhile . . . what's left of me? Just a *nobody's son.*

chapter thirty-four

REFLECTIONS OF CONSCIOUSNESS

The fire has gone out and darkness has filled our tent. The last vaneyaras, coming back from the Yule Festival, go back to their dwellings. I am still here awake under the blankets, listening to each one of them as they make their way in. A few hours later, Luis comes back too. He whispers my name, but I pretend to be asleep. I wait immobile until his breathing becomes regular and heavy.

Now, everyone is sleeping except for me, obviously. Sleep has escaped me because I can't think about anything but the beating I've received lately. Unbelievable. I don't even have time to enjoy the moment. Within a few hours, I know that it will be confirmed I am not as special as everyone thought. As if that wasn't bad enough, Maya basically told me I am not the one for her; not bad actually, just sad and disappointing.

A sudden snap gets my mind off my troubles. I hear feet dragging through leaves, and I see a shadow coming out of nowhere. A tall, skinny silhouette, whose profile fades into smoke. It's Antédios; he found us!

I go to stand up, but an invisible force stops me. I try talking, calling, screaming, but not a *hiss* nor any sound comes out of my mouth. I remain powerless, as the shadow comes closer to the tent, becoming bigger and bigger. A thin and corpse-like hand breaks through the leathers, throwing the entrance open. A cackle breaks the silence. The demon's face appears in the doorway, his hungry eyes and lips forming an evil smile. For a moment, he glances at my friends, passes over them. He bends over me, first over my feet, then my chest, holding my face in his icy cold hands.

"Akasha," he whispers in a chilling voice.

I finally find the strength to react. Freeing myself from the paralysis, I push him away with both hands.

I open my eyes; it was just a nightmare! I grab Uerabog, and turning where Antédios was, I spot a kuspaf, one of those creatures seen in my swamp vision. At that point he runs away quickly, fleeing from the tent. I look at Maya, then Luis, who are both still sleeping. I am too angry to let him go; I get up and chase him.

I dart out of the tent wearing only my pants. The night is so cold that it feels like a sharp, cutting blade, but my rage is intense, making me forget everything else. I see the creature entering a grove of trees, and with my heart beating out of my chest, I run after him holding my sword ready to fight. He's an incorporeal being, and the blade would probably pierce right through him, but it doesn't matter. I need to vent and focus on the enemy, focusing all my frustration on him.

The Nagha is deserted again, and the sentinels are busy guarding the perimeter outside the circle, so they don't even notice me. I crouch behind the bushes, moving forward silently. I look around and search everywhere, but that creature seems to have disappeared into thin air. I advance watchfully, go past the circle of protection, and after a few steps, I find myself in a totally different place. By the Nagha borders, the forest seemed serene and sleepy, now it has suddenly turned dark and animated by shadows that crawl and creak among shrubbery. In the distance, I hear inhuman grunts, roars, and growls. Someone is out there crying; many white eyes are watching from the branches over me. As I turn the sword in the dark, it glints faintly, causing the creatures that surround me to retreat. I try to go back, but I realize that the path from which I came is no longer there, as if swallowed by the woods.

I hear joyful laughter. I hold my breath, moving through the boughs, until I spot a group of hamadryads bathing in a crystal-clear pool of water. They behave like little spiteful girls, splashing water at each other and swimming in circles creating small whirlpools. I am surprised to see that the water around their slim bodies shines with clear light.

I remain there, mesmerized, staring at them until I get enough courage to ask for help. But, as soon as I walk close to them, the fairies start screaming, quickly jetting out of the water. One of them stops for a second and stares at me with her purple eyes. I try to talk, but she runs away too. Within an instant, all the fairies have disappeared into the trunks of surrounding plants and the forest shakes like an earthquake. Then, silence. I am alone and desperate once again.

I am so panicked that my head begins to throb. I walk up to the water source, crouching by the banks. I don't know what else to do, so I decide to stay there and wait for dawn. I glance at the body of water, observing my reflection that vibrates in the current. I spot something in the glowing tracks left behind by the hamadryads. Something takes shape slowly, rising from the bottom. It's the silhouette of a man, who's swimming up to the surface. I jump back, falling on my behind. I am still holding onto Uerabog, ready to fight.

A head full of gray hair and a face with a sparse beard surfaces from the water. His blue eyes wander around. My heart skips a beat. I can't believe it, it's my Uncle Victor! I fall down on my knees, crying his name out loud. He stares at me, as if he needs a moment to realize who I am.

"Leonardo!" he yells, smiling.

I abandon the sword on the shore, and I jump in the water toward him. We embrace each other, crying in sweet release.

"Thank goodness you're alright! What are you doing alone in the forest?"

"I got lost, but what about you? I thought you were . . ."

"Dead," he completes my sentence. "Let's get to shore, I have a few things to explain to you."

We swim back to the shore and sit down on the rocks, keeping our legs in the water. My uncle looks at the blade that's by my side.

"Where's your father?"

I shake my head, looking down. He sighs, looking up.

"Leonardo, you have to be ready. The path of the Akasha is . . ."

"No, Uncle Vic," my voice is shaking, but I have got to tell him.

"Don't worry, Leo. I know you're scared. It'll be alright."

"Uncle Vic, you're wrong. I am not the person you all think I am."

"Leonardo, we've talked about this . . ."

"No," I interrupt him again. "I am sure of it now; I can feel it inside of me. I am not the Akasha."

I feel a knot in my throat strangling me. My uncle caresses my head.

"It's normal and right to doubt yourself. The strength of a man resides within the fear of not being able to be who he wants to become."

"But I'm not . . ."

"You have been, and you will be."

Silence. I want to cry, but I can't even do that.

"The Sidhits have turned off," I whisper.

"I don't think so," he smiles, pointing to a lump in my pants pocket.

Shocked, I touch it. It can't be the Sidhits, I threw them out! I pull out the leather sachet with the magical triangular symbol and let the spheres roll out on my palm. The eight Sidhits radiate their colorful lights and fill me with energy.

"We all aspire to become great men. You, Leonardo, were born to be one."

I look at him unable to comprehend the Sidhits palpitating between us.

"Be free and shine bright like the sun, the moon, and the water. Mirror what's in your heart. Remember that there is always hope." He caresses me again, then vanishes into a burst of water.

"Uncle Vic!" I scream, desperate. "Uncle Vic!"

A blanket is thrown on my shoulders. I turn around, grabbing my sword. It's Luis who, in a white undergarment, looks at me with a sad expression.

"I followed you. May I sit with you?"

"My uncle was here; he was here with me. My uncle! Did you see him?"

Luis crouches next to me, scratching his bald head.

"I saw that, but it wasn't your uncle. It was you."

"I don't get it." I get up quickly, almost losing my balance and falling in the water. "It was my uncle, and he was here! We hugged each other, we talked and . . ."

"It was you, or at least what you should be."

I let myself fall on the ground.

"What are you saying?"

"This is hamadryads' magic. The water they bathe in gains magical powers, and it is capable of waking the conscience of those who see their reflection in it."

"My conscience?"

"I knew it was you," he explains with pride. "The Akasha, I mean. Nobody can escape their own truths and your conscience has chosen to resemble your uncle to convince you to listen to it."

I dry my face and start biting on a piece of blanket I am wrapped in.

"Finally, you've come back," he says, glancing at the Sidhits flare, now filtering through my closed fist.

"But Druir told me that . . ."

"Druir chose to tell you what you wanted to hear. There are none so blind as those who will not see, and you needed to hit rock bottom before you could come back up."

I go to speak, but I change my mind. Now, I am even more confused than I was before. I also feel relieved, as if this was the truth I had been looking for all along. I open my fist as the Sidhits levitate.

"What am I supposed to do, Luis?"

"I don't know," he says, shrugging. "You are the one who has to choose which kind of man you wish to become."

chapter thirty-five

THE ISARA RIVER

We wake up at the crack of dawn and find our clothes washed, mended, and folded by our bedrolls. A dense fog rolled in over the village, hiding trees and tents under a gray curtain. Even though the sun is not up yet, I can tell the day will be awful: light rain is pattering on the leaves, cold air blows over the trunks whipping through tree canopies.

Nobody seems to have noticed what happened last night. Not even Maya, who didn't wake up at all when Luis and I got back. It's for the best since I've decided to keep this secret between us for now. What happened has really shaken me up and I need time to absorb it.

After a breakfast of milk and fresh fruit, Janani, Suma, Kubra, and a few more vaneyaras, lead us to the river down a steep hill. Trees and bushes alternate with giant and fluorescent mushrooms that, in the mist of dawn, light our path.

Among trunks, we spot goofy little pigs with turtle-like saggy skin, small horns, and mauve-colored fur with darker spots. There are dozens of them running around smaller mushrooms, making agonizing sounds that break my heart.

"What are those?" I ask Kubra, who's walking next to me.

"Skuoks."

That name sounds familiar. I must have already heard it from Luis in one of his usual rants.

"What kind of sounds are they making?" adds Maya, who seems to be quite interested.

"They're crying," Suma giggles, handing us one.

"Crying?"

"Yes, it's in their nature. They cry because they feel ugly!"

"What do you mean?"

376 Davide Simon Mazzoli

Suma explains that those tiny animals, who look so cute and funny, are actually huge whiners who spend their lives in a self-pity party because they feel they're ugly. He tells us that, once upon a time, the woods were full of them, but then monstrous creatures invaded the forest and unfortunately, the skuoks's population began dwindling.

After a long walk, we finally reach the shore of the Isara River. The sun is trying to peek through the clouds that cover the sky, but the grayness seems to thicken. What at first was just a light rain, is now an actual downpour that feeds the fast and swirling waters of the river, making waves crash against the rocks. I notice dozens of big canoes, made of faded wood, placed ashore.

Luis is talking to Tribal Chief Janani who, standing tall by his side, listens to him while slowly shaking her head. Whatever it is that she's denying him, he doesn't seem to give up. Rather, he keeps talking to her, pointing at something toward the river, as if trying his hardest to convince her of something. As soon as I realize what he wants to convey, I see him ask a vaneyara for help with pushing a canoe on the water.

"What do you think you're doing?" I ask him, tightening my fists. "You are not thinking about riding these waters, are you?"

"We have to go down the river and then cross it. What we are looking for is on the other side of it."

"And there are no bridges?" asks Maya, more worried than I am.

"No," the tribal chief intervenes, the feathers of her head-dress glistening in the rain. "No bridge unifies the two sides of the forest. On the other side of the river, there are creatures who must remain there."

The vaneyaras mumble something to one another, while looking at us suspiciously.

"We have welcomed you and protected you without asking any questions. But now that you have chosen to follow the river, I wish to know where you are heading," the chief says, moving back by Luis' side.

"We have to meet . . . someone."

"Who are you looking for?"

"Don't make me say his name out loud," he replies, squinting. "I do not wish to alarm your children, holy Janani."

The vaneyara immediately turns somber. Her blue eyes dart toward me.

"You are embarking on a dangerous journey. The river is flooded, and it could swallow you before you have a chance to cross it."

"I know, but this is the only way."

"I'll go with them," Kubra comes forth, followed by his brother. "There's something in this boy that tells me we have to help him."

"No," the chief stops him by raising her hand. "No child of mine shall follow them to their fate."

"But the boy is part of our fate! I know you have perceived it, too. His Yuth is . . ."

"Enough!" Janani cuts him off.

I squint at Maya, noticing her uncertain and scared expression. Maybe she's become suspicious, but she hasn't found the courage to ask me anything.

Silence has set in on the group of vaneyaras who are accompanying us, leaving the river to speak for all of us. Luis is standing inside the canoe, with the rain streaming down the brim of his hat, striping his pursed face. I know he'd prefer to avoid the river as well, but we have no choice; this is the only way.

"Come on guys," he says, stretching out his hand toward us. "We need to reach our destination before sunset."

We walk by the vaneyaras who move aside, bowing their heads, as if observing a funeral procession. Kubra and Suma watch us with regret. I sense their wish to tell me so many things, but there is no time left to talk. We get in the canoe and

Luis, armed with two long paddles, pushes the boat toward the center of the river.

"May our Yuth enlighten your path and protect you all," Janani says, offering the salute.

The remaining vaneyaras mirror her gestures, and within a few seconds, they all vanish behind the splashes of waves that already drag us into the violent river.

The challenge begins immediately. The canoe is sucked into eddies and pushed toward the rocks jutting out of the surface. Luis orders Maya to sit in the center, while I must stay put at the stern. He takes position in the bow, to balance the weight of the canoe and avoid flipping. Using the paddles, we try to stay away from the rocks as much as possible but keep ending up crashed against them. The rain pours down, stinging our faces like needles, and the sky is now torn apart by blue lightning that burns the shadows of the forest. For a moment, I think I spot dozens of silhouettes spying on us from the shore, but then lightning wipes away my fear, revealing only a thicket of trunks and bushes. The canoe starts to fill with water, and Maya tries hard to empty it out by hand.

There are horrifying moments where we are overwhelmed by rapids that almost flip us over and shatter the boat. Then, the rain stops at last, the storm moves away, heading toward the mountains behind us. We float down, letting the flow, now less impetuous, lead us. Maya and I, exhausted and scared, surrender like dead weight on the bottom of the flooded canoe. Anxious, Luis is sitting down and checks that the bag with all the potions, the Grimoire, and his staff are still there. Maya stares at me, without moving a single limb, her wet curls drip water down her face and shoulders, making the purple dress stick to her skin. Even though she's weary, she is still beautiful. I look at her, finding it hard not to feel a hint of resentment toward her. She played me, deceived me, and for what? I shake these thoughts out of my mind. She touches me lightly, making me wince. Her bracelet jingles while our eyes meet again, silent yet full of unspoken words; so many lies between us, so many secrets that wish not to be revealed.

"You know, I got them by the way," she says suddenly, with a hint of embarrassment in her voice.

"What?"

"The rings. I ended up finding the gnome's pavilion."

From her pocket, she pulls out two rings with white flowers that now, with closed buds, resemble two stones set in a silver band.

"They closed . . . how come?" Maya asks me, surprised.

I remain quiet observing them, while I think back on Ialon and what happened between us.

"Well, this one is yours," she says, handing me one.

"And what is this supposed to mean? We no longer have to act like a couple, right?"

She answers with a sad smile, still stretching her arm out to me. I pick up the ring and place it on my finger without thinking about it too much. I put a paddle in the water, and I pretend to be busy maneuvering the canoe. We let the water slip us away quietly, watching the shore and the river. Hours go by. We munch on some fruit and berries the vaneyaras gave us. Then, during the afternoon, Maya and I, tired and drained, fall asleep, while Luis still vigilantly guards our journey.

A jolt wakes me up. The sky is painted with sunset colors and the current is becoming vigorous like it was earlier. I think I can hear the rumble of a waterfall in the distance. I turn toward Luis when, a few feet away from the canoe, I spot the back of what seems to be a big fish with blue scales coming out of the water. It only lasts a moment, but it's enough for me to see the dorsal fin made of veils. Then, the creature disappears among the waves.

"Luis! Did you see the . . ."

"Don't move," he murmurs with eyes wide open, slowly pulling the paddles out of water. "Do not intrude under any circumstances."

"What did you see?" Maya asks, opening her eyes.

"Mermaids," he hisses.

In that very moment, the canoe becomes surrounded by three dark figures who swim at the bottom of the rough waters. Mirroring Luis, Maya and I lay down on the flat surface of the canoe, without uttering a single word. We look at each other, and with our ears immersed in the flooded bottom, we hear their nails scratching the hull and their whispers mixed with the rushing water sound of the river. These are bloodcurdling sounds. We stay there, immobile, and terrified, for what seems like hours, until they finally go away. Luis sighs, deflating his chest like a balloon.

"Are they gone?" asks Maya, who looks very pale.

"I think so."

"You told me that mermaids were in a lake," I exclaim, moving a wet tuft of hair from my forehead.

"And they are. Mermaids live in the abyss of the *Nerthuris Lake*, at the foot of the flooded ruins of the *Apsu* city."

"And what are they doing in this river?"

"They must have gone upstream by way of the *Gomin* waterfall, heading toward the Isara source."

"How can you go upstream a waterfall?" Maya asks.

"They are elemental, and they have the power to command the water and become part of it."

"So why are they going up the river?"

"I don't know, but it is not a good sign. They must have sensed danger coming from the mountains."

I look behind me, over the river, the forest, and I scan the jagged profile of the dark mountain tops.

Everything happens very quickly. The current abruptly increases, pushing the canoe up in a leap that catches us off guard. The boat rocks violently, rotates on itself and throws me out into the river. The impact is jarring, and the icy cold water feels like thousands of needles all over my body. I try hard to keep my head above water, the waves, however, ravage me and take me far from the boat. Luis and Maya are screaming out my name, trying to stretch the paddles toward me. I reach out, grab the wood, but the cold has already stiffened my fingers and my grip eludes me. I open my mouth to yell, but the waves nearly drown me. Luis jumps in the water, holding one hand on the edge of the canoe, which now rotates in the current, out of control.

"Don't give up, Leonardo!" I hear him cry out loud, stretching the paddle close to me once again.

With all the strength I can muster, I fight against the current, and with a push, I swim back to Luis. I hold onto the edge of the paddle but, in that very moment, thin and cold fingers grab my ankle, dragging me to the bottom.

Air comes out of my mouth in a mute scream that only blows a column of bubbles. Shadows of mermaids, with long hair moving like seaweed, swim around me. Their tails are wide and thin, so colorful they dazzle even in the darkness of the waves. My lungs burn and my head is about to split in half from the pain. Before I lose my sight, I see the deformed face of the creature who comes over me: small white eyes and a giant, shark-like mouth. Just when I think it's all over, the mermaid stops me; her appearance turns human, and after staring at me for a few seconds, she kisses me. My lungs fill up with air, and for a moment, I feel as though I'm coming to my senses.

Still attached to her lips, I reach the surface so quickly my ears feel like they are about to explode.

"There he is!" Luis yells.

I look around in confusion and I see that I'm right in front of the canoe. Maya is desperately crying, while Luis, shielded by his magical staff, reaches toward me and takes me away from the creature's embrace. I turn toward the mermaid and see her gorgeous face, right before she vanishes in the frothy waves.

"Leonardo!" Luis slaps my face. "Leonardo, are you OK?"

"I'm fine!" I tell him, blocking his hand. "They didn't hurt me."

Luis sits in front of me with a shocked expression on his face, while Maya throws her arms around me, sobbing out of fear. Meanwhile, the boat keeps spinning out of control, overtaken by the current.

"It's incredible," the lusogham says suddenly. "Mermaids don't usually spare their prey."

"I was about to drown, and they were ready to eat me," I explain out of breath. "But then, one of them stopped and kissed me."

At the word kiss, I feel Maya's grip loosen up immediately.

"She kissed you?" Luis asks shocked.

"Yes, it felt as though something was searching my mind, going through my thoughts."

"They recognized you," he says in whisper.

"What do you mean?" Maya asks, "What did they recognize?"

The boat stops suddenly, making the three of us bump into each other. I look over the edge and spot the angelic faces of the three mermaids who, with their hands holding onto the sides of the canoe, are leading us away from the current, toward the other side of the river. Maya, scared, comes closer to me, while Luis stares at the creatures' diaphanous beauty: they have dark blue eyes, and their faces are crossed by two vertical lines that, even though it looks like tribal paint, are actually part of their tropical fish features.

The mermaids push the canoe toward the entrance of a cave, which blends in with the greenery so well we would have never been able to spot it without their help. The entryway is so low that we have to duck our heads to fit through. The water is calm, and the light is dim. We slide on the mirror-like surface that is dark as night and go through natural columns of limestone that look simply ghostly. In the darkness, on a few ledges, red flames glow, casting light on small alters of clay statues and skulls. On a black rock, idly lays the rotting carcass of what was a huge sea snake. I see the surface rippling into a whirlpool, and I understand that our presence must have bothered some ugly beasts' banquet.

I shiver while moving away from the edge of the canoe and notice that, from the depths of the cave, come beams of sunset light.

We proceed slowly, until we arrive where the bend of the river ends. Here the shore is rocky, and a steep cliff rises out of the chasm overlooking the forest. Plants and bushes crowd the breach, following the rays of sun and rooting their tendrils in the water. For a moment, the sight of this window of light reassures me. Then, the canoe stops abruptly, scraping on the rocky bottom. I turn toward the darkness from which we came and spot the silhouettes of mermaids watching us in silence. I raise my arm to thank them, but they jump backward and disappear in the waves.

"Where are we?" Maya asks in a whisper.

Luis stretches out his arm, pointing his staff to the shore. In the wild greenery, a few feet from the water, there is a portal hollowed out of the rock; a short stairway and arch make the entrance to an unknown place, brightened only by lanterns made out of skulls.

Luis slowly gets out of the canoe. He turns on the light of his staff, and with water up to his knees, he proceeds toward the doorway of what must be the entrance to the lair of the Dark Sorcerer.

My heart is beating ninety miles an hour. I help Maya climb over the edge of the boat and we follow our friend, quietly, all the way to the stairway. It's cold, and in the air, I can sense something that I don't like.

chapter thirty-six

TRAPPED LIKE RATS

"Watch your step."

It's the only advice Luis gives us, going up the slippery stairway. I unsheathe my sword, hold Maya's hand, and follow Luis through the narrow entrance arch. As we pass by, the flames that crackle in the skulls extinguish. Darkness swallows us, as Luis tries to light the path with the white sphere of his staff.

We find ourselves walking down a very tight hall with open niches of every shape and size along the walls. Some of them are closed by rusty fences, while others show a glimpse of mummified cadavers of armed warriors. I tremble while Maya squeezes my arm, her eyes glued on the corpses.

We move through the thick quiet darkness without uttering a single word, interrupted only by the squeak of mice and the sound of flapping bat wings. Then, suddenly, a groan. Luis becomes still; he turns toward us, his eyes wide open, as he holds onto his staff.

"Whatever happens, don't look up," he tells us, without moving his lips.

In that very moment, I feel a gust of freezing air above us: something clammy almost touches my head. The torches on the wall light up in a quick sequence, bathing the hall in dark reflections from their red fire. I look around, and I am finally able to see where we are. It's a catacomb!

Even though Luis warned me, I can't resist, and I slowly look up. Monstrous souls shine on the ceiling, and attracted by the lit torches, jump down, into the mummified corpses placed in the niches.

"Bad sign, really, really bad sign," Luis whispers.

"What's going on?" Maya asks, terrified.

"Exactly what I feared. The Dark Sorcerer is awakening the dead."

Metallic screeches of armor and sharp blades sliding from their sheaths echo throughout the hall. Luis searches the bag of potions.

"Leonardo, back against back. Maya, in the middle. Don't let them get close!" he tells us while still rummaging.

I follow his orders with my heart jumping out of my chest. Warrior cadavers begin to crawl out the depths of the walls. Their helmets reveal decomposing faces, and long dusty hair flows on their dented armor. I take a step back, grabbing my hilt, but I bump into Luis's back. Uerabog's blade is crossed by a glimmer, as if to give me strength.

"Be brave, Leonardo!" he screams, throwing one of the vials on a cadaver.

On contact, this liquid petrifies and dissolves the dead one into ashes, but it's not enough to stop the others from coming closer. One of them jumps on me, trying to slash my chest with his saber. Fortunately, I manage to parry and with a mighty blow I make its head crumble. Another zombie quickly comes toward me, but with a fluid move, I amputate its arms by the elbows, making it disappear into a puff of dust. Maya looks at me in shock, unable to move, while Luis keeps fighting and destroying the enemies' helmets with the sphere of his staff.

I turn around just in time to deflect the spear of a warrior who's darting toward me. I break it in half with one single hit, then I pierce his chest from side to side, shattering him as if he were made of glass. Meanwhile, Luis tries to cast spells on the zombies, but nothing happens, as usual. We keep fighting, defending ourselves to the point of exhaustion, with Maya between us who tries to do her part by knocking a couple of them over the head with a broken spear. Then, suddenly, the light becomes dim. The dead stop as if hypnotized by a mysterious curse.

A man's laughter, which quickly turns into a monstrous roar, echoes from down the hall.

"Come here!" Luis shouts, pulling me closer to him, with Maya still in the middle, protected by our bodies.

In front of us stands a silhouette darker than darkness itself, with two glowing embers for eyes. It's huge, with horns on its head and two big, bat-like wings. We walk backward, while Luis raises the staff, increasing the intensity of the white beam. But it's all useless: the shadow is still a shadow, as if no light could reveal it. There is a moment of hesitation; the thing lingers, analyzing our defenses. Then, darkness sets in. The monster, turning into a dark cloud, envelopes us in a vortex of black insects that sting us everywhere. I see Luis desperately shaking his staff, while Maya calls my name, crying. She is farther from me.

An image takes shapes in my head. My hand searches for the belt and grabs the leather sachet in which I feel the Sidhits pulsing. I hold them tight in my fist, and with all the strength I can muster, I throw them over our heads.

The attack stops immediately. The magical spheres hover briefly, then explode in an energy bubble that squashes and dissolves the cloud of evil insects. Thunderbolts ignite the walls, crackling the stone and disintegrating all the warrior cadavers into puffs. I get up, my eyes burning, while the Sidhits come back down from the ceiling and gently land in my open palm.

"How did you do that?" Maya asks, scared, looking at the spheres in my hands. "Leonardo?!"

I am about to make up an excuse when Luis interrupts me with a scream.

"Look over there!" he exclaims, stretching his arm toward something incredibly small on the ground. "Those insects were nothing more than the minions of this evil homunculus."

My thoughts focus so fast it makes my head spin. I get down on my knees near Luis, grabbing the unconscious sprite from his hands that he is about to smash.

"Sbacot!" I call him, slightly shaking him. "Sbacot, are you there?"

"How do you know his name?" the lusogham asks me incredulous.

The homunculus slowly turns toward Luis and barely opens his little eyes.

"Who are you?" he murmurs, still blinded by the magic of the Sidhits.

"It's me, Leonardo."

"Leonardo? . . ." he asks puzzled, pointing at Luis's long white beard.

"No, Sbacot," I take the tip of his long nose with my fingertips. "I'm here."

A weak smile stretches over his thin lips and makes his eyes sparkle like two tiny black pearls.

"What's going on, Leonardo?" Luis stands up quickly. "How do you know this homunculus, servant of the Dark Sorcerer?"

"First of all, I'm nobody's servant," Sbacot sits up, dusting off his maroon velvet jacket. "And my Master is not a dark sorcerer."

"Your Master is Weldos?" I ask him in shock.

"Your Master is a demon!" Luis roars while pointing the shiny staff at him. "Stay back! You have no idea how dangerous this creature can be. He's full of his Master's black magic. Let me destroy it!"

"Where in the world did you find this cuckoo?" Sbacot asks me, taking off in front of us.

"Don't listen to him!" Luis screams, covering his ears with his hands. "He's hitting us with a curse to make us go crazy!"

"Well, it seems to me you're already on that path, my friend!" the homunculus teases him.

"Stop it! And you, Luis, calm down! Sbacot is a friend, we have nothing to fear."

"But, if he's a friend," Maya comes forth, "Why did he attack us with those monsters?"

"Simply because I didn't recognize him. These are tough times and my Master set up a few tricks around the dwelling to protect himself."

"What tricks? That was pure black magic! Leonardo . . ." Luis pulls me by the arm. "No known power can awaken the dead from their tombs."

"Don't you get it yet? Those were just illusions created to keep away meddlers like you!" Sbacot giggles.

"Yes, illusions that almost killed us," Maya adds.

"Oh, give me a break . . . you're all still alive," the homunculus says, making light of the situation.

"Certainly not thanks to you or the Dark Sorcerer you serve!" Luis screams.

"Oh boy, are we still on that Dark Sorcerer thing? My Master, Weldos, is anything but that. Legends that surround his character have been created with the sole purpose of giving him some well-deserved privacy."

Luis stares at him perplexed, his face gray as a rock.

"Anywho, where are the Guardians?"

"Guardians?" Luis asks. "You know of the . . ."

"Shhh!" the homunculus stops him by raising his hand. "Leonardo, answer me. Where are the Guardians?"

I grind my teeth so hard my eardrums begin to ring.

"What about Dagonis?"

I slowly shake my head, closing my eyes.

"They're all dead, Sbacot."

"Oh, for the Great Dragon's sake . . ."

We are all left speechless for a few minutes, until Luis breaks the silence.

"Can you please tell me why this homunculus knows so much about you and the Guardians?"

"Follow me!" Sbacot intervenes. "Let's go talk somewhere quieter."

I turn toward my friends. Maya has a weird expression, as if she has figured out that I am hiding something from her. Luis bites his lip, frowning at me while looking sternly as if searching for answers.

"Are you sure we can trust him?" he asks me, ogling at the homunculus who's ahead of us, flitting in the hall.

"Yes, because he was the one to give me the Sidhits."

"Wha . . . the Sidhits?" he asks me in shock. "The Dark Sorcerer's servant had the Sidhits?"

I nod with a half-smile.

"So? Are you coming?" Sbacot yells.

We follow the sprite down the hall, until we get to what looks like an underground cathedral. Rows of carved columns extend along the nave and rise to the ceiling in rib-like vaults. We quickly cross the sanctuary; I hold onto my sword while Luis has a firm grip on his magical staff.

"Come on, we're almost there!" Sbacot tells us, pointing to a dark wood door, lit by two small torches.

The statue of a dragon is mounted on it, and the architrave that frames it is inlaid with eight colorful stones that, for some reason, remind me of the Sidhits. On the wood of the door, I discover a carved symbol that is identical to the one on the sachet that holds the spheres.

"Come on in. And remember, don't touch anything."

We find ourselves in a very intimate place, warm and cozy, lit by a fire burning in the hearth. It really doesn't look like the atrium of a dark sorcerer.

In the center of the octagonal room, there is a huge firepit placed under a large copper fan. Smoke rises like a snake and disperses over the stone arch of the ceiling. Scattered all around the room on colorful carpets are couches, chairs, furniture, tables, and desks full of books, weird metallic objects, and parchment paper rolls of every size. The walls are lined with

shelves full of gimmicks and ampoules. From every corner of
the ceiling, drop chains and pulleys from which hang mysterious machines, skeletons of flying monsters, and bunches of
dried herbs that release a smell of dust and pollen.

In the blink of an eye, we have a cup of steaming Panaka in
our hands. Sbacot flies around bombarding us with questions.
Maya and I get comfortable on two sunken armchairs, while
Luis stays standing, nervously rocking with his staff.

I sip the beverage and begin telling the whole story, asking Maya for help. After a while, Luis starts to calm down as
well and intervenes here and there to clarify a few details. The
whole time, Sbacot just nods, remaining quiet and listening intently to every single word. Although I am deep into the story,
I choose to omit what happened in the hamadryads' lair; that's
a secret that I haven't revealed to Maya either, and I have the
feeling that this is not the right time to talk about it. I glance at
Luis and see that he too agrees with my choice.

"Incredible!" The homunculus is amazed. "So, then you decided to seek advice from Weldos, even though you are scared
of him?"

"Yes," Luis replies on everyone's behalf. "Druir, my order's chief, saw in the stars that your Master is in everybody's
destiny."

"We came here because Weldos is the only one who can
take us back home," Maya points out. "Leonardo forgot to
mention the most important thing; he's not the hero you all
have been waiting for. We ended up here by mistake!"

Sbacot looks at me, puzzled.

"Have you really renounced your . . ."

"He hasn't renounced! Is it possible that no one understands?" Maya interrupts him furiously. "He never was The
One!"

But the homunculus continues reasoning, as if Maya had
never opened her mouth. "Then how come the Sidhits answer
to your will?"

392 Davide Simon Mazzoli

Maya hesitates for a moment. Then, she turns toward me, piercing me with her gaze. "Leonardo, is there something you wish to tell me?"

I can't utter a single word.

"I'm afraid to tell you that Weldos has disappeared," Sbacot murmurs, catching our attention.

"Disappeared?" Luis echoes him.

"When I came back here, I found our house completely abandoned," the sprite explains. "Last news I have from him dates back quite some time ago."

"News?"

"It's all written there, in his Grimoire," he says, pointing to a big book placed on a lectern behind him. "I have waited for him for days. I even went looking for him, but nothing. I fear Weldos might have left this world."

We are all speechless. Maya, staring into space, murmurs something I can't even hear. I get up and cautiously walk toward the leather-bound book. On the cover, the same triangular symbol, inlaid on the sachet and the door, shines incandescently.

"What does this symbol mean?"

"It's the Tricarium, the symbol of the Great King, gifted by the Elohims."

I focus on it, letting my thoughts sink in.

"Do you know where the Tower of the Guardians is?" I ask.

"It's in a secret village. Only a few know of its location."

"We have to find it!" Luis exclaims. "The new Guardians are our only hope to . . ."

"The Tower has been destroyed, the Nayaka has been shut off and the order of the Guardians has been annihilated," Sbacot interrupts him. "Everything is written there, in the Grimoire. This is the last thing written by Weldos before he vanished."

"Destroyed? So, what are we going to do now?" Luis asks, letting himself fall back on a chair.

"We can't go home anymore, can we?" Maya adds desperately.

"Maybe there's a way," Sbacot reveals, giving her hope. "I could check the Grimoire and see if there is a spell able to open the portals between the two dimensions. But you must be really sure that's what you want to do."

"How is that possible that the order of the Guardians has fallen?" I ask, reemerging from my thoughts. "My father told me about warriors, new Guardians even."

"Leonardo, did you hear what he said?" Maya, now very agitated, intervenes. "He can take us back home!"

"They must have been betrayed by their secret keeper," Sbacot explains.

"Who was it?" Luis asks.

"It was a 'secret keeper,' lusogham. How am I supposed to know?"

I think back on the words spoken by my Uncle Victor and his fear that something terrible could have happened to the Oghandum, the hamadryad I saw in my dream.

"The Oghandum!" I whisper.

"How do you know about the Oghandum?" Luis inquires, surprised.

"Do you know where it is?" I ask.

"Of course! The Oghandum was one of the hamadryads' queens and the whole Nemeton Forest cried her death for centuries."

"She's not dead. She just turned into a specter, but she's still here, in Midendhil."

"How can you possibly know all these things?" Luis asks me, even more surprised.

"She's the one who betrayed the Guardians. Their Tower is in the kaladar overseen by the Oghandum!"

"Leonardo, please . . ." Maya slowly turns me toward her. "Why are you doing this?" Her eyes sparkle while she caresses my face with both hands. "We decided to go back home.

Remember what Druir told you? Midendhil's destiny is not on your shoulders."

"Sbacot, can you let my friend go back to her world?" I ask, still looking at her.

"Sure, I can try."

Her hands leave mine as if suddenly they had become scorching hot.

"Maya, this is my home. Now I know, and no kiss nor promise can make me change my mind."

Her gaze becomes empty: lost, betrayed. Tears run down her cheeks, and her mouth is trembling so much she can't speak.

"Try to understand me, Maya. For once in my life, I finally know what I am supposed to do."

She doesn't give me time to finish my thought. She turns and runs away, slamming the door behind her.

"Maya!"

I chase after her in the dark chamber, going back through the narrow hall where we fought against those zombies. I call her, begging her to stop, but she doesn't slow down. She runs crying, passing through the entrance arch and vanishing into the cave.

"Maya!" I scream again.

I follow her into the cave, along the riverbanks, and then up the hill with all the green vines. I clamber up behind her, toward the opening now wrapped in the darkness of the night. I call to her to the point of exhaustion, still climbing up the hill that leads out, into the forest. In my haste, I slide on a muddy rock. I lose my balance and fall, rolling all the way down to the shore. I get back up screaming, as I see Maya disappear among the trees.

I start climbing up the hill again, but this time it's a bit harder. Luis and Sbacot appear in front of the catacomb stairway.

"Leonardo!" Luis calls me.

"Maya . . . Maya went up to the forest!" I exclaim, while fumbling with my fingers through the bushes.

"The forest?!" Sbacot yells. "We have to find her immediately!"

I reach the top, and out of breath, roll onto the humid ground of the underbrush. Darkness hides everything under its mantle, and no light can illuminate the forest. Luis and Sbacot catch up to me.

"Let's split up, but don't go too far from here," the anxious homunculus tells us.

We separate, quickly sinking into the deep, dark green foliage.

"Maya!"

At the same moment I call out her name, I spot something moving close by: a shadow that seems to go away with the sound of sobs. I unsheathe Uerabog, and making room among the bushes, I go after her up to a small clearing surrounded by brambles and twisted trunks. Maya is squatting on the ground, her back turned toward me, shaking by violent sobs.

"Forgive me," I whisper, putting the sword back in its sheath. "I didn't mean to hurt you."

Nothing. She doesn't turn, as if she didn't even hear me.

"I must stay here, Maya. I need to find out who I really am and follow my destiny."

I crouch down next to her, and I massage her back.

"Do you understand that?"

I feel the vertebrae of her spine sprout like a ridge under her dress. A laughter hisses in the silence. I pull my hand back, repulsed, then the head of curly hair turns slowly toward me, revealing the skull-like face of the shaman kaptur. He smiles, while already annihilating me with his lidless, evil eyes.

chapter thirty-seven

THUNDER AND LIGHTNING

I jump back, unsheathing Uerabog again, while kapturs's torches ignite and shine all over the forest. They move, sizzle, surround me and block every way out. The shaman writhes on the ground, howling in pain like a wounded beast; his bones break and become longer, while the curls that covered his head begin to tear off in handfuls, and soon the creature turns back into his skeletal and repulsive appearance.

"It was just a matter of time, my boy," he pants with a terrifying voice. "I knew you were going to be mine, sooner or later."

I go to grab the Sidhits, but two kapturs hold me still, blocking my arms, pulling the sword and spheres out of my hand throwing them on the ground. I recognize one of them, because I cut off his hand. I see him shake with rage and he growls in my ear like a beast ready to tear me to pieces. With a slow, yet powerful, clapping of hands, the Dum emerges from the darkness. His evil eyes are two pinpoints that shine in the bloody mask that dons his face.

A beam of light shines and the shaman's body is illuminated by an incandescent vapor that wraps him in a maelstrom.

"*Adara!*"

To that command the spiral is molded into a sphere of purple light that separates from his body, shaping itself into his own appearance.

"Find the demon Antédios and tell him the boy is here."

The ghost takes off high above us and disappears through the tree canopy. The magician walks around me, devouring me with his eyes. The other kapturs grunt and stomp their feet on the ground in a scary tribal dance. The Dum smirks amusedly, enjoying the moment.

Suddenly, a strange buzzing resounds from the depth of the forest, coming closer and closer. Within a second, it overcomes the screams of the savages, while a dark cloud engulfs the clearing. The two kapturs who hold me prisoner, fall to the ground, prey of Sbacot's càndemus, who mercilessly enter through their noses and eyes, biting them like a swarm of deadly insects. In the chaos, I manage to free myself. Luis jumps off the branch, ending those two kapturs with a couple of blows from his staff, then runs toward me.

"Hurry, Leonardo! We don't have much time."

A flame darts above our heads, whipping through the air. The càndemus immediately dissolve, Sbacot is lying on the ground, burned. The shaman stays still with a raised hand from which emits a swirl of pyroclasts, with the other hand he's squeezing Maya's throat. She is cyanotic against his chest.

"Don't touch her!" I scream.

Luis stops me, yanking my arm. The shaman steps back, tightening his squeeze around Maya's neck.

"You caused me so much trouble, boy. Too much . . ."

"Let her go or I swear I'm gonna kill you all," I say in a voice that doesn't sound like mine.

The shaman hesitates. He opens his mouth to talk, but it expands in an unnatural way, as if in a deadly scream. I look down on his boney chest, which now bulges as if his heart is about to burst out of it. His skin stretches out and a big black stinger pops out of his ribs, slicing him. Maya falls down and crawls toward me, scared. Meanwhile, the kapturs howl, alarmed, and point their weapons against an enemy I have yet to see. The shaman crashes down on his knees, eyes empty as death. Behind him, the mashuis' leader stands proud and powerful.

"Shaman, this is the fate of everyone who dares to stand in the way of RavaKhan."

With the firm gesture of his sabers, RavaKhan chops his head off; it rolls down to my feet. The cadaver of the shaman falls to the ground. From the wound, riverlets of red flow toward the bushes then ignite into walls of fire. I spot the black shadows of the other mashuis through the flames. We are surrounded! The Dum's scream of rage and revenge echoes in the confusion and sets off the battle.

The clash is terrible, and we are right in the middle of it. I get up as the flames already burn my face, protecting Maya behind me. Sbacot, who's up again, is fighting side by side with Luis to shelter us.

"Run!" he yells at us without turning.

With my temples and heart pounding, I grab my sword and hold Maya's hand. I try to get away, but RavaKhan throws me down with a thrust of his tail. I roll toward the sachet with the Sidhits that the kaptur had taken away from me and thrown on the ground. The mashuis is faster; he grabs my arm and squeezes it so hard he almost breaks it. Maya screams and walks backward, vanishing in the crowd.

"Maya!" I cry out loud.

"Kill them all, but don't touch the female human," RavaKhan orders his subordinates. "The Dark Lord wants her too."

"Leave her alone!" I exclaim, slumping down from the pain.

The fight is extremely violent. The mashuis are slaughtering the kapturs and soon the Dum is forced to retreat. We are the only ones left in the clearing. Luis and Sbacot are still fighting fiercely, trying to keep the mashuis away. Maya is behind them with her back against a trunk, swirling the sword of a dead kaptur, screaming out loud. One of the monsters jumps off a branch over her.

"Watch out!" I shout.

But the mashuis is already on her. He takes her weapon and picks her up on his shoulders. I try to free myself, but RavaKhan's grip is too strong.

Just when it seemed to be over, something incredibly fast, darts past me. I follow the trajectory till I see the feathers of an arrow sunk in the back of the mashuis that captured Maya. I watch him fall heavily to the ground, lifeless, while a wave of hope fills my heart again.

A battle cry explodes in the clearing, and down from the trees come dozens of vaneyara warriors who throw themselves at the mashuis in a direct attack. Kubra and Suma run to Maya's rescue. I find the courage to roll on my side and free myself from RavaKhan's hold. The Sidhits are on the ground between us. The mashuis looks at me with enjoyment, slowly twirling his sabers. The walls of fire become taller and isolate us from the rest of the battle, but I am not scared and hold Uerabog with renewed energy.

"Don't believe for a second that old piece of rust can keep you away from your destiny."

"Actually, my very own destiny is calling me through Uerabog."

I jump on him. The poisoned harpoon comes toward me. I raise the blade, and with a backflip, I parry the hit, but he throws me a series of vigorous blows that I dodge by stepping back. The harpoon aims at my back once again. I elude it, turn, and try to chop his tail off. The monster avoids Uerabog by whipping the air and another blow from his saber slices toward my legs. I jump up with both feet, divert the attack with my sword, and guide his blade till I thwart it to the ground.

"My Lord wants you alive, don't complicate things for me, human."

In no time, the other saber moves quickly toward my side. I sidestep and counterattack with a manipulative hit. Then, I thrust myself forward, aiming at his heart. Our swords clash mid-air in a rain of sparks. The blow of the monster is powerful and almost breaks both my arms. He pushes me to the ground, behind the cross of our blades, but I resist. At that point, RavaKhan twists his wrist to disarm me, moving both swords up. I can feel the hilt slipping out of my fingers. My uncle's voice is speaking to me. I can hear his teaching: "*Work on your grip!*"

I grab onto the sword, place my foot on the mashuis' chest and jump backward. I twirl, straighten out my sword, and with all the strength I can muster, I throw myself at him, piercing the blade through his chest. The shock is evident on RavaKhan's pale face, as the dark blood starts flowing out the deadly wound. His saber falls out of his hands and his mighty body drops, lifeless.

"Leonardo!"

I turn around; it's Maya who, safe and sound, runs toward me through the flames.

"Maya!"

Suddenly, her eyes are open wide. She screams. I turn but RavaKhan's tail is faster and transfixes my shoulder. The blow makes me spin, and a twinge of pain blinds me, as if incandescent lead has been injected into my veins. I collapse to the ground, while the mashuis pushes himself up, laughing. My sword is still in his chest and the blood is flowing out of his mouth as well.

Maya throws herself at me, calling for help, but the walls of fire flare again, confining us in the circle, along with the mashuis.

"Nobody can defeat RavaKhan, the *Boneshredder*!" he roars.

Anger and pain mix in an alchemy that pushes me to the limits of consciousness. With a burst of energy, I rush against the monster and push him back. I grab the hilt of my sword and sink the blade deep down to the handle. I feel the mashuis' body convulse and tremble under the spasms of death, while the tail rises like a cobra behind me, and swoops down on me. I unsheathe Uerabog, and with a violent and unsteady blow, I chop off his harpoon.

The hit makes me lose my balance. I roll amongst the leaves, exhausted. Maya, far in the distance, calls out my name. I hear the loud crackling of breaking wood, and something collapses. The flames roar. Then, only cries. Venom is rushing through my body, all the way up to my head, it burns my temples and shuts my brain down in a lethal grip. I barely manage to turn onto my side. The Sidhits are still on the ground, only a few inches away from my fingers. They shine brightly. Behind them, Maya is stuck underneath a trunk surrounded in flames. She is crying desperately, and with her arms stretched out, she tries to reach me. I attempt to drag myself toward her, but the pain is too strong. I call for help, but nobody can hear me. Here, in the middle of the fire, nobody can see us either.

"Poor little babies," a woman's childish voice suddenly says. "Two hearts and a fire . . ."

Silischia! My sight becomes foggy. I squint, then open my eyes wide: three dark silhouettes stare at me from afar, pulsating like my nightmares. I hear a laughter that pierces me to my bones. Antédios is here.

"At last, here we are, at the end of everything, Akasha," the demon hisses, as he walks toward me. "You've battled and fought to die like this, lying like an animal, killed by the betrayal of the hybrid you had defeated."

His bare feet move close to the sachet with the Sidhits, but a white blaze whips through them, forcing Antédios to step back. I stretch out my fingers and grab them. Their energy quickly fights against the monster's venom, slowing its fury.

"The mashuis' poison is cursed, and not even the Sidhits will be able to block it forever. It takes someone powerful, able to counteract anathemas like this one." He bends over me, while the curls of smoke wrap up around me, caressing me. "Surrender them to me, Leonardo, and all of this will just be a bad dream. My Lord Kenat can save you, but you must trust me."

"Don't listen to him, Leonardo!" Maya shouts from afar. "Whatever he's telling you, don't listen to him!"

"Shut up! You pathetic little brat!" Silischia growls, using magic to tighten the grip that holds her prisoner.

Maya screams out in pain but doesn't give up.

"Resist, Leonardo, resist! Do it for me!"

"For you?" Feghin asks her, laughing at her. "How can you say that after everything the Akasha has done to you?"

Maya doesn't pay attention to him. Instead, she stares at me, as if trying to give me strength to react, to fight back.

"Your mother died because of him," the evil sorcerer confesses.

Time stops. That sentence, which has been lightly whispered, sounds like it was screamed loudly in my ears.

"We knew he was close by, but we needed to blend in with the humans to find him," Feghin smiles. "Your family proved to be the perfect fit."

Silischia crouches down in front of Maya. She slides her open palm in front of her face, and for a moment, her countenance changes back to Cynthia's, the terrible stepmother.

"Did you do your homework, little brat?" she mocks her as she bursts out laughing.

Maya's expression changes from scared to enraged. Tears of anger fill her eyes. She tries hard to get out from under the trunk, but she can't. Behind the wall of fire, the battle between mashuis and vaneyaras is still going strong. Luis and Sbacot see us and try to pass through the fire. I can hear them while they call us. But nothing. There is nothing else we can do.

"Give me the Sidhits, Leonardo, or I swear this time there won't be a spell strong enough to save your friend," Antédios threatens.

I look at Maya. She's furious and crying, while Feghin laughs and Silischia makes fun of her, singing something horrible. Rage begins to rush through me. I feel my hands burning, black flames crackling in my palms. Antédios gets up and takes a step back.

Within me, the desire for revenge grows. All the thoughts in my head are erased, except the one to kill. I want to tear apart, slaughter, and destroy. I get back up, wrapped by the fury of what is burning inside of me.

I glance at the battlefield. The witch and the sorcerer stare at me, frozen by fear. With a gesture of my hand I throw them both into the flames. Then, I turn toward the demon, who bows down immediately at my intensity.

"I beg you to come with me, oh great Akasha. Kenat awaits you, along with the Sidhits you hold."

I take a look at the weird spheres that shine in my palm. A cry catches my attention. I raise up my other hand ready to kill, but the sight of the human stuck under a trunk prevents me from going forward. Her face brings back memories from another life. A past, or maybe a future, that doesn't belong to me but that I can recognize. A smooth laughter, like a caress, echoes in my head. On my lips, I can sense the warmth of a kiss.

"Maya!"

The demon suddenly looks up. In a moment of consciousness, I squeeze the spheres in my hand. The light of the Sidhits fights against the black fire that traps me, then irradiates my arm and through my body. Every bit of rage disappears in an instant. Lightning and a wave of energy expand like an explosion, putting out the fire. I fall to the ground, no more strength left in me.

When I open my eyes again, Suma is holding me over his shoulders, while Luis helps Maya to stand back up; her leg is injured, and her face is covered in soot. Our eyes meet for a moment, then we lose each other again.

"Akasha, let's get out of here before the demon comes back," Sbacot says, flying around me.

"The Tower . . . take me to the Oghandum."

The mashuis' venom is spreading again. I feel life leaving my body, more and more with every second that goes by. I hold onto the Sidhits, but I can sense that even they can no longer save me.

We escape through the trees blackened by the fire. A mashuis jumps out at us, ready to slaughter us, but Kubra runs to our aid and hits him with an arrow between the eyes.

"Hurry!" he says, protecting us.

We keep running, while I'm still on Suma's back. In the flickering of the shadows that fill my mind, I see something chasing us. It's Antédios! I try to warn my friends, but I don't have the strength to talk. Kubra is busy fighting, while Luis, Maya and Sbacot are ahead of us leading the way. I spot the demon pointing his finger at us, as he opens his mouth. A red bolt of lightning hits Suma's head. We collapse to the ground, rolling among the bushes. Kubra and two other vaneyaras run to our rescue. Suddenly, confusion takes over: bows and arrows darting everywhere. Kubra tries to revive his brother, but there is nothing else we can do.

Antédios is getting closer. His curses race by us, sharply cutting the darkness of the night.

"Hold on, Leonardo," Kubra whispers, his eyes flaring with rage and pain.

He picks me up and we run away. The demon frees himself from the vaneyaras who were left behind to protect us and he glides among the bushes, followed by a pack of mashuis. They are close. Very close.

The Sidhits, which I am still squeezing in my hand begin to burn, but I fight against the pain and the temptation of letting them go. A ribbon of white light drips from my hand like sand. Soon, the trail we leave behind turns into an incandescent vortex whirlwind that raises a barrier between us and our enemies.

"Hurry!" I hear Luis shout. "This way!"

NAYAKA

It all feels like a dream. My eyelids are heavy, and every sound is muffled and echoes as if my head is stuck in a bucket. Maya. My thoughts focus only on her. I try calling her, but words won't come out of my mouth.

Kubra has yet to stop running; my ear is pressed against his chest and his heart is beating like a hammer. We have run through trees, crossed crevices, jumped over trunks, and climbed up steep paths. I can hear the river flowing nearby, and the faint rumble of the waterfall in the distance. Sbacot is still flying around me to make sure I don't stop breathing. His tiny hands caress my head, and he whispers for me to resist and not give up.

The white light from the vortex created by the Sidhits still glows in the darkness we are leaving behind. It still burns in the dark heart of the forest, preventing the demon and his creatures from coming forth.

"This way!" Luis suddenly shouts.

For a moment, I feel like I'm sliding backward, but Kubra tightens his grip, and running out of breath, he climbs over a slope of rocks. The roar of the Isara River becomes more powerful, and I finally see it. We proceed in line, balancing on a rocky ridge over the river. I spot its black water, speckled with the sparkles from the moonlight reflection. We follow the flow of the river when a deafening thunderclap stops us in our tracks. Behind us, the whirlwind of white light still pulsates, but now there is also a red beam blinking underneath, in an attempt to fight against it.

"It's the demon!" Kubra exclaims. "We gotta hurry!"

I see Luis lighting the path with his staff. Maya is holding onto him. They are going down the slope. Kubra follows them with big steps, and within a few seconds, we are back deep in the woods. Trunks and bushes dart past my side, while the moon peeks at me from the open shreds of the green canopy.

"There it is!" I hear Luis panting.

"Leonardo, are you there?" Kubra asks, lightly shaking me.

I move my head with difficulty, as if my skull were welded to my spinal cord, and at last, I see it. The Oghandum. Everything looks just like it did in my nightmare: a big, dark, and twisted plant sinks its roots deep into a black rock outcropping, overlooking a putrid pond that once must have been the bend of the river, but now is just a swamp. It's on the edge of the forest; behind it, only a couple of shrubs, then an expanse of rocks and brambles that end with an overhang opening onto what seems to be a giant lake or even the sea. Next to it, the Isara flows through the rocks, leaping into space as a raging waterfall.

We move along the shore of the pond, being careful not to disturb the water. We struggle to climb up the black rock. Then, we reach the foot of the tree. Maya, with her arm across Luis' shoulder, stares into space, shocked.

The Oghandum appears before us in all its gloomy majesty. The trunk is withered with a gash as big as a cathedral door that tears it in half. Inside, there is only a black void with the stench of mold and stale air.

"The tree is dead and abandoned. Let's get in!" Sbacot says, flying in it.

There is a dull sound, then the homunculus is expelled out with bullet speed.

"How dare you enter without asking permission?" a bleak voice whispers suddenly.

Behind us, we hear the mashuis' screams getting closer. The white light no longer glows, darkness of the night is all that's left. I signal Kubra to let me down, but I remain hanging from his arm, forcing myself to endure the pain that is slowly killing me.

"Let us in, Oghandum," I say at once.

From the smelly laceration in the tree, comes a ghostly figure, slightly wet, glinting in the moonlight. She's a pale woman with an emaciated face and long dirty hair that hangs down to her torn clothes. Her eyes are vacant, but they stare at me as if full of questions and suspicions.

"Who are you, human, asking with so much attitude to enter my kaladar?"

"I am the Akasha."

"Impossible." She studies me.

Sbacot is back flapping around her, ready to throw one of his tantrums but, with one hand gesture, she paralyzes him mid-air, like a tiny statue.

"I can read your mind. What you are looking for is lost; hope is no more and those who protected it have been killed."

A sharp pain pierces me from side to side. I collapse on the ground, defeated in agony. Maya leaves Luis and comes to me. She is holding me tight. Her tears wet my cheeks. I glance at our intertwined fingers; the flowers of the rings have bloomed. I look up at the Oghandum, who stares at us, puzzled. She crouches down, turning Maya's face toward hers.

"I know how you feel," she says, gazing at her. "Once, I loved a man so much I surrendered who I was."

"The Dark Lord," I whisper. "You loved him . . . you gave him your Yuth, and he betrayed you by destroying the place you preserved."

The specter stands up, her expression on the brink of rage.

"How do you know my secrets?"

"I told you," I say, showing her what I have in my fist. The Sidhits shine even brighter, cutting the darkness that surrounds us. The grim expression of the hamadryad becomes softer. "Don't let it all end this way," I beg her, still holding onto Kubra. "There is one last possibility, and you know that."

The Oghandum hesitates. She walks between us, passing us. She looks over the cliff above the swamp. The wind makes her clothes flutter and blows through her hair. The mashuis's barks are getting closer and closer; it's only a matter of seconds now.

"You bring hope where hope is long lost."

"There is always hope," I murmur in agonizing pain that doubles me over.

She turns toward us. Her eyes sparkle.

"Do you think there's still hope for me as well?"

The Sidhits quiver in my palm. I speak as if channeling someone else.

"Oghandum, Midendhil has always forgiven you."

"I let die, the one thing I promised to guard . . ."

"But you have already paid the price for a fault that did not belong to you."

A single tear slowly slides down her cheek. She picks it up on her fingertip and throws it over our heads, backward inside the black hole in the tree. A light bubble starts to burn, becoming so big it illuminates the entire opening. A glowing stream pours out the entrance. It flows among us, wets the hamadryad's feet, and goes down through the putrefaction. Something in the Oghandum changes. For a moment, she turns into the fairy she used to be.

"Listen, Akasha. I shall not do this for Midendhil, nor for what you represent," she says, hiding her emotions. "I shall do it for the love this girl has for you. Make sure you deserve it."

I am speechless. I look at Maya, then at Oghandum again. In that moment, a shadow appears behind the hamadryad. Antédios in on the other side of the pond. The mashuis are with him, still busy with a few vaneyaras who have not stopped fighting.

"Now go. I'll take care of them."

Kubra picks me up again. Maya hesitates letting go of my hand. Luis helps her stand back up. Sbacot recovers and leads the way in the tunnel of light. In a moment, we find ourselves at the edge of a barren field that extends beyond the tree. The enormous ruins of what used to be the wonderful palace of the Guardians now appear on the edge of the cliff overlooking the great lake. Among domes, colonnades, and giant statues of Annunaki, stands a high tower surrounded by a spiral staircase, on a massive, truncated pyramid. The grandeur that it emits is supernatural.

"Up there, Leonardo," Sbacot tells me, pointing at the top of the tower. "You have to get up there and give the Nayaka its light back."

I try to stand, but the poison has sucked all the energy out of me. The Sidhits vibrate in my hands, as if recognizing where we are and the mission that awaits us. Kubra holds me up.

"I'm here with you, Akasha. Resist," he whispers while holding me up by the shoulders.

We run toward the Tower of the Guardians. The field is disseminated by the signs of an ancient battle, chasms blackened by explosions, and skeletons of monsters and warriors who died during the clash. The palace before us is huge. Some parts have collapsed, while others are darkened by fire. We walk through the archway that leads to the yard of the tower when a scream overpowers every other sound. We all turn together. Antédios has managed to cross the Oghandum's barrier and now runs through the dark field that divides us, raising his arms. Behind him, there are a few mashuis, immediately followed by the vaneyaras survivors who are still fighting.

"Luis, help Leonardo," Kubra says. "I've got your back."

The vaneyara's blue eyes look at me. "I believe in you, Akasha."

I feel myself being handed off between friends. Luis holds me by the waist and puts my arm around his neck.

"Come on, Leonardo. If there is still a chance to save us all, it's waiting up there," he encourages me, looking up at the tower. "Give me a hand, Maya!"

She comes toward us, limping. A line of blood spots her dress on the leg that was crushed by the tree trunk.

"Are you OK?" Luis asks.

She doesn't reply. She grabs me on the other side, and together, we enter the tower. Luis illuminates the path with his staff and Sbacot leads us through the maze of corridors. He flies back and forth, stopping us before impassable paths, trying to find the quickest way. Nobody talks. We are all focused on moving as fast as possible, while the sounds of the battle coming from outside penetrate through the empty rooms.

We climb the dusty and steep rock stairway. The mashuis's venom has paralyzed my arm and the whole right side of my body. I no longer feel pain. I am very tired and wish to be lulled into the oblivion that is calling me. However, Luis keeps slapping me, to make sure I don't pass out.

We pop out in an outdoor area by the spiral stairway that wraps around the central staircase. Before us is the battlefield, which burns due to Antédios's curses. Among the fighting shadows of mashuis and vaneyaras, I spot seven giants, darker than midnight, moving along with their mantles made of flames.

"The Dumongorths!" Sbacot exclaims, giving voice to my fears. "The demon has evoked the black souls of the seven ancient Viceroys!"

"What?!" Luis asks, choking.

We rush up the stairs, with my wobbly legs and dragging my feet. The close-by noise of paws stomping on the rock and the grim barking of mashuis catches us off guard. Sbacot looks over the edge of the stairway.

"The mashuis! They are climbing on the tower."

I can tell Luis feels totally lost. He glances at me, at Maya, then at Sbacot again.

"Don't worry," the homunculus tells us with a sparkle in his eyes. "I'll take care of them."

Immediately, he turns into a cloud of small càndemus and jumps down. We hear the monsters howl and cry out. We follow their screams as they fall, smashing onto the ground.

Luis, Maya, and I keep going up. We are close to the top, very close. A few more steps and we will have made it. Out of nowhere, two flames flare up, followed by an explosion. Before us appear Feghin and Silischia who, stretching out their hands, are about to hit us with deadly curses.

Maya doesn't give them time to open their mouths; she throws herself on the witch, grabbing her face with her nails. Silischia cries out loudly, rolling with Maya down the stairs. Feghin leaps with his hands already shining with a blue beam, but Luis hits his hands with his staff, and points it at him.

"*Nirasha!*"

Unexpectedly, a ray of light gushes out of the sphere and strikes the sorcerer, throwing him against the wall. I fall but crawl up the last steps, until I am finally on top of the tower. In the middle of a vast area, there is an altar made of stone from which rise thin tips holding a cloudy crystal, delicate and afloat. I drag myself to the center. I grab onto the altar, get on top of it, and kneel under the stone. I raise the Sidhits and . . .

"Don't do it, Akasha!"

Antédios appears in front of me: his face is tense, his eyes staring at my movements. The smoky mantle twirls, whipped by the wind.

"Surrender the Sidhits to me. It's all over now. You have no idea what will happen if you turn on the Nayaka."

"I do know," I whisper. "I know what I'm doing."

"Why do you want to give false illusions to the people of this world?" he asks, slowly coming closer to me. "Why do you want them to believe there is still hope?"

"There's always hope."

"But not for you, Akasha. You're dying and you gave up on your destiny. You were meant to rule side by side with my Lord."

"No, you're wrong. This is my destiny!"

He tries to stop me, but I raise my hands and hurl the Sidhits against the floating stone above me. A sparkly vortex surrounds us, a fiery column comes down from the sky and floods me and the crystal. Antédios shouts, the tower shakes. The light is intense, and an invisible force pushes me to the ground, but I resist by holding my closed fists up high. I feel the stone shake, then I see it crack. The Sidhits move around us, faster and faster. The murky surface of the crystal crumbles, revealing its heart of fire. The heart of a star. The Nayaka.

The globe palpitates and emits a deep rumble, which is also soft and delicate at the same time. A sound that goes deep into my chest. Energy is released through a magnetic wave that shifts the air. The glow is very strong. Underneath us, the monsters scream in fear, while the vaneyara survivors celebrate the victory.

A black arm cuts the white thunderbolt, and enraged, jerks against me. Antédios pulls me off the altar, throwing me to the ground. With his face deformed by rage, he grabs my head between his hands, ready to make it explode with some curse. I am about to die, but I am ready. I am ready for anything now.

In that very moment, a lightning bolt tears the sky and strikes the demon. It hits him right in the chest and throws him backward with incredible strength. I try to get up, but I can't. The silhouette of a man appears among the bolts shining everywhere: tall, with a long vermilion robe that goes down to the floor. On his head, he wears a pointy headpiece with a golden halo around it, as if a crown. He turns his back to me, but his figure irradiates so much power that I physically feel it. Antédios recovers from the hit, and quickly becomes terrified. The shattered pieces of the stone that are around us begin to levitate, floating midair as if weightless.

"It is written that you cannot meddle in his destiny," the demon mumbles, still on the ground.

"The boy is not ready to fight yet," the stranger replies calmly, lifting him up with only the movement of his fingers. "Kenat will have to wait."

The two of them face each other. Antédios tries to speak, but he's too afraid.

"Go now, evil snake, and bring my message to your Master."

With a subtle gesture, Antédios is thrown across the darkness of the night, screaming. The wizard turns around, his black silhouette against the light of the Nayaka that shines immaculately. Crawling on my behind, I try to retreat in fear. He comes closer and leans on me. Finally, I see his face; he's wretched, with a gray goatee, but it's his irises that really terrify me. They are red like blood and burn like the flames of hell. He places his hand on my forehead. I try to scream, but every pain goes away, almost disappearing completely. The last thought that forms in my head is a name. Weldos.

Then, it's dark again.

TIME TO CHOOSE

Amber. Amber is the color that fills my eyes yet again. I no longer feel pain and all the fear I have felt is just a memory of past events that may have never happened.

I open my eyes, slowly. A pink gleam floods the piece of sky above me. The light of the Nayaka pales my friends' faces. They are exhausted and leaning over me. I recognize Luis, Sbacot, Kubra, and then her, Maya.

I sit up.

"Slowly, Leonardo, be careful," Luis scolds me, while helping me straighten up.

We are still up in the tower; the star burns behind us. Before us is the panorama of the forest with the dawn breaking in the background.

"The Nayaka is shining again," suddenly a deep voice says.

The wizard is standing by the edge of the tower. His red eyes are staring at me.

"This is Weldos," Sbacot whispers satisfied, flapping around my head.

"The free people of Midendhil shall awaken," he continues, imperious. "Soon, they will answer the call of the one who will unite them under his guidance."

I stand up carefully. My friends are holding me. I feel Kubra's hand on my shoulder.

"Now it's up to you, Leonardo. You must choose who you wish to become. Will you continue your path as the Akasha that Midendhil has been waiting for, or will you go back to the other world, fulfilling the life that your Uncle Victor wanted you to have?"

I look at him, surprised. How does he know about my uncle's desire?

I look at my friends. They don't say anything, but in their eyes, I can see what they think. Maya walks toward the edge of the tower. Her gaze is lost on the canopy of the forest that wakes in the morning breeze. I go slowly next to her, remaining by her side. She doesn't look at me, but her hand reaches out for mine, and holds it tight. Then, she nods lightly, her curls becoming tousled in the wind. I glance at her profile, bathed in the pink reflection of the sky. Her eyes sparkle, but her expression is still on the world we have before us.

"You and me, Leonardo," she whispers. "You and me till the end."

acknowledgements

The creation of the Midendhil saga, and the writing process of this first book, have been a hard, exciting and, at times, delicate mission. As in all the best adventures, I have been incredibly lucky to have great companions by my side.

I would like to thank **JuLee Brand**, my wonderful publisher who believed in my novel from the first moment. For a foreign author, publishing in the United States is a dream, an almost impossible mission that JuLee, with her strength, has made possible.

I would like to thank also the wonderful team of **W. Brand Publishing**, for following me and my work along all the publishing process. You guys did an amazing job!

I would like to thank **Brunella Costagliola**, a dear friend and certainly one of the greatest supporters of Midendhil. She took care of the translation of the novel in English and, with her incredible perseverance she found the way to deliver my novel to the USA. Thank you Brunella, you are in my heart.

I would like to thank my father **Valerio**, my mother **Fawzia**, and my sister **Lucrezia**. From the youngest age, you have always supported, pushed, motivated, and dreamed with me. Without you, guys, I wouldn't be here.

I want to thank my family. My wonderful wife, **Alice** and my two little Americans **Leonardo** and **Alexander**. Within you, is the entire meaning of my life.

Thank you, **Alice**, for being my true love, my best friend, my partner, my confidant, my balance and my most severe critic. Without you, I'd be lost.

Thank you, **Leonardo** and **Alexander**, because your births have changed everything for the better, turning me into the man I always hoped to become. This book is for you and I hope that, in time, you both will be proud of your Papi. Keep dreaming, sons, life is a beautiful adventure to discover together with your loved ones.

Finally, thank you to you, **readers**; if you've made it this far, it means you believed in my work. A writer is nothing without his readers. So, thank you, thank you very much from the bottom of my heart.

Leonardo, Maya, all of their friends, and the great Magic of Midendhil will be waiting for you in the next adventure!

Davide Simon was born in Milan, Italy, in 1980 but he has been living in Orlando, Florida, with his family for the past decade. At the end of the 1990s, he began working in the entertainment industry as a set designer, sculptor, and project manager in the theme park and entertainment sector.

While his career as a writer and director of TV shows and fiction has been expansive and fulfilling—he has worked with MTV, SKY, and other networks—his career as an author has truly been the most rewarding to him.

His book titled *Radio-grafia di un DJ che Non Piace (X-Ray of an Unlikable DJ)* was published by Rizzoli and became a bestseller in the first ten days of publication. Then, his thriller *Lo Specchio del Male (The Mirror of Evil)* was published by TEA, and that same year, MonDadori also published his book titled *Non Mollare Mai! (Never Give Up!)*. These three books have been published in Italy.

After the success of his novels, Sperling & Kupfer published the first book of his YA fantasy saga *The Magical Lands of Midendhil*, which was then translated and published in Bulgaria by Egmont and Brazil by Saraiva Group. Thanks to the great feedback from the readers, the first Midendhil book became the night show theme of Mirabilandia, one of the most successful and important theme parks in Europe.

Davide Simon Mazzoli is also a screen player and movie director. He produced the movie *On Air: Storia di un Successo (On Air: A Success Story)*, which was based on his novel *X-Ray of an Unlikable DJ* and distributed by Medusa. For this movie, he received the Best Director Award at the 13th Magna Græcia Film Festival.

He recently published in Italy the novel *Uccidi il Male (Kill the Evil)*, the first book of a thriller series by publisher La Corte Editore. For the international market he created *Benny and His Friends*, an educational picture book series by Moon Publishing, an imprint of Rusconi Editore.

Davide Simon Mazzoli is also a founder of tech brands specialized in entertainment, virtual reality, and augmented reality formats for new worldwide development.

When not writing, directing, or producing, you can find him spending time with his beloved kids and wife, enjoying all that Florida has to offer.

Coming Soon:

Book Two

The Magical Lands of Midendhil

The Path of the Akasha

Made in the USA
Middletown, DE
23 October 2022

13324599R00257